The MICAL Formation

M. Lawrence

Chapters

Prologue

Langford Bullfinch stood perfectly still on the deck of his sailboat as the sun set over Abraham's Bay on Mayaguana Island in the southern Bahamas. The waters of the bay were the lightest turquoise blue and, at this time of day, as smooth as a glassy mirror stretching from the white, sandy shoreline all the way to the reef, nearly a quarter of a mile out to sea. At the reef, the change in the bay was dramatic, with the turquoise glassiness giving way abruptly and violently to the crash of waves on the reef. Just beyond the white frothiness, the much darker blue of the open ocean warned of the drop-off in the depth of the water to hundreds, or even thousands, of feet. The natural beauty was enhanced all the more at sunset, when the sky became red and long golden fingers of light raced towards the reef. It made for a dramatic, postcard-worthy view on this late December evening, but Langford did not notice. His eyes scanned the shoreline warily.

That's not to say that Langford couldn't appreciate the sunset and beaches in this tropical hideaway. He was an avid diver and sailor, and had marveled at the natural beauty of Mayaguana ever since he first arrived over thirty years ago. He had been a young Marine officer on a cushy reward assignment after some very hard years fighting in Vietnam. Back then, the island was a sleepy, US military outpost being slowly decommissioned. Langford had spent several lonely, but happy years as the post commander, presiding over the closing. No tourists visited this lonely island. From time to time, boaters stopped by on their way to more exotic destinations. To them, Mayaguana was just another of hundreds of small, untouched, tropical islands in the long

Bahamian archipelago. Langford knew there was much more to the place than met the eye.

He walked cautiously to the bow of his sailboat, the Maelstrom, to get a better view of the coastline. Thanks to him, this was no longer just a deserted stretch of rocky shore, but a construction zone. In the thirty years since he had flipped the power switch off on the air base generator and taken the last US military flight back to Florida, Langford had left the Marine Corps and become a rich and powerful real estate developer. Now he had returned to this little island with big plans. Until recently, the only man-made structure in the bay had been a small, concrete dock that the local islanders called the "government dock" because the British navy had built the original one back in the 1960's. An immense warehouse, a dredged marina basin, and a series of fenced-off supply yards and construction equipment facilities now dominated the small Abraham's Bay harbor area.

The sun set and the water morphed in to a black sheet, broken only by the ripples off the hull of his sailboat or occasional splash of a fleeing fish below the surface. Langford shivered a bit, partly from the cool breeze that came in off the reef, but also from an odd feeling that had been growing in him all day. During his days in Vietnam, Langford had developed a sixth sense to danger. Outwardly, nothing had changed around the marina construction site or around the island in general. Nevertheless, over the past few days he felt a steadily growing tension in the air.

Out of the corner of his eye, Langford caught a glimpse of unnatural movement along the beach at the other side of Abraham's Bay. He froze instinctively, and strained to hear and see more clearly what was at the water's edge. After thirty seconds intensely peering off into the dusk, he confirmed his fear. They were coming for him. How many, Langford could not be sure, but at least two motorized Zodiac rafts had quietly put into the water from where they must been hiding in the mangroves along the bay.

The Zodiacs seemed to be picking up speed as they got further from shore and into deeper water. They were closing in fast. Langford took a deep breath and assessed the situation. The information he had about Mayaguana was too valuable to be given up if he was captured. His only thought now was how to send a message and a very important file. With a swift turn on his heels, he rushed down into the cabin of his sailboat. A framed picture on his desk momentarily caught his eye. It was a picture of himself with his late wife and his daughter, Jennifer, taken up on the deck of the Maelstrom several years ago. Jennifer and Langford hadn't spoken for a long time, but she was the only person he could trust. Next to the picture was his satellite phone. Grabbing the phone from his desk and turning it on, he hurried back on deck to get a signal while plugging a small USB drive into the phone to upload the file.

He punched in Jennifer's cell number, pulled up the text message screen and started typing. The green glow of the screen bounced off his face, and he lamented that he was leaving his attackers no doubt of his exact location – no time to think about that now! The first Zodiac was only a hundred meters from the sailboat and Langford saw three figures crouching low in the raft. The dark metal of machine gun barrels glinted in the moonlight. He hit the send button and watched as 'Sending…' pulsed on the screen for what seemed like an eternity. 'Message Sent' finally flashed.

"Mission accomplished," Langford whispered quietly. He didn't have a minute to lose. If he took to his skiff, a small Boston Whaler with a good outboard motor on it, he might be able to get through the break in the reef and out into open seas before the Zodiacs reached him. In the open water, he'd have the advantage and could lose them fast, and then find a cove in which to lay low.

Phone in hand, he jumped in the small boat and yanked on the pull cord to start the motor. It roared to life, and with a feeling of triumph, Langford gunned the engine. He had only motored a few yards when splinters of wood exploded around him, as automatic gunfire rang out. Bullets whizzed past his ears. Looking back, the Zodiac rafts were just yards behind him. Masked shooters were taking aim as they steadied themselves against the sides of small boats, jostling over the waves in the wake of Langford's larger Boston Whaler. Langford opened the throttle to full, turning back around to see how close he was to the cut in the reef. The water ahead of him looked like a black abyss. Through the darkness, he could just make out the grey froth of large waves crashing against the reef. He'd need to turn hard to the left to make the cut, and hopefully slow his attackers.

He pushed on the rudder to turn…nothing happened. The boat didn't respond but continued straight ahead. Langford's blood turned to ice in his veins. He looked down in the dim light to see what was wrong, and realized he had been set up. Somebody had attached a small but sturdy chain between the engine mount and the boat. He had been sabotaged!

He shoved frantically with all his strength on the engine rudder, but to no avail. The boat continued furiously straight ahead. Glancing back, he expected to see his attackers right on his tail, but they had slowed their pace and were now quite far behind. With his heart in his throat, Langford looked ahead to see the waves on the reef, just a few feet in front of him. Before he could bail out, his Boston Whaler smacked into the first coral head of the reef wall with an earsplitting bang. As wood cracked and the engine whined, Langford was thrown into the air. A fraction of a second later, the gas can on his boat exploded in a ball of flames that engulfed the reef. After a few moments, the flames were extinguished as the Boston Whaler sank quietly under the waves. The sounds of the night ocean settled over the tranquil bay once again.

Chapter 1

Jennifer Bullfinch's cell phone chimed in the darkness of her bedroom apartment in Cambridge, Massachusetts. It was still early evening, but she purposely made it an early night. She had two final exams tomorrow – her last two of the fall term. So after a kickboxing workout, which was her preferred method of stress relief, Jennifer spent a few hours reviewing at her favorite study nook in Aldrich Hall, the main classroom building at Harvard Business School. Just as night fell, she had walk briskly home through Harvard Square and down Garden Street past the Observatory to her sparse, but comfortable, apartment on Fenno Street.

Before attending graduate school, Jennifer had helped run the Atlanta real estate empire of her father, Langford Bullfinch. In the last real estate boom, the pressure Jennifer felt had been intense. So when it came time to find a place to live before starting classes, Jennifer sought somewhere peaceful and away from the hectic campus social scene. The quiet, family neighborhood of Huron Village in Cambridge, on a pretty, tree-lined street several miles away from the business school and the bustle of Harvard Square suited her perfectly.

The cell phone chimed again from the window sill where she had set it before drifting off. Jennifer drowsily looked over at the phone and sighed, her plans to get a good night's sleep foiled again by the miracle of modern connectivity.

"Should have just turned the damn thing off," she mumbled to herself, as she slid out of bed and walked over to the window. She checked the incoming phone number on the screen. It was unfamiliar, and a little strange. The number had a lot of digits, as if sent from a phone somewhere outside the United States. She opened the text message and read: "MICAL 09/7" on the glowing screen. A text file was attached to the message. She double tapped on the file to read it. It looked like computer programming code – just lines of numbers. She had no idea what it could mean, and the odd sender's number convinced her that the message had come to her by mistake.

She thought about ignoring the message and going right back to bed, but her sense of responsibility would not allow it. And, someone somewhere in the world might be expecting a reply. When it didn't come, they'd be texting or calling to disturb her evening yet again. She hit the send button and the strange number dialed back. She watched the "Dialing…" message flash a few times across the screen, and then put the phone to her ear. A recorded female voice spoke: "The number you have dialed is either out of range or out of service. Please try to dial again." The accent was vaguely British.

Jennifer pressed redial. Same message.

Looking at the phone in her hand, she gave a mildly confused and frustrated look to the empty room. Well, she had given it at least a half-hearted effort. If it was truly important, the caller would either turn their phone back on and see her missed call, or would realize they had texted the wrong number.

She peered out her bedroom window and looked up and down Fenno Street. It was quiet as usual for a December evening. A strong, sudden winter wind blew down the street. It whipped the branches of a large oak tree just in front of the triple decker apartment, scraping them loudly against the railing of the small deck off her bedroom.

Jennifer set the phone down on the window sill, but then thinking better of it, picked the phone back up and set it on the nightstand beside her bed. Now she could answer the thing when it inevitably rang again without having to get up. She crawled back in bed, re-checked that her alarm was set for 6AM, closed her eyes, and slowly drifted back to sleep while mentally reviewing her exam notes.

Jennifer awoke to her alarm and quickly got ready for the day. She bundled up against the wind and trudging out the door, walked to campus in the light snow that had fallen since she looked out the window the night before. She hadn't slept well, waking up several times and instinctively looking over at the phone to see if another message had arrived. None had.

Her Real Estate exam was up first for the day, and despite that Jennifer hadn't even really studied for it, she was not worried. Jennifer had been working in real estate her whole life, and had learned the business from the ground up from her father. Langford Bullfinch got his start in the real estate business in the early 1980's in Atlanta soon after he left the Marines, literally swinging a hammer himself to build homes. Soon he had accumulated enough money to start developing entire neighborhoods in the fast growing Atlanta suburbs.

Some of Jennifer's earliest memories were of tagging along with her father and watching with fascination as graders and bulldozers cleared roads and lots. She was the only child of Langford and Julia Bullfinch, and her father had groomed her to one day take control of his growing business. Developing lots and homes soon led to developing apartments and office buildings. When the city won the bid for the 1996 Olympics, Langford Bullfinch had already positioned the company, now grown to the point it could be called "Bullfinch Property Group", for tremendous growth. Langford was a dedicated mentor. He had included Jennifer in everything from polished meetings with bankers to all-out, shouting-match arguments with gritty sub-contractors about exactly how much should be paid for a job.

Aside of making her a formidable businessperson, those experiences had turned out to be good preparation for her classes at school as well.

Jennifer arrived at school, walked into Aldrich Hall and slid into one of the many study tables built in to the long, wood paneled corridors. She flipped quickly through her Real Estate class notes, confirming in her mind, for the thousandth time, that she would ace the exam. Less confidently, she started reviewing her Finance exam notes. Jennifer knew a lot about commercial banks and the practical side of finance. She had herself applied for, been granted, and managed numerous construction loans, permanent mortgages and even a few simple interest rate swaps for many real estate deals. But this kind of finance was different – more like physics than banking to her mind. She started working on a sample problem one of her friends, a former investment banker, had given her as a study aid.

As she finished a set of review problems, Jennifer's phone rang. It was 7:45AM and her first exam started in just 15 minutes. The name Bennett Wilson Baker III popped up on the screen as the incoming caller. B.W., as he was called, was the General Counsel for Bullfinch Property Group, or what was left of it anyway. B.W. had also been Langford Bullfinch's business partner for many years. When Langford started his real estate business and needed a lawyer he could trust, B.W. offered to help out for a stake in the projects rather than for a fee. Those ownership stakes had turned out to be shrewd investments, and as the company and its fortunes grew, so did B.W.'s wealth. He became not only an important advisor, but also a part of the core team.

The consummate southern gentleman, B.W. was a formidable mixture of good ol' boy and cunning intellectual. Despite his back woods upbringing, he worked his way through Vanderbilt

University, back when such a thing was still possible, and then found a way to put himself through law school at Yale. Jennifer had always noted with some wonder how his accent would change depending upon the setting. Smooth, polished and reminiscent of Jimmy Carter when in high level meetings, it would somehow devolve to a growling twang when dealing with more pedestrian matters. Much like Langford, he had been somewhat underestimated by the Atlanta Establishment when he first came to town. B.W. took advantage of that miscalculation with a vengeance. Within a few years, his name was mentioned often as the best attorney in town, even with Langford as his only client. As B.W. was something of a surrogate grandfather to Jennifer, she quickly answered the phone.

"Jennifer? Are you there?" B.W.'s voice had the soft 'Jimmy Carter' tone. He sounded concerned and Jennifer was immediately uneasy.

"Yes, B.W. I've just got a few minutes before a final exam. What's the matter?"

"Jennifer, I've terrible news, so I better just come out and say it. I got a call from Mayaguana just a few minutes ago. Your father is missing."

Jennifer sat in stunned silence holding the phone to her ear and fighting back tears that immediately began to well up in her eyes. "Missing? What happened?" she asked trying to stop her voice from cracking.

"No one knows yet, dear. Colin Steele, that runway contractor we've got down there just called to let me know, but he really didn't have much information as yet. I hate to say it, but he said the initial report from the Bahamian police is that... well, they found some debris from what looks like Langford's Boston Whaler, and there's no sign of him anywhere. They're presuming…well, they're presuming he's gone", B.W. said in a hesitating voice.

"Never", she said flatly, and regaining some of her composure. "You've known my father his whole life. He was an expert on the water, and he knows that bay like the back of his hand. You know that's not possible."

"I know. It certainly doesn't sound like Langford. But listen, there's some other news you need to know which might change the picture," B.W.'s tone changed subtly from concerned grandfather to concerned lawyer. "Yesterday we got official notice from the China Global Development Bank. The company your father set up in The Bahamas has missed payments and they're going to foreclose on the whole Mayaguana project in 30 days."

"What?" Jennifer gasped incredulously.

"Look, you need to get down here right now," B.W. said in a tone implying more of an order than a request. "We have a conference call with the bank at 9PM this evening. You and I need to put our heads together in person before that call."

Jennifer was already packing up her notes before B.W. finished his sentence. "I'm on the way."

Chapter 2

Only a few hours later, Jennifer powered on her cell phone as the plane she had rushed to catch in Boston touched down and taxied all the way from runway five to the terminal at Atlanta's Hartsfield-Jackson International Airport,. It was 11:45AM. She had a missed call from B.W. She dialed him back quickly while the plane was still pulling up to gate T8, thankfully close to the main terminal building.

"B.W., it's Jennifer. I'm just pulling up to the gate. Saw I missed a call from you."

"When it rains it pours," sighed B.W. into the phone. His usual drawl sounded tired and worn already. "Colin called again from the island. It looks like we are going to have a mutiny on our hands soon. Workers aren't getting paid, and trouble is brewing."

"Who is Colin, again?" exclaimed Jennifer, with a harsher intonation than she intended. She was beginning to feel a little overwhelmed with the complete lack of details she had concerning the Mayaguana project.

"OK, OK, I forget you've been even less involved with this project than me. Truth be told, I don't know much more than you about what has been happening on that crazy island. Just get over to the office as soon as you can so we can go over the loan documents."

After what seemed like a much longer journey on the Atlanta commuter rail than anticipated, the train pulled up to Buckhead Station. Jennifer stepped quickly on to the platform and headed up the escalator, emerging on to Peachtree Road. She was just around the corner from the Fidelis office tower, and for the first time in the hour or so she had been in Atlanta, it occurred to her how nice the weather felt compared to what she had left in Cambridge. It was sixty-eight degrees and sunny in Buckhead with a gentle breeze. It was light windbreaker weather, and downright tropical compared to the thirty-four degrees and freezing rain that had stung her face getting in the cab outside the business school.

The Fidelis Tower on Peachtree was Langford Bullfinch's crowning achievement as a real estate developer. Completed just a few short years ago, it was the biggest bet in a long line of big bets that Langford had pulled off over the course of his career. For Jennifer, it had also been a special project because it was the biggest development in which she played a major role. The building was beautiful in its architecture and design. One of the very first floor-to-ceiling glass office towers in Buckhead, it was designed by the rock star architect Jean-Paul Michel, and had garnered national attention when it opened. The building photographed amazingly well. Jennifer had enjoyed seeing the building on the cover of several magazines, even though she and her father normally didn't put much stock in the appearance of a building.

Her father had his eye on this parcel near the corner of Peachtree Road and Piedmont Road in Buckhead for years, along with many other developers in Atlanta. The parcel itself, to the casual observer, had been nothing special - just an old empty lot with a few trees and an old shack on it. But to those watching the trends and patterns of growth around Atlanta, it was the front line of the next wave of commercial development in the city's most exclusive district.

The problem, as all those developers keeping their eye on the parcel had found, was that it was owned by the most cantankerous old man in Atlanta. Raymond Barnes was about eighty years old and had been a caretaker on the old Joyeuse Estate, the lands of which sprawled about the northern edge of modern day Buckhead. In the late 1950's, when part of the lands of the estate were purchased to build one of the nation's first shopping malls, Barnes had somehow managed to wrangle himself a few acres at the far end of the estate to live. He received a constant stream of offers to buy the property, which he always refused, usually in a rather loud and rude manner. As offices, restaurants and shops sprang up around the empty lot, Barnes sat on the porch of his small shack glaring at the traffic.

Langford and B.W. felt they also had to make an attempt to buy the property for Bullfinch Property Group. Langford despised the unsavory nature of the on-going battles for the lot, but the competition for the few remaining undeveloped acres in the heart of Buckhead was too important to ignore. So, on a hot and hazy Sunday afternoon, Langford and B.W. drove Langford's old pickup truck over to Barnes' lot. They found him sitting on his porch as usual with two hound dogs laying in the shade and a rifle conspicuously leaned against the wall of the shack next to his rocking chair. Curiously, there was also a very nice Nikon camera setting on a small table next to him.

The conversation was predictably icy, despite the thin veneer of southern hospitality that prevented Raymond from throwing them off the porch and having his dogs chase them back to the truck immediately. But Langford was determined not to give up, and put on his best charm offensive.

As the conversation gradually warmed up, it also turned out that Barnes had served with the Marines in the Pacific during World War II and then in Korea. Although he had enlisted as an infantryman and seen some of the toughest fighting as a part of the MacArthur and Nimitz island-hopping campaign, he had somehow ended up as part of an aerial reconnaissance team. He

14

had learned the art and science of photography, snapping and analyzing photos of Japanese defenses on the island chains of the South Pacific Ocean. Even more coincidental, after hours of rambling war stories, they figured out that Raymond and B.W. had both been in the same Marine division later on in the Korean War. B.W. had been captured and had spent several months in prison in China before being released in a prisoner exchange. Barnes seemed to vaguely even recall the incident and the shared kinship of battle warmed him a little more to the idea of selling his land to Langford and B.W.

Not long after that visit, Barnes indeed sold the property to Langford. The Fidelis office building plans were put into action. Despite many ups and downs along the way, the tower was soon constructed and nearly fully leased.

Waiting for the elevator, she took a brief moment to look around at the beautifully framed photos showcasing some of Barnes' photography of exotic locations in the Pacific during World War II and the Korean War. Some wall space to display his photography had been a part of the final deal in his sale of the property to Langford. The elevator doors opened, Jennifer stepped inside, and headed up to the forty-seventh floor.

Chapter 3

The elevator doors opened and Jennifer walked into the granite and marble tiled foyer. She turned left and walked towards a glass wall with the "Bullfinch Property Group" logo etched in it, and a door with stainless steel handles and hinges. Jennifer pulled out the key card she hadn't used for almost two years and swiped it on a sensor pad on the wall. She was happily surprised to hear the door lock click open, and she pulled the steel handles to walk inside. The receptionist desk greeting her was empty. A few years ago, the company had needed the entire floor, but now they leased just one of the suites, and even that was more space than needed. Her father's odd obsession with the Mayaguana Project had caused him to sell off nearly all their other properties, including this office tower. He had also been forced to shrink the staff. It was now a two person company: B.W. and Langford. To Jennifer, it was eerily quiet in the office. No hustle and bustle, and no phones ringing.

The clicking sound of foots steps against tile floor broke the silence. B.W. emerged from down the hallway. He was not as tall a man as Langford, but B.W. had been a high school football hero in his youth, and still had a solid frame. He was just a little stockier than Jennifer remembered and his grey hair was sparser than when Jennifer had last seen him. But one thing hadn't changed: B.W. was dressed in a sharp, grey, pinstripe suit with a regimental striped tie. While Langford Bullfinch had never felt comfortable in a suit and tie, and therefore rarely wore them, B.W. always looked like he just stepped out of a Brooks Brothers catalogue. Even now, with no one else in the office, B.W. just couldn't bring himself to wear business casual. He came over to Jennifer and gave her a long, tearful hug.

"I still can't bring myself to really believe he's gone," B.W. choked somewhat melodramatically.

"B.W., until we get some more details, let's not write Dad off just yet," said Jennifer, a little annoyed at him. "But we have a lot to talk about."

"You're right," said B.W. stepping back from Jennifer and straightening his tie. "There is a lot of work to be done, and no time to cry about things now. We have eight hours before the conference call with the China Global Development Bank," he said, looking down at his Rolex Oyster Perpetual wristwatch.

"What do you know about this bank?" Jennifer asked.

"Honestly, not much. Your father took on this loan without really consulting me. I've been digging around the office for hours, ever since I got the notice from them of default, but I have only been able to find the term sheet summarizing the loan details. Without any of the full documents, it's hard for me to do any serious lawyering yet."

"Well, you're going to have to do your best. Let's start with what we do know."

"Everything's in the War Room. Let's go take a look."

Jennifer and B.W. walked down the hall to a large conference room they called "The War Room." It was one of Bullfinch Property Groups few splurges. In a corner room with views overlooking the Atlanta skyline and the green, leafy western side of Buckhead, the effect was breathtaking. The interior walls of the room along the hallway were also glass with stainless steel accents, but by pressing a button from the control panel, the glass walls would turn translucent grey to provide privacy. The non-window wall at the far end of the conference room was paneled in

17

rich mahogany. Also controlled from a button on the table, one of the wood panels could retract revealing an 84 inch flat panel monitor. The chairs along the conference table were high backed, black leather, with mahogany accents on the arm rests linking them decoratively to the wood paneled wall. To the left of the projector screen, another wood paneled door opened up to reveal a wet bar and small, fully-stocked refrigerator. A set of leaded crystal tumblers and decanters set on one of the shelves. Just below them were enough china place settings for each of the 16 chairs at the conference table, available in case of a working lunch. Jennifer remembered how Langford had never felt very comfortable with the material excesses of the War Room, but B.W. had insisted, so he went along. And he did eventually have to admit making a superficial good first impression was, unfortunately, often necessary.

Jennifer walked to the end of the conference table and picked up the loan term sheet. It was not comforting. The terms looked absolutely Draconian to her. The loan amount on the top line of the term sheet was for a staggering $150 million, and the fine print seemed to indicate that foreclosure proceedings, in this case, would be initiated after just 30 days.

"I can't believe Dad would ever have signed this loan," Jennifer said, looking up from the sheet at B.W.

"Well, you'd better believe it. I've been on the phone with Tyler King all morning. His firm has done quite a bit of work in China the past few years, so he knows something about the legal environment there. His assessment is that we're in trouble."

Tyler King was a partner at the law firm of Jennings, Kidder & Holt LLP, one of the world's most powerful law firms that also happened to be based in Atlanta, with over eight hundred lawyers in their downtown office. King had been a great help to Bullfinch

Property Group when they needed to engage a firm for larger deals. Jennifer knew Jennings, Kidder had done a lot of work recently in China, and seemed to remember reading they had opened an office in Shanghai.

"Let's get Tyler back on the line. I've got a few questions of my own," Jennifer said as she sat down in one of the black leather chairs and pulled the speaker phone towards her. She pulled up his number from her contact list and dialed on the speaker phone.

"Hi there B.W." said Tyler's cheerful voice with just the faintest southern drawl as he picked up the line. "I thought I scared you enough for one day.," he joked.

"Hey, Tyler. It's Jennifer along with B.W. this time," said Jennifer. "Good to hear your voice again after a few years. B.W. has given me a recap of some of what you've covered, but I really need to ask you a few questions myself."

"Hope I can help, Jennifer. Shoot."

"How are the bankruptcy laws in China? Do you think we'll get fair treatment in the courts there?"

"That's hard to say. Rule of law, as you or I might view it, is still an evolving concept in Chinese courts, especially when it comes to dealing with foreigners. From the limited information you have, it's also hard to tell where your case would be heard, but it seems likely to be handled by the courts of the Wubei Province, where the China Global Development Bank is located. If the court system you were dealing with was in Shenzen or Shanghai or some other more well-known and foreign investment friendly area, it might be easier to tell. However, I think you should operate on the assumption that you will not be treated fairly, and any appeal to a higher court system is not likely to be granted for a long time, if ever."

"That's not encouraging. What about this strict foreclosure law. Can we fight that?"

"I doubt it. You're used to laws that protect the borrower. That's not the case in a lot of other countries. It's still borrower beware. And since the bank has what appears to be about $75 million of your cash in their account, I think you'll have little success fighting the foreclosure or recovering any of the escrow."

"Hmm. Well this project is actually located in The Bahamas. Couldn't we try something in the court system there?"

"I don't think it will do much good. The Bahamas is still, from a juris prudence sense, connected to Great Britain, and the Privy Council in London serves as the Supreme Court for The Bahamas. But given the amount of leverage the bank has over you in China, I doubt you'll get very far. And, to be honest, The Bahamas legal system is a bit convoluted as well. No major firms have any offices there as it's dominated by a handful of really well-connected local firms."

The conversation with Tyler went on for over an hour, but with little resolution. In the end, Tyler told them he would get in touch with a lawyer from their new Shanghai office to see if they could shed any more light on the problem. But for now, Jennifer and B.W. were no closer to any answers, or a good strategy for handling the fast approaching conference call with the bank. Over the next few hours, they poured over what information they could find, as well as some notes and general documents about Chinese lending laws that Tyler had emailed over. Soon it was 7PM. The winter sun had set early over Georgia. They took a brief break to walk down the hill to a local restaurant and pick up some dinner, which they brought back to the conference room to enjoy. Jennifer got each of them a Coke out of the fridge in the wet bar and they ate while continuing to review what little information they had. Soon, it was 8:55PM. Conference call in five minutes.

Pulling up the conference call number B.W. had been given earlier that morning, he dialed. A few seconds later, a recorded voice said something in Mandarin. B.W. gave Jennifer a 'here goes' look and dialed in the pass code. The voice said something else they didn't understand, and after a brief moment, classical music came across the speaker phone.

"I guess we're on hold?" said B.W. in an uncertain tone.

At 9PM exactly, the classical music stopped. "Hello, who is on the line please?" inquired a female voice.

"This is Bennett Wilson Baker the Third and Ms. Jennifer Bullfinch of the Bullfinch Property Group," answered B.W. in his best authoritative tone. "We were told Mr. Li Hong would be speaking with us."

"Yes. Hold please for Mr. Li."

After a few moments, a male voice came on the line.

"Ms. Bullfinch, Mr. Baker, this is Li Hong, the President of China Global Development Bank," the banker said. His accent, Jennifer noted, had faint traces of British pronunciation that came through the Chinese accent.

"Mr. Li, I just got notification yesterday afternoon from our Bahamas office of your bank's intent to foreclose on Bullfinch Property Group project on Mayaguana Island. Sir, I must let you know that a tragedy has struck our company. Mr. Langford Bullfinch, our President and CEO, has gone missing as of yesterday evening…and though I hate to say it, the Royal Bahamian Police Force is inclined to believe he may have died in a boating accident off the reef of Mayaguana," B.W. said into the speaker phone. He paused expecting some kind of response. None came. "In light of this terrible setback, we are calling you to ask that your bank grant some leeway in dealing with the loan, and thought we might be able to work with you to…"

"There will be no leeway, Mr. Baker. The internal problems of LIC Development are not the concern of my bank," interrupted Mr. Li curtly.

"Mr. Li, this is completely unreasonable," Jennifer broke into the conversation. "We fully intend to remedy this situation and get current on our payments." Jennifer actually wasn't sure if that really was what she intended to do, but she felt she had to say something to buy some time.

"Ms. Bullfinch, there is no remedy for this, as you call it. We are taking over the project, which has very little value even as a work in progress, and we are retaining the funds in the escrow account to make good on the rest and minimize our losses," Mr. Li said in an icy, matter-of-fact tone that was absolutely infuriating Jennifer.

Jennifer was turning red in the face in her anger. B.W. put his hand on her arm as if to remind her to stay calm. He opened his mouth to take the next turn in the conversation, but before he could, Jennifer forged on. "Then I am informing you that we will be fighting this tooth and nail over the next 30 days to the fullest extent possible."

"Ms. Bullfinch, we initiated this process after the interest payment was missed nearly two weeks ago. You have 15 days, not 30," said Li in his icy, quiet, even-toned voice. "And, as neither of you are actually officers of the company in question or signatures on the loan, I am done dealing with you. This call was intended merely as a courtesy. You should take my advice in this matter, and it is this: your father has squandered a fortune on this hopeless project. Don't waste whatever precious little you have left trying to rescue it."

The line went dead as Li hung up on them. Jennifer and B.W. looked at each other in silence. Jennifer swallowed hard and took in a deep breath.

"He sure does know how to rub salt in a wound," B.W. said, breaking the silence.

"Yeah," Jennifer said looking out the window at the lights of the Atlanta skyline. They both fell silent again for a few moments, each of them processing what had just happened.

"I hate to say it, but maybe he has a point," B.W. said softly, looking down at the conference table.

Jennifer looked at him and thought how painful this must also be for B.W. Langford and B.W. had known each other most of their lives, and worked closely together as long as Jennifer could remember. He looked haggard and worn. Despite his sharp dress, he seemed to slump in his chair, like a beaten man. Jennifer realized at that moment that she was on her own in this battle. B.W. didn't have the fight or the energy that Jennifer sensed this was going to take. She gently suggested he head home for the evening.

After B.W. left, Jennifer worked a while longer, trying to recall if she had ever heard of the LIC Development Company that Mr. Li had referenced. Eventually, she shut her laptop and settled in her old office just across the hallway. Sitting down on the comfortable couch where she had spent many nights, she pulled an old photo album off the end table. The album had photos from Langford's time spent on Mayaguana while he was the sleepy outpost's commanding officer.

In particular, one picture always piqued her curiosity: her father on a boat dock with two other people – a Bahamian teenage boy and another young military officer. Once or twice Jennifer had asked him who those particular people were, but he always brushed off the question and changed the subject, so she stopped asking. After looking through the album several times, she noticed that this picture was missing.

Soon a wave of tiredness overtook her. Jennifer set the album aside and laid her head down on the stuffed arm rest of the couch. As she drifted to sleep, a lone tear ran slowly down her cheek.

Chapter 4

Jennifer woke to the sound of the alarm on her cell phone at 6AM. She had been far more exhausted than she realized, but despite sleeping on her favorite old couch, which was usually very restful, she had not gotten a good night's sleep. She sat up and rubbed the back of her head, which felt like something was boring into it, only to realize something actually was boring into her head – a bobby pin. She was always leaving them in her hair on accident, and this night, it cost her some much needed rest.

She showered in the simple but elegant bathroom near her office. Just as she was finishing up, she heard her cell phone ringing from the teakwood bench next to the shower. She wrapped a towel around herself and grabbed the phone. It was an unfamiliar number, from somewhere with the area code "242".

"Jennifer Bullfinch," said Jennifer using her standard telephone answer line when she did not recognize the caller.

"Miss Bullfinch, my name is Colin Steele. We've never met, but I work with your father down here on Mayaguana," said a man's voice. The voice had a business-like tone.

"Nice to hear from you, Mr. Steele. You'll have to pardon me because I only first heard of you yesterday from Mr. Baker," Jennifer said. She paused, saying nothing more since she was not exactly sure what this person wanted at 6:45 in the morning, but mostly sure it had to do with money he was owed.

"I'm calling you because I understand you are now responsible for this project in place of your father," he explained. His tone was now all business and growing harsher.

"I suppose. We are still trying to get a handle on things up here in the Atlanta office," Jennifer replied, hoping he didn't know that "the Atlanta office" consisted of a woman who hadn't been involved with the project at all since she left the company in protest at the poor investment it seemed to her and a semi-retired lawyer who basically felt the same way.

"Well I suggest you get that handle very quickly, Ms. Bullfinch. Your contractors here are all two weeks or more overdue on their paychecks from your father, and you're going to have a real trouble on your hands very soon if you don't get things under control."

Jennifer took a split second while Colin was chastising her to think. She needed to turn the tables on this guy fast and put him in his place. Her experience with contractors like Colin was that they talked tough over the phone, but face to face, they could usually be handled much easier. Also, having a young woman go toe-to-toe with them usually threw them off enough for her to gain an advantage.

"Don't you worry yourself, Mr. Steele," said Jennifer brusquely. "I'll be in Nassau this morning, and I'll be chartering a plane to the island in the afternoon. I'll be happy to address everyone's concerns in person, so you just have them ready."

There was a brief pause on the other end of the line, and Jennifer felt like she had precipitated the desired effect. She meant for the chartered plane comment to subtly signal that she had plenty of money at her disposal. Whether or not it would sink in to the skull of this Neanderthal was another matter.

"Fine. We'll be eagerly awaiting your arrival, and you better bring cash because I doubt anyone will accept a check…" Colin said with some sarcasm.

Jennifer hung up the phone before he could get anymore snarky comments in. She had been thinking about getting down to Mayaguana to put some eyes on the actual place, but some uncharacteristic uneasiness had been holding her back. Colin's call had been just the jolt she needed.

It was just after 7AM and she wanted to catch the 9:30AM flight to Nassau. Thankfully, there were still some clothes in her office closet. She dressed quickly and loaded all her clothes and laptop into a backpack. With a last look at the empty, scaled-back offices of Bullfinch Property Group, she headed out the glass doors to the airport. She made good time to the airport. After quickly getting $500 out of the ATM once she arrived, she hurried to the gate, arriving just before the attendant closed the jet way door.

The flight from Atlanta to Nassau was only about ninety minutes. The plane was soon on the ground and taxiing to the terminal. She turned on her cell phone to see what would happen. After a few seconds of searching, her phone had 5 signal bars on a network called "BTC." Jennifer dialed B.W.'s mobile phone.

"Good morning B.W. I've just landed in Nassau."

"I figured you had headed down there when I got to the office this morning and you were gone. I do have to say, I'm a little concerned. I think we really need to just stay focused on the legal battle from back here in Atlanta, and not run around on that god-forsaken rock of an island," B.W. gently scolded. His orneriness seemed to indicate he had gotten some wind back in his sails after a night's rest.

"Colin Steele called my cell phone early this morning, and I thought it was best to get down for a face-to-face meeting right away, seeing as it will be the Christmas holiday soon. Exactly

27

what do I have to work with here, B.W.?" Jennifer knew he would have an exact figure of what few funds Bullfinch Property Group had remaining.

"Well, not much right now. We have twenty thousand in cash, and as far as I can tell, that's all we're going to have for a while. We may get some of that business insurance policy, but I would say that is weeks or months away. Even if we break our lease on the office and hold a fire sale for the furniture, it won't be significant. I doubt we could even get an emergency line of credit, since we don't have any assets."

"Keep working on our options, and keep on top of Tyler. I'm going to find out exactly what people down on Mayaguana think we owe them. And, I'm going to get to the bottom of what really happened to Dad," Jennifer said. "I'll get word to you from the island." She hung up after B.W. reluctantly wished her luck, asking one more time for her to return to Atlanta. She gathered up her backpack and headed off the plane with no clue what to do next.

Chapter 5

The line to get through Customs and Immigration was a lot slower than Jennifer had hoped. Once she finally reached the front of the line and walked up to the counter where a sour-faced Bahamian lady asked for her passport and immigration card, things got worse. Jennifer had checked a box on the card that indicated she was traveling to The Bahamas for business. When the sour-faced lady questioned what kind of business and Jennifer explained she had to handle some contractors for a real estate development, a long inquisition followed. After several minutes delay as the customs officer made a few phone calls and queries, Jennifer was finally allowed through. She went out past baggage claim and found herself in a small lobby. Inside the lobby were a few benches with some Bahamians lounging in them as they waited for people to arrive, and a few counters for rental cars and shuttles to the larger resorts. Jennifer had absolutely no idea where to go from here. She had made it to Nassau, but Mayaguana was, as her review of the country's geography on the internet had told her, over three hundred miles further south.

"Ms. Bullfinch?" someone asked from just behind her. Jennifer turned around to face the voice and saw a Bahamian man walking up to her from down another hallway on the opposite side of the lobby.

"Yes," said Jennifer, in a quietly surprised manner.

"I thought you might be. Colin said you were coming in on the morning flight from Atlanta, but he had no idea what you looked like. I see a bit of your father in you, though, so I made a smart guess," the man held out his hand to shake. "I'm Obediah Gibson. I work with Colin Steele on Mayaguana."

"Ah. Nice to meet you, Obediah," said Jennifer flatly, now more on her guard. Colin was clearly no friend, so chances were this gentleman fell in the same category.

"Just call me Obie, for short. Well, Colin said you were chartering a plane to head down to Mayaguana this afternoon. I was in town taking care of some things, but I need to get back down to the island soon. Mind if I hitch a ride?" Obie inquired in an easy manner.

Jennifer quickly sized up her new acquaintance. Obie looked to be in his early forties. He was just about six feet tall, and had the bulky frame of someone who looked like they might do heavy construction work. He was dressed in old jeans and sneakers, a short-sleeved striped Izod shirt, and a Miami Heat baseball cap. He had a breezy smile on his face, and Jennifer decided to take him at face value – nothing sinister behind his request.

On one hand, Jennifer was not thrilled about having an agent of the enemy with her for the rest of the day, especially if she was on the phone with B.W. or Tyler King talking about sensitive information she would not want to get out to the public. On the other hand, having Obie along would solve her problems of complete ignorance about the basic logistics of getting from this lobby to Mayaguana. She decided letting him tag along with her on the charter might also give her a chance to massage a little information out of him as well, and maybe even build some good will.

"Sure. Which charter company did you use to fly up here?" she asked, hoping her question did not reveal she could not name even one air charter company in The Bahamas.

"I can hook us up with a guy over at General Aviation."

"Great. Let's head over there," Jennifer said, hoping she continued to give off the impression she knew her way around at least a little.

Her charade did not last long. As they walked by a small newsstand, Jennifer's eye caught a headline on a local newspaper that made her draw her breath in surprise loud enough that Obie noticed and looked her way. The headline read: "MICAL Secession Movement Heard in Parliament"

"MICAL?" Jennifer mused, half to herself and looking at Obie with an inquisitive air.

Obie replied as if they both should be familiar with this headline, "Yeah. The big debate is in Parliament today. Of course, you know there's still a long way to go after that, even with some positive headway the next few days."

Jennifer felt she could go no further without potentially walking into a land mine and doing worse damage to her reputation should Obie take her for some kind of fraud. It was better to ask the dumb questions early on. "I'm sorry, but I have been focused on many other projects at Bullfinch Property Group, and I am just getting up to speed on this one. What exactly is 'MICAL'?"

"Oh, I see," said Obie, sounding a little unsure of how he should respond. "MICAL is a region of the Bahamas. The most southern region, and in fact, you'll get to see it first-hand this afternoon."

"You mean Mayaguana Island is a part of this MICAL?" Jennifer said, trying to keep the emotion out of her voice at piecing together a part of the text message clue.

"Of course! It's the M, in MICAL. Mayaguana, along with Inagua, Crooked Island, Acklins and Long Cay form the MICAL region. It's a small group of islands, all pretty close to each other," laughed Obie, looking pleased at being able to give an impromptu lesson on The Bahamas. They continued the conversation as they walked out the door and down the road towards a small, yellow building that read 'General Aviation'. Jennifer continued to delicately pump Obie for information.

"So tell me a little more about this secession movement."

"Well, as you know, the southern Bahamas is pretty un-developed compared to the rest of The Bahamas. The islands down there have been nearly deserted since Columbus sailed by. The problem, so to speak, is that a lot of Bahamians, meaning those who come from the islands in MICAL, feel real strong about their heritage and attachment to their home. So, even though there are almost no jobs, a lot of the natives still want to live there. Maybe fish a little, or just retire there one day to relax. Now as you know, being American I suppose, when you've got a lot of retired folk in one area who need support and services, but there's no industry to speak of to make jobs and such, the government ends up spending a lot of money to support just a handful of people," Obie continued his lesson, and Jennifer was rather impressed with the clarity of his explanation. He was well spoken but Jennifer noticed that as he relaxed during their conversation, he dropped a lot more "have's and "is's" sounding more like what Jennifer thought someone from a Caribbean island might sound.

"So that explains to me why the rest of The Bahamas might want to see MICAL out on its own, but not why MICAL would want to secede. How do you make a new country work when there's no economy?"

Obie laughed out loud and shook his head. "Oh boy, you really been working on other things and not paying much attention to what's going on down here in The Bahamas. You're company's one of the big reasons. Maybe the biggest!"

Now Jennifer was really perplexed and more concerned than ever. Not only had her father gone and bet the ranch on a deserted island in the desolate backwater of the Southern Bahamas, a place even other Bahamians thought might be OK to see go away, but he also had apparently gotten tangled in a serious political mess. An entire region of a country was looking at this bankrupt project as a key reason to become their own nation. She may have figured out what 'MICAL' meant from the text message, but clearly, there was much more to learn.

"So the people in the region are pushing for secession because they think projects like ours will make the region economically self-sufficient?" she asked.

"That's right. For the past ten years, everybody down that way has been looking at the next country over – the next island over – just thirty or so miles: the Turks and Caicos. Mayaguana's just a stone's throw from Providenciales, one of the hottest hot spots in the Caribbean today. They figure a new airport, a few hotels, and soon the MICAL islands will be thriving," Obie explained.

Jennifer knew the Turks and Caicos Islands, as she had been there a few years ago to go scuba diving. When her father had first mentioned working on Mayaguana and Jennifer had found the place on a map, she too, noticed how close it was to Providenciales. Merely being close-by to "Provo", as it was called for short, did not seem like enough justification of the project. Provo's growth had been jump started un-naturally by money from the drug trade. And, there were many other islands in the area, many even closer to Provo than Mayaguana, that were just as undeveloped and could easily also become great resort locations. She had urged her father to find an empty stretch of beach on Grace Bay, considered by many to be one of the most beautiful beaches in the world, and build a hotel there if he felt like he just had to do a Caribbean resort project. There were lots available, and there seemed to be growing demand for hotel rooms on the island. Her suggestion fell on deaf ears.

They arrived at the General Aviation building and Obie approached a Bahamian man sleeping on a bench outside the building under an awning. He was wearing black denim jeans, an old pair of Air Jordan's, and a white shirt. Upon a closer look, the white shirt also had epaulets on it and a pair of wings embroidered above the pocket. A pair of silver-rimmed Randolph aviator sunglasses with bayonet temples finished off his pilot look. Apparently, he was the very pilot Obie was looking for, because he walked up to the gentleman and gave him a gentle kick on his Air Jordan's to wake him up.

"Hey man, there's no sleeping on this job. Better get your ass up. We got places to be," Obie yelled, laughing.

The pilot looked up slowly from behind his sunglasses. "Man, I don't know just who you think you are strutting around here giving orders. This ain't your office. When you down Mayaguana, you give orders. When you at my office, just ask nicely," the pilot growled, glaring at Obie. He didn't get up from the bench. Jennifer thought for a moment he might really be upset at being kicked. The pilot put his head back down as if he was going back to sleep.

Obie stood in front of the pilot and crossed his arms shaking his head. "Ha. Fine, cousin. Would you do this young lady the honor of gracing us with your tremendous piloting skills." He said with mock over-politeness.

"For her…I suppose," replied the pilot, getting up slowly from the bench and winking at Jennifer from behind his glasses.

"How gracious," Obie said. Turning to Jennifer, he motioned towards the pilot. "Ms. Jennifer Bullfinch, may I present our distinguished pilot for today, Mr. Tony MacDonald. He also happens to be my cousin."

"Charmed, Madam," said Tony, now grinning broadly at Jennifer and holding out his hand.

Jennifer smiled at the exchange, and shook Tony's hand. "I'm sure. Looks like we're in experienced hands for our flight down to Mayaguana," she said, playing along a little.

"Your chariot awaits," Tony gestured towards the doorway leading into the yellow building.

"How much did Obie tell you this flight was going to cost?" Tony asked, now a bit more serious.

"He didn't," replied Jennifer before Obie could open his mouth.

"Ah. Well, my rate to go down to Mayaguana is twenty-five hundred dollars. Cash."

Jennifer thought nervously that she only had the five hundred she had taken from the ATM in the airport, and not much more in the bank. "How about I have the money wired today?" she asked.

"Well, that's not really acceptable," said Tony, looking even more serious. "I mean, I know you owe a lot of people money already. I'd feel more comfortable if you could pay up front."

"Oh come on, man. Stop this foolishness!" Obie chimed in. "You know she's good for a lousy twenty-five. And we need to get down to Mayaguana soon, not after you've finally gotten a wire payment."

Tony looked at them and considered the situation for a moment. "OK. Here's the deal. You pay me cash for the gas now, and then wire another twenty-five hundred later today" he offered.

"How much is the gas?" Jennifer asked.

"Three hundred." Tony replied without blinking an eye.

"Deal. Let's get going on this chariot of yours."

They walked out the door towards the parking ramp as Jennifer sent B.W. a quick text from her phone telling him to wire the money to an account number Tony had readily available. As they walked up to the plane it appeared they were going to take to Mayaguana, Jennifer observed to herself it was hardly a chariot. Being somewhat familiar with the more common types of aircraft from her father who liked planes almost as much as boats, she recognized this as a Piper Aztec. Jennifer was no pilot, but the plane looked very old and tired, and not maintained to a level that inspired confidence. The paint job, which was white with red accents, was very faded, and had scratches and rust marks showing around the joints. At least the plane had two engines, for which she was thankful.

Climbing inside she saw the six seats looked worn and uncomfortable. She sat down inside the plane, which was still cool from the morning air. Tony stored her backpack and a few other items in a stowage hold in the nose of the plane and then climbed in the pilot's seat. Obie took the co-pilot station. The fuel truck came over and an attendant in a jumpsuit hopped out and began to fill up the tanks. Once he was done Tony handed him the cash from Jennifer. The fuel truck drove away and Tony made a few quick checks and then cranked the engines. The engines sputtered to life with a few puffs of black smoke. He revved the engines and spoke on the radio to the tower. As the plane taxied forward towards the runway, Jennifer noted that, much like the worn exterior of the Aztec, a lot of the cockpit gauges appeared to be worn out as well. Particularly concerning to her were the fuel gauges, which indicated both fuel tanks were empty, even though Jennifer had just watched the attendant top them off.

"What did you get us into here, Dad?" she asked herself. Tony turned the nose of the Aztec down the runway. The Aztec buzzed down the runway and lifted smoothly off the ground, just past the same Airbus Jennifer had arrived on, now getting ready to depart back to Atlanta. She watched Lynden Pindling International Airport fade away as they climbed upwards and out over the ocean. Tony turned the plane south, and soon the entire island of New Providence was lost as hazy heat and the blue ocean overtook the landscape. Despite the condition of his plane, Tony quickly impressed Jennifer with his piloting skills. His aura of easy confidence translated well into his flying, and he was much more meticulous and attentive to the details of his cockpit than his laid back attitude suggested. She was still nervous about the broken fuel gauges, but she felt comfortable enough to relax a bit. Obie turned about in his seat to continue their earlier conversation over the droning of the propellers.

"So, you were telling me about the MICAL secession movement. Do you think it's really going to happen?" Jennifer coaxed Obie.

"I only know what you can read for yourself in the papers. I told you in the airport the reasons for the movement, and why the government seems inclined to let the region go independent. But I doubt without the leadership of Carty the run for secession would ever have gotten off the ground."

"Carty?" Jennifer enquired.

"Carty Wallingford-Rolle. He's the Member of Parliament who represents the MICAL region. He's been the MP for many years, and most would have said with little accomplishment for the people of MICAL. But recently, he quietly built up support for secession, and then launched a blitzkrieg political campaign. Obviously, it's been very successful, since, as you read on the headline, there have been months of debate in Parliament but it's now nearing a vote."

"Once the vote is complete, what happens then?"

"Well, once the legislation releases MICAL to be independent, there will be a ceremony signing the final documents formally releasing the islands from The Commonwealth of The Bahamas, and before that ink is dry, it's a done deal. Mayaguana and the other MICAL islands will be their own sovereign country."

Obie sat back in his seat and looked out over the ocean. Jennifer sat back in her seat as well. What he had just told her was very concerning. If Mayaguana became its own sovereign country in just a few days, her situation was even more desperate than she had thought. Once this little chain of islands was independent, she doubted they would look favorably on her still poking around trying to figure out what happened to her father. Any claims of land ownership might not be honored, making chances of saving her company even slimmer than she had hoped.

"So, obviously, I don't know much about The Bahamas, and even less about Mayaguana. Can you give me the ancient history lesson, before this whole secession movement?" Jennifer asked. Obie seemed eager to continue to show off his local knowledge, so why not take advantage.

"Certainly. I can go back a long way, all the way to before Columbus when the island was just inhabited by Arawak Indians, but we'll fast forward to more recent times," Obie said, starting to sound like a history professor. "The current inhabitants of the island trace their roots back primarily to the nearby Turks and Caicos Islands, and many were also freed slaves who found their way south. The first settlement was recorded in the early 1800's, when two sisters who got tired of being bossed around by their drunkard husbands sailed a small boat over from Provo and set up camp on the east end of the island. The island population grew slowly, and a few other small settlements sprouted, but no more than about two hundred people ever inhabited the whole place, living as simple fishermen and farmers."

"They sound like hearty souls!" Jennifer said, impressed by the pioneer spirit. It didn't seem quite as surprising to her that their descendants might seek independence.

"They are, even today," Obie agreed, and then continued. "Much later, Mayaguana Air Station was initially established just after World War II ended. The emerging Cold War left the Caribbean seas as hostile territory, where Soviet submarines prowled, coming uncomfortably close to US waters through the deep water channels around The Bahamas. The first thought was the base could serve as a southern hub for the US military, and soon Seabees arrived on the shores with bulldozers and pavers. Within months, the US Navy had paved the longest runway in the world at the time – over seventeen thousand feet long – and got ready to base long range bombers on this remote outpost. As the Cold War heated up and Cuba looked like it would be causing more and more trouble, the air station at Mayaguana was further built out, with a complement of PT boats docked just south of the runway in Abraham's Bay."

"And that's where my father's development is primarily located, right?" Jennifer broke in.

"That's the place. He is resurfacing the runway so tourist jets can land, and getting the old PT boat marina area ready for mega yachts. You'll see when we land," Obie answered, going on with his history lesson. "Now, the Cuban threat gradually diminished, only to be replaced by an even greater threat as Soviet submarines became more and more brazen in the Caribbean. I guess the fear of a nuclear missile attack from the sea dominated the minds of generals and analysts in Washington, and there was little old Mayaguana, already a nice foothold and seemingly just the right place for a missile tracking station. So in the mid 1960's, the air station again saw a surge of activity as a string of towers were established along one of the island's highest ridgelines. Of course, the public message was that these towers were to track NASA rockets as the space program kicked into high gear, but the crews manning the base and the locals from the island knew differently."

"Wow, so my father probably knew all about this, even though by the time he got to the island, the base was shutting down," Jennifer said.

"I would assume so. Since the base closed, Mayaguana has been a relatively uninhabited island with just a couple of hundred people in a few settlements. You know what they call Mayaguana? Its nickname, I mean?"

Jennifer shook her head no.

"They call it 'God's Back'…because it's so desolate, God must have turned his back on it."

Obie turned back in his seat as he and Tony began a heated discussion on Nassau politics. The drone of the propellers on the Aztec mesmerized Jennifer for a few moments before she fell asleep.

Chapter 6

The trade winds above the Mayaguana Passage just south of Crooked Island jostled the Piper Aztec as it cruised across a clear blue sky. Jennifer roused from her sleep and looked at the clock on her phone. It was early afternoon, so she guessed they must be getting close to Mayaguana. She noticed the Aztec was descending. Looking out of the front window of the cockpit, she saw they were approaching a large island. Soon, the coastline of the northwest corner of the island was clearly in view.

Jennifer had to admit to herself that it was a stunning site. The dark, blue hues of deep-water ocean met with light, blue fingers of shallow, sandy seabed. Along the coast, white crashing waves smashed and splashed over limestone rocks at the base of tall cliffs overlooking the ocean. A small lighthouse stood at the very tip of the northwest point of the island. Past the lighthouse to the north, three smaller islands stood out along the reef line, just about a quarter mile from the beaches of the north shore of the island and creating a half- moon shaped, protected bay.

Jennifer looked out further and realized she could not see the other end of the island. It seemed to go on forever. She began to appreciate how large the island actually was. This was no tiny private island like the ones owned by famous actors and rock stars. This was a vast landmass, and for the first time, Jennifer could see how it might actually be its own country, not even considering the other islands making up the MICAL region, each of which were also as large, or even larger than Mayaguana. She also felt that, at least from the air, the island did appear stunningly beautiful – the kind of place people indeed might want to vacation.

The Aztec cruised from the northwestern point towards the south and east, and Jennifer could now make out the runway and a lot of construction activity to the south of the runway along a very large, shallow, bay. From the little time she spent learning about Mayaguana, she figured this must Abraham's Bay. She looked down at the bay and her heart skipped for a moment as she saw her father's sailboat, the Maelstrom, still anchored in the bay near a small, concrete dock that jutted out from the shoreline. The beauty of the place was lost to Jennifer at that moment, and she reminded herself that among the natural wonders of the reef and tranquil beaches there was deadly danger. For the first time, it occurred to her that danger might also find her on this island, just as it apparently had found her father.

Jennifer noticed that most of the runway was torn up or under construction. There were orange barrels and cones marking different areas, and construction equipment at different locations working on the various sections of the runway and airport.

The runway operation, as extensive as it was, seemed dwarfed by the activity near the new port. A new road leading from an equipment yard near the airport wound its way to the coast and the area Jennifer thought was supposed to be a marina for recreational boats. But the work in progress appeared to be much more extensive than she considered would be needed.

The Aztec made a last shallow turn on to its final approach. Tony lowered the flaps on the wings as the plane descended below the ridgeline running along the south side of the runway. Her thoughts were interrupted as the plane touched down on a roughly graded, thin strip of old runway that had obviously been left as the temporary useable part during the resurfacing work. The buzzing drone of the propellers was drowned out by the rumble of the tires along the bumpy surface.

Tony slowed the Aztec and taxied over to a small dirt parking area marked with a few cones, some tie-down chains and a fire extinguisher. As they climbed out of the plane, an old green Land Rover pulled alongside. The driver opened the door and walked over, leaving the vehicle still running.

"Ms. Bullfinch, I'm Colin Steele. We spoke on the phone," he said to Jennifer, extending his hand. His tone was business-like and although he was speaking cordially, his expression was stone-faced.

"Yes, I recall," Jennifer replied coldly, shaking his hand and looking him in the eye.

"I'm sorry we have to meet under such unpleasant circumstances," Colin said in an almost imperceptibly warmer tone.

"Thank you. I suggest we get down to business, Mr. Steele. I believe you said you would have consolidated issues and grievances on behalf of the other contractors here," Jennifer was in no mood for false sympathy.

"I've got unpaid invoices at the office. I'll drive you over there and we can go over everything," Colin said, getting back into the driver seat of the Land Rover and closing the door. Jennifer took her backpack out of the stowage hold and climbed into the passenger seat of the Land Rover. Tony unloaded some packages Jennifer had seen him stow back in Nassau. It was two large sacks of fast food hamburgers and two pizzas, which he traded to another Bahamian who had driven up to the other side of the plane in an old Toyota Hilux SUV, for a small, red cooler. Obie had exchanged a few quick words with Colin, and got into the Hilux along with the burgers and pizza. Tony gave a quick wave good-bye to Jennifer as she drove away with Colin.

The green Land Rover sped along a dusty road that ran out away from the old runway and up the ridgeline to the south. It was a quick drive up the hill, and Jennifer and Colin sat in an icy silence. As the Land Rover reached the top of the ridgeline, Jennifer could see two reasons why this location had been chosen for the head office of the operation. For productive reasons, the ridgeline view back to the north allowed for the entire runway to be surveyed. Looking towards the south over Abraham's Bay, the marina construction could also be overseen very nicely. But putting good business sense aside, it was also a gorgeous view. Maybe even a million-dollar view once the office site wasn't needed and luxury vacation homes could be built along the ridge. The office was a simple trailer, much like those Jennifer had worked in on many construction sites in Atlanta. Colin parked the Land Rover in front of the trailer.

"Welcome to the LIC Development Headquarters," he said, somewhat dryly, opening the door and shutting off the Land Rover. Colin got out and walked purposefully towards the steps leading up to the entrance door of the office.

She took a moment to consider Colin Steele before getting out of the Land Rover. As much as she disliked his attitude, she had to admit that he was handsome. Just about 6 feet tall, with light brown hair, and light green eyes, Colin looked like a former athlete. He had broad shoulders that reminded her of a swimmer's build. His clean-cut, v-shaped look was juxtaposed by his rugged, construction worker appearance. He was wearing a green, short-sleeved polo shirt that had some kind of dive bar logo on it, a pair of worn-looking Dickey work pants, and brown Caterpillar work boots. This made him something of a contradiction to Jennifer: an odd mix of former frat boy and blue collar workman. His athletic build gave him a youthful appearance, but Jennifer guessed he was probably a few years older than her, somewhere in his late 30's.

They sat down at some desks inside and Colin began to give her a basic overview of the project and where the costs were most concentrated. He seemed to sense already that she really didn't know much about the project, because his explanations started at a very basic level. Jennifer was glad for this, as she was figuring out a lot about the overall project without having to admit she was as uninformed as she actually was. There were well over a hundred various invoices overdue, ranging from a few hundred dollars to tens of thousands of dollars.

Despite his clear explanation of the project, it was also clear Colin was no accountant. As Jennifer expected, given his only real responsibility was the airport, he knew very little about the other invoices. She sat with a calculator while Colin read out the invoices, often accompanied by his sarcastic commentary, and handed her one from time-to-time for a closer read. After two hours she sat back and looked at the numbers. It was a grim financial picture.

The total amounts were unfortunately quite significant. It looked like Langford was behind by about well over eight million dollars. What was most confusing to Jennifer was where those millions were owed. It looked like a very small amount was owed to various general suppliers for things like food, household supplies, and some payments on a few leased all-purpose trucks. The airport area represented another half a million dollars, most of it to sub-contractors that Colin had hired, such as the paving crew and a company that had shipped in and was operating the asphalt plant to produce the material to pave the runway. That left the marina construction, by far the biggest culprit, with the balance of the outstanding bills. It was difficult to say exactly how much and what companies were owed money, because most of the marina-related invoices were in Chinese characters.

"So, if you've got the new runway work, then who is in charge of the marina part of the development? My father seemed to handle the general support, since most of those bills were directly to him, and you are managing the airport, but I have yet to hear about or see the marina project manager," Jennifer asked Colin. It was another question she wished she didn't have to ask.

"Now that is a good question," Colin said, looking serious rather than sarcastic for the first time in several hours. "Maybe we should take a drive around now that you've seen this stack of bills?"

Jennifer looked at him to try and read what was behind this proposal. He looked earnest. "OK. I think that would be very helpful" she said, putting down the notepad she was using to tally the bills. Now that she knew a lot more about what was going on based on the invoices, a site visit would be helpful.

They walked out of the office and Colin called Jennifer to the edge of the ridgeline overlooking Abraham's Bay. He started pointing out all of the various places and equipment related to the development, which could easily be spotted from where they were standing, thanks to a swath of brush that had been cut down for just such a purpose on either side of the ridgeline. Jennifer looked down towards the marina. She could see a lot of activity: trucks rolling about, workmen directing the tying of re-bar, large excavators continuing to dredge various portions of the marina basin. Just inland from the marina activity and a few hundred yards south along the bay was a work camp, with several rows of trailers similar to the headquarters offices. Even further down the bay to the south, and directly on the water, was another strange building. It was a huge, corrugated aluminum monstrosity that looked like a warehouse of some kind.

"What is all this?" Jennifer said looking over at Colin, and failing to keep the incredulity out of her voice.

"That's what I have been wondering for a few months now. Supposedly, it is to serve as a huge workshop and materials warehouse during the construction of the mega-resort. You can see the layout of the whole complex. The actual marina, where all the dredging is going on with those excavators, looks very large to me. Like it will eventually be able to handle commercial ships, not just yachts, recreational sailboats and sport fishing boats," Colin shared his thoughts.

"And even that housing complex. It looks fairly large. How many workers are on this project?" Jennifer asked, now that Colin seemed open to offering up some of his knowledge.

"On the whole project? I don't really know. For my part at the airport, I've got twenty, though they are mostly off island now. There are a few security guards, some housekeeping staff and a few office workers as well, so maybe another fifteen. But that housing complex you're looking at," Colin said, waving down at the rows of trailers just off the bay. "That is just for the crew working on the marina. I guess there might be over one hundred."

"Does that sound right to you? I've never worked on a marina project, but it seems like a lot of people even for what looks like a much larger project than I thought."

"I've never worked on a marina project either, but I agree with you. To be honest, I was hoping you would be able to shed some light on that side of things," Colin looked up from the extensive construction operation and over at Jennifer. "I have been working on the airport for months, and very closely with your father, but I have never seen a set of plans for the marina anywhere."

"And so, again, who is the project manager? You must work with them," Jennifer prompted.

"I told you - I really don't know. It's like a completely separate operation on the other side of this ridge. There's a foreman, a guy named Mr. Wu, who doesn't talk much. As best I can tell, he's in charge. I think we should drive down there so you can get a closer look and form your own opinion of what's going on," Colin said walking back towards the Land Rover.

Jennifer took a long look at the site, another look at her father's empty sailboat, and then turned to walk over to the Land Rover. She opened the door and stepped up to get into the SUV. As she did, the airport project on the other, inland side, of the ridgeline caught her eye again. It suddenly occurred to her the difference between the two operations. The airport work had ground to a halt. Colin, no longer able to pay his crew, had equipment just sitting idle where the work had left off when the money for the project dried up. Colin and a few of his key people, like Obie, were the only ones left, as most of the others had gone back home to Nassau to find paying jobs. That was what Jennifer would have expected – no different than what she had seen in other projects that ran out of cash. So then why was there so much work still going on at the marina? She had seen clearly the huge stack of unpaid bills - bills presumably to pay the same people down on the bay toiling away, apparently working for free for almost a month now. She got in the Land Rover and thought about the possible options as Colin drove down a narrow dirt road that ran along the ridgeline towards Abraham's Bay.

The Land Rover jostled its way down the road, and Jennifer sat in silence looking out the window towards the ocean. Towards the base of the ridgeline, the road curved south, heading directly to the beach. Off to her right, she could see the sky was now a deep orange, and the sun had turned from bright yellow to bright red as it lowered towards the water off to the west. It was now late afternoon, and this time of year the sun would soon set completely. Jennifer's heart began to race just a little. The day was nearly over, and she was no closer to any answers. At this rate, fourteen more days would go by very quickly, and she would have lost the project, lost the fortunes of an entire company, and have lost her father with no explanation. She glanced over at Colin, set her jaw, and renewed her determination to get to the bottom of things fast. They pulled up to the marina site, and Colin stopped the Land Rover. They both looked out the windshield at the workers. Everyone she saw looked Asian. No Bahamians, no American ex-pats. She looked over at Colin, and he looked back at her nodding his head.

"That's right. They are all Chinese," he said, reading her thoughts. "Just like all those invoices for the marina operation are all payable to Chinese companies. In case you are wondering, that is not common here. Even if a foreign company is allowed to manage a project in The Bahamas, they must hire a lot of Bahamians to help."

"Drive down to the housing area," Jennifer told Colin. Apparently, the marina crew might even work at night. There were several portable light sets arranged around the marina basin, which was drained out so some excavators could deepen the area. A few groups of workers were gathering around in different clusters talking and going over notes on notepads. It looked to Jennifer like a shift-change briefing as the day crew changed over to a night crew. The Land Rover pulled to a stop just outside the housing area. Jennifer counted fifteen trailers.

"How many did you say they sleep to a trailer?" she asked Colin.

"I think about eight. Four sets of bunk beds. But if they're hot bunking, could be twice that. That last trailer they use for a kitchen, and one is a kind of office or meeting room," Colin said, divulging that he had been quietly observing the activities of the camp.

He continued driving along the dirt road past the work camp towards the large warehouse at the edge of the water. Unlike the work camp, there was a chain link fence around the warehouse that went right up to the water's edge, which at that part of the bay was not sand, but 'iron shore.' Iron shore, Jennifer had learned, was limestone that had hardened into a dark, volcanic-looking mass of rock along the edge of the water. The water was deeper in this part of the bay, and as darkness continued to fall, it looked black rather than the beautiful light turquoise blue of earlier this afternoon. Jennifer estimated the two story warehouse was at least seven hundred feet long and two hundred and fifty feet wide. That made it nearly two hundred thousand square feet. On the top of the building were several large ventilation fans which worked in conjunction with several large air condition units along the edge of the building near a row of storage sheds and shipping containers. At the end furthest inland, there was another large shed from which a loud humming noise emanated. An exhaust pipe coming out of the top told Jennifer there was a generator inside powering this warehouse. There were no windows anywhere, just a few sets of large, roll-up doors.

"Why do you think they need so large a warehouse here?" Colin asked Jennifer, looking at her with over-probing eyes.

"I have no idea. I told you, I am new to this project," she snapped at him, annoyed that he was prodding her after she thought they had come to an unspoken understanding that she was clueless about this development and trying to learn from Colin, not the other way around.

"And why would it go right up to the edge of the water like that?" he continued as if thinking out loud and ignoring her snapping. "I mean, it looks fairly permanent to me, so it's not like they plan to tear it down once they are done with the marina. And if I were building a resort, I really wouldn't want this large warehouse just a little way down the bay from my tranquil, island outpost marina."

Now he seemed to be really trying to push Jennifer's buttons. It was working. She spun around and stared Colin in the eye for a moment. Before she could think of a retort, he spoke up again.

"Here comes Mr. Wu."

Jennifer got out of the SUV and walked over to the chain link fence. A tall, mean-looking man stepped out of a large shipping container. He lit a cigarette as he walked towards a door that led into the warehouse. "Mr. Wu! Can I speak with you?" she yelled to him over the clatter of machinery.

Mr. Wu looked over at Jennifer and squinted at her through the dust and sunlight. Slowly, rather reluctantly, he walked over towards her, until he was just in front of her with the chain link fence between them.

"Yes. Can I help you?" Mr. Wu asked suspiciously.

"Mr. Wu, I'm Jennifer Bullfinch. With my father missing, I am in charge of the project. I'd like you to show me around your work site, and I'd like to see what's in that large warehouse," Jennifer said trying to sound forceful but friendly.

"Certainly. Let us check the access roster to ensure you are allowed," Wu said, pulling out a clipboard.

Jennifer was flabbergasted and infuriated, as she could swear Wu had smirked a bit when he said this. She looked as Wu ran his finger down a list of names of workers who apparently were granted access to this fenced off area.

"I am sorry. You are not listed on here. Perhaps someone from your company can add you?" Mr. Wu told her, showing her the clipboard. A memo apparently signed by her father did list out a series of names, but of course, not hers.

"Mr. Wu, I don't think you understand. I'm sure you know my father was supposedly in a boating accident. I am running the project in his place. I order you to show me inside," she said, dropping the friendly tone entirely.

"If you are in charge, then you will be able to produce proper documentation from LIC Development, and then I will be happy to show you around. But now, if you will excuse me, I have much to do." Wu turned on his heels and headed back for the warehouse, leaving Jennifer silently glowing red with rage.

Colin looked on with some amusement. "Well, now at least you see what we've had to deal with down here."

Chapter 7

Jennifer knew her next stop must be to examine the Maelstrom. Collin dropped her off near what he called the 'government dock' saying he would return after finding Obie for a quick meeting. Thankfully, as she arrived to the dock, the sailboat looked perfectly normal, and just as she remembered it from her many days spent aboard. However, the Boston Whaler that had been Langford's favorite 'run-around' accessory to the larger sailboat was conspicuously missing from its normal tie down.

The deck of the sailboat was clean, and the white fiberglass of the hull looked like it had recently been waxed. Her father always had been good about maintenance. The Maelstrom was a forty-four foot long Beneteau Idylle. Langford heard about the opportunity to get this beautiful sailboat through another real estate developer in Charleston. He jumped at the chance. Jennifer still remembered their first voyage from Charleston down to Savannah, where they had kept the boat ever since.

The vessel drafted five feet and nine inches, and she estimated now at low tide there was about two feet between the keel and the sandy bottom, so it looked like someone had dredged out the channel to the government dock from the reef about eight feet at low tide. The channel up to the mysterious warehouse, in contrast, looked even deeper - like it could be thirty or forty feet deep. That was commercial ship depth. Jennifer stopped to read an inscription in the concrete block forming the start of the dock. It had been written with a stick in the freshly poured concrete many years ago and it read: Lt. Cdr. Smythe, H.M.R.N., August 11, 1962. She had forgotten that Obie had mentioned the British had also manned a small outpost on the island. For a while, the US base here had a contingent from Her Majesty's Royal Navy even after The Bahamas became independent in 1973. The old dock was now crumbling apart, expect for areas where new concrete had been poured over the top as temporary reinforcement.

Jennifer stepped over a rusted tie-down that was being used to secure the Maelstrom and climbed aboard. Still, she could notice nothing amiss. The sails were neatly tied and covered. Jennifer opened the door to the cabin and went below. Again, everything appeared to be in order and as she remembered it. The interior of the boat was done in teak wood, well-oiled over the years so it had a glistening, dark shine to it.

She examined the navigation station, which was a desk built in to the wall just before the steep stairs leading out of the cabin to the aft deck. Langford used that station as a work desk, since even when they were on vacation sailing he usually had continued to work on future real estate deals. Mounted to the wall above the desk was a West Marine VHF radio and handset, and next to it was a base station for a satellite phone. The phone was missing from the base station, but the number was written on a label on the base. She pulled out her phone, and compared the phone number with the one that had sent the text file. It was a match! The strange text message and the file had indeed been sent from his satellite phone. She forced herself to refocus and continue her investigation.

Jennifer finished examining the desk. There was a navigational chart of the waters around Mayaguana, but with no significant markings in it. At the back of the desk were a few books: *The Bahamas Investment Handbook and Business Annual*, *The Bahamas Sailing Guidebook*, *Goode's World Atlas*, and for some reason, a college geology text book.

There were also two framed pictures: one of Langford, Julia and Jennifer taken about five years ago, just before her mother became ill. The other she remembered had been the photo missing from the scrapbook in his office. It was of him, another military officer and a Bahamian taken near this very dock. She turned on a brass retractable lamp mounted to the wall by the desk and picked up the picture, looking closer at it.

"That photo goes back a long time, when Major Langford Bullfinch was the most feared officer at the Mayaguana Air Station," a voice from behind Jennifer said.

Startled, Jennifer spun around to find the speaker. A man stood looking down at her from the top of the deck stairs.

"Who are you?" she demanded loudly, hoping the fear she felt was masked by her best commanding tone of voice.

"Oh, I'm very sorry. Didn't mean to scare you. I shouldn't have surprised you like that, especially given the unfortunate recent events," said the man, not answering her question. Jennifer now had recovered from her surprise enough to notice he had a British accent.

"So, who are you?" Jennifer demanded again, looking back towards the galley out of the corner of her eye wondering if there might be a kitchen knife readily available.

"Right, sorry. My name is Michelson, Ian Michelson - Professor Ian Michelson, actually. But back then, I was Lieutenant Michelson of Her Majesty's Royal Navy. That's me in that picture standing next to your father," said the man, smiling broadly.

Jennifer looked quickly down at the picture she was still holding. The other officer did look like it could have been this same man, when he was thirty or so years younger. In the picture, he was a clean cut looking military man in his early twenties, while the person looking down at her from the cabin door looked like an aging rock star. He had long shaggy hair, which was mostly gray, and an ear ring. He still had the same piercing gray eyes, and the same slight, thin build from the picture. Also as in the picture, he was wearing a pair of khaki shorts with deep cargo pockets, but instead of a neatly pressed uniform he had on a white oxford shirt with only a few buttons carelessly buttoned, and rubber-soled deck shoes.

"That may be," she conceded. "But why are you snooping around his boat?" she pushed.

"Ah, yes. I was walking by heading to my own boat – that's the one docked just behind you – and saw someone inside here. I figured it might be you," Ian said. He stepped back out of the doorway, clearing the way for Jennifer to come up the stairs on to the aft deck. He bowed slightly and waved his hand in an exaggerated 'come forth, your majesty' manner, and said "Won't you come up on the deck, and we can make a more proper introduction, Miss Bullfinch?"

Jennifer shook her head yes as she set the photo back on the navigation station desk. She climbed up the stairs warily, but determined to be cordial enough to find out more about Professor Ian Michelson.

"How did you know I was Langford's daughter?"

"It's a small island. New travels fast. And besides, I've been aboard this boat many times before and recognized you from the other picture on the desk."

"So what are you doing on Mayaguana, you obviously haven't been here all these years since that picture was taken if you are really a professor!"

"No, No! Goodness no. I left the same day your father did. Headed back to England, and found my way back to University. Never really left, I suppose. I got my master's degree in geology, then a Ph.D., and then I got a position on the faculty. Been teaching and conducting various bits of research ever since."

Ian had a nervous, halting way of speaking. If he were an American, it would have been extremely annoying, but his posh British accent somehow made it more acceptable and amusing.

"So what brings you to Mayaguana all these years later?" Jennifer asked, still uncertain why a British professor would be poking around a half-built marina in The Bahamas.

"Ah – well that's my research. When I was here as a young Naval officer, I got interested in geology from countless hours, days, months, of walking along the shores of this island and noticing the different geological conditions and patterns. It became something of a rather serious hobby for me, and certainly helped to pass the time. When I went back to England, and needed a doctoral thesis, I thought of this place. I've been conducting research around this part of The Bahamas ever since."

"So I guess you and my father became friends here?" Jennifer asked, still trying to learn more.

"We did become very good friends indeed. I meant what I said about him being the most feared officer at the base. When he arrived, the previous commander of the place had been letting things go - no discipline, no maintenance. I suppose one couldn't blame him, but all the same, just because you're on a tropical island outpost doesn't mean the rules and regulations are gone. That was certainly the attitude your father had when he took command. He made his presence felt I can tell you, and to me no less than any of the others. I was a young lieutenant, and far more interested in my rock-hounding than in real work. I am proud to say your father saw some potential in me and set me straight. We started accompanying various patrols around the waters; we set up work details to whitewash and fix old buildings and equipment. Really gave everyone a sense of purpose. Took quite a few months and a lot of struggling, but he set this ship right, so to speak."

"That sounds like my father. And about your research…?"

"Nowadays, I have been working on a thesis about the geological formation of this entire island. You see it's really rather unique. Most of the islands in The Bahamas are essentially worn down coral reefs. The place is like one long sand bar, and the islands look like how you might expect - very shallow, with little in the way of elevation. Mayaguana is quite different. You've noticed, I'm sure, the bluffs, or cliffs along the northern shores? Yet on parts of the south side of the island, you've got a more shallow, typical Bahamas beach environment?"

"Yes, now that you mention it."

"Right. Well, that's because this island sits along a fault line, tectonic plates, as it were. The edge of two plates runs right along this island, and where one plate has slid up on top of the other, that's your bluffs on the north shore."

"Fascinating," said Jennifer, although she was not really all that fascinated. "So what does that mean?"

"Well…nothing, really…I guess. It's just interesting to geology professors like me I suppose," Ian answered, seeming a bit disappointed Jennifer wasn't as enthralled about the subject as he.

"You're just here on your own then? Alone doing research?"

"Oh, no - I wouldn't say on my own. My university, the Royal School of Mines, in London, is backing my research," Ian paused looking at Jennifer for a moment before continuing, "And your father has been quite helpful as well."

He looked down at the deck of the sailboat, and then back up into Jennifer's eyes, gauging her reaction to his last comment. Jennifer was really not sure how to respond. On one hand, this man had known her father for many years, and he had a way of looking out for old friends. On the other, it was unlike him to just fund academic research for no reason. Especially if it was very expensive research, which based on the covered up equipment on Ian's boat tied off nearby, she was guessing it was.

"Really?" she probed, "What was his interest in your findings?"

"Oh, I think he felt as though some academic published articles would be good publicity for the island and good for real estate development perhaps. And I take a lot of depth readings and soundings that will be useful for the marina," Ian offered.

An awkward silence hung in the air for a few moments. Jennifer still found this hard to believe, but this whole thing had been so out of character of her father, maybe it was true. She was saved from commenting on this back to Ian by the sound of a vehicle approaching. It was the Land Rover, being driven quickly down the hill by Colin Steele. He pulled up next to the sailboat and rolled down the window.

"Hi there. I've been looking for you," Colin said through the window. "Good day, Ian."

"Mr. Steele," replied Ian. He said it cheerily, but his face read rather blankly.

"And I see you have returned from another of your excursions," Colin pressed.

"Quite so. I was just out in the Caicos Passage taking a few readings."

"And where is your lovely assistant?" Colin asked, smiling slightly.

"Oh, she's still aboard, finishing up a few notes," Michelson said, not returning the smile.

"Assistant?" Jennifer asked.

"Yes, I have a graduate student who's been working with me for several months now here also. She's not really an assistant, more of a junior colleague. Mr. Steele enjoys poking me in the ribs a bit about her," Michelson answered.

Jennifer looked over at his boat and saw that there was someone coming up from the cabin. As the person emerged and Jennifer could get a clearer look, she started to realize why Colin was giving Ian a hard time. The 'junior colleague' was a stunningly gorgeous young woman. She looked to be in her late twenties, with long dark hair. As she turned to walk towards the bow of the boat, Jennifer noted she had Asian features, and she was dressed in tight cut-off jeans shorts and a bikini bathing suit top.

"…Speaking of poking…"Colin said crudely under his breath, but loud enough so Ian and Jennifer could hear him.

"Dominique!" Ian called to her, "Come over here and meet Jennifer Bullfinch."

Dominique, who had not been paying attention to the three talking near the sailboat, looked up slightly startled. Her head

61

swiveled in an almost mechanical manner, surveying the scene, from Colin in the Land Rover, over to Ian and Jennifer on the deck of the sailboat. When she got to Jennifer, her gazed fixed on her for a few moments with a slight frown on her face. She suddenly smiled, and waved over at them as if it had clicked who Jennifer Bullfinch was. She walked up to the side rail of the boat and with manicured, bare feet hopped lightly on to the concrete government dock. The adoring look on Ian's face as she walked gracefully towards them told Jennifer that Colin was probably right about the relationship between Dominique and Ian.

"Hello, Ms. Bullfinch. I was very sorry to hear about your father," Dominique said, walking up to Jennifer. She was tall and slender, but looked quite muscular to Jennifer, like a triathlete. She had a noticeable accent that seemed to be mostly British, but with a very faint Asian undertone. She extended her hand.

"Thank you," Jennifer answered perfunctorily. She took hold of Dominique's hand and shook. Dominique had a strong grip, and Jennifer guessed she probably did some strength training along with the triathlon regimen.

"Jennifer, I hate to break up the party but we have some more things to review up at the office," Colin cut in the conversation, throwing open the passenger door from the driver's seat for her to get in the Land Rover.

"Good to meet you both," Jennifer said quickly to Ian and Dominique as she slid into the passenger seat and closed the door.

"Right, good to meet you," replied Ian. Dominique nodded to her in acknowledgment.

Colin drove back through the sandy marine construction site leaving a trail of dust as he headed towards the large, fenced off warehouse and parked the car a few feet from the edge of the water. Jennifer saw a crude set of stairs had been carved into the rocky, iron shore leading down into the water. A small skiff was tied off at the steps. Jennifer looked back through the cloud of dust towards her father's sailboat. Dominique was still standing at the edge of the government dock as if she had been watching them drive away, while Ian looked busy fumbling with some equipment.

"So, you've met our staff geologist and his love interest. What do you think?" Colin asked looking over at her as he parked the SUV.

"They seem harmless enough, though I can't say I understand what interest my father would have in funding the academic research of a geologist, even if they were old friends," she said to Colin, curious as to why he seemed so interested.

"Maybe so. I don't really understand his work myself. He spends days away on that boat of his with Dominique. I used to think they were just out there naked sunbathing, but I guess he has actually published quite a bit of findings based on his work here. I understand it's a bit controversial though for some reason," Colin mused.

"How so?"

"Well, your father once mentioned to me that the professor's theory about Mayaguana being some kind of different geological formation than the rest of the islands around here either makes him brilliantly correct or dismally wrong, and most other geologists seem to place him in the latter category," Colin said looking over at her.

They drove back up the ridgeline to the office trailers. As Colin turned off the engine, Jennifer could hear the land line phone ringing at her father's desk. She quickly ran inside the office and grabbed the phone off the receiver.

"Hi!" she exclaimed breathlessly, expecting to hear B.W. at the other end.

"Ms. Bullfinch, my name is Carty Wallingford-Rolle. We have a lot to talk about."

Chapter 8

Jennifer was caught by surprise at the caller. Two days ago the name Carty Wallingford-Rolle was completely unfamiliar, but having learned he was leading the charge for MICAL secession from The Bahamas, she felt rather surprised and even a bit honored by the call. She thought for a second about what to say to him.

"Mr. Wallingford-Rolle, I have heard a lot about you. How can I help you so early this morning?" she asked, trying to balance formality and pleasantness in her response.

"Please, call me Carty. I think we will be getting to know one another quite well very quickly, so let's dispense with the pleasantries right off, shall we?" Carty replied. He had a distinguished tone to his voice, which sounded a lot more like the recorded operator's voice she had heard when trying to call her father, rather than Obie's coarser, distinctly island tone.

"And just why is that, Carty?" Jennifer asked, now on full alert.

"We shouldn't talk over the phone about this. This is a face-to-face kind of conversation. I think you should come to Nassau immediately so we can meet and talk in person. I guarantee it will be enlightening for you," Carty said in a suave, but matter-of-fact voice.

"I'll fly up at first light tomorrow morning. When can we meet?" Jennifer asked, hoping Tony MacDonald and his Piper Aztec were somewhere in the vicinity and could come pick her up soon.

"Just call me when you land, and I'll be sure to be available at my office. It's just off East Bay Street. Are you familiar with Nassau?" Carty inquired.

"No, but I can find my way around. Text me your office number and address to my cell phone," Jennifer told him, and read off her mobile phone number.

Jennifer hung the phone back on the receiver on her father's desk. She looked up from the desk to see that Colin was in the office, sitting quietly at his own desk. She hadn't noticed him come inside.

"Sounds like we're going to Nassau," Colin said, leaned back in his chair with his feet up on his desk, smirking at her.

"What 'we' *Kemo Sabe*?" Jennifer said frowning at him, annoyed he had invited himself into her conversation and now on her visit to Carty.

"Look, your father's company, which is also your company, still owes me a lot of money. Maybe it's not a lot to you, but without it, a lot of my workers go hungry, and I go bankrupt. So like it or not, I'm along for the ride," Colin said softly but sternly.

"Well if you're along for the ride, you'd better not be dead weight. Get Obie and see if he can get in touch with Tony MacDonald. We need to charter his plane first thing tomorrow."

"Yes Ma'am!" Colin shouted, standing up from his desk in mock uncoordinated nervousness. Jennifer just shook her head as Colin left the office to go find Obie.

The call had re-energized Jennifer, and even Colin's silly sarcasm and reminder of the impending doom of the project did not really bother her much at the moment. She picked the phone back up and dialed B.W.'s office number. Sure enough he answered.

"How are you making out down there?" B.W. enquired into his end of the line.

"It's a mess here, B.W.," Jennifer laughed, happy to hear his familiar voice. "There are still a lot of things that just don't make sense, and I can't believe Dad would have run a project like this."

"What's the damage?" B.W. asked, getting right to the point.

Jennifer summarized the mess the project finances were in and the confusion the entire crew seemed to have about who was in charge.

"What are you planning on doing now that you've at least seen the place and taken a good look at the financial records? I really could use your help back here." B.W. asked.

"Well, I've met more than a few characters on this island already, but I think it's time to go back to Nassau and do some more detective work. I went aboard the Maelstrom this morning," she choked a bit on the last part.

"How'd she look?" B.W. asked gently.

"Just like normal. This whole accident sounds more suspicious than ever, but his Boston Whaler was gone," Jennifer said, lowering her voice as she spoke into the phone.

"Be careful, Jennifer," B.W. warned. "You're in the lion's den down there."

Chapter 9

Tony's Aztec touched down and taxied back to the yellow General Aviation building where they had departed the day before.

Jennifer turned on her cell phone and waited for it to get a signal. After searching for a moment the letters "BTC" again appeared next to five signal bars at the top of her cell phone screen, indicating she was connected to the Bahamas Telecom network. A few seconds later, the text message from Carty popped up with his office address and phone number.

Jennifer and Colin thanked Tony for the flight after Jennifer texted B.W. to have yet another payment wired to Tony's account on top of the fuel money she had paid him. They walked down the street the quarter mile or so to the Domestic Terminal at the main airport area to rent a car, and Jennifer realized she had spent almost seven thousand dollars on travel in less than twenty-four hours. At this rate, she could understand how her father may have had trouble keeping the project afloat, even with a loan to help. Everything just seemed so expensive, and the necessity of coming back and forth from Nassau to Mayaguana every few days at five thousand dollars per round trip was staggeringly costly. She put it out of her mind for now, knowing there was really no choice in the matter if she was going to get to the bottom of this mess.

At the Domestic Terminal, they rented the most reasonable car available, a Ford Focus, which was still far more than Jennifer had wanted to pay, but she and Colin both agreed they wanted to get to Carty's office rather than wait around for another, cheaper rental car to be returned.

They walked hurriedly out of the terminal, keys in hand, after Jennifer put the car on her credit card and an elderly Bahamian lady had excruciatingly slowly processed her rental contract. Colin hopped in the driver's seat, much to Jennifer's relief. She noticed as they walked out the door that in The Bahamas, as in England, cars drove on the left side of the street, which was a little unnerving to her, especially not knowing her way around. Luckily, it was soon clear that Colin did know his way around Nassau very well. He seemed very comfortable driving along the narrow, busy streets as they got closer to downtown, where an offensive driving style was clearly the only way to actually get anywhere. Some of the streets were marked with signs, but most were not. Somehow Colin wound his way through what he called "Over the Hill" until they got to a road called Shirley Street. It was one way, and completely jammed with cars, trucks and buses. He made a right hand turn on to a cross street, and then another immediate right on another busy road called East Bay Street.

Jennifer was turned around by now, as Colin made a last turn on to a less busy street marked Fowler Street. Fowler Street was lined with nondescript looking buildings, some reasonably new, and some that looked like they might have been homes many years ago, but now were converted to offices or local shops. After a few blocks, Colin pulled in front of one of the newer - but still rather shabby - office buildings and parked the car behind a black SUV. A small sign out front of the office read "Wallingford-Rolle Law Offices."

"Well, we're here. What do you think Mr. Carty Wallingford-Rolle wants?" he asked.

"I've been trying to figure that out the whole way here. I have no idea. Maybe he's worried about the future of the project with my father gone. It sounds like it was a cornerstone of his bid for secession."

"I guarantee he's worried. Your father never mentioned Carty to you?" Colin asked, again looking closely at Jennifer.

"No. But as I have told you for the hundredth time, when he insisted on going forward with this crazy project, we really stopped talking at all. It drove us apart."

"I can tell you since I have been on Mayaguana, Carty has visited several times. He and your father had a lot of close conversations. I have no idea about what, but they clearly knew each other well."

"And why didn't you tell me this?" Jennifer demanded, angry that Colin was holding back information.

"I just did," Colin said, looking her straight in the eye.

Jennifer met his stare, and then opened the car door. "Well I'd appreciate it if you don't let me walk into any minefields, since you seem to know all about them, and you also seem to be latched on to me until you're paid. You know it might just help you to work with me."

"Who says I'm not working with you?" Colin shrugged, getting out of the car.

Just then, the front door to Carty's law office opened, and two very large muscular men wearing dark suits stepped outside. One looked up and down the street, and the other held the door. Jennifer looked closely and saw they were both wearing ear pieces, and she caught a glimpse of a holster underneath one of the men's suit jackets. The man looking up and down the street nodded to the other holding the door, and soon two other men emerged from the office, talking closely to one another. The tallest of the security guards, for that was clearly what they were, briefly looked over Colin and Jennifer, but apparently decided they were harmless. He walked around the front of the black SUV, pulling off two flag covers on either side of the hood as he went around to the driver's side door. Two small blue, black and yellow Bahamian flags unfurled and fluttered lightly in the soft breeze running down Fowler Street. The two men talking in the doorway shook hands, as the second security guard moved from the office door to the SUV, opening the rear passenger door and holding it open. The taller of the two men who had just shaken hands noticed Jennifer and Colin, and enthusiastically waved them over to the entryway of the office.

"Ms. Bullfinch, I presume? I am Carty Wallingford-Rolle. You've arrived just at the proper time. Please allow me to introduce my close friend," said the gentleman. He turned to the other man he had been speaking with and put his hand out indicating towards Jennifer. "Mr. Prime Minister, may I introduce Ms. Jennifer Bullfinch."

"Ah, Ms. Bullfinch," said the Prime Minister. "Please allow me, on behalf of the entire Commonwealth of The Bahamas, to extend our deepest sympathy. Mr. Wallingford-Rolle was just telling me about your father's apparent accident up south."

"Thank you," stammered Jennifer, a bit taken aback.

"If there is anything I can do to help personally, just ask. This man here can get in touch with me at any time," the Prime Minister continued, putting his hand on Carty's arm. With that, the Prime Minister got into his SUV, the security guard closed the door, and got into the passenger seat. Two Bahamas police force motorcycles with blue lights flashing pulled up in front of the SUV, and they all drove off down the street.

"Welcome to my offices. And a rare treat indeed to meet the Prime Minister. Normally to get an audience with him takes quite some doing, but we're old friends and he had just stopped by my office this morning on the way to another meeting," Carty exclaimed, beaming at Jennifer. He extended his hand. Jennifer took it and Carty shook her hand warmly. "You made good time getting up here from Mayaguana. Let's have a seat in my office and have a talk, shall we? And I see you brought Mr. Steele - very good, very good."

Carty held open the door, and Colin and Jennifer stepped inside. Carty's law offices were very plain, much like the outside of the building. The floor was covered in a grey builder's grade carpet, and the walls were simply painted in cream with a lighter white color trim. His reception area was small and consisted of one plain, wood paneled counter and two old leather chairs with a small end table between them. A bored-looking young Bahamian woman sat behind the reception desk filing her nails and watching a newscast from a Miami television station on a flat panel TV mounted to the wall for entertaining clients while they waited. Carty led Jennifer and Colin back to a small conference room, with a window looking out on the side alleyway. He offered them a coffee from a Bunn coffee maker he had sitting on top of a filing cabinet in a corner of the conference room.

In contrast to the plain vanilla surroundings of his office, Mr. Carty Wallingford-Rolle himself was anything but plain. Jennifer guessed Carty was about six foot three inches tall and slender, making him appear even taller. His dark hair had strong flecks of gray in it, adding to his distinguished gentleman aura. He was wearing a very expensive Brioni suit, with a palm tree print Hermes tie, and dark Gucci leather shoes. He poured himself a cup of coffee in a Styrofoam cup, sat down in the chair at the head of the conference table, and leaned back, smiling broadly at Jennifer.

"I wish we could have met under more pleasant circumstances, but I am very glad to make your acquaintance in

72

person all the same," Carty said. In true Bahamian fashion, even with important, time sensitive matters to discuss, it was clear to Jennifer that Carty was going to chat a bit and get to know her before getting down to business. Idle chit chat at this particular moment was infuriating to Jennifer, but she felt it was better to let Carty lead the conversation, no matter how frustrating.

"What did you think of Mayaguana, now that you have had a chance to see it?" Carty asked.

"Very beautiful. I can see why my father thought it would make a great vacation destination," Jennifer answered dutifully.

"Indeed. The most beautiful island in all The Bahamas, if you ask me. I was born and raised there, you know."

Jennifer had not known, but she found it not coincidental.

"In fact, the P.M. likes to call me his 'Man from Mayaguana'," Carty laughed, continuing his chit chat.

"And what do you think of the project itself?" Carty continued.

"Well, I haven't made up my mind on that one yet," Jennifer answered. Carty leaned forward in his chair and looked at Jennifer, still smiling.

"Why not?" he asked.

"I can't seem to make much sense of it. Massive infrastructure works, but not much accomplished if you want to get tourism started on the island. My father was a brilliant developer. It troubles me he seems off course on this one," Jennifer answered honestly.

"Who said anything about tourism?" Carty asked, now looking very serious, the smile gone from his face, and leaning even closer towards Jennifer, his palms flat on the table.

" Well…I guess…that's what I have always understood about the project," Jennifer said hesitantly.

"So you really know nothing about this whole thing then? You mean your father told you this was about tourism? Hotels?" Carty asked, looking a bit incredulously.

Jennifer was now completely on edge. Here again, another strange character from her father's past seemed to hold secrets she knew nothing about. Carty's cheerful, outgoing, politician demeanor was gone, and he looked dead serious. She decided to test the waters.

"I've heard about your secession plan," she offered, not sure what his reaction would be.

Carty sat silent after she spoke, looking at her intently for a moment.

"That's right. Of course you are by now I'm sure familiar with my plans for the MICAL region," Carty responded slowly. He regained his politician's demeanor and continued. "I have great hopes for the place. It has been ignored for hundreds of years, but I believe, and your father believed, that its time has now come."

"My father shared your vision?" Jennifer queried.

"He did. You mean to say he never mentioned any of this to you, his daughter and successor to the family empire during all the time you spent together?" Carty asked, with some misbelief evident in his tone.

"Never. I knew he spent some time here while he was in the military, but he never spoke much about it other than he enjoyed the sailing and diving," Jennifer did not want to tell Carty just yet her true feelings about the folly of the whole endeavor.

"But surely then he must have told you about me. I mean, we knew each other from way back, when I used to go spear fishing with him around the island," Carty looked her in the eye, like he was trying to read her thoughts as he spoke.

Suddenly, the picture from her father's desk came back to her mind. Carty was the young Bahamian on the boat deck along with her father and Ian Michelson. She felt perhaps Carty was offended. Perhaps he had placed more importance behind the relationship from so many years ago than her father had. But still, not wanting to have to make something up on the spot just to spare his feelings, she felt sticking to the truth was still best.

"Since you know my father, you know he is the kind of person who looks to the future. I'm sure if I had spent more time here with him, it would have come up." Jennifer said, hoping it was the right way to smooth this rough patch in the conversation and move on.

Colin, who had sat quietly observing the conversation so far, chimed in now, maybe feeling he also needed to diffuse the issue and change course a bit. "Mr. Wallingford-Rolle, perhaps you could help us out while we are here in Nassau. We're hoping to find out some more about the company that Langford Bullfinch started here in The Bahamas to operate the development. As I'm sure you know from some of your own visits to Mayaguana, my runway work down there has been significant. I am very sorry Langford has gone missing and the project is in disarray because I had a lot of respect for him. But I have my own business to worry about. Now that he is gone, maybe for good, the finances are a mess. Jennifer has been very helpful in trying to get this straight, but we've hit some stumbling blocks. Since you are a lawyer, maybe you can help us track a few things down."

Carty shifted his intense stare over to Colin. "I can tell you both all about the company, Mr. Steele, since I am one of its officers," Carty said in a quiet but deliberate tone.

Jennifer and Colin exchanged brief glances of surprise. Carty looked at them, a small smile again cracking his distinguished features.

"Yes, Ms. Bullfinch. Mr. Steele has got right to the heart of the matter. This is in fact why I called you this morning, although I assumed you already knew," Carty said, opening a thick manila file folder he had on the conference table. "Here are the articles of incorporation, and the business license. All Bahamian companies must have a Bahamian citizen as a partner. I am that partner for this company, not to mention its legal counsel."

Jennifer looked down at the paperwork, which established "LIC Development Company, Ltd" as a legal corporation in The Bahamas. Jennifer groaned to herself at the thought of more international legal tangles to work out in just a few days, and during a holiday season. She could hear the cash register in Tyler King's office ringing happily and using up more and more of her remaining funds. She knew it had to be done though, and all these documents would later require careful reading, but she had too many questions of Carty Wallingford-Rolle at the moment to begin dissecting legal documents.

"So you are the Member of Parliament for this region, and leading the drive for independence, and you are a partner in the project which is to be the key economic driver of the new MICAL state. Sounds like my father, or this project anyway, was very dependent upon you," Jennifer told Carty as Colin sat nodding his head in agreement.

"Maybe so. But rest assured that I, as much as your father, wanted to see this project succeed. Being so closely involved was, to my mind, the best way for me to help ensure its success."

"And ensure you become the king of your own country!" Colin blurted out, naming the elephant in the room that Jennifer had felt better to leave alone.

"Look, I called you here to explain this entire situation, not be judged and accused by the likes of you, Mr. Steele," Carty growled at Colin, the suave politician momentarily replaced by a menacing mask with smoldering eyes.

Colin met his stare.

Jennifer glowered at Colin for inserting himself into a conversation when he should have just sat quietly, but it was too late now. Carty looked at her and leaned back again in his chair.

"Ms. Bullfinch, I am not the only partner your father has in this venture. Perhaps you are also familiar with a geology professor, Mr. Ian Michelson."

"We met this morning. He's sailing around the island with his assistant doing random geological research. You're telling me he is also a partner in the development, and not just a geologist for hire?" Jennifer said incredulously.

"I am. But let me assure you his research is not at all random."

"Right, I know. He's got some theory about tectonic plates colliding and causing the cliffs on the north side of the island. I'm sure it makes for a good doctoral thesis. I was surprised that my father has been funding his research. That was out of character for him."

"Well, perhaps not," Carty said, smiling. "What I am about to tell you must be kept absolutely secret." He looked at each of them closely, clearly relishing the effect his words had on Jennifer and Colin's faces. Carty Wallingford-Rolle was a natural born politician with a great flare for the dramatic, and this was right up his alley. Jennifer and Colin both nodded in agreement, and after a theatrical pause, Carty continued with his bombshell. "Our good professor's research on tectonic plates is a giant cover story."

"A cover story?" repeated Jennifer, now thinking perhaps Carty was either a con artist or just slightly mad.

"Yes, a cover story. You see, the reason the cliffs on the north shores of Mayaguana are so high, and that the island is tilted, so to speak, had nothing to do with tectonic plates, or at least that's not the interesting part. In fact, what is pushing up the island is one of the largest oil and natural gas fields in the world."

Chapter 10

Jennifer and Colin looked at one another after hearing the bombshell Carty had just dropped on them. Colin looked at Carty and gave a short, sarcastic laugh. "Come on," he snorted. "This is preposterous. What are you trying to pull here?"

Carty stood up and looked down his brow at Colin. "I didn't realize you were an expert in this area, Mr. Steele."

"I'm not, but neither are you. What I do know is that the waters of the Caribbean have been combed for sixty years or more by real experts, and some of the richest, most powerful oil companies in the world. They've turned up nothing in the entire MICAL region. How is it that you have managed to find this sprawling oil field everyone else has missed?"

Jennifer looked over at Carty. Colin was making good sense to her. Still, she couldn't help but think that perhaps Carty was telling the truth. It would explain a lot about why her father would undertake this project. A small, glimmer of hope began to form in her heart, but she forced herself to keep calm and not let on to Carty or Colin her feelings. Knowing her father, even a remote chance at unlocking one of the biggest oil fields in the world would be just the kind of thing that would bring out the risk-taker in him.

Carty began anxiously pacing about the room and looking at a map of The Bahamas on the wall, his eyes fixed on the bottom right corner, where Mayaguana stood out alone at the very southeast end of the archipelago. He looked back at Jennifer and Colin, sitting at the conference table, and drew himself up, as if to start a long lecture or sermon.

"Well, let me tell you a story, Mr. Steele, and perhaps you'll begin to see the truth. You see, back over thirty years ago, when Langford Bullfinch was in charge of a nearly deserted air base on Mayaguana, and the good professor was an under-employed intelligence officer, I was a young man who had some good part-time work helping out around the base. You see, the whole reason for the air base was to keep tabs on Cuba, and maintain a decent place for a fleet of bombers to rearm and refuel should the US ever need to launch a proper invasion of the place. But with Cuba's influence already quite diminished by that time, there really wasn't much going on at Mayaguana. So, the military found another mission for the bored personnel on the island – security details for private oil companies who paid the government to send along a few armed guards or the occasional escort ship. Now, being around water my whole life, I was pretty handy with boats and had sailed around every island from the southern Bahamas to Haiti and Cuba many times. I could be of help to the crew with deck hand work and the like. Soon, I was included on many of these missions."

"You mean, you were accompanying private oil companies as they operated around Mayaguana over thirty years ago?" Jennifer asked.

"Exactly," Carty answered her, still grinning.

"Then how come there have never been any major oil drilling operations anywhere in the whole area?" Colin asked, still clearly certain Carty was telling a tall tale.

"Calm down, Mr. Steele, I'm getting there," Carty said, with a broadening Cheshire cat grin. "Now these oil companies, as our Mr. Steele so aptly has pointed out, were searching for evidence of oil by using sonar and soundings on the ocean floor. For many months they'd searched with no finds. But then one day, not too far off the bluffs of the northern shore, the readings started to show positive signs! The crew from the oil company was excitedly talking amongst themselves at this amazing find they'd made. 'Largest field I've seen…incredible…vast…' Those were the kind of things they were saying. Of course, we from the base were merely observers to this all, and they paid us little attention, so long as we helped on the deck and kept a good watch for any other vessels. So excited, they were, that even as we warned them about a huge squall baring down on our ship out deep in the Mayaguana Passage, they would not leave the area until they felt like they had clearly identified the location, and could return with more precise equipment. The storm came upon us quickly, and it was one of the worst I have ever seen."

Carty looked at Jennifer and Colin, seeming pleased that his riveting 'tale of the sea' had grabbed their attention.

He continued, "Caught in the storm, one towering wave ripped through the hull and split the ship in two. I jumped from the deck into the ocean, and thought I was done for. I grabbed onto a large piece of the hull floating near me, and managed to hang on. I didn't see anyone else in the water, and I was sure everyone else had drowned. The boat disappeared under the water in a matter of minutes. I held on to my piece of hull for dear life, and somehow, when the squall died down, I was still alive. I started swimming to shore, which I could see miles off in the distance thanks to the height of those bluffs. Well, who should I see also alive and trying for shore, but Ian and your father. They had managed to get a hold of a few life jackets, and they were slowly kicking towards the coast. After many hours of struggling against the waves and the currents of the Passage, we washed ashore like three drowned rats. We were the sole survivors! After we got ashore and realized the crew, the ship, and its equipment were lost, we also realized we were in possession of a very great secret."

"You mean the existence of the oil field?" asked Colin.

"Yes. The sunken boat turned out to be the straw that broke the camel's back, so to speak. The oil company left the island a few weeks later, having never known that what their crew had discovered. Soon thereafter, the United States government notified the base that it was to shut down for good within the year. Before Langford and Ian left the island, we all agreed that the secret of the oil field would remain with us until we could find a way to do something about it," Carty ended his story with a satisfied look.

"And this project on Mayaguana is that something? And LIC Development is 'Langford, Ian, and Carty'?" Jennifer reasoned.

"Exactly."

Colin had been getting restless sitting next to Jennifer and blurted out again in his blunt fashion, "This is quite a story you've called us here to listen to, but so far, it's just raised two nagging questions in my mind. First, why tell us if you're sitting on top of this great find? And second, it appears to me that you might gain personally if Langford Bullfinch is out of the picture."

"My, my, you are a tough customer," Carty laughed. "And as usual, you pose the hard questions, whether it's getting paid in full for your contract work, or gently accusing me of murder." He looked more seriously at Colin.

Jennifer, despite sharing some of Colin's suspicions, found herself buying Carty's story. His flowery language and politician's flair for the dramatic made her believe her father might have seen something in Carty that suggested he could indeed pull off seceding an entire region of The Bahamas into its own country. She also felt that Carty was the kind of person you could get more out of with subtlety, than Colin's blunt, accusatory, and confrontational questioning.

"I am convinced his disappearance was no accident. But I also won't jump to any conclusions about your involvement as quickly as Mr. Steele here. But I do want to hear why you are telling us all this," Jennifer said quietly to Carty.

"Ms. Bullfinch, I need your help. It is that simple," Carty answered her, lowering his tone to match hers.

"My help? I hardly think I can be of help here, especially to you. All I want is to find out what happened to my father and stop this bank in China from taking everything," Jennifer told Carty.

"And all I want is to bring real, economic freedom to the people of my home island," Carty said, smiling again, but still looking quite serious. "And I think our two goals may be mutually supportive. Ian has been mapping out this oil field for years now, coral head by coral head. No small task given he had to do it secretly and without the resources of a huge international oil company behind him," Carty explained to Jennifer, looking back at her from the map.

"It has taken years of work, and millions of dollars – your father's millions of dollars – to undertake this effort, and without that work, we could never hope of getting a drop of oil out of the MICAL Formation, not before others find out what we're doing," Carty went on.

"And by others, you mean the Bahamian Government?" Colin asked.

"That's one interested party. I suppose you can imagine that if they ever found out about the vast wealth sitting just under the surface of the poorest region of the country, they would put an end to my secession plans and nationalize the whole operation!" Carty exclaimed.

"So that's the reason for the secrecy and the secession plan. You'd never be able to cash in on this knowledge without the MICAL Formation being in another country – your own country!" Jennifer said, things now becoming more clear.

"Our own country, Ms. Bullfinch, our own country. But despite the years of work we have already done, there is much more to do. I called you here for a simple reason. I do not know anything about what has happened to your father, but as his representative, I must ask you to continue to fund the operations. The preparations to begin drilling must continue as scheduled, or the newly independent MICAL will not be able to sustain itself," Carty explained, nodding his head as Jennifer's expression indicated she had drawn the final conclusion.

"So my father may be missing, but you still need his company's money," Jennifer concluded.

"Precisely. We cannot afford any setbacks at this critical and historic juncture."

"What was the estimate of the value of the oil field. How much money are we talking about here, Carty?" Colin asked, again driving right to the point.

"Ian has estimated about 6 billion barrels."

"At today's market price, that's several hundred billion dollars!"

"Quite so, Mr. Steele. Now it doesn't all come out of the ground at once. The professor estimates we can bring out about one half of a percent of the total reserves per year, or about 30 million barrels a year. That's billions of dollars a year, or even tens' of billions, if we can get production up or prices rise," Carty said, looking pleased.

"Well I hate to disappoint you, but my father appears to have spent his entire fortune on this venture already. What little he had left is tied up in a bank account in China, and that bank is about to foreclose on the project. So all of this day dreaming may be in vain," Jennifer broke back into the conversation after doing the math in her own head, and her mind flashing to the data file accompanying the text message file from her father.

"That is most disappointing to hear, but perhaps we can find a way forward," Carty said, with his now familiar Cheshire-cat like smile that Jennifer had come to realize was a semi-permanent expression for him. "In regards to this bank and their impending foreclosure, all I can say is, we must find a way to resolve this whole situation without losing control of the project. Ms. Bullfinch, we simply cannot – cannot – falter at the finish line. There is far too much at stake."

Chapter 11

At that moment, their conversation was interrupted by Jennifer's cell phone ringing. It was B.W. Jennifer asked Carty if she could use his private office to take the call, answering as she walked into the small room and closed the door.

"Jennifer, are you there?" B.W. was asking with his usual drawl.

"Hi B.W., what's new?"

"Just checking up on you. I guess you are still in Nassau then?"

"We are. We're meeting with Carty Wallingford-Rolle," Jennifer explained.

"Who's that again?" B.W. asked, sounding confused. Jennifer had forgotten that B.W. was still in the dark about all these players, and especially this new development of the oilfield. But she felt it might be best to keep this quiet until she'd found out a little more. B.W. could get over-excited rather easily.

"He's the member of parliament whose district covers Mayaguana. He's the one leading the charge on the secession plan for the whole MICAL region."

"Secession plan? MICAL? Jennifer, I think you are wasting precious time down there meeting with all these characters. It was all well and fine to take a look at the site, but we have real work to do now. I think you ought to come back to Atlanta today. We can get a legal team together and really try and fight this thing," B.W. was clearly frustrated, but Jennifer felt like he was just grasping at straws. The real work was here in The Bahamas.

86

"Don't worry, B.W. I'm making good headway here, and finding out a lot of information. I'll get back up to Atlanta soon, but armed with more knowledge and some good local contacts," Jennifer said, trying to sound soothing, but not patronizing, to the old man.

"Then I'll keep working things from my end. But take my advice when I say don't trust anyone," B.W. gave his parting thoughts to Jennifer before hanging up.

Jennifer shook her head at the phone, walking out of the office and back into the conference room where Colin and Carty were standing by the map on the wall. Carty pointed out to Colin where he thought the oil field boundaries might be.

"I think you may be exactly right, Mr. Wallingford-Rolle. Our needs may just be coinciding, because I will bet when I solve the mystery behind my father's disappearance, we'll clear up your funding troubles as well," Jennifer announced as she saw the two men browsing over the map.

"I thought you might see it that way," said Carty. "You seem to have a game plan in mind already."

"I do. I need to see the police report investigating my father's disappearance. That's my next stop."

"The Commissioner of police is a close friend of mine. I'll let him know you are on the way over and to be sure he gives you whatever you need," pronounced Carty, seemingly again proud to display his well-connectedness. "I'd go along, but I do have a lot of work to do in preparation for the secession vote. We're coming up on the holiday break, and it's the last and most significant item on the parliamentary agenda before the legislative session breaks for the holidays." He walked them to the door of his office, and they agreed to talk again later in the day.

Jennifer and Colin walked out onto the street, now baking in the noon tropical sun, even in December. The door to Carty's office swung shut and the last wave of cold from his air conditioned office hit Jennifer, feeling briefly refreshing. Colin shook his head at her.

"You don't really trust that crooked politician, do you?" he asked.

"I think our interests are temporarily aligned, and that may be enough," answered Jennifer after giving it some thought.

They walked towards the car, parked alongside the road, and Colin fumbled for the keys in his pocket. Jennifer walked around the front of the car to the passenger door. She looked at Colin over the roof, and mentioned something that had been bothering her.

"You know, the whole time I spoke to Ian by the dock this morning, he never said anything about the partnership or about this oil field."

Colin stopped patting his pockets for the keys for a moment and looked thoughtfully down at the car. Before he could comment, Jennifer's cell phone beeped indicating an incoming text message. She took out her phone to look at it. Suddenly, the quiet of Fowler Street was broken by the whining of several motorcycle engines. Four motorbikes whipped around the corner. Tires squealed as two of the bikes blocked the front of the car and the other two pulled up alongside the car. The motorcycles, which were fast 'sport racing' style motorcycles, were ridden by drivers dressed in black jumpsuits, black ski-masks, and goggles hiding their faces. Colin could see the two bikers who had pulled up next to the car were dismounting and heading for Jennifer.

"Jennifer! Watch out!" he yelled to her, as she looked up from her phone to see the commotion. She didn't have time to react before two of the bikers were on top of her. One biker grabbed Jennifer by the arms. The second biker, shorter and slighter of build, went to rip the phone out of Jennifer's hand.

Colin jumped over the hood of the Focus and grabbed the larger of the assailants, hoping to break his grip on Jennifer. Jennifer, about the same size as the biker going for her phone, fought back impressively by throwing herself backwards against the car and using the leverage of the door to kick the biker square in the chest. Colin landed a hard right hook on the larger biker, who staggered under the force of the blow and loosened his grip on Jennifer enough for her to break free. She gave the biker a hard kick just below the knee, knocking him to the ground. Both bikers lay momentarily stunned.

"Get in the car!" Colin yelled to Jennifer, hitting the unlock button on the key fob and throwing the passenger door open for her. Jennifer scrambled inside as Colin threw himself across the hood of the car back to the driver's side. He opened the driver door and swung into the driver's seat.

"Nice kick. I'm impressed," Colin said, with surprised admiration.

"Thanks. Kickboxing class. Now will you get us out of here!" Jennifer yelled, as the window next to her shattered from the blow of the large biker. A second blow bought his gloved hand through the glass, groping for Jennifer's arm. Colin fumbled with the ignition.

"Get us out of here – NOW," Jennifer yelled again at Colin. Finally, the key turned, and Colin obliged, stepping hard on the gas pedal. The wheels squealed and smoked as the car lurched away from the bikers, knocking aside the two motorcycles blocking the street.

"What was that!?!" Jennifer exclaimed, looking down at her bruised wrist, the cell phone still in her hand.

"I don't know, but buckle up, because it's not over yet," Colin said, glancing at the rearview mirror. Jennifer heard the whining engines of the racing bikes again. She used her elbow to smash away the remaining glass in the passenger window. Looking into the side mirror she saw the four motorcycles closing in fast.

The Ford Focus was up to eighty miles an hour, which on the quiet narrows of Fowler Street, seemed much faster. Even more unsettling, the end of the street was coming up fast, leading to a busy intersection at the bridge to Paradise Island, home of the sprawling Atlantis Resort complex. Colin whipped the Focus down a single lane street, called Hall Lane, lined by a concrete wall. Colin cursed silently to himself. This little side street led directly to Shirley Street, and as usual it was at a standstill with traffic. He knew if they got stuck in a lunch hour traffic jam, they were done for. He looked over at Jennifer and wondered just how much this woman knew, and if she really understood the danger they were in. This car chase was only the beginning.

"We're going to have to stay off the beaten path, otherwise we'll never shake these guys," he said.

"What does that mean?" Jennifer asked, hoping Colin's driving skills were up to the task.

"It means we're in for a rough ride. We're going to have to stick to side streets, where hopefully I can find a place to hide us. On those motorcycles, they'll be able to zip right through Nassau traffic."

"Yeah, I noticed," said Jennifer dryly, giving Colin a bit of his own medicine as she looked at a line of cars up ahead.

The Focus came upon the Shirley Street intersection within seconds. Glancing in the rearview mirror, Colin saw three of the four motorcycles were just a few feet behind him. He made his decision in a split second, and gunned the engine. It was an act of desperation: he'd either slam into cross traffic and kill them both, or whip the car across Shirley Street into the first cross street he came upon. The car rocketed out into the intersection, and time seemed to stand still. Colin slammed on the brakes and yanked the steering wheel hard to the right. The tires on the Focus screeched and the back end started to fish tail as it crossed the first lane and turned into the far left lane. The rear of the car shimmied and hit a small retaining wall at the curb of Shirley Street. With a loud smash of broken glass, the tail light broke against the concrete wall. From behind them, they heard the deep blaring of an air horn from a truck and the screeching of brakes. A huge tractor trailer skidded by the car in the lane they had just crossed, jerking to a halt just in front of the Hall Lane intersection, blocking the four pursuers from turning down Shirley Street.

Jennifer looked at Colin with raised eyebrows, slightly sweating. Colin looked a little shaken, but determined. He stepped on the gas to take advantage of their good luck, leaving the intersection and the bikers behind quickly. Colin turned left down the first cross street he saw, and continued to weave through as many back alleys as he could find. After several minutes, with no signs of the motorcycles, he crossed a busy intersection at Carmichael Road, and turned onto another quiet side street. After going a few blocks, he pulled the car into a dirt driveway behind an unpainted concrete block garage hidden by dense palmettos and a bougainvillea hedge.

Putting the car in park, Colin exhaled, breaking the silence in the car. Jennifer sat quietly in the passenger seat, still clutching her phone, in shock from the entire incident.

"I think we've lost them. We should be safe here for a while," he said, turning the car off.

"Where are we?" Jennifer asked. She had become completely disoriented as they raced through the Byzantine streets of Nassau.

"Obie's house," Colin answered, now smiling at her. "Let's get inside and get ourselves together." He opened the door and got out. Jennifer did the same brushing aside broken glass from the window as she got up from the seat. She closed the door, and the last remaining bits of glass fell from the window onto the ground. Colin came from out of the garage with an old tarp he threw over the car. They walked from behind the garage to the house next to it. It was a one story, concrete block, yellow-painted house and looked similar to several others on the street they had passed. Colin picked up a flower pot near the side door containing a lone pineapple plant, and retrieved a key. He unlocked the door and set the key back under the pot.

"I guess you've been here before?" Jennifer commented.

Colin just shook his head yes and opened the door, motioning for her to go inside. The inside of Obie's house was as simple as the outside appearance. The side door led directly to the kitchen. Jennifer looked at his refrigerator and saw several pictures held by magnets. Most of the pictures were of two small children and a woman.

"Obie has a family?" she asked.

"They live in the states, in Florida," Colin said as he shut the door.

Jennifer continued her survey of Obie's place. It was quite utilitarian, and looked like he didn't spend much time here. The few windows were shut, and the curtains drawn. It was sparsely furnished, with a small kitchen table, an old looking sofa and an even older looking TV setting on a small folding card table in the living room just off the kitchen. In the corner of the living room was a desk with a computer, printer, and a heavy looking file cabinet with a lock on it.

Jennifer sat down, emotionally exhausted, at the kitchen table. "So what do we do now?" she asked, in part just to help herself think.

Colin Steele looked at her from the kitchen where he was peering cautiously out the window over the kitchen sink through a dusty venetian blind. He turned away from the window and frowned.

"Now?" he said. "Now, I think, it's time you and I had a talk."

Chapter 12

Carty Wallingford-Rolle had just sat down at his desk in his office on Fowler Street after showing Jennifer and Colin to the door when he heard a terrible racket out on the street. He set down the cup of coffee he had poured and quickly hurried back to the front door of his office. The street was empty, but he heard the roar of engines and the sound of squealing tires far off down the street. He opened the door and looked up and down the street. Some broken glass littered the gutter, but all was now quiet.

He went back to his desk and sat down, a bit puzzled. He opened up the folder on his desk containing the legislation for parliament consisting of the official articles of release, recognizing the MICAL region as a separate and independent state from The Bahamas. He sighed to himself. There was still so much work to be done, and very little time before he must appear before parliament to read the legislation. Just as he was getting out his red pen to make an edit, his phone rang.

"Law offices of Carty Wallingford-Rolle," he said cheerily into the phone. He took a mental note to fire his receptionist who had obviously left for lunch just after Jennifer and Colin had arrived, and had still not returned.

"Ms. Bullfinch and Mr. Steele just left your office?" a voice on the other end asked, but seemed to already know the answer.

"That's correct. How did you know that?" Carty asked, confused and trying to place the voice, which sounded disguised.

"Never mind that now. We have important things to discuss, and not much time if you still want to be the inaugural prime minister of the new MICAL state...."

Chapter 13

Colin sat down at Obie's grey Formica kitchen table and looked at the floor while gathering his thoughts. Jennifer Bullfinch was obviously in a lot more trouble than he thought when she got off the plane yesterday. What she believed was a simple fact finding mission to see who was owed what money on her father's bankrupt project had nearly taken her life. He looked back up at her. She looked nervous, but she had regained most of her composure quickly after the chase. He had realized soon after they met he was dealing with a very smart woman, and he doubted he could tease any information out of her through winding, leading conversation. Better to take a direct approach and see what happens.

"Jennifer, I have to believe there is something you are not telling me," Colin started out, breaking the silence.

"Me?" she said incredulously. "You're the first paving contractor I've met who seems to have been trained in evasive driving maneuvers."

"All I want is to get paid, so I can pay everyone else I owe money and save what little reputation I have in the construction world," he answered carefully. "I didn't realize that might cost me my life."

"You don't need to stick around to babysit me just to make sure your check is good. I can take care of myself, and when I clear this whole mess up, rest assured you'll get your money along with everyone else," Jennifer snapped at him.

"Oh come on. I'm not going to leave you stranded in the middle of Nassau."

"I didn't ask for your help, Colin. And I certainly didn't ask you to come along with me."

"So much for the direct approach," Colin thought to himself miserably. He knew he needed her help and whether she liked it or not, she needed his help too. But her stubbornness, or his mismanagement of it, was threatening to implode his only real hope. He drew in a breath, and consciously softened his features, unclenching his jaw.

"I know," he said quietly. "I shouldn't have been so accusatory. But let's face it, we were just attacked by a gang of bikers, and I think they were after you."

"Yeah, strange isn't it?" Jennifer said, tentatively seeming to react positively to Colin's new tact.

"Who texted you just as we were leaving, by the way?" Colin asked curiously.

"Oh, it was just B.W. asking me to call him. I assume it was just a delayed message since he had called me just a few minutes earlier."

"Probably so," said Colin. "Can you think of anyone else who might have knowledge or information about this project?"

Jennifer thought about the text message from her father the night of his death. It now seemed clear the message he sent contained important information, or at least someone thought it was important. But she thought about B.W.'s warning to trust no one. Could Colin really be trusted, she wondered. After all, they had only met yesterday, and she really didn't know much about him yet. She decided discretion was the best course of action, and did not mention the text message to Colin.

"I don't know. After hearing Carty, I can only assume this has something to do with this oil discovery", she reasoned aloud, giving Colin only part of her thoughts.

"Right. And we do need to get in touch with Ian. Why he didn't say anything, like you mentioned as we were walking to the car, seems a bit suspicious," Colin added to her thought. He sat back in the kitchen chair, satisfied he had gotten Jennifer back working with him, at least for now.

"So, are we still a team?" he asked, smiling at her. Colin decided it was not the right time to continue to press Jennifer any further for real information.

"We're a team," she said, laughing a bit. "But the team's not going to get anywhere sitting around Obie's kitchen table! You seem to know your way around Nassau. So where to next?"

"I think that stop to the Commissioner may be the right thing to do, especially now," Colin said, getting up from his chair. He went to the door and looked over a small wooden plaque with brass hooks on it. Looped over one of the hooks was a set of car keys.

"I hate to do this, but I think Obie will understand," he said, taking the set of keys from the hook and replacing them with the keys for the rented Ford Focus. "We need a new set of wheels. One those bikers won't be looking for."

They locked up Obie's house and walked through a side door into the garage. The keys Colin took from the kitchen were to a plain looking Toyota Tercel that sat looking a bit dusty in the garage. Colin threw up the overhead garage door, and Jennifer was relieved when the Toyota started with no problems.

They were soon headed back through the streets of Nassau. Jennifer noticed Colin took particular pains to keep to the smaller, less busy roads, and she was again impressed by the way he could easily navigate his way from one alley to the next without getting lost. They stayed quiet in the car, each keeping a sharp lookout for the black-outfitted bikers, but all seemed quiet. Soon the alley Colin was driving down opened to a busy thoroughfare. It was East Street, near the northern central part of New Providence Island, and Jennifer saw a large acqua-green building just in front of them – the Central Police Station. Colin pulled the Tercel through a back gate into a parking lot next to the building. He parked the car in an empty spot underneath a large dilly tree and looked over at Jennifer.

"Look, Carty's not the only one who knows the Commissioner of Police. I happen to have met him a few times myself, and while I think he may be able help, I think we should be a little careful when we talk to him," Colin said.

"You do the talking, then. I just want to know if they have any more news about my father. I only care about those bikers because it seems like they could be related to whatever has happened to him," Jennifer ended the conversation opening the door and getting out of Obie's car.

Chapter 14

Professor Ian Michelson was a nervous and suspicious person by nature. His time as an intelligence officer had magnified those qualities. Michelson sat on the deck of his research boat in Abraham's Bay, and watched the plane carrying Jennifer Bullfinch and Colin Steele away from Mayaguana to the northwest towards Nassau, their destination. At the bow of the boat, sprawled seductively across a towel wearing a very scanty bikini was his assistant, Dominique, who sat up briefly to remove her top for an even tan.

"Siren," Michelson said softly to himself as he looked away, mildly embarrassed, even though he was certain she knew he would see her removing her top, and had done so on purpose. She loved teasing him, and he knew it.

Aside of the pleasant distraction of this beautiful woman, Michelson was having a hard time concentrating on the job at hand. He was beginning to think that he, perhaps like Jennifer and Colin, was no longer safe on the island. Obviously, Langford Bullfinch had not realized the depth of the danger bearing down upon him, and it looked like it had cost him dearly. Ian Michelson had no intentions of letting the same fate befall him. He made up his mind at that instant. He must leave Mayaguana immediately, especially now that Colin was gone with Jennifer. Another night spent here could be disastrous. He needed to get back to someplace with a lot of people, where he knew the terrain. His office back at The Royal School of Mines in London seemed like the right place. Even though people knew to look for him there, he felt he could avert trouble better in the city than in some isolated location. More importantly, there was some information in his possession he needed to deposit somewhere safe as soon as possible. If he moved fast, he could be pulling his boat into the marina on Provo in The Turks and Caicos in less than an hour.

He looked at his beautiful, young, research assistant at the bow of his boat. What should he tell her? Should he bring her along? Dominique had been one of the few bright spots in his lonely life this past year. Ian had never married, always being a bit too wayward. In the Royal Navy, he had moved around, and the nature of his job, always keeping secrets and never being able to tell people exactly what he did or where he had been, made it difficult for him to develop any real relationship with anyone. When he became an assistant professor, the constant stream of young undergrads and later, graduate students, was just too tempting for him to settle down with any one person. But time had caught up with him, and the past few years, his long, solitary trips around the waters of Mayaguana had made him long for a real companion. Perhaps it was the setting: The gorgeous blue water, the powdery beaches, grilling fresh caught lobster on a driftwood beach fire in the evenings. It made him yearn for someone meaningful to share these experiences.

Almost as if on cue, Dominique arrived at his office doorway back in London. She was looking to become a geologist, and although her academic background was a little hard to decipher, she seemed to have some financial background in the energy industry. Within a semester, she had gained his trust as a competent research assistant, and even a bit of a confident. He began bringing her on his trips to Mayaguana.

He could never remember exactly who had made the first move, but the rush of their blossoming romance was exhilarating. She was almost half his age, and he felt invigorated by her youth. Ian approached his work determining the geological extent of the MICAL Formation with new, dogged determination. Long hard days at sea seemed so much more enjoyable when he was looking forward to passionate evenings ashore. At first, he continued his pretense with her, that he was there researching the unique geological characteristics of the formation. But soon, he found himself sharing more and more of the truth about the real goals of his research. He found some of her knowledge of the energy industry very helpful, and as he picked her brain to ensure he was going about his soundings of the MICAL Formation properly, she seemed to clue in to what was going on. Her intelligence, beauty and companionship became more than the lonely professor could stand. Michelson was reluctant to leave her behind.

'Besides,' he justified to himself, 'I can use an extra set of eyes crossing the Caicos Passage to get to Provo.'

The crossing from Mayaguana to Providenciales could be a little dicey. Normally, boaters started early in the morning when the seas were typically calm. But this late in the morning, even tied to the dock in Abraham's Bay, his boat rocked and strained against the ropes securing it to shore. Winds like that meant they would have to proceed across the passage, some twenty-five miles, very slowly. That meant more time in treacherous open waters.

"Dominique! Better get dressed. We're going to head over to Provo this morning!" Michelson exclaimed to her, trying to sound nonchalant and as if he had been planning this trip all along. This was the normal protocol for them. They rarely left the dock without turning on their sounding equipment, and Dominique's normal duty was to sit at the laptop computer attached to the sensors and read and track the data.

Dominique looked up at him puzzled. "Now? This morning?" she said raising her eyebrows at him.

"Afraid so, my dear. I thought I mentioned that a few days ago. I have to head back to London for a spell."

101

"I need to go ashore for a few minutes. I've left some things with Mr. Wu," Dominique said, smiling at Michelson as she put her top back on almost as seductively as she had removed it earlier.

Michelson sighed and shook his head OK reluctantly. He was going to be glad to get her away from Mr. Wu for a while. Wu seemed to think the authority he had as the senior manager of the Chinese work crew extended to selecting his choice of pretty women to spend time with, and he and Dominique had been spending just a little too much time together for Michelson's liking. Since they were both Chinese, it did not surprise him that Dominique enjoyed spending some time with a fellow countryman from time to time, but Wu seemed to have some stronger influence over Dominique that Michelson reluctantly chalked up to their shared culture. Nonetheless, he did not really approve. Now he had a good excuse to get Dominique away from Wu for quite some time.

Dominique walked by Michelson and hopped lightly off the side of the boat and onto the concrete dock. He looked at her as she walked away. Her beauty was so delightfully distracting to him, but he cleared his mind and thought about the trip ahead of them. There would be people watching them leave, but once they got further east along the coast, they would likely be out of direct site of anyone on land until they were almost to Provo. That was good and bad. Would anyone realize he was fleeing the island and try to intercept him at sea? That's what he would do were he the pursuer…no witnesses, and perhaps no one would even realize he was missing for some time. He began, as quietly and subtly as possible, to prepare the boat for departure.

He glanced at the clock on the cabin wall and swore quietly to himself, noticing she had already been gone for almost thirty minutes. The wind was picking up. The palm trees at the water's edge began to sway and the boat was rocking noticeably more than earlier in the morning. He walked up on deck and tried not to look anxious as he scanned for Dominique. Just as he was about to really start losing his temper, he saw her walking towards the dock. Michelson allowed himself a quiet sigh of relief and began throwing off the lines. He couldn't bring himself to be mad with Dominique, though, so when she walked up to the boat, he held out his hand to help her aboard and smiled.

"Finally!" he said, using a mock exasperated tone to disguise the real exasperation he was feeling in the pit of his stomach.

"I hate to say it, but I feel absolutely terrible – in my stomach" whined Dominique, apparently oblivious to the frustration she had caused Michelson by taking so long to return. "I really can't bear the thought of jostling around on this little boat. I'll get terribly seasick. Can't we just stay here?" She gave him a pouty look, suggesting if they did what she wanted, she'd soon feel better and Michelson would be in for some fantastic sex.

At first his jealousy of Wu reared its head in his mind, but quickly he dismissed the feeling.

"I'm afraid not, and the wind's picking up a bit. I need to get out to sea now to get across the passage. You mean to tell me you're so sick you're going to miss a trip to Provo and London?" Michelson asked.

They quarreled back and forth for several minutes, but in the end, Michelson shrugged his shoulders in a 'suit yourself' manner and said, "OK. Don't worry, darling. I will only be gone a week or so…Quick trip to give a lecture and keep up the old tenure status."

Dominique seemed to be relived he gave up on making her come along, and smiled coyly at him as he threw off the last line, and got himself situated. He gave a quick wave over his shoulder to Dominique as he steered towards the dredged channel out to sea. The research boat was a sturdy, reliable craft, but Michelson was mentally prepared for a rough ride, as the waves were picking up even quicker, and he wanted to be able to hold about 30 knots if possible.

He piloted the boat out into the bay, and through the cut in the reef at the southeast end of Abraham's Bay. Getting through the reef always required some good concentration since they had not yet gotten around to marking the break in the miles long line of coral. Once out into open ocean, Ian Michelson's spirits lifted a bit as Mayaguana disappeared behind him. Michelson steadily pushed the throttle on both engines forward until the boat was cruising quickly over the waves, making good time to the container post in Provo. Next stop after that was the International Airport and direct to London on British Airways.

Chapter 15

Jennifer Bullfinch and Colin Steele sat in two comfortable, leather chairs across the desk from the Commissioner of Police, Brian T. Crawford. Commissioner Crawford was a big, imposing man. In his crisp, tan uniform, he fit his role well. He looked across at them, listening intently as Jennifer and Colin took turns explaining how they felt Langford Bullfinch's disappearance was very suspicious, but that they, or at least Jennifer, refused to believe he had died in a boating accident as an initial report by Commissioner Crawford's investigators suggested. The Commissioner nodded, jotted down a few notes from time to time, and seemed, at least to Jennifer, open to their suggestions. After about ten minutes, however, her perceptions were proven wrong.

"Enough, enough," Commissioner Crawford broke into their explanation as Colin was finishing up with his list of reasons why Langford would not have killed himself or had an unfortunate accident, "Look, we've done a complete investigation. It was a boating accident. They happen here all the time, especially with visitors who don't know the waters. The case is closed."

Just as Jennifer looked like she was about to say something she might later regret to Commissioner Crawford, her cell phone rang. It was B.W. again.

"Please excuse me," she said, seeing that Colin and Commissioner Crawford also seemed to look relieved that she had a phone call providing a momentary 'time out' in a conversation that looked like it was about to boil over into unpleasantness. Jennifer stepped outside into a waiting area near the door of Commissioner Crawford's office.

"Hi B.W.," she answered, sounding cheerful for him, despite her growing exasperation.

"Jennifer? How's it going down there, dear? You know I get antsy when I don't hear from you for a while," B.W.'s comforting drawl came across over a slightly static cell phone connection.

"Oh, you know. I'm meeting with the Commissioner of Police down here, and I think I'm going to have a long battle to clear up Dad's disappearance. But as far as saving the project goes, I'm still no closer to an answer. Just more muddied waters."

"What do you mean?" B.W. inquired.

Jennifer regretted her last comment. She had opened the door, so now she would have to tell B.W. about the meeting with Carty and this new, crazy development of the oil field.

"Well, the last time you called, I was meeting with a Bahamian named Carty Wallingford-Rolle. Apparently, he and Dad went way back, to his time as post commander at the Mayaguana Air Base. Did he ever mention that name to you?" she decided to ease into this new development.

"Well, let me see…" B.W. mused, "Other than you mentioning him just today, no, I can't say I recall that name when your father spoke about his time on Mayaguana. But, you know, he wasn't one to talk about the past much."

"I'm not surprised," Jennifer said, and then in a quieter tone continued on, "But there is something this gentleman Carty told me this morning that I am surprised Dad never mentioned to you…"

Back in Commissioner Crawford's office, as the door closed behind Jennifer so she could take her phone call, Colin Steele looked across the desk at the Commissioner.

"OK, what's going on here? You're giving her the run-around, but I think you and I have known each other long enough to shoot straight," Colin said, dropping the pretense he didn't know Commissioner Crawford very well.

"Look man, you know that we always speak off the record. What are you doing bringing this crazy woman into my office with no warning?" Commissioner Crawford shot back.

"You have no idea what I've been through this morning with her. We were attacked in broad daylight on Fowler Street by a gang of masked men on motor bikes!"

Commissioner Crawford's eyes widened and he looked at Colin with disbelief.

"That's right," Colin continued, secretly pleased his statement had the desired effect on Commissioner Crawford. "And just moments after the Prime Minister himself had been in that very spot. Once I could beat them off for a few seconds, we sped off in the car, but they followed us."

"Are you fooling with me? Because you know that if you're really telling me this, there are things I will have to look into," Commissioner Crawford said carefully to Colin.

"This is no joke," Colin said shaking his head. "I think at least one of them was hurt severely by a truck on Shirley Street when I managed to shake them."

"I'll have someone check at Princess Margaret Hospital, quietly of course, and see if we can use that as a lead," Commissioner Crawford said, scribbling down a quick note on a pad at his desk.

"I doubt you'll find anything, these are pros."

"Well, I guess you'd know. What do you need from me?" the Commissioner asked setting his pen back down on the leather blotter that covered his desk.

"I need to know everything your investigators found about Langford Bullfinch and his project on Mayaguana. You know I've been keeping my eyes open down there, but I get the feeling you haven't been blind that strange things have been happening there. This attack on us this morning was no coincidence."

Commissioner Crawford looked down at his desk a little uncomfortably. "Look, Steele, we did a real investigation. There are no clues, nothing out of order, no leads. Langford Bullfinch is gone."

Colin looked at Commissioner Crawford. He had an odd look on his tough face that Colin had never seen before. Crawford was hard to read, but Colin felt some vibe coming across the desk at him. He sensed uneasiness in the Commissioner.

"You've got no idea who might have been after her today? No connection to something similar happening to her father?" Colin pressed.

The Commissioner continued, "I've got nothing. Take that lady back to the States today, and do what you can to convince her to stay there. Besides, in a matter of days, the whole MICAL region will be another country…not my problem anymore."

The door to Commissioner Crawford's office opened after a quick knock that did not wait for an answer. Jennifer hurried back inside the office putting her cell phone away.

"I apologize for taking so long out there. B.W. worries about me, and he wanted to talk about a lot of business issues that are bubbling up with my father gone," Jennifer explained, sitting back down in the empty chair next to Colin.

"That's OK. I think we are done here anyway," said Colin, shooting a cool look at Commissioner Crawford as he stood up from his chair.

"Done?" repeated Jennifer a bit incredulously.

"Yes, Ms. Bullfinch," broke in Commissioner Crawford. "I was just finishing explaining to Mr. Steele that we'll be happy to provide you with a copy of our investigation report, but I'm afraid there's just not enough reason to warrant re-looking the case. Being new to Nassau, you may not realize that this year has sadly been a record year for violent crime, and we just don't have the resources to re-open investigations without significant new developments in the case. I'm very sorry."

Jennifer looked at Colin. He slowly looked back at her, and gave her a slight shrug of the shoulders as if to say, 'well, we tried.' Jennifer, putting aside her now fully developed dislike for the Commissioner, extended her hand purposefully. Commissioner Crawford shook her hand, and Jennifer thought for a brief moment he looked distraught, but quickly regained his pleasant, but stone-faced composure. Colin murmured something about 'catching him later' and they walked out of the office, leaving the Commissioner at his desk.

They emerged outside into the growing heat of the day. Jennifer felt like this stuffy, closed, secret-filled island was beginning to choke her. Her head was spinning slightly, from the heat as much as the muddled confusion of The Bahamas. Not sure what to do next, she posed the question to Colin.

"Well, unlike you, I have never been much of a student. But in this case, maybe a little research will help us," he answered her,

109

pulling out his phone and checking the time. "Someone I know may be able to give us some background."

"Research? What are you talking about?" asked Jennifer.

"We only have one lead to follow, and that's the oil field. The guy I want to go see, well he's a petroleum engineer who also does some teaching at the College of The Bahamas. He might be able to give us some ideas about who has interest in oil in The Bahamas."

Chapter 16

The College of The Bahamas campus was a picturesque setting, the centerpiece of which was a large, yellow colonial style building with towering, white columns. Upon seeing it for the first time, Jennifer thought what a nice place it would be to study for a few years. As they drove to a small parking area aside of the main campus building, she looked around at the groups of students walking to class and sitting in small study groups underneath large royal palm trees. It made her miss being back at school, even though it would be months before it was warm enough in Boston to sit outside and enjoy the campus.

Colin parked Obie's car, and led the way towards a smaller, white and yellow building out of view from the street. A small sign next to the door read "School of Chemistry, Environmental & Life Sciences." They walked inside and entered a corridor with identical half panel doors with frosted glass windows along both sides of the corridor. They walked along the corridor until Colin stopped in front of a door with the name "Prof. Harold Rajkumar, Ph.D." on the door. Colin raised his hand to knock on the door. Before he could, Jennifer grabbed his wrist and stopped him. They had sat in an uneasy silence in the car driving down to Poinciana Drive where the campus entrance sat at a busy intersection

"So just who is this, and why are we here again?" she pressed in a quiet tone, her blood pressure beginning to rise.

Colin looked like he was making a concerted effort to restrain himself from rolling his eyes. "Look, newbie, Dr. Rajkumar is an expert on energy issues in The Caribbean. If there's some kind of oil field off Mayaguana, I'm going to bet he knows about it. And if you want to find out what happened to your father, the smoking gun has to be this oil field."

"Coming here was a mistake. I never should have just let you drive us over here without asking more questions," Colin's reaction pushed Jennifer over the edge. "I am running out of time, Mr. Steele. I only have a few days to rescue everything my father invested in this crazy project and to find out what has happened to him before MICAL is an independent oil kingdom. While I appreciate your conspiracy theories, I do not have time to sit down and chat about the history of Caribbean oil exploration with some crackpot old prof…!"

Before Jennifer could finish, the door opened into the room, and a tall, good-looking man in his mid-forties stood in the doorway.

"I can hear you, you know, through the door," he said, not cracking a smile. "But please, come inside my office and you can at least have the decency of finishing your conversation in some more privacy."

Professor Rajkumar swung the door to his office fully open, and stood to the side, motioning them inside with a sweep of his hand and a slight, somewhat theatrical bow. The professor looked like he had been interrupted during a late lunch at his desk. A bowl of chicken souse and a cup of tea sat to one side of his desk, while a report he must have been reading over lunch sat on a leather desk protector with a yellow highlighter next to it. It was a sparse, but comfortable and distinguished looking office. The linoleum tiled, institutional looking floor was covered by a thin, woven grass mat. A bamboo and wicker couch rested at the edge of the mat against one wall accompanied by matching end tables and a brass lamp, lending a tropical feel to the room. A large oil painting of a Caribbean port-city street scape hung over the couch. A gym bag with a pair of running shoes poking out of it set underneath one of the end tables provided some evidence behind the professor's slight, but athletic, build. Behind the professor's desk was a built-in bookshelf. It was filled primarily with technical books on engineering, but there were also a few small framed pictures of the professor and a smiling woman.

The professor walked over to his desk and sat down in an ergonomic office chair and casually, but deliberately clicked off the flat panel monitor at the other side of his desk, which would have been visible from the two chairs he motioned them to sit in. As she sat down, Jennifer looked over towards the window, noticing the view into a small, garden courtyard, was quite tranquil. On either side of the window were two framed diplomas, indicating the professor had attended the University of Miami as an undergraduate and Tulane University in New Orleans for his graduate schooling. He looked like he may have just returned from a lecture wearing dark pin striped pants, a white shirt with the sleeves rolled up, and a tie with black and red stripes. The matching suit jacket was hung on a polished wooden valet standing in the corner of the office by his bookcase. He sat down, gently pushed his bowl of souse to the side and leaned forward pressing his fingertips together.

"Now, Mr. Steele, are you going to introduce your companion?" he asked, still blank faced, "Or do you two need to finish your conversation? I believe the young lady was concerned about wasting time with a 'crackpot old professor', was it?"

Jennifer opened her mouth to apologize, but Colin spoke up quickly.

"Professor Rajkumar, may I introduce Ms. Jennifer Bullfinch. Ms. Bullfinch, Professor Harold Rajkumar," Colin interjected.

"Professor, it's been a long time since we last spoke. I do hope all is still well with you and Mrs. Rajkumar?"

"Ah Colin, thank you so much for asking, and I cannot say how grateful we both will forever be to you for your help," Rajkumar answering, now breaking into a soft smile.

"Oh, it was nothing," said Colin quickly. "But I do need to tell you that Jennifer and I heard something very interesting this morning, and I thought of you immediately."

"I'm flattered," responded the professor, smirking a little at Colin amusedly.

"You see, it sounds like there is some potential for oil exploration in the MICAL region. Is that possible?" Colin asked.

"Ah. That is indeed an interesting question. Not normally something that would interest you, Mr. Steele."

"I know, I know. It is a long story, but I am helping Ms. Bullfinch, and I think oil fields in the MICAL region may be a factor in her…situation," Colin said, not wanting to reveal too much to the professor.

"Very well, then. I do think I had better give you a bit of background," said Professor Rajkumar. He stood up from his desk, and pulled a geographic atlas down from his shelf. He opened up to a tab which showed a two page map of The Bahamas and surrounding Caribbean Sea.

Professor Rajkumar cleared his throat, as if he was ready to present a very long lecture to some colleagues, and began earnestly accounting the history of oil drilling in the Caribbean. Jennifer began to feel her blood pressure rise, but she restrained herself, trusting that Colin would not have brought them here for an afternoon lecture when he fully understood the pressure they were under, and that the attackers from this morning were still out in Nassau looking for them.

"The history of oil exploration in The Bahamas goes back to just after World War II," the professor began his lecture, "when merchant marines and naval officers who had patrolled the waters during the war returned home. Some of those gentlemen became executives at oil companies, and they were familiar with the waters, so naturally, some sights got focused on the Caribbean Sea for exploration. For the next ten years or so, from 1946 until the late 1950's, The Bahamas saw a lot of oil exploration by the biggest oil companies."

"Was some of that exploration in the waters around Mayaguana?" Jennifer asked.

"Some of it, but not at first," explained Rajkumar. "You see, the deeper the ocean floor, the harder the testing and extraction, and the best test results seemed to be coming up further to the west, closer to Cuba and Florida than to Mayaguana. And as you may know, the Caicos Passage and the Mayaguana Passage are some very deep water. The seas can be rough at times. Back seventy years ago, that was a more serious obstacle than today. That said, over time, even the waters around Mayaguana saw some exploration."

"So we've heard. Did the oil companies ever find anything?" Colin asked, seeming even more interested than Jennifer.

"No," said the professor flatly, pausing, and looking back and forth at both of them intently, as if to gauge their reaction from the bluntness of his answer. Jennifer looked over at Colin with slightly raised eyebrows, but said nothing.

Rajkumar saw his statement had the dramatic effect he had desired, so he continued on, "However, just because 'Big Oil' didn't find anything back fifty years ago doesn't mean that there can't be oil."

Colin turned his head and raised his own eyebrows back at her to say 'You see.' The professor got up again from his chair and pulled a binder from his bookshelf. He opened it to another map of the Caribbean Sea, which had many different sized and colored boxes outlining different parts of the sea.

"On this map are the different areas tested for oil. Look at the seas between Florida and Cuba - do you see how many different areas of interest there are?" asked the professor, pointing to the map.

"None of them are anywhere near Mayaguana. They're all near Cuba and Florida, like you said," Jennifer commented as she ran her finger down the line of boxes from Andros Island to just north of Cuba.

"Yes. For nearly twenty years, test wells were done along this corridor, if you will, running generally from north to south along the western edge of The Bahamas. Although undoubtedly crews did some testing in the eastern part of The Bahamas near Mayaguana, not enough tests were conducted, and the few tests done were never conclusive enough for the big oil companies to pursue drilling rights in the area. "

"But there really wasn't ever much actual production oil drilling in The Bahamas, in the west near Cuba or in the east, right?" asked Colin.

"That is correct. The lack of drilling in the west, despite the evidence that there are significant oil deposits there can be explained rather simply: there has never been a clear national boundary between The Bahamas and Cuba. The oil companies were worried that any real gushers would be claimed by Cuba to be in their territorial waters, regardless of any rights granted by The British government. And that problem exists to this very day. Hence little off shore drilling has occurred."

"But you said earlier that despite big oil companies finding little evidence, you thought there might still be significant oil reserves in the eastern Bahamas around Mayaguana," Jennifer pointed out with a mildly confused look.

"I did. You see, the early tests in the west and near Cuba, seemed so much more promising than the early results in the deeper waters of the east, that many years were spent focused on mapping out the western oil fields. From the 1940's all the way until 1973, as a matter of fact when The Bahamas became an independent country, a lot of effort was put into carving up the waters by a few large companies," said Rajkumar, leaning back in his chair a bit as he felt more at ease with his guest audience.

"But while independence may have been wonderful for the people of The Bahamas, it threw the oil industry into a bit of turmoil. There were many doubts amongst the executive at the major oil companies about any further investment in drilling in The Bahamas. At the heart of the issue, as in so many problems of this region, was politics. No one knew for sure if the newly independent country would retain its functioning legal system or if the new leadership might try to nationalize profitable industries for themselves. So, with that potential instability and the absence of authority of The British government behind the oil field agreements in question, it seemed to many oil executives that if they really hit a gusher and could finally get some profit out of all this exploration expense, either Cuba would be right there to make a claim that the oil field was in their waters, or a corrupt Bahamian government would squeeze any profit for themselves."

"Wouldn't the oil companies assume that America would step in and protect their oil fields? I mean, weren't most of the big oil companies exploring in the Caribbean from America?" Jennifer pressed.

"Ah, you Americans have such short memories," Rajkumar quipped, smiling light heartedly for the first time. "Even until the early 1980's, the effects of the Cuban Missile Crisis still loomed over the whole region. While the US certainly had no fear of Cuba, most politicians seemed to think that Cuba might use any excuse they could to stick it to America a bit. A lucrative oil field might certainly have been just enough justification for that kind of a confrontation. And, as in the Cuban Missile Crisis, it could easily escalate. So, I think in their internal calculus, the oil executives assumed no one would come to their aid, and any investment would be lost. That really meant that from the time it became evident that independence for The Bahamas was not only likely, but imminent, oil exploration really dropped off."

"Well that explains why no more exploration occurred in the western waters, but not in the east, where Mayaguana is, and far away from any maritime border confusion with Cuba," said Colin, beating Jennifer to the punch on that question.

"There could have been. Really, there should have been. And but for one small research group casting doubt, I think exploration would have occurred."

"One small research group?" Colin echoed.

"Yes. In the world of oil exploration, it's impossible, or at least not very economical, for the geologists working for the oil companies to keep tabs on every potential new find. So, these private industry scientists at the big oil companies do a lot of reading. They read all kinds of academic findings, thesis papers, scientific journal articles, etcetera, which are published by students, professors, and smaller, independent researchers. In the early 1980's, just as the oil companies had gotten over their fears of maritime boundary disputes with Cuba and jitters that the newly independent Bahamian government might do something crazy like nationalize industries or become a socialist banana republic, something interesting happened. A small research group, privately funded it seems, began publishing articles that showed clearly there was little to no probability of rich oil fields in the east around the Mayaguana and Caicos Passages."

"What did this group of researchers find that could put such a damper on any further testing?" Colin asked, now really interested and engaged in the conversation.

"The findings, and I do use that term loosely, were that the geological constitution of the ocean floor around Mayaguana was wholly unsuitable for the formation oil, or any fossil fuels for that matter," replied Rajkumar, his voice tinged with some obvious disdain.

"How did they conclude that?" Jennifer chimed back in.

"Their theory was that the same white, sandy bottom that makes the water so crystal clear and the beaches so beautiful was the culprit. Or more specifically, the lack of vegetation on the sea floor, was the problem. Without those millennia of decaying organic material being slowly compressed and formed beneath layers and layers of hard rock and sand, it was not possible for oil to form in any significant quantities," the professor said, pointing to a picture in the margin of the atlas showing a picture of a white sand beach, as if it were evidence.

"That sounds kind of reasonable to me, but you seem to think otherwise," said Jennifer.

"Yes. To my mind, it is a completely baseless theory," said Rajkumar without hesitation. "You see, much of my own geological research has been funded by my home government, back in Trinidad, since as you may know, the petroleum industry is so critical to our survival. And the fact is, despite all these silly claims by every country in the Caribbean about who has the clearest waters and the whitest, crystal sandy beaches in an effort to win over the most tourists, from a scientific standpoint, the ocean floor throughout the entire region is essentially the same."

"So that means that if there is oil in abundance in the waters off of Cuba or Trinidad, which it seems there is, then there should be – or at least could be – oil also in abundance in the waters around Mayaguana," said Colin in a slow, soft tone, as if he were reasoning this through as he said it.

"Precisely, at least in my academic opinion," answered Rajkumar, smiling slyly at Colin.

"And this one group of researchers, with seemingly wrong, or at least questionable conclusions could discourage the entire industry from looking for oil in the eastern Bahamas?" asked Jennifer.

"Well, yes," the professor said. "It can take millions of dollars to do real testing, not to mention a lot of time. There were more fish in the sea - so to speak - to pursue that seemed more likely to pay out with a gusher. So, the ocean around Mayaguana lay quietly undisturbed."

"Then since the 1970's, there has really been no interest in oil in The Bahamas at all," said Jennifer.

Professor Rajkumar nodded his head yes, and looked at his watch. "Oh my - I have a lecture to give in two minutes. How time does fly with such interested students with whom to chat!" he exclaimed, smiling at them.

"Professor, I can't thank you enough. This has been very helpful. Sorry for just stopping by like this," said Colin getting up from his chair.

"For you, Mr. Steele, anything," said Rajkumar, also getting up from his chair to usher them out.

"Professor, just one last question," Jennifer cut in, "Do you still have any of those old research publications that discouraged the oil exploration around Mayaguana?"

"Certainly," he answered, hastily pulling another binder down from his bookshelf after running his finger along the neatly labeled rows of books and binders. "Here is their most significant paper. They got it published in the scholarly journal 'Geology' in 1986. From that point on, a few counterargument reports and papers were published, but every time, this group was able to defend their findings and discredit their attackers."

Jennifer looked at the title page of the article. The research group was called the Oceanographic Stratification Research Institute, with an office in Austin, Texas. "Do you have any idea who the actual researchers are at this Institute," she asked Professor Rajkumar, typing the address into her smartphone.

"I'm afraid not. I was just finishing my graduate work at that time, and not very well attuned yet to the industry, especially to privately funded scientists. They tend to be rather secretive since, as you might expect, there is often a corporate agenda behind them with the money for the research," he said, rolling down his sleeves and buttoning them so he could put on his suit coat.

Slipping on his coat, the professor picked up a binder full of PowerPoint presentations printed out and stapled together from off the bookshelf behind his desk, and motioned them to the door, leaving his still uneaten lunch on his desk. Colin and Jennifer walked into the hallway. Rajkumar followed them out, stopping to close his office door and quickly lock it with a key he produced from his pocket.

"I hope I've been able to help you. I'm not really sure what's going on, but I will leave you with this parting thought: It's my own opinion, but I consider it an educated one, having now spent years researching the entire Caribbean to determine the feasibility of oil drilling. The waters around Mayaguana do indeed have significant potential for oil production, despite anything you may have heard to the contrary."

With that, Professor Harold Rajkumar gave a quick nod, smiled goodbye, turned sharply on the heels of his black leather dress shoes, and walked smartly down the hallway to a double door which he dramatically flung open, calling out for a group of students to settle down and take their seats. The doors swung shut behind him, and Jennifer and Colin were left alone in the quiet hallway.

"So maybe Carty Wallingford-Rolle isn't completely full of shit after all," Colin said, turning to look at Jennifer with a grin on his face.

"Maybe not. If he really believes there is a significant oil field surrounding the island, and may have some information suggesting he is correct, it would certainly explain why he would like to lead a secession movement and become the first Bahamian oil sheik," Jennifer reasoned aloud.

"That's what I was thinking too. But I'm also thinking we had better get moving. Obie's car has been sitting out in the parking lot for some time now while we chatted with the professor. The gang looking for us just might have figured out to look for his vehicle," Colin said a little softer.

They walked out the door of the School of Chemistry, Life Sciences & Environment and walked calmly but quickly to the car. Jennifer noticed Colin's head seemed to swivel subtly as if he were scanning their path the entire way. They said nothing to one another until they were driving down Poinciana Drive, comfortably anonymous amongst the bustle of cars on the busy thoroughfare. Jennifer had another lead now: an address in Austin, Texas from twenty-five years ago for the offices of an innocuous research group that was probably long since dissolved. She thought for a moment on her next move. It was now getting late in the afternoon, and she was one day closer to losing everything to the bank.

"Why would Carty tell us all about this oil field?" Jennifer asked, opening up the primary question on her mind to discussion with Colin. "I mean, if you were sitting on billions of dollars of oil, and you had a chance to have it all to yourself, and maybe even have it as the economic engine behind your own small kingdom, why…why would you tell us?"

Colin shrugged his shoulders as he drove calmly down the street, turning down a different, random, side street from time to time to throw off anyone following them. "I don't know. Maybe he knows the Chinese bank really plans to take over the whole place, and he's hoping you actually do have the money to somehow stave them off?"

"Maybe. Money can make people do strange things. Look at my father. This project seems to have sent him haywire," Jennifer mused.

"The Caribbean makes people do strange things. Trust me, I've seen it a million times. Level headed, normal people come down here and it's like the mesmerizing sand and blue waters changes them into different people. They make bad decisions they never would make at home – they start using drugs and spending more money in a few weeks than they make all year. I've worked on projects for some very savvy businesspeople. But after a few months here, reason goes out the window," Colin said, but immediately regretting it once he finished. It probably stung Jennifer, which was not his intention.

"I'm starting to think its time I get out of the Caribbean, because my reasoning might just be starting to go out the window too, and I've only been here two days," said Jennifer, " I think I know what I have to do. Can you drop me off at the airport? I'm going to catch a plane to Texas tonight," Jennifer announced, resolute in her conviction to track down this research group and find out what she could.

"Do you think you're leaving me here in Nassau? Remember, I am still owed a lot of money by your company, so if you're going to Texas, I'm going to Texas."

Jennifer looked over at him to see if he was joking. He looked dead serious. "Oh come on. You don't need to follow me around to make sure you get the money my father owes you. You know where to find me now, and I hope you've figured out that I have principles. I will make good on all those unpaid invoices, and you're first in line."

Colin made a sharp u-turn and headed back towards the airport. He looked troubled, more troubled than Jennifer expected. She started to wonder if perhaps he was in even more dire financial straits as a result of this project going under than he had let on.

"Sorry. I'm coming along. Like it or not. We're a team now, right?" said Colin after a moment.

He gave Jennifer an easy smile, but she sensed he was still quite uneasy inside, just hiding it well. She thought about putting her foot down, but then thought better of it, and decided if Colin felt so strongly about coming along, then maybe it was best to let him. Besides, once they were back in the US, if things got uncomfortable between them, it would be much easier, and safer, to ditch him. Riding in his friends borrowed car in the rougher parts of Nassau where she was still turned around and at his mercy, it seemed poor judgment to fight too hard on this one.

"Suit yourself," she said, returning the smile. "But you're paying for your own ticket. I'm not adding to what I already owe you," she jabbed at him, allowing some mild sarcasm in her voice.

"Don't worry. I still have a few dollars left," he retorted back. The sun was low in the sky and the shadows of the buildings were long as they drove west towards Pindling Airport. Jennifer hoped they'd be able to catch a flight to Miami, and from there, they might make it to Austin this evening.

Chapter 17

Ian Michelson breathed a sigh of relief as the British Airways jet landed at Gatewick Aiport outside of London. Despite having worked all over the world, he always felt a sense of calm when touching ground back in the United Kingdom.

He looked down at his well-worn, brown leather legal briefcase. He had been using that briefcase to travel the world for thirty years. Now it carried the hard drive that could make all the years of slaving away worthwhile. The last year of data he had gathered was stored on it. Because if the profligate investment in the past year, that data was the vast majority of the information needed to begin drilling. When put together with a series of other files he had collected, Michelson could unlock the biggest oil field in the western hemisphere. It was the key to his professional and financial future. Once the wells in the Formation were pumping out oil based on his findings, he would be rich beyond imagination. But more important than that, he would become an instant academic celebrity in the geological community, and finally be given the respect he deserved. He held the briefcase a little tighter than usual as he walked through the airport and headed for the taxi cab stand. Despite the rainy, gray London day, but he couldn't help but smile.

His turn finally came up in the long queue waiting for a taxi, and as he sat down inside the cab, he gave instructions to drive to the Royal School of Mines.

The past few days had been extremely unsettling. Langford disappeared, his daughter stormed onto the scene poking around everywhere, and rumors surfaced of the Chinese bank taking control of the entire island. It had confirmed in Michelson's mind that he must get this critical data off the island and secure back in London right away.

Soon, his cab was closing in on the Royal School of Mines. His office was in the basement of the Aston Webb building, a part of the sprawling, urban Imperial College in the heart of London. Although nicely decorated and furnished, his office was small, with just one half window peeking out to the sidewalk. The building itself, a part of the prestigious university since it's completion in 1909, was just steps away from Albert Hall. It was an impressive building that housed classrooms, lecture halls, offices and laboratories where some of the most important research in the world was conducted – a juxtaposition of a classic Edwardian architecture with cutting edge, twenty-first century technology. The taxi was fast approaching a traffic circle at the intersection of Exhibition Road and Prince Consort Road.

"Hi there, can you turn down Exhibition? I'm going to get off at Imperial College Road," Ian called to the cabbie. The cabbie gave him a nod and followed the roundabout, pulling to a stop at the curb. Ian pulled on a grey half zip sweater he had brought along with him as the only winter clothing item he had in his island wardrobe. The gray, rainy morning was breaking just a bit, but the winter chill was still biting as Ian got out of the cab and headed towards the rear entrance to the Aston Webb building. He zipped the sweater up fully, put his head down, and walked quickly towards the unobtrusive rear entrance. Thankfully, it was a quiet day. There were few students, or anyone else for that matter, walking about. He walked inside the building, and made an immediate turn down a side staircase which led to the basement. Opening the door to the stairwell, he looked down a long, empty hallway. The last remodel of this basement space had been in the 1960's, and there was a distinctive institutional feel to the hall. His office was just three doors down on the left. Taking out the door key, Ian walked quietly down the hall and turned towards his office door.

Ian gently and quietly slid his key into the lock and stepped inside, softly closing the door behind him. He quickly surveyed his entire office, looking carefully about the room for anything out of place. Nothing appeared to have been moved or taken. He walked over to his desk and stared down at this desktop computer and keyboard. His computer, which he left on twenty four hours a day, three hundred and sixty five days a year, whether he was going to be away from his desk for a few hours or a few months, hummed softly. He logged on, plugged in the hard drive, and began to backup the data from it on his desk top along with the years of other files he had collected of the oilfield. Ian leaned back in his desk chair, pressed his fingers together, and closed his eyes to finally relax.

Chapter 18

Sixth Street, in Austin, Texas on a Saturday night was always a lively place. Even in the winter with a light rain falling, there were still plenty of students celebrating the end of the semester before heading back home. There were also plenty of twenty and thirty-something's enjoying the long strip of bars and restaurants in the center of Austin. Jennifer and Colin drove slowly down the street taking in the scene as they made their way to the north of the University of Texas campus and the 'Oceanographic Stratification Research Institute" address.

As they approached the address, they found a tree lined street, not very well lit, and also not very busy. Evening had settled across Austin and even the edges of a normally bustling campus were sleepy. Jennifer was surprised their search had brought them to this place. It seemed like a regular neighborhood, not an area you would find an office or a research center. Several cars and pickup trucks were parked along the edge of the street, and a few lights were still on in various windows. The dim, bluish glow of a television illuminated a living room window from one house.

"Does this make sense to you?" Jennifer asked, looking over at Colin. "I expected to find the OSRI offices in some downtown office building."

"I had the same thought, at first. But I think this may make more sense than it seems," Colin said slowly, as if beginning to work things out in his mind.

"Isn't that where the place is supposed to be?" she asked.

"Yeah, I think so," said Colin, still driving south down a road called Speedway Street and past the intersection where the address indicated the OSRI office should be located.

"Shouldn't we stop, then? See if we can confirm it's the right place?" Jennifer asked him, getting annoyed.

"I think if we drive just one more block south, it will make more sense why the OSRI might have its office in this neighborhood, rather than somewhere else," he said. "Besides, it's better reconnaissance to make a quiet first pass at the place before stopping and barging our way in."

As they drove slowly down the street and out of the tree lined row of homes, a series of brick, institutional buildings emerged. She read a sign in a green lawn off of the sidewalk and next to a large building that read 'Center for Petroleum Engineering and Technology, University of Texas.' Jennifer wondered how Colin seemed to know how this would happen. This construction contractor continually surprised her.

"Seriously, how did you know that!" Jennifer exclaimed, pointing to the sign, and looking over at a now broadly smiling Colin.

"I've spent a little time in Austin," Colin laughed. "Makes a little more sense now, doesn't it?"

"It does. So you're thinking that the OSRI has some connection to the Center for Petroleum Engineering and Technology?"

"Whoever is the brains behind the OSRI did some research, or studied, or taught at the center. It's one of the premier places in the world for ground breaking research with anything to do with the oil industry."

"Well that was a good bit of detective work. But I think we need to get back to the intersection to see if we can find out some more."

"My thoughts exactly," Colin said, turning the car at the next intersection. He turned back north at the next street and found a spot to park in front of another University building.

"Best go on foot from here," he said, turning off the car. They got out and walked up a block to the corner where they believed the 'office' of the mysterious think tank was located. Jennifer continued walking towards the corner, but stopped as she felt Colin's hand on her arm, gently holding her back.

"Look, I think we need to be a little cautious. The OSRI was publishing papers about Mayaguana years ago. The likely thing is that whoever was behind that group is probably long gone, and I doubt we'll be finding any evidence they were ever here. But just in case someone is still around, we really don't know anything about them. And, I think it would be best if they didn't suspect we're checking them out," Colin said, looking earnestly at her from the shadows cast by a lone street light at the corner.

"Yeah, I don't disagree. What are you suggesting?" Jennifer said, looking him. In the dark night, he seemed to blend in with the shadows. She noticed he had subtly pulled her out of the circle of light cast on the concrete sidewalk by the street lamp and out of line of sight of the corner where they thought they might find the OSRI. It was a little un-nerving. He seemed different. Less happy-go-lucky and more serious than the snarky guy she had come to know over the past few days. It also occurred to her she really didn't know him well at all, and she felt a twinge of anxiousness well up in her stomach.

"Why don't you let me go alone? I'll check everything out, and meet you back at the car," Colin proposed.

"Not a chance," Jennifer said flatly, despite her misgivings. Colin opened his mouth to protest, and Jennifer held up her hand to him in a 'talk to the hand' manner. Colin closed his mouth without another word. They started down the block together, and Colin couldn't resist telling her quickly and with a smile,"I should have known better."

The buildings at the corner where Jennifer's smartphone had told them they should find the offices of the OSRI looked like apartments, and as they got closer, Jennifer was sure they were following a rabbit hole that was likely to lead to a dead end. Her heart sank a little as they looked at what appeared to be a vacant building. It was a four-plex building of condos or apartments, and based on the architecture and plain brick front facing the street, she guessed the apartment was built in the 1970's. The sidewalk in front of the apartments was cracked, and grass and weeds poked through. The windows looked old and dirty. It was clear the buildings, whether inhabited or not, were not particularly well maintained. She turned to Colin, and tried to read the look on his face.

"We're wasting our time," she said, trying not to sound crestfallen. Colin did not answer her, and looked like he was deep in thought. He stopped just across the street from the four-plex, and shook his head slightly, almost as if to himself, rather than in answer to Jennifer. He looked across the street and his eyes panned back and forth from the front of the apartments to the back of the building and a low, chain link fenced back parking lot. There were no cars parked in the small parking lot behind the apartments.

"I think it's worth a closer look," Colin said, still with his head on a swivel, slowly scanning the scene. The street looked empty. There were no people outside, and only a few cars had passed by. They casually crossed the street at the corner crosswalk. A narrow concrete sidewalk led along the front of the apartments, with a small cinder block entry way landing by each door. At the corner of the building, near the first front door, was a square, silver, metal mail box with four slots on it – one presumably for each apartment. With a quick look up and down the street to verify that it was still deserted, Colin walked to the mailbox and examined it. After also looking up and down the street, Jennifer followed him and read the mailbox over his shoulder. She suppressed a gasp. Only one of the four letter box slots was labeled with a small card that that read: "Oceanographic Stratification Research Institute."

Colin turned from the mailbox and walked back towards the street corner, subtly waving Jennifer to come along with him. They turned the corner, and Colin went directly to the gate in the chain link fence behind the apartments. He lifted the horseshoe shaped latch securing the gate, pushed it open and walked into the back yard as casually as if he lived there. Jennifer hesitated for just a moment on the sidewalk in front of the open gate, and then followed Colin. This was taking a turn she was not comfortable with, but she also felt like protesting out on the sidewalk, in the flood of the light of the streetlamp on the corner of this very quiet street, was not a good idea. Colin closed the gate and quietly lowered the latch back in place. He walked towards the back door of the apartment furthest from the street and fumbled in his pocket as if looking for a key. There was a light over the top of each of the four back doors of the four-plex, but the last one – the unit which according to the mailbox label they had just read held the office of the OSRI and under which Colin now stood - was burnt out. The other back door lights were very dirty and covered in cobwebs, so that they both now stood in a shadowed area, and nearly out of sight of any passers-by. Jennifer's heart was starting to race, and she feared what Colin was about to do. From inside his pocket, Colin pulled out a small metal object that looked like a pocket knife. He pried a small blade from out of the center of the knife, and quietly pressed the end of the blade into the lock of the door.

"What the heck are you doing!" hissed Jennifer, realizing that Colin was about to pick the lock and break into the apartment. "Put that damn thing away!"

"We're not going to find out anything else by just snooping around out here and peering in some grimy windows," said Colin in a firm whisper.

"Who are you?!? We cannot just go around breaking into houses. What are we going to find out from inside the Austin police holding cell?" Jennifer whispered back, putting her hand over the doorknob to stop Colin from working on picking the lock.

"Have I led you astray yet? We flew all the way to Texas. We need to know just who is behind this think tank, and start to put together the pieces of this puzzle. There's an interconnecting thread here: from the island, to the oil field, and now to this dingy apartment. We're close to putting it all together!" Colin appealed to her.

Jennifer didn't answer, but she reluctantly took her hand off the door handle to signal he should go ahead and finish the job. Her heart was pounding in her chest, and she cringed in anticipation of Colin's lock picking attempt, sure that the noise of the scraping metal and prying would rouse attention. She looked away from Colin to keep an eye out, but no sooner had she had turned her head when she heard a gentle click. To her surprise, Colin was pushing the door open slowly, and with impressive stealth. He held the small knife open in one hand, his other still grasping the door handle, and keeping the door just ajar. Jennifer's fear of being seen overtook her and she pushed on him to urge him in the room and off the street. Colin looked back at her, and leaned in to her ear.

"We don't know for sure there is no one inside. You have to be patient. Stay cool," he whispered, giving her a reassuring smile. Being told to chill out made Jennifer furious, and she opened her mouth to tell Colin he was going to get them both thrown in jail when some passerby noticed what they were doing and called the police, but something held her back. Jennifer could defer to experience and demonstrated success, and over the past few hours, Colin had been showing a fair amount of both. Maybe it was his tough-guy, construction working, handy-man ability, but he seemed remarkably comfortable in this situation. He didn't seem to be guessing how to pick that lock, he *knew* how. Her thoughts about Colin were interrupted as he slowly opened the door six inches, and proceeded to wait for ten, long seconds. Nothing happened. With his foot, he gently pushed on the door and it slowly swung open, bumping against a stop. The empty apartment stared back at Jennifer and Colin in quiet darkness. Colin walked inside, guiding Jennifer by the arm in behind him. In the shadows, he motioned for her to stand by the wall near the door, as he slowly and quietly shut the door, carefully ensuring the door handle made no noise as it secured.

The room in which they stood looked sparsely furnished, and its purpose was a little hard to infer from its contents. There was a tattered futon against one wall, a work-station style office desk against another, and a rolling office chair that had been repaired with duct tape pushed underneath it. A large, five drawer filing cabinet sat next to the desk. On the opposite end of the room, a kitchen table was accompanied by a few metal kitchen table chairs with yellow plastic cushions. Even in the dark, it could not be mistaken for anything luxurious. It also looked like it had been ransacked. There were some drawers and cabinet doors left open, some papers scattered about, and an over-turned chair.

"I think we need to risk a little light," Colin said quietly, looking over at Jennifer. "We're going to need to really look around to figure anything out, and I doubt anyone will notice this late at night." He nodded towards a light switch on the wall near Jennifer. She shook her head in agreement flipping on the switch. The room lit up instantly from a series of track lighting running the length of the room's ceiling. In the brighter light, it still appeared like a badly decorated, messy, crash pad. But there was a certain utilitarian functionality about the place that made it different from some typical college student's apartment. Rather than posters of rock bands or cheap prints of famous artwork, on the walls hung a series of maps. The maps were oceanographic charts of the area around Mayaguana, and were marked with red pen, colored tape, and sticky notes as if some intense and in-depth analysis was done using them. Upon closer inspection, Jennifer realized that the maps were tracking oil field testing in the ocean. There were numerous points on the charts marked with depths, coordinates, and other technical notes that Jennifer could not quite understand. A few bare spaces suggested some of the maps had been removed.

Colin whistled softly through his teeth. "Did I tell you? Well we've certainly found something here." His eyes scanned the walls, and then focused on the desk. There was a vintage computer monitor sitting on it, and a dusty keyboard and mouse, but no CPU. Along the wall were stacks of banker-style file boxes. Some of the boxes looked older, with a fake wood grain printed on the cardboard. Others were just white or gray cardboard, and looked newer, with crisp edges and box tops that hadn't creased or caved in from the weight of being stacked on one another. He walked to the filing cabinet and pulled on the drawer. It didn't budge, but the sound of the metal bar of the interior cabinet lock banging against a stop could be heard faintly in the quiet of the empty apartment. Colin again pulled out the small pocket knife, inserting the tip into the filing cabinet lock. It popped open almost immediately, and he slid open the top drawer. Jennifer stood to the other side of the open drawer and they both looked inside. It was full of manila file folders, neatly labeled with various dates. Pulling out a file that had the date 9/88, Jennifer noted the tab read "OSRI Pubs".

"I'd say this confirms we're in the right place, if the maps on the wall weren't conclusive enough," Jennifer said, looking over at Colin. He nodded in agreement. Opening up the folder, Jennifer pulled out several typed reports bound together with alligator clips. They were all red rubber stamped "DRAFT". Jennifer set the opened folder on the desk. As she flipped through the draft documents, she recognized them as articles for scholarly journals, similar to the ones Professor Rajkumar had in his office back at The College of The Bahamas. She flipped quickly through the rest of the alligator clipped reports. They all seemed to be drafts of other publications in the long running debate that, as the professor had remembered, occurred in scholarly journals about energy, oil and gas for years between the mysterious OSRI and various other academic sparring partners.

"Do you see any names? Any idea who we are actually dealing with yet," Jennifer asked Colin, who had pulled out several folders from the filing cabinet himself and was thumbing through them.

"No. There's a lot of material here, but it all seems pretty anonymous," Colin said, still flipping through a stack of papers. "We don't have all night either. We should find out what we can and get out of here within the next few minutes."

"What is this, Mister Big Time Cat Burglar? You're the one who broke in here and turned on the lights! Now you get nervous about someone noticing!" jeered Jennifer quietly as she smirked at Colin. She felt he had been slowly taking over her operation, and it had been getting more and more uncomfortable that this relative stranger was starting to dictate what she did. In any situation that would have been annoying, but given the many pieces to this puzzle and the quickly running hourglass counting down to MICAL independence and the bank foreclosure – well, this really wasn't the time for some knucklehead to start calling the shots. Despite Colin's emerging and - she had to admit grudgingly to herself - impressive skill set extending beyond general construction, she enjoyed taking a shot back at him just to let him know this was still her show. It seemed to have the desired effect.

"I'm just saying," Colin came back with a barely detectable defensive whine, "that we don't want to stay here all night shuffling through boxes of files, especially since I would say someone has been here reasonably recently."

"What makes you say that?"

"Look over at the kitchen floor. Neither of us have walked over that way but there are footprints and they haven't dried yet. Someone's been here since it started raining," Colin said matter-of-factly, jerking his head slightly in the direction of the referenced evidence.

She looked in that direction and saw the footprints. Her skin crawled. The minutes ticked away as they searched the files, and felt like hours. Small, innocent noises out on the street seemed louder and louder to Jennifer, and she felt herself begin to jump at the normal sounds of an apartment building at night. She still had no names or clues as to whom or what group was funding all of this research and acting under the front of the OSRI. Her frustration grew. She took a long, hard look around the apartment. There had to be a better clue somewhere than reading innocuous and seemingly sanitized lines of research notes and journal publications about oil exploration and underwater geology.

There was no personalization to the room. It was purely functional, almost like some kind of research command center, where the occupant came to review data, do analysis, and then store the results. It also seemed like the apartment had been used for this purpose for many years. Surely, Jennifer thought to herself, people can't come here for years without leaving something behind that would give a clue to their identity. She walked around the room making an effort to look with a different eye. Rather than focusing on the maps, the technical data, and the pictures of Mayaguana Island, she made herself look at the room from the perspective of the mystery tenant.

Her eyes fell on the bathroom door at the other end of the apartment. Walking to the door, which was ajar, she slowly pushed it all the way open and flipped on the light switch. A fluorescent light flickered to life. A quiet hum echoed in the small bathroom, which was now bathed in a white light, growing in intensity as the bulb warmed up. She scanned the room, but it looked like a normal bathroom with the typical items you might expect to see. It had linoleum flooring, and a shower/tub with a sliding glass door that looked like it could use some glass-cleaner. A partially full tube of toothpaste sat next to a white porcelain sink on the vanity. She opened the medicine cabinet, which sat behind the vanity mirror, but found nothing more conclusive - a box of band aids, a bottle of aspirin, and some aftershave.

Jennifer stopped her scan for a moment, looking at the medicine cabinet. The aftershave suggested that a man was at least here some of the time. None of the items looked like things you might find in a woman's bathroom vanity. Nor did the small quantity of items look like more than enough for one person. She concluded whoever stayed here working from time to time was probably a single man. Not much to go on, but at least it was a start.

Walking back out into the main room of the apartment, she noticed Colin had his head down, pouring over another stack of files he had pulled from one of the file boxes. By his silence, she knew he had not discovered anything important yet, so she decided to continue her examination of the apartment. The kitchen was in the corner of the room near the door they had entered. This was a studio apartment, and an older one. There was nothing separating or delineating the kitchen from the living area of the room save cheap linoleum floor in the kitchen area as opposed to a dirty, worn, green carpet covering the rest of the room. Similar to the bathroom, it was nearly empty. A few rusty pots, pans and some old ceramic plates and cups were in the drawers underneath the kitchen counter. She opened a pantry door above the counter. A clear glass canister half-filled with sugar sat on one shelf. An unopened blue package that looked like crackers was next to it. Jennifer read the label: Huntley Tea Biscuits. This was interesting. It wasn't the type of thing you'd expect to see in a typical American pantry. She proceeded to the refrigerator. She opened the door, but the old refrigerator was set at such a high temperature the air inside it barely seemed to feel any colder. It was empty, save for one small jar sitting in the door shelf. Picking up the jar, Jennifer read the label: Devonshire Clotted Cream. Her mind began to race. She walked briskly back to the bathroom and picked up the tube of toothpaste: Gibbs SR Toothpaste.

"Colin, what do Tea Biscuits, clotted cream, and Gibbs Toothpaste all have in common?" she asked, looking for some confirmation about her suspicion without having to lay it out clearly for him and sway his opinion.

Colin didn't look up from the file he was reading to answer her. "I don't know. I've never heard of any of them, but I don't think that's the answer you're getting at."

"They're all British products."

Colin looked up from his file. "So you think whoever stayed here was also British?"

"I'd say it's highly probable. None of those brands are readily available in Texas, or anywhere in the US for that matter."

"Well unfortunately, coming from the Caribbean, there are lots of people of British decent. It's a start, but I'm afraid that doesn't narrow the field too much," said Colin, clearly not as excited as Jennifer.

"It's a British man. He had some aftershave – a British brand of aftershave – is in the bathroom as well. So that narrows the field by half!" Jennifer shot back with a faint look of triumph on her face. "Come on now. Don't play dumb just because you didn't figure this one out…a British man, who's a geologist, who has known the waters around Mayaguana intimately for years. There's only one suspect in this case now!"

"Maybe so. So Ian Michelson has been coming to this hideout for years while he did research from time to time at the University," concluded Colin.

"He must really be brilliant. It's one thing to be able to prove to yourself, and a group of tough investors to boot, that there's a massive oil field right under their noses. That takes a very smart scientist. But to then be able to alter the data just slightly, and be able to publish these journal articles convincingly enough to throw the rest of the world off the scent…well, that's a genius," Jennifer continued. She was quickly becoming certain the oil field was for real, as Carty had claimed.

"So does any of this lead to your father's sudden disappearance?" Colin pressed.

"I think Michelson was making a play to keep control of the oilfield for himself. He had all the technical data, and he had personally scouted nearly the entire field on his boat," Jennifer said, looking over the maps on the wall as she spoke as if picturing him on his converted fishing boat, out taking soundings.

"Do you think when your father's money began to run out, Michelson, and maybe Carty along with him, decided they were better off without him, and they are behind your father's mysterious boating accident? And now Michelson is the only person who knows all the locations of the oil fields around Mayaguana?" Colin continued her thought. He paused for a moment to consider the idea.

"Sounds like the best explanation we have so far," Jennifer answer unwaveringly. "But for now, I think I should try and get back to Mayaguana and confront Michelson. It's clear that this rumored oil and my fathers' disappearance are linked."

"You're right. Let me call Obie so he can make sure that guy doesn't head out to sea on another week long geology experiment," Colin laughed, pulling out his cell phone and dialing Obie.

"Hey, man," he said into his phone when Obie answered. "Where's Michelson at?"

He listened for a few moments as Obie spoke from the other end, and then scowled as he reproached Obie. "What do you mean? How could you let that happen? Obediah...I'm disappointed....Yes, in you. Look, get out there and track him down. Right...I'll call you soon."

Colin hung up. Jennifer had not known Colin Steele for long, but she could tell he was furious.

"He's gone!" Colin growled, giving Jennifer a sidelong glance as if he couldn't bear to look her directly in the eyes. "I can't believe Obie would let that happen."

"Why would Obie think to keep Ian on the island? And how could he even if he wanted to?" Jennifer asked, a little surprised at Colin's reaction. "I don't think you can really be upset with him." She was always able to keep calm and reason better when others flew off the handle a bit. It was a part of her leadership tool kit she had learned from watching her father.

"Yeah. Yeah, you're right," Colin answered. "Well, do you still want to head back to Mayaguana?"

"Do you think Michelson is gone from the island for good?" she asked.

"My guess is yes. And it also makes me very suspicious of him. At first I doubted he had anything to do with your father's disappearance, but now, I'm not so sure," Colin said.

"I think we've learned all we can here. The missing CPU for this desktop might have been the Holy Grail, but he must have taken it with him. There's not much real information in all of these paper files and maps. It looks like all of the disinformation he used to throw people off. And it's time to get going while it's still the dead of night. It doesn't seem to make sense to go back to Mayaguana if Michelson is gone. What's our next move?" Colin asked, looking down at his watch. It was 3AM.

"We try to find Michelson. Where do you go when you're on the run?" Jennifer posed the question to Colin.

"You go to someplace familiar, but big enough you can hide in the crowd," Colin replied, deep in thought trying to reason through Michelson's options.

"London. He went to London. It's a big city. He knows it well. It's his home turf advantage," Jennifer answered. Her mind was made up on exactly what she had to do. "If we get an early flight out of Austin to a major hub, we can be in London today."

"Lead the way," Colin said.

Chapter 19

Carty Wallingford-Rolle sat at his desk sipping a cup of coffee, thoughtfully considering the phone call that had just ended. As a young man, he had felt a calling to be the Prime Minister of The Bahamas. But now, he was near to accomplishing something even greater than that, becoming the founding father of his own new nation.

The one room school house in Abraham's Bay, the largest settlement on Mayaguana Island, had been his favorite place to spend time as a boy. In Carty's childhood, Mayaguana felt a lot different than it did today. The US military base had a staff of hundreds, which kept the island humming at a very comfortable pace. The schoolhouse in Abraham's Bay had been a benefactor of this bit of economic activity. Base commanders had established a tradition of donating a fair amount of their staff's time to making sure the school house, among a few other buildings important to the local community, had been well-maintained and supplied. A newcomer to the island might have been very surprised to see how modern, well-appointed, and well run the academic program on Mayaguana had been in those days. To Carty, it was an illuminating oasis in the desert of the humdrum life on a small island. He walked to school as soon as his chores were done, stayed as late as possible, and spent many a Sunday afternoon after church sitting at his desk reading text books, periodicals, and newspapers, which thanks to the almost daily US Air Force flights in and out of the island, were delivered quite regularly.

Even working part time at the military base as a high school student, Carty found his zest for learning set him apart. The children of Mayaguana were well educated for simple islanders, but Carty's natural intelligence enabled him to function at a much higher level, and he was first in his class. It was no wonder then, that Langford Bullfinch and Ian Michelson had found Carty a top notch companion, not to mention a first class local guide, while escorting and conducting missions in the waters around the island.

By the time Carty was leaving the island to attend college, his mind was constantly at work struggling with how the great secret he and his two companions shared could be leveraged to catapult him to greatness. That he would be great, he had no doubt, and with the secret of the riches below the waters of his island, he believed he could become a legendary leader, not just in The Bahamas, but the whole of The Caribbean. After his graduation from the University of Miami with a degree in Political Science, he stayed on at Miami to attend law school.

While a student in Florida, Carty had been a voracious defender of The Bahamas, driven by an intense internal pride for his home country. Many, especially in Florida, viewed The Bahamas as a drug fueled Sodom and Gomorrah resulting from the prevalent trafficking in cocaine through the chain of islands from Columbia to Florida. While Carty couldn't help but admit that certainly some in The Bahamas turned a blind eye to the drug runners, and many benefitted themselves, he resented the disparaging image of his beloved, beautiful island home.

But after establishing his law practice in Nassau, he soon became jaded with his own country. He had always believed the Government of The Bahamas functioned as a shining example of a newly independent country operating its own exemplary Parliamentary system. What he found most disturbing as a young lawyer, was that the many Americans he had met in Miami who laughed at The Bahamas as a funny, little, corrupt dictatorship, were more correct in their assessment than Carty could have imagined.

From the bottom to the top, corruption reigned supreme, riding roughshod over the many laws, regulations and systems that had been put in place so carefully over hundreds of years. The rules that were followed were enforced as a tool to be used by a rich and powerful few to keep everyone else out of their business. And that business, while it might have had legitimate arms, was always financed at its heart by smuggling. Carty didn't mind so much that the downtrodden, work-a-day Bahamians made a little money from time to time, like a dock worker being paid a few hundred now and then to look the other way, but what really bothered him was the hypocrisy of the big time players, who were nearly all politicians, and many of whom were lawyers like himself. The judges of the Bahamian legal system were nothing but a group of well-paid lap dogs. The crooked lawyers made sure that even if a few of their drug cartel partner's foot soldiers had to do some time every now and then, just to make things look good, nobody of any real influence ever saw a single day in prison, or even the courtroom for that matter.

Carty simply refused to sink into that world, despite many opportunities, and much pressure to do so. As a result, his law practice barely paid the bills. He had a small trickle of clients and most could not pay for the services they needed. Carty took on their cases anyway. Their problems were usually mundane and trivial, but the legal and political system was so busy burying all the dirt that it could take years for small, but legitimate, claims to get their day in court. Carty went through dark periods in those early days as an angry, young lawyer, working long hours just to keep the lights on in his office. His hopes of becoming a powerful politician, and continue on his calling to the highest office, were nearly dashed.

But after several years of being the lawyer to the poorest of the poor Bahamians, a glimmer of hope appeared from handling all of these charity cases. The Bahamas is an "archipelago nation" comprised of over seven hundred islands, but only one island mattered: New Providence, where the capitol city of Nassau had been a center of Caribbean commerce, government and culture for over five hundred years. Bahamians from New Providence enjoyed the wealth and security that came from being at the center of their nation's seat of business and government. For Bahamians from the other 699 islands, life was much more difficult, and subsistence living in a rustic kind of poverty was the norm. Government benefits, programs and services, and more recently the wealth effect of millions, maybe billions, of dollars from the drug trade all seemed to be centered around Nassau, and rarely, if ever found its way to the poor inhabitants of the "Out Islands." As a child of Mayaguana, one of the furthest out islands from Nassau geographically and emotionally, these were Carty's people.

Despite his morose demeanor and belief that his outsider, incorruptible reputation was an anchor weighing him down, Carty did manage to win a lot of small victories. From sheer will, his relentless push against the slow, bureaucratic and corrupt system often made his comparably small demands easier to grant by the judges and government officials, just so he would go away and leave them alone to get back to the really profitable business of graft.

These small victories were not small to his clients, for whom a few hundred dollars could represent a significant windfall. Their gratefulness knew no bounds, and word of mouth about the 'miracles' that young Carty Wallingford-Rolle was performing in the big city spread like wildfire amongst the country folk of the Out Islands. Carty's reputation as a modern day Robin Hood was soon legendary, and rumbles began to arise for him to run for Parliament to represent his home district, MICAL, comprising the islands of Mayaguana, Inagua, Crooked Island, Acklins, and Long Cay.

Those five islands held the dubious distinction of being the poorest of the rural poor, a kind of Bahamian Appalachia. Mayaguana, in particular, had a reputation of being one of the most isolated and inaccessible of all the Bahamian islands because of the deep water passages surrounding it.

In Carty, the oppressed people of these lonely islands had found one of their own who had what it took to stand up to the Nassau political machine. The rumbles calling for Carty to run for office became shrill demands early in 1986, an election year. Carty felt that perhaps his calling was still achievable, but he himself still had no money, and his potential constituents had even less. He didn't need much to win the MICAL seat, but he needed something. Votes could be, and typically were, literally bought in Bahamian elections. Candidates would hand out thousands of dollars to voters in their district in the days, hours and minutes before election booths opened, which was a campaign tactic that proved understandably effective. Carty believed that his grass roots support might overcome this tactic, meaning that the MICAL voters would certainly take his opponents money, but once they went to cast their votes, they would still choose Carty. More concerning was coming up with enough of a war chest to pay the tribute to the power brokers in Nassau necessary to ensure they stayed out of his way and allow the votes to fall where they may. This could be tens of thousands of dollars, which he was not sure how to find.

His thoughts turned to his old companion, Langford Bullfinch. Because of the secret they shared, he had kept in touch with Langford from time to time. Carty knew Langford was starting to do well for himself in real estate. Carty was never one to ask for handouts, but he believed in his heart that winning the MICAL seat in Parliament could mean a lot for Langford and Ian, not to mention himself. It seemed to Carty the right time to go hit Langford Bullfinch up for a sizeable political donation. Carty had a well-rehearsed speech ready to make his pitch to Langford, but it was entirely unnecessary. Within five minutes of their phone call to discuss the issue, Langford had readily agreed he would back Carty in his election. Money was wired to Carty's bank that afternoon, and he went to work on his first election campaign.

He was elected as the Member of Parliament for MICAL by a landslide. However, Carty's role as the rogue outsider in Bahamian politics was just beginning. Since he had no real history or affinity for either of the two main political parties in the country he had run as an independent. Although this had caused some concern to Langford, Carty was a persuasive operator, and ultimately, Langford backed off and contained his consternation. Carty not only delivered the victory, but also proved continually that his acumen as a politician was remarkable. His status as an independent, which would have prevented most from winning a seat in parliament, proved to be his greatest weapon.

The election, though a landslide for Carty, had been a close one for the two political parties, the Free National Movement, or FNM, and the Peoples Liberation Party, or PLP. The PLP, which had been in power since The Bahamas became independent in 1973, had previously held twenty-five or more of the thirty-six seats in Parliament. In this election, however, the tides had begun to shift, and the PLP took only eighteen, while the FNM won seventeen seats, and Carty, the one independent, held his seat. That meant for the PLP to ensure legislation they wanted to enact had enough votes to pass uncontested in a draw, they often had to have Carty's vote as well. Never had so much attention been paid to his backwater district.

Also during Carty's early years in Parliament, an idea had taken hold of him that he simply could not put out of his mind: MICAL independence from The Bahamas. To Carty, the idea made perfect sense. The rest of The Bahamas wouldn't even notice if MICAL was no longer a part of The Commonwealth, and many would be happy to see it go away, as it was a net taker of precious government resources without giving anything back in the minds of most in Nassau. Geographically speaking, the MICAL region was so far away from the rest of the islands of The Bahamas it could easily be sliced off with no national or maritime boundary issues. And, it was actually closer to the Turks and Caicos Islands, which were still a British protectorate. To the east, Cuba was another close neighbor. Neither would feel threatened by yet another tiny island nation in The Caribbean, especially one with just a few thousand people spread over five islands.

The only thing that would ever stop The Bahamas from gladly jettisoning MICAL would be if the secret oil field became known. Carty had worked for too long to let that happen now. The MICAL secession plan had been carefully nurtured by him for years. Indeed, it had been a tightrope walk the entire way. On one hand, he was a Member of Parliament and representative of the people and of his country. Should things be construed the wrong way, a push for secession could be considered treason. On the other hand, he believed independence was the right thing for the people of MICAL. Those poor, forgotten souls would become stewards of a great natural resource, and Carty imagined them living like the lesser princes of an oil state like Kuwait or Dubai.

Carty knew his Bahamian people well. He knew they loved to talk politics, and that there would be eager listeners to even casually mentioned hints of independence. The radio stations of Nassau spent many hours in the day airing political talk shows with very lively debate from guests and callers. This programming was listened to by nearly everybody in the country, and was interrupted only by the broadcasts of Parliamentary sessions and political rallies, which of course, fueled the next few weeks of political talk shows. Carty knew he could sway opinion through the medium of the political talk show, but only if he controlled the content and timing.

He had done just that, and masterfully for many years now. His strategy was founded on his understanding of how quickly news could travel from the many and disparate islands to Nassau, and how the 'telephone game' played into that word of mouth medium. Carty never spoke in public about his desires for MICAL independence, and certainly never in Nassau. He made trips down to the southern Bahamas every few weeks to visit his constituents. From time to time, he made sure to make it to a local watering hole, of which there were surprisingly many given the small population. Carty was a sociable fellow, and of course, a very smooth talker. Before the night was out, someone in whatever bar he visited would be loudly arguing the merits of MICAL independence, and no one could put together that it had been Carty's quiet, silvery tongue that had planted the seed in the minds of his chosen target.

Normally, in The Bahamas, if a boisterous and controversial political debate broke out (or at least more boisterous and controversial than usual) it would be open for discussion on the radio the next morning, with a constant stream of callers to put in their two cents. Here, Carty again used the services of his campaign financier, Langford, to slip just enough money to the radio hosts and producers to make sure the subject never made the news. This, of course, only infuriated the people of MICAL all the more, and reinforced Carty's political rhetoric that they were the ignored, backwater of The Bahamas.

In this way, Carty ensured the desire for secession was constantly bubbling just below the surface, and ready to be uncorked at the time of Carty's choosing. Of course, he had to grudgingly admit to himself, he wasn't entirely in control of this situation. He remained dependent, financially anyway, upon Langford's checkbook, which kept him in office.

For Carty, this was better than being indebted to the wealthy establishment of Bay Street Boys or the few political godfathers in Rawson Square. The Bay Street Boys, a nickname of the old colonial ruling elite, lost direct control of the government of The Bahamas after independence from Great Britain. However, this small group still controlled nearly all of the wealth. Neither they nor the leaders of the PLP or FNM were people to whom Carty ever wanted to be indebted. Most politicians in Nassau could line their pockets very quickly and go from rags to riches within one five year term, but Carty understood that staying above graft, bribery and political favors was critical to his strategy. His reputation as a clean politician was what endeared him to the people of MICAL and allowed him the freedom to play the maverick when needed.

Carty leaned back in his leather desk chair, thoughtfully sipping from his coffee cup. For a man who had walked a tight rope for many years, it was as if he had suddenly realized there was no net beneath him. The phone call he had just received was not entirely unexpected. Langford and Ian had presented the China Global Development Bank, or CGDB, and its autocratic President, Mr. Li, to Carty at a posh dinner meeting at Café Matisse. Carty's sensed trouble right away. In fairness, Langford and Ian seemed to understand that they were letting a shark into their swimming pool, but there seemed to be no choice. Langford's money was not nearly enough to undertake the infrastructure the three partners knew would be needed to ensure Mayaguana could support the extensive oil operation that would fuel its economic engine. And the CGDB promised what the three partners, and especially Carty, needed as much as the loan itself: secrecy.

On the cursory phone call that just ended, Carty was informed there was to be a meeting in China, at the bank headquarters. Carty had just been requested, or maybe ordered was the more accurate term, to ensure that his new acquaintance, Ms. Jennifer Bullfinch, was present at the meeting. This meeting would be no luxurious French dinner with a '62 Rothschild to warm the conversation up and a '50 Chateau d'Yquem to seal the deal. This was going to be an unpleasant foreclosure meeting, and Carty was mentally prepared to fight tooth and nail to keep his vision alive. As for how he could corral Ian and the younger Bullfinch, get them to China, and convince them to cooperate was another matter altogether. But he knew that whatever happened, one thing was certain: MICAL independence, and his position as the Founding Father of the Caribbean's only Oil Kingdom was on the line.

Chapter 20

Ian Michelson sat at his office desk in London turning over the recent events in his mind. He knew he would need to talk to Carty soon – very soon – to get a good read on the wily Bahamian politician. Without Langford and his money behind their whole scheme, Michelson wasn't entirely sure how he and Carty could get things to completion. They each had their own vices, and Michelson had sensed right away that power was Carty Wallingford-Rolle's. If Michelson could just make sure everyone involved remembered clearly that without him, they were years further away from tapping into the ground, he would be OK. Only Michelson had access to the entire data set that would be necessary to begin drilling operations

The portable hard drive containing the final MICAL Formation data set next to him on his desk. He pulled down a thick and boring looking textbook from his bookshelf, entitled *A Geographic Study of North Dakota*. He opened the cover, to reveal that it had been hollowed out. He placed the hard drive inside, closed the cover, and set the book back on the shelf.

Michelson decided it was time for a bite of dinner. His favorite Indian restaurant in London was not too far away, and they delivered to the University. He called in for a chicken Tikka Masala with garlic na'an, which a friendly voice told him would be at the back door of his building in twenty-five minutes. That was just enough time for him to shower up. Michelson didn't keep a flat in London since he had been there so infrequently the past few years. Instead, he had his favorite leather club chair and a matching large, leather foot rest in his office where he would catch a few winks when he was tired. Conveniently, there was a full locker room in the lavatory down the hall, so he could get away with living for short periods of time in his office. If anyone else at the University knew, they never said anything. Soon, he was enjoying the best dinner he had eaten in months, sitting in his club chair, and listening to Mozarts's Eine Kleine Nachtmusik playing through his computer. He set the empty carton on the small table next to his chair and drifted off to sleep, the exhaustion of a very long few days catching up with him.

Sometime later, Michelson stirred from his sleep. It was still dark outside, but he could not tell exactly what time it was. He thought he heard a noise coming from the hallway. He strained to listen, but the hall was silent again. He closed his eyes and readjusted his position in his chair, settling in to go back to sleep. The distinctive scrape of a key being inserted into the door lock sounded in his ears. Before he could sit up in his chair, the door to his office flung open. Two figures rushed inside, only their silhouette's visible from the dim hallway light. The largest of the figures was at Michelson's chair in an instant, towering over him menacingly, while the other had gone right to his bookshelf. Michelson rose to get out of his chair, when a thundering blow to the chest knocked him back down. A right hook to his jaw knocked his head sideways and into the padded leather edge of his club chair. His head began to swim, his vision blurred, and the room closed in around him. He collapsed into his chair, unconscious.

Michelson dreamt the uneasy dream that is the human mind's way of self-preservation in a truly traumatic situation. He was on his boat, just off the southeast point of Mayaguana. To Michelson, it was one of the most beautiful places in the world. It was also the best reference point from which to head northeast around the furthest end of Mayaguana and around the horn to the north, where the Caicos Passage met the open seas of the Atlantic Ocean. The waters of Southeast Point were crystal clear, and the sand was pure white. He stood at the console of the research boat, steering it slowly to follow the outside of the reef as it curved around the point. To his left, the small island the locals called "Booby Cay" in reference to the bird, the brown booby, which sometimes inhabited the place. To his right, the open ocean of the passage looked a different shade of blue, much darker from the deeper, sudden depths. It always fascinated Michelson how quickly the ocean floor dropped off at this particular island. It was not uncommon for the depth to go from 50 feet to 500 feet within a matter of yards. Diving "walls" as scuba divers called them, surrounded nearly the entire island. In fact, as Michelson himself had discovered, that was the Mother Nature's geographic clue hinting to the oil reserves that lie below the waters surrounding the island. In particular, the cliffs along the northern coast were so high, and the diving wall so pronounced, because of the upward pressure exerted on the earth by the force of the oil and natural gas beneath the surface.

To his left, movement caught his eye, and keeping the boat slowly moving along parallel to the reef, he looked over to see a flock of flamingos take flight. They took off in a pink formation, at least a hundred birds, flying in a winding, loping pattern for about a quarter of a mile to another stretch of white sandy beach interrupted only by a thick, grey trunk of driftwood that had washed up on the beach in the last hurricane. Arriving to their new feeding ground, the flamingos touched down as gracefully as they had departed their previous hunting ground. Michelson loved watching this particular flock. This part of the island was their regular haunt, since the shellfish they fed upon were so plentiful. Despite the beauty of the place and the sun rays glistening off the sand, bad weather threatened. A front line of dark, menacing storm clouds billowing high in the sky was on the horizon, moving fast towards the island. The locals knew better than to get caught so far from Abraham's Bay with that kind of weather setting in. Michelson knew better also, but he was running behind schedule, so he was banking on his skill to collect his much needed data readings quickly, and on the powerful engines on his boat to get back to the safety of the bay before the storm hit.

Michelson stood mesmerized by the flamingoes for a minute, but soon recalled he had work to do. Dominique needed to turn on their equipment so it had time to power up properly before they hit the area north of the cay where he would start his data collections. He set the friction on the steering wheel and stepped down into the cabin to make sure she was getting everything set properly. As soon as he poked his head into the cabin, he picked up a very odd vibe. Dominique looked like a child caught with her hand in the cookie jar. She quickly hit a key on the keyboard of the laptop she was using at the workstation, and Michelson noticed it was the computer he used personally, as opposed to the more ruggedized Panasonic Toughbook he kept just for doing research on the boat.

"Oh…hello…my love," Dominique stammered, looking up from the desk. As she turned, the childish look of nervous embarrassment melted away and by the time she looked him in the eye, Dominique had managed to turn on a smoldering gaze of raw sexual desire. "I was hoping you'd come down here…to help me." She got up from the small stool at the desk in a fluid graceful motion, undoing the hook of her bikini top as she stood, and letting it fall gently to the floor to reveal her breasts to Michelson.

"What were you doing down here, my darling?" Michelson asked, slowly coming down the stairs. He quickly glanced at his personal laptop screen, but it just showed the desktop picture of him and Dominique embracing each other on the beach at Grace Bay in Provo during one of their recent weekend escapades. "We need to get the equipment powered up. We're just about around the southeast point."

"Couldn't it wait, for just a few minutes?" Dominique asked softly, in her most sensual tone.

Michelson took a moment to take in her beauty. He thought about how wonderful making love to her felt, how he enjoyed feeling her soft, naked skin. Even the gentle rocking motion of the boat turned him on when she set the mood this way. Coming down the stairs, he put his arms around her waist and kissed her deeply. Putting his suspicions out of his mind, they moved in a graceful embrace to the small day bed at the bow of the cabin. Dominique sat down of the edge of the bed, and then lay back, pulling him gently down and on top of her. Kissing softly again, she pulled his hand seductively down her thigh.

Suddenly, the boat rocked violently, flinging them both against the cabin wall. As Michelson recovered himself, he saw a look of panic in Dominique's eyes. He hoped she didn't see the look of panic in his own. Looking out of the port hole, Michelson realized the storm had come upon them much quicker than he anticipated. A line of rolling waves began rocking the boat to and fro, stronger than the initial wave which had broken their embrace, and getting even stronger. Michelson stood up, holding on as best he could, making his way back to the console to get control of the boat and turn them for home. As he reached the stairs, heavy rain drops began battering against the plexi-glass console windshield. The sky, which had quickly become almost as dark as night, lit up suddenly as a long, crackling thunderbolt struck down very near them. The sound of thunder rolled across the skies, shaking the boat with each heavy thud and pounding against his chest…

…Michelson awoke drowsily from his unconscious dream. His eyes opened slowly, as he realized he was not at sea during that terrible storm, but still in his leather club chair back in London. The faint, gray light of dawn shined through the window. He realized he must have been unconscious for some time. The office was empty and the intruders gone. He was alone. Presently, however, it also registered in his mind that someone was pounding on his office door with a steady thud, as a muffled voice from out in the hallway demanded that he open the door. Michelson sat up and collected himself. Unlike his last set of visitors, whoever was at the door was probably safe since they were knocking rather than just breaking the door down.

"Just a minute!" he called out. "I'll be with you in just a minute, so hang on." He got up slowly from his chair. His entire body ached. He gingerly rubbed his ribcage, fairly certain he had a bruised rib. He held his jaw and gently opened his mouth. Calling out to his visitors had hurt tremendously, but at least his jaw wasn't broken. He drew himself straight and took in a slow deep breath. It hurt, but he could manage.

He glanced over at his desk. The CPU was missing. His next thought was his hard drive hidden in the book on his shelf. With a great effort, he got up from the chair and walked unsteadily behind his desk. He pulled the textbook from the shelf, and knew the moment he lifted it that the hard drive was gone. The book felt light in his hands, in stark contrast to his heart, which weighed heavily as he opened the book and confirmed the hard drive was indeed gone. His only consolation was that some of the data was still on his server in Texas, and a few files remained on the laptop on his research boat docked back in the Turks and Caicos. But there was no doubt, this was another alarming setback.

He walked slowly over to the door, surveying his office as he went. Other than the missing hard drive and CPU, it looked the same as when he had fallen asleep after dinner the night before. Standing in front of the door, Michelson stood staring blankly, weighing in his mind one more time if he should really open it.

The pounding by the visitors in the hall continued. He held his head up straight, turned the handle, and opened the door.

"Ian, we need a word with you. Right now." It was Colin Steele. Next to him stood Jennifer Bullfinch with a look on her face that worried Ian his jaw might end up broken this morning yet.

Chapter 21

Michelson stepped to the side of the doorway, motioning Jennifer and Colin inside his office. Jennifer took the lead and brusquely walked in. She had just spent the past fourteen hours on a long plane ride from Texas imagining what she would do when she finally found the professor, and in nearly every instance, it ended with her pounding his face in. As she turned to look at Michelson to commence the thrashing, she realized someone had already done the job. For a brief moment, she was at a loss for words trying to calculate what may have happened to him since they last saw him on Mayaguana, less than two days ago. Colin was the first to get a word out.

"You look like you've been worked over pretty good. What happened?" Colin asked as he walked into the office behind Jennifer, sounding genuinely concerned for Michelson, much to her annoyance. She was still convinced she was staring at a snake, and a few bruises on him were not going to evoke any sympathy.

She took a longer look at Michelson making a closer assessment. He was doing his best to stand up straight and look nonchalant, but clearly, he was in quite a bit of pain. The left side of his face was bruised and his jaw slightly swollen. She waited to hear his response, gathering more data points to make her assessment of the situation. In the first place, she was surprised they found him so easily, right at his office in the heart of London. Jennifer had been quite skeptical when, as she and Colin landed at Heathrow and were deciding what should be their first move to locate Michelson, Colin had suggested trying the Royal School of Mines. But here Michelson was, and looking quite a bit worse for the wear. Yet again Colin proved to be more capable and perceptive than Jennifer gave him credit.

Jennifer took a quick survey of Michelson's office, and had to admit, it was a comfortable place. In contrast to the British institutional feel of the hallway, Michelson's office had the aura of a private library in an exclusive London club. A very large Persian rug covered most of the floor, and a dark walnut half-panel wall ran along all sides. A dark green, almost velvety paint covered the upper half of the wall, and Michelson's desk and bookshelves were also of a dark mahogany wood. This, combined with his leather club chair and footstool, gave the office a very warm, rich feel. The walls were adorned with various hunting trophies, old wooden cricket bats, African art, framed parchment maps of various places around the world, and two crossed fencing sabers. Along the interior wall, a small fireplace took center stage, and some glowing embers and a few wisps of smoke drawn up the chimney hinted it had been burning not long ago. The scene suggested to Jennifer the trophy room of an Edwardian era National Geographic Society explorer or perhaps some kind of colonial military officer's mess showcasing the regiment's far flung outposts around the world. It did seem a fitting office for this strange, lonely man who had spent his life traveling around the world, as a modern day military officer and explorer of sorts.

Michelson didn't answer Colin right away, but walked slowly over to his desk, sitting down with some effort, and using the desk to steady himself. The silence hung in the air as Colin and Jennifer waited for Michelson to speak. Jennifer got the feeling he was using the time to determine how he wanted to answer. Michelson looked at her from behind his desk, realizing she was staring at him. He answered her gaze with his own intent look, as if he was trying to read her mind. Without breaking his gaze at Jennifer, he finally spoke.

"And, what brings you and Miss Bullfinch to my office doorstep on a cold winter's day here in London?" Michelson responded without really acknowledging Colin's question. His tone was nearly flat, his words measured and even, giving them a rehearsed and theatrical feel, as if he was reciting lines from a well-studied script. His answer infuriated Jennifer, but she kept her emotions flat, not wanting to give Michelson the upper hand, as she now realized his intent gaze and opening lines were intended to draw some kind of tell from her. For the first time since she had met Michelson, she sensed how absolutely cunning he was. Jennifer sometimes wondered over the past few days why her father had thrown his lot in with him. Michelson appeared exactly like the kind of person who would have repelled her father: a sloppy academic, with a penchant for young girls, and a clandestine nature that lent his words and actions a tenor of mild paranoia. But there was tougher and shrewder man underneath the professorial garb and obviously, he didn't trust them anymore than they trusted him.

"We came here to find you. We needed to talk to you, and when we heard you had left suddenly from Mayaguana, we were concerned," Colin answered, mildly exasperated. "And it looks like that concern was justified. You didn't look beat up when we saw you on your boat just a day ago."

"Well you have found me then. And thank you for the concern, but I am fine as you can see," Michelson responded a bit curtly, finally breaking his intent gaze on Jennifer and looking over to Colin. His stern look softened a bit, and gingerly rubbed his bruised jaw for a moment. "Now, what is it you want to talk with me about?"

"We know you have been throwing people off the scent of the MICAL Formation for years, under the guise of the OSRI think tank. I think you need to start explaining yourself from there," Jennifer said, getting to the point in her brisk, business-like manner.

"Do you indeed know that," Michelson retorted with the slightest look of amusement. "And just what do you want to know about this OSRI and the MICAL Formation?"

"Carty Wallingford-Rolle told us all about the oil field in the waters around Mayaguana. He told us how you, and he, and my father found out about it. Carty couldn't hide his fear that news of the oil field will get out, and he will lose his chance at leading a newly independent MICAL state. And you...you went on the run as soon as you could break away un-noticed. You were also on Mayaguana when my father was last seen. I'd say that means you have a lot of explaining to do."

"So you've gone and interrogated Carty, and now you're here to interrogate me so you can determine whether one or both of us got rid of your father for our own diabolical purposes. You're quite the junior detective, Miss Bullfinch. Brilliant." Michelson said quietly, as if to himself.

"Since you are here, and you obviously came to get answers, I suppose I can oblige," Michelson continued. He looked over at Colin.

"And thank you for your concern, whether genuine or not. I am fine, and I've taken worse knocks than this."

"So you were attacked. We were, too – in Nassau. Who was it?" Colin asked, seeming to take Michelson's promise to be honest with them at face value.

"I don't know for sure," Michelson answered. He wasn't ready to give away that his hard drive had been stolen, so a little less honestly, he continued, "And I don't know exactly why. As it appears you have discovered, I have devoted my career to two things: mapping out the MICAL Formation to determine exactly how much oil is under that sand, and keeping the rest of the world at bay. I have been successful in the first mission. I have detailed readings on nearly the entire MICAL formation, after many, many years of work."

"And the second mission, to keep the existence of oil around Mayaguana a secret? Have you been successful in that?" Colin pressed.

"I thought so until now. You clearly have done a bit of homework, and figured out that the OSRI think tank was really just me. The sole purpose was smearing anyone who began poking their geological nose around Mayaguana, or anywhere in the MICAL region for that matter. Forgive my 'junior detective' jab, Miss Bullfinch. That was actually a good bit of work. It was much easier to remain anonymous back when I started my subversive campaigns thirty years ago, but in the age of the internet, it became a challenge. I pulled everything I could off line, keeping things as analog and paper as possible. I wanted to ensure I could keep people away from our find, but never let it be known who was behind these academic attacks."

"Yes, that still confuses me," said Colin. "Why such secrecy?"

"Langford, Carty, and I agreed if someone knew that I was the scientist making fools of anyone who started looking around the geology of the southern Bahamas, they might well link the three of us together. Until we were ready to start working on Mayaguana to launch the project, we wanted to keep the place quiet, sleepy and anonymous. For Carty, in particular, it was most important that he not be associated with my geological ranting about MICAL.   His political future might be put in jeopardy. I don't suppose Carty mentioned that when you interrogated him?" Michelson smiled at the two of them, seeming to loosen up a bit.

"Now the project to put in place the infrastructure needed to drill in those waters is finally in progress. But within the past few days things seem to have gone terribly wrong. What do you think is going on?" Jennifer asked, taking advantage of Michelson's moment of lightheartedness to seek a direct answer.

"Somebody outside of Carty, your father and me knows about the MICAL oil field," Michelson looked back at Jennifer and Colin earnestly. "Since you've tracked me down to London to confront me about this whole fiasco, let me put it more plainly: I have no idea what has happened to Langford, and I had no motive to do harm to him. We'd known each other for many years, long before you were born. While I may have been the only one to work nearly full time on 'the dream' of MICAL oil making us all rich, your father certainly backed me financially without question. He was my friend, a good man, but what's happened to him – if he died in an accident on the reef, lost himself out at sea, or something more sinister has happened, I have no idea."

Jennifer sat down on the edge of Michelson's desk, thinking deeply about his justification of his innocence. "So, that still leaves Colin's original question: who is after you? Because whoever that is, it's the same people who attacked us in Nassau, and it's the same people who I think are behind my father's disappearance."

Silence filled the room as Jennifer contemplated her own question, Michelson sat looking exhausted and relieved to be able to just sit quietly for a moment, and Colin studied the office as if subtly searching for clues. Breaking the silence, Jennifer's cell phone rang out harshly. She pulled the phone from her pocket to look at the number. It was a 242 area code: The Bahamas. She paused for a moment as the phone rang, and then decided it was best to answer. Carty Wallingford-Rolle's distinguished voice was at the other end of the line.

"Miss Bullfinch. Carty Wallingford-Rolle here. I'm so sorry to call you in the middle of the night like this, but it is quite urgent I speak with you. I'd like you to meet me at the Executive Air Terminal at the airport. We need to talk," Carty said, sounding smooth and polished as ever, but with a hint of forceful urgency behind his tone.

Clearly, Carty assumed she was still in Nassau. She thought momentarily about letting him continue to believe that, but then decided it was better to tell Carty the truth and see what his reaction was.

"I'm not in Nassau, Carty. I'm in London. With Ian Michelson," she responded without letting any emotion or suggestion sound in her tone. She waited for several seconds, enjoying the fact that it was now Carty's turn to figure out how to respond, and it was obviously causing him some angst given the long silence on the his end of the line. When he did speak, he surprised Jennifer a little.

"Perfect," he said. "Michelson was my next call. I assume your phone has a speaker. Please put me on it so I may speak with you both."

Being unable to think of a reason not to oblige, she looked over at Colin and Michelson, who were both hanging on her words to Carty. "It's Carty. In Nassau, he has something to tell us," she announced and pressed the button on her phone to activate the speaker, holding it up slightly to the room. "OK, Carty. You're on speaker. Go ahead."

"Ah, well. Good morning, I should say to you all. You must be having a coffee together. It's quite the middle of the night

168

here in Nassau," Carty led off, sounding a little bit uncomfortable with his impromptu address to a larger audience and still unsure why Michelson and Jennifer were in London together at a very early morning hour.

"Good evening, Carty. I know you lawyers like to work late, but I'm surprised to hear you doing business at this hour," Michelson joked uneasily into the speaker phone from his club chair, still nursing one side of his ribcage that was clearly bothering him after his encounter.

"Hi, Mr. Wallingford-Rolle. This is Colin. I'm here too," Colin announced, seating himself in Michelson's wheeled, reclining desk chair.

"I see the gang is all here…or there, I suppose I should say," Carty continued, beginning to regain his smooth banter. "Well, let me get right to it, then. I was contacted by the China Global Development Bank just a little while ago. Mr. Li, the President of the Bank himself, has requested we meet with him at their offices in Wuhan, China."

"What does he want to meet about? I had a very unpleasant phone call with Mr. Li just days ago. He seemed very intent on taking the land on Mayaguana and everything else along with it since the loan my father took out is in default," Jennifer explained, somewhat cautiously.

"Well, he wasn't entirely clear on the matter with me. But he seemed to want to discuss how China Global Development Bank could 'partner' with the Government of The Bahamas. Since he knew I was a partner on the Mayaguana deal, or a at least a silent partner with some clear standing in the Government as a Member of Parliament, he contacted me," Carty explained, making it all sound rather matter-of-fact.

"And he wants us to go China? Just to meet in person?" Michelson asked incredulously.

"Right, this doesn't make sense," Jennifer said, shaking her head. "He's taking over the project. He's keeping every penny my father ever pledged or spent. Li's not taking any prisoners. Believe me, if you had heard him lay into me, insult my father, and tell me plainly he had no sympathy or interest in working together, you wouldn't be flying off to China for a friendly meet and greet."

Carty sounded a little taken aback. "I don't think this is just a 'meet and greet' as you call it, Miss Bullfinch. Perhaps reason has set in, and he understands to make anything of the Mayaguana project once he's taken it over, he'd better have the people that know the project best helping him."

"And at any rate, I think the three of us stand a better chance showing our value, than just me alone," Carty pressed on after a few moments of silence on the phone.

"I say we make it a team of four, because you're not leaving me out if there's a chance I can get some of that back pay you owe me for the runway work!" Colin chimed in, smiling broadly, and reclining back in the desk chair with a look of satisfaction on his face.

"Perfect!" Carty exclaimed, his smile coming through the phone line. "We haven't a moment to lose. Li Hong asked for us to meet him as soon as possible."

"When do we need to meet you in China, Carty?" Jennifer asked, trying to keep the spending-fatigue overcoming her enthusiasm and drive.

"It just so happens, I have the Prime Minister's ear right now, and he's taking a small 'stay-cation' as they're called these days at his home out east. He's given me use of his jet for the next few days. Since this trip to China is in the best interest of the people of The Bahamas, I think we shall take it. I'm on the way to the airport now. Meet me at Farnborough at the executive terminal in ten hours. We'll head right to Wuhan from there." Carty hung up, clearly in a rush to get over to the executive terminal and get the pilots moving and on their way quickly, in a most un-Bahamian fashion, and at a most un-Bahamian hour.

Jennifer pulled up the world clock function on her smartphone and looked at the time in Atlanta. She already knew the time there, but did it as more of a gesture. Whenever she felt a little homesick, which was more often than she would have liked anyone to know, she would often pull up this page and look at the little clock that told her the time back home. It was 1AM, and she imagined the invitingly quiet streets of Buckhead at this hour. She made a mental note to check in with B.W. in a few hours, and put her phone away. To her surprise, no sooner had she put her phone away than it began to buzz. She pulled it back out and saw a text message from none other than B.W. himself: "Jennifer – Are you up? B.W." it read. Something must be on his mind, and it's probably the petty cash account, she mused.

"Pardon me for a moment, gentlemen, it's my father's Atlanta business partner. He gets nervous if I don't keep in touch with him, and he just texted me. I'd better call him, since the last he knew I was in Nassau," she announced to Colin and Michelson. She walked to the office door and stepped into the hallway. She hated talking to B.W. with others around, especially since it could be a little touchy. She hit his number, and the international assist rang it through after a moment.

"Hello?" B.W.'s voice came through. Jennifer had expected him to sound a little drowsy, but his voice was crisp, with no hint of sleepiness.

"Hi B.W.," Jennifer said cheerfully. Hearing his voice lightened her spirits again, even though she knew it was likely to be a tough conversation. "What are you doing up so late?"

"Oh, you know me when I get to worrying on something," B.W.'s southern drawl came over the phone. I suppose you're up enjoying a night out in Nassau? I was hoping you'd be back in Atlanta by now, so we could tackle this Mr. Li character. You know time is running out!"

"I know, B.W., and you have to trust me. I am doing the best I can to save the project – and find out what happened to Dad," Jennifer hesitated to take a breath before continuing,"…but I'm not in Nassau, and I'm not coming back to Atlanta soon, not at least in the next few days…I'm in London."

"London!! Jennifer, this is ridiculous. I need your help back here. We're dead in the water! And you're off globe-trotting," B.W. chastised. He was clearly running his best guilt trip on her. And even though she knew she was doing the right thing, the guilt trip still made her feel bad that she was leaving B.W. alone to suffer helplessly in their empty, luxurious, office. She could picture him still showing up each of these past few days, dressed in his three-piece suit, soldiering on in the face of certain impending doom. There was really nothing else he could do.

"Well, I think I may be on to something. And I have discovered a lot – a whole lot – about Dad and what went on around Mayaguana for years in secret. For starters, I think the MICAL Formation may actually be a real oil field worth billions. I went to Austin and found a fictitious think tank funded by Dad just to keep people away from the island. But there's really no time to go into it now.   I promise I will be back to Atlanta in just a few days, and I'll be able to explain even more," Jennifer said, trying to be soothing.

"In 'secret'? What does that mean? You've been to Texas in just the past day? Jennifer, I do believe you have gone crazy. We are about to go under, lose millions of dollars and whatever the sand on that god-forsaken rock in The Bahamas is worth, and you're going on like this is some kind of silly game of hide and seek," B.W. began to put on his more stern, fatherly voice.

Jennifer did not back down, "B.W., I told you, I'm not entirely sure of the whole story, but I'm putting the puzzle pieces together. I will be back at our office in a few days and we can really turn things around."

There was silence on both ends of the line for a moment before B.W. continued with a quiet reprimand, "Jennifer, I'm disappointed in you. But if you want to go flying around the world, wasting time and money playing detective, then so be it."

He hung up in disgust before Jennifer could protest.

Chapter 22

Nine hours later, Jennifer, Colin and Michelson were in a taxi cab headed for Farnborough Airport. Jennifer had received a text message from Carty that he was in the plane taking off with an estimated arrival time of about 5PM London time. They had been able to get a little sleep and it had done wonders for Michelson, who looked like a new man, recovering quite a bit from the attack the night before. Colin had regained some of his sharpness, and Jennifer had to admit she felt better for the rest as well. She got the feeling, one long plane ride to China aside, they might be in for a marathon over the next few days. What might come of the meeting with Li, she really wasn't sure, but it would be significant. If Li changed his tone, then something must have happened to make him move away from his hard line stance. If he was the same, cold, hard-nosed banker looking to take the project out from under her, then she would be down to just a few days left to find a life line.

Despite the refreshed feeling after some rest, the mood in the cab was still tense between Jennifer, Colin, and Michelson. They chatted a bit about Mayaguana as Michelson told a few harmless, funny stories about the challenges of the project, which Colin filled in with some colorful detail from time to time, but the conversation remained quite superficial. Jennifer was frustrated they still did not know who was behind the attack on her and Colin in Nassau, or now, Michelson in London. Despite his bruises, her suspicions that he might still be somehow connected to her father's disappearance were not entirely gone. The fact that Michelson alone seemed to have all of the data needed to turn the project from a bankrupt folly on a worthless rock into a Caribbean oil kingdom still seemed like a reasonable motive to take his partners out of the picture. Carty, too, might do very well by getting rid of her father and Michelson, assuming he could keep control of his plans to become the Prime Minister of his own, new oil-wealthy country. The text message from her father remained a complete mystery as well. Thinking about how far she was from any resolution, she became anxious, but resisted the urge to pull out her phone and confirm at the date and time.

The taxi pulled into Farnborough, and Jennifer was impressed with a very modern looking private air terminal. It looked like a giant, metallic and glass wave at the edge of the aircraft parking apron. They got out of the taxi, and of course, Jennifer had to pay as Colin and Michelson seemed to have no money. At 5PM precisely, a Gulfstream jet elegantly touched down on the runway and taxied towards the terminal. They went through the terminal to the lounge, to see Carty walking down the steps of the jet, looking polished as usual in another expensive looking Brioni suit. Jennifer wondered to herself if Carty spent all of his income on bespoke clothing. Walking towards the lounge and pulling up his collar against the cold, British winter breeze, he saw the three waiting for him and broke into a broad, oily smile.

"Well met, my friends," beamed Carty at the group. "I hope you have some scones and breakfast tea ready to load up the galley. It's going to be a long flight and we'll still be on board when breakfast time comes around."

"Carty, can't you stop being a slippery politician and get real for one moment?" Michelson rolled his eyes at Carty's theatrical greeting. "Just what is going on with this sudden meeting?"

"Oh, Ian, you do insist on being so businesslike, especially for an academic," Carty said, shaking his head but still smiling at his old colleague. "Let's get all the immigration paperwork taken care, and we'll have plenty of time to talk on the way."

Fifteen minutes later, they were all aboard the Gulfstream, taking off just as a muted sunset began to cast long shadows on the chilly airfield. The two Bahamian pilots, Jennifer noticed, were sharply dressed in uniforms and both looked like they could also double as bodyguards in a pinch. The pilot had done a very thorough walk-around and pre-flight inspection as the local airfield FBO truck refueled the jet. The co-pilot had completed all the proper flight plans, filed the immigration paperwork, and checked weather along their route. Their efficiency and professionalism was in stark contrast to Tony MacDonald and his flyboy, lackadaisical, slipshod style. Soon the jet was cruising at four hundred and fifty miles per hour at forty-one thousand feet.

Wuhan was six hours ahead of London time, so it was well into the evening there. The pilot stepped into the cabin to let them know they would be flying for eleven hours, not including a refuel stop in Turkey. That would get them to central China, landing at the Wuhan Tianhe International Airport in the early afternoon the following day just in time for their late afternoon meeting at the bank's headquarters. After the pilot had returned to the cockpit and pulled a small panel door closed for privacy, Carty got up and went to the galley at the front of the cabin. Ever the gracious host, not to mention showman, he produced a cold conch salad appetizer, broiled Bahamian lobster, chilled champagne, and fresh baked guava duff with espresso for desert. Clearly, the Prime Minister's plane was kept at the ready to travel in style. They sat down to their dinner and Carty broke the tension as he opened up the conversation to the business at hand.

"I believe we have the China Global Development Bank re-thinking their harsh stance on our overdue construction loans," he announced, with a hint of triumph in his voice at delivering this good news. He sat back in his leather chair, and took a slow, deliberate slip of champagne.

"Yes, you mentioned as much on the phone. I don't think we believe you," Michelson said, including Jennifer in his 'we' with a wave of his hand in her direction. Jennifer nodded, and reminded herself to stay pleasant, if for no reason than to tease information out of Carty.

"You know, I think Mr. Li has done a little homework on real estate loans and courts in The Bahamas, and come to the very sound realization that without us as a partner in the deal, his bank would have quite a bit of difficulty in just taking the property. And once they'd taken it, ever getting approvals to do anything with the land would be quite difficult without a good local partner. Sometimes the convoluted waters of my little island can work in your favor," Carty answered, taking another sip of champagne, and seeming to consider this the final word. He leaned back even further, extended his long legs, and gazed out the window with a look of smug satisfaction.

Chapter 23

The Gulfstream landed at Wuhan's Tianhe International airport under clear, afternoon skies. Like London, the air in Wuhan promised to be brisk, and the pilot had told the group it would be just over fifty degrees Fahrenheit, and could get quite cool in the evening, down into the low forties. Jennifer was relieved there was no snow on the ground. She stepped into the surprisingly spacious lavatory of the Gulfstream a few hours before they had landed to slip back on her sweater and be sure she looked professional for the meeting. Looking in the mirror, she crinkled her nose for a moment in dissatisfaction. After several days constantly on the move, she was looking a little worn and windblown from the time on the island. Thankfully, the same bobby pin that had ruined her night's sleep on the couch in Atlanta was still lost in her mane. She fished it out and used it to secure her hair in place enough to appear businesslike.

Emerging from the lavatory, she noticed she was not alone in bundling up as Michelson had put back on his half-zip sweater and Colin had donned a grey sweatshirt he had with him since Austin. The jet taxied up to the far end of the main terminal building. The terminal was a large, long, concrete and glass structure, with rows of airliners parked along it and jet ways connecting them to the building. Jennifer was surprised at how bustling and busy it was, with hundreds of people milling about handling baggage, servicing the planes and doing the myriad of other jobs needed at a major international airport.

As the Gulfstream came to a halt, a uniformed woman walked out of an automatic sliding glass door in the terminal building. She stood waiting for them near an all-weather, red doormat. When the pilot opened the door to the jet and pushed the stairwell down, the woman waved them to her. As they approached, she gave a slight bow of her head, and motioned them through the glass doors into a small waiting area. As Jennifer walked by the woman, she noticed her uniform was official and military, and not some kind of flight attendant uniform as she had first thought. The woman followed the group inside and pointed out a row of benches for them. Jennifer realized the woman must be with the immigration department. As they were sitting down, the immigration officer spoke to them in Mandarin. Jennifer was about to ask her if she spoke English, when a familiar voice next to her answered in Mandarin. Jennifer raised an eyebrow as she glanced to her side, unable to entirely contain her look of surprise. Colin Steele had pulled yet another trick from up his sleeve.

"She'd like all of our passports. Normally, this would be some trouble, since we are supposed to have visas, but apparently Mr. Li has cleared things for us," Colin explained, digging a well-worn passport out of his inside jacket pocket. Jennifer rooted through her pack for her passport, which had seen a lot of use the past few days. Michelson already had his passport out, making Jennifer suspect he also understood enough Mandarin that he knew what the immigration officer asked before Colin's translation.

"You speak Mandarin?" Jennifer asked, smiling at Colin.

"When you spend months working on an island where nearly all the rest of the inhabitants are Chinese, you pick up a few phrases," Colin answered, smiling back a bit awkwardly. The thought was ushered out of her mind as two men wearing dark suits walked into the waiting area. The shorter and more slender of the two stopped at the door, looking around the room from behind a pair of sunglasses. The taller, more muscular man, wearing an understated pin striped suit, walked up to the benches and stood in front of Carty.

179

"Mr. Wallingford-Rolle welcome to Wuhan," he said in very clear English with an accent that Jennifer would have called 'Californian'.

"I have been asked by President Li to escort you and your companions directly to his office for your meeting," he continued.

He turned and gave a stern command to the immigration officer, who quickly stamped the last two passports, handing the stack to their escort. He thumbed through the passports and returned them to each of the visitors.

"Your pilots must remain here. There is a lounge for them, which also has some hotel-style bedrooms for resting," the man said to Carty, still not really acknowledging the rest of the party.

"Please follow me. We have two cars waiting." With no further ceremony, he turned and walked towards the front door to the lobby area. After following a short hallway, they emerged onto the bustling pick up and drop off aisle at the very end of the main international terminal building. Hundreds of people were getting into and out of cars, taxis and buses along the terminal. Two black sedans efficiently waited for them just a few feet from the doorway at the curb.

The driver of the rear sedan stepped out, opening the rear passenger door. The pin-stripe suited escort motioned for Jennifer, Colin and Michelson to get in the back seat. He motioned Carty towards the first sedan, now also with its driver holding the rear passenger door open.

"I guess our government official gets the red carpet treatment, even if the entire population of the 'government' he represents is outnumbered by the people at this airport, " snorted Michelson, his irritation by their Chinese hosts' clear deferential treatment of Carty evident.

"Don't make a big scene here, Ian. I just want to get to this meeting and find out what he really wants," Jennifer said in a quick hushed tone, voicing her concerns more than she cared. They got into their respective cars with no further comment. Only Colin, Jennifer noticed, looked noticeably concerned about the seating arrangement. But he said nothing and clambered in the back seat of the car, closing the door as he sat down next to Jennifer. Through the front windshield, they watched Carty settle himself into the lead car. Much to Ian's annoyance, Carty sipped on a cup of what looked like a Starbucks coffee that apparently had been waiting for him.

The two cars pulled away from the busy airport and on to an even busier four lane highway heading south towards the city of Wuhan. Worldly person though she was, Jennifer was not very familiar with China. She was surprised to see an urban canyon of large office towers as they drove closer to the city. The skyline of Wuhan put Atlanta's skyline to shame. The highway wound along fields and canals, passing factories, little villages, and orchards. Villages soon gave way to major industrial buildings and vast apartment complexes. The highway made a sharp turn to the east, and a large bridge spanning the wide Yangtze River came into view. Some of the road signs were in English as well as Chinese, so Jennifer knew they would be in the Wuchang District of Wuhan once they passed the bridge. Wuchang was the central business district of the city and the location of the headquarters of the China Global Development Bank. She pulled out her phone. It was 3:30PM local time and the meeting was at four. They were right on schedule. She looked ahead through the front windshield to see if Carty's sedan was still in front of them, but it was out of view. Their driver had an earpiece in, and had chatted quietly on his cell phone for nearly the whole ride, seeming oblivious of his three passengers in the back seat.

The sedan crossed over the bridge, giving Jennifer an excellent view up and down the mighty Yangtze River. Like the highways around Wuhan, the river was bustling with barges and boats of all sizes carrying cargo up and down this major waterway. She noticed Colin looking intently up and down the river as well. As they hit the east bank of the river, the driver took an exit ramp to the south and continued down a secondary street for several blocks. At a small cross street, a traffic signal in front of them turned red, and the driver slowed the car to a stop.

Suddenly and violently, the sedan lurched forward with a terrible crashing sound of colliding metal and glass. The back windshield burst into a thousand pieces. Jennifer was thrown forward, only her seat belt preventing serious injury. Her head snapped, and for what seemed like a very long time, her vision blurred from the whiplash. As she began to regain her situational awareness, a shout erupted from next to her.

"Michelson! Open your door, and get out! Hurry!" Colin roared.

Jennifer looked at him, momentarily confused and wondering why it had to be Michelson to open the door. Then she realized why. From a small alleyway near the intersection, a second car was barreling towards them. It would hit Colin's side of the car at full force in seconds. Michelson sprang into action. He opened the door and was out of the sedan before Colin had finished yelling. Michelson yanked Jennifer, with much greater strength than she had imagined he had, from out of the back seat and away from the wrecked sedan. Colin scrambled out of the car behind them. A moment later, the second car slammed into the side of the sedan, which skidded out into the center of the street.

Jennifer looked in the front seat of the sedan and saw their driver slumped over the steering wheel, with blood splattered across the door window and cracked front windshield. Her head was still spinning, but she looked around to see if Colin and Michelson were hurt. They were both lying on the ground, having flung themselves out of the way of the three car pileup. Thankfully, they both looked unharmed. The passengers from the two cars that had hit them were getting out of their own vehicles unhurt.

As Jennifer tried to stand up to get a better look at the terrible accident scene and call an ambulance for their driver, she felt someone grab her arm to help her up off the pavement. It was one of the passengers from the first car that had hit them from behind. As he pulled her up, his grip became uncomfortably firm. Jennifer was about to thank him, when she felt another firm grip on her other arm. The two 'helpers' lifted her up and then slammed her against the wrecked black sedan. Before she could react, she was pinned to the car by the two strong men. One of them quickly began searching her, rooting through her pockets and pack, while the other pressed her harder against the side of the car so she was completely immobilized. Within seconds, the searcher's hands emerged from her pack with her smart phone. The searcher paused to look at the phone as if to confirm it was the item he was looking for.

His head snapped suddenly to the side from a surprise right hook by Colin. The phone flew from the searchers hand on to the pavement as the man fell to the ground. Jennifer gave her immobilizer a swift and powerful knee to the groin that would have made her kickboxing instructor proud. The man howled and doubled over in pain, releasing his grip. She hit him again hard. He fell to the ground whimpering, and Jennifer jumped away from the car.

"Gun!" roared Michelson from nearby. Jennifer and Colin looked around to see two men from the second car that had hit them emerging from their vehicles with handguns drawn.

"Run to the alleyway," Colin yelled, pointing to a narrow side street that wound into a labyrinth neighborhood of apartment buildings and small shops. Michelson ran into the traffic lane next to them and waved his arms to try and slow the oncoming line of vehicles just long enough for them to cross the road. Luckily, the scene of the accident had created enough rubbernecking drivers and pedestrian by-standers that they could cross safely and run into the alley. Colin pointed out Jennifer's phone, making sure she grabbed it up off the ground as they ran across the street.

A shot rang out; then another. A bullet ricocheted off the concrete blocks of the building on the alleyway corner. Jennifer ducked her head instinctively, feeling certain either she, Colin or Michelson would soon fall from a gunshot wound. Their assailants were right on their heels, following across the street and too close to keeping missing them for long. A third gunshot rang out, but this time the sound was so close and deafening it left Jennifer's ears ringing. She looked over at the sound to realize the gunshot had come from a semi-automatic handgun Colin Steele had just produced from inside his jacket. He fired back at their pursuers.

Colin's return fire had the desired effect. The assailants stopped cold in shock for a moment, and the cries of bystanders became louder as chaos ensued on the street. The growing crowd of bystanders quickly dispersed. Traffic that had slowed to get a look at the three smashed cars squealed their tires trying to get away from the gunfight. In the mass confusion, Colin led them quickly away from the scene through twists and turns of alleyways in the urban maze.

While the main thoroughfare where they had been ambushed was crowded and busy, once in the inner city neighborhood, it was surprisingly quiet, and nearly deserted. They passed a few groups of old men sitting outside of store fronts smoking cigarettes and talking quietly, and a few women doing chores. In the middle of the work day, it appeared most people were gone from this residential zone. Colin directed them down another small side street, and they slowed from their all-out sprint. He looked back over his shoulder. The street behind them was empty and quiet. They slowed to an inconspicuous walking pace and at a small, empty cafe they gathered under the awning of the entrance. They were largely blocked from view of the street by a menu board, some tables, and chairs. The three companions faced each other. Jennifer noticed that Michelson, by far the oldest, did not seem even out of breath, and Colin's typical happy-go-lucky face looked hard and serious. They had to regroup and figure out what to do.

"You have a gun!?" Jennifer asked in a hissed, incredulous whisper at Colin. "How do you have a gun? And why?"

"Oh, I always carry a gun," Colin said, shoving it back into his jacket, apparently into some kind of concealed holster. "In my line of work, you just never know when it might come in handy."

"I thought your line of work was construction?" Jennifer said. Colin didn't respond, but looked around them, his head back on a swivel as it had been in Nassau after their encounter with the masked motorcycle attackers.

"I do believe we're going to find Mr. Steele is full of surprises," Michelson said in an odd tone that suggested he knew what some of those surprises might be.

"Enough about me. Let's get this little pow-wow going, because I don't think we should stay in one place for long. Those

185

two men who were shooting at us are not just going to give up and go home, and they probably have help by now. They'll be all over this neighborhood looking for us and I'd hate to have to shoot our way out of another situation," Colin said, refocusing the conversation on the matter at hand.

"Jennifer, this is the second time I have been nearly killed because someone wanted to get a hold of your cell phone. I let you keep your secrets when I asked you about this the first time back in Obie's house, but it's time to come clean. What's on your phone that is so valuable someone would kill for it?" Colin asked point blank and looking Jennifer straight in the eye with an interrogating gaze.

Jennifer was speechless for a moment and caught off guard. It seemed like a long time ago, back in her apartment on Fenno Street when she had been awakened by the cryptic message and mysterious text file. She hadn't trusted anyone, not even B.W., enough to mention the text message, and she certainly never planned on telling Colin, who she hadn't even known a few days ago. Still, things had taken a dramatic turn. She was no closer to uncovering the mystery of her father's disappearance, and no closer to saving her company from ruin. And now, she was being shot at on a street corner in central China. Perhaps it was time to more fully enlist Colin's help.

"I don't know exactly," said Jennifer, admitting it to herself as much as to Colin and Michelson. "But I got a strange text message, which I believe was from my father, the night he disappeared. The message made no sense to me. I flew down to Mayaguana right away to try and figure out what was going on. You know the rest of the story."

Colin looked at her for a moment, as if gauging whether or not she was telling him the truth. It dawned on her for the first time that, as much as she did not trust him or any of the other characters she had met in the past few days, he very well might not trust her either. Michelson, standing just to the side of their conversation keeping watch over the street, broke his sentry duty for a moment, looking back and forth at them with curiosity at this new development.

"What did the message say," Colin asked. It sounded more like an order than a request, and normally Jennifer would have bristled at his tone.

"It said 'MICAL' followed by the numbers zero, nine and seven. There was a slash between the nine and seven. I figured it was just typos or he pocket-dialed me, given our lack of communication the past few years" she answered. She thought about mentioning the text file as well, but she still didn't feel comfortable enough to disclose everything to Colin and Michelson.

"Any ideas?" she asked him after a moment of silence, keeping the sarcastic doubt out of her voice as best as possible.

Colin looked at her intently for a moment, but didn't answer. He looked up and down the street to double check they were still safe and alone.

"I think you two must get to that meeting with Li at the bank," he said, seeming to have made up his mind about the situation, but saying nothing about the text message.

"Are you serious? This really no time to joke," said Michelson incredulously.

"I'm dead serious. You both need to walk into that meeting and play it as though absolutely nothing happened. If anyone inquires, just admit we were in a small fender-bender along the way, but play it down as no big deal and get on with the meeting with Li and Carty," Colin said, indeed looking dead serious.

"So the message didn't mean anything to you either?" Jennifer pressed again.

"I'm not sure exactly what it means yet, but I have a few ideas. Obviously somebody wanted that phone of yours more than they wanted us to make it to the bank's office. You still have the phone, so that's something. I think you need to find out what Li says at that meeting. Ian, you need to go along too as you were invited as a partner in the deal. Get a good read on Carty. I think we're all suspicious that he avoided this whole mess rather nicely," Colin answered.

Jennifer had to admit to herself that Colin was making sense. He seemed to have hit on a good point about Carty as well. There was a part of her that was disappointed though. Somehow, she thought maybe this mysterious construction contractor would have noticed something in the message that told her what happened to her father. If it had meant something to him, he was keeping it to himself. But his advice on continuing to the meeting was sound.

"I guess that means we need to figure out where we are, and how we can find our way to the bank headquarters," Jennifer said, trying to get back in control of the situation. She looked up and down the street as if to get her bearings, and then began to pull up the GPS map on the smartphone.

"I think you should keep that phone out of sight and avoid using it if possible," Colin said. He looked down the street. "To get to the bank headquarters you just need to walk about six blocks that way. You'll come out on Zhangzhidong Road, a main roadway in the business district. Turn to your left and go down that road a few blocks. You will see the bank's office tower if I am not mistaken. It's about thirty stories, so you shouldn't miss it."

"How can you possibly know that?" Jennifer asked, a look of confused amazement on her face.

"I told you our friend might surprise us," Michelson chimed in, smiling at them.

"Never mind that now. You need to get going to make the meeting. If you hurry, you'll be just a few minutes late," Colin answered, looking down at his watch.

"Aren't you coming with us?" Jennifer asked, simultaneously worried and suspicious.

"I wasn't invited to the meeting, so I'd just be hanging around the lobby anyway," Colin said with his familiar smirk. "Besides, there's something I need to check on."

"Where should we link up?" Michelson asked.

"Back at the airport. I think we need to try and stick close to Carty, especially since his jet is probably still our best way out of here," Colin answered.

"You think we can trust Carty even that much?" Jennifer asked.

"I'm not sure any of us can trust anyone, but I think if you keep with him, no one will try anything else while we're in Wuhan. Whoever is behind this, they'll need time to plan another ambush," Colin answered, again seeming to make a lot of sense to Jennifer.

"Text me if anything else happens. Keep your message general, as if someone else might read it. I might not be able to confirm I get your message," Colin stated.

They had been talking in front of the little café for several minutes now, and people were starting to notice. Jennifer saw a few curious faces peering out of some of the windows. She knew they stuck out badly in this place. The sooner they got to a busy road where there might be a few other foreigners for them to blend in amongst, the better. They broke up their impromptu planning session, with Colin heading back the direction they had come.

Jennifer and Michelson continued down the road as Colin had directed them. They walked in an uneasy silence, both to avoid attention, as well as from the continuing shock of the situation in which they found themselves. The alliance between Jennifer and Michelson, although strengthened by the shared battle they had just fought, was still tenuous. Jennifer felt like she was walking into a den of thieves, surrounded by the power-hungry Carty, the mysterious Professor Michelson, and this wildcard, Chinese banker. She wished B.W. was here to help. Her father had been the true master of situations like this, but now that he was gone, she'd take the help of anyone she could truly trust.

Chapter 24

Jennifer and Michelson found their way to Zhangzhidong Road without incident. As Colin has said, it was a major business road. There were many people hurrying about among the tall buildings lining the road. A few blocks to their left, they saw the looming tower of the China Global Development Bank. Like many major business signs she had seen so far in Wuhan, the name of the bank was blazoned across the top of the building in both Chinese and English, making it conveniently easy for them to make sure they found the proper building. Jennifer, who considered herself an expert on modern office buildings, had to admit the tower was impressive. It looked recently completed, perhaps within the last five years, and would have blended in well in any modern US city. Its ground floor was two stories, promising a large atrium-style lobby. The ground floor exterior was polished granite and stainless steel, while the rest of the floors were tinted, low emission glass. The top floors were similar polished granite with metal accents to balance against the ground floor finish.

The building sat back about one hundred feet off Zhangzhidong Road, creating a nice buffer between the busy road and the building entrance, which was beautifully landscaped with large trees, park benches, and huge jade planters. They walked through a large revolving door entrance and into the atrium. As Jennifer suspected, its high ceiling made for an impressive entry. There were four elevator banks in the center core of the building. A large, sleek, frosted glass panel security desk sat just before the elevator banks, controlling access to the upper floors. A building directory was above the desk, in both Chinese and English. Jennifer gave the directory a quick scan. It appeared the entire building was occupied by various divisions of the bank. She glanced over at Michelson as they made their way to the security desk.

"Here goes," she said, trying to sound confident and cheerful. Michelson did not answer. He just nodded his head slightly as if to say yes. They checked in at the desk, and soon were given a temporary visitor badge to put on before being ushered towards one of the elevators. As they stepped into the elevator, it automatically knew which floor was their destination and the doors closed quietly. An LCD panel on the wall played a Chinese newscast, ran streaming stock ticker symbols, and presented the weather for various cities around China and the rest of the world. As the elevator came to a graceful halt and the door opened, Jennifer's heart raced. She stepped out into a central executive suite. A female receptionist looked up from her desk inquisitively at Jennifer and Michelson. Jennifer walked purposely to the desk and noticed that guests arriving to this floor for meetings were greeted with an impressive view of the Yangtze River, a very leafy green central park, and a rising skyline of similarly modern high rise towers juxtaposed against a series of colonial, historic buildings from Wuhan's past. The message was clear: Wuhan was on its way to becoming one of the biggest and most important cities in the world, and the China Global Development Bank lorded over this growing metropolis.

"I am Jennifer Bullfinch and this is Ian Michelson. We are here for a 4PM meeting with Mr. Li. I'm sure he's worried that we did not arrive with Mr. Wallingford-Rolle, but we hit some traffic on the way from the airport," Jennifer announced to the receptionist, assuming she spoke English. It appeared to possibly be a false assumption as the woman gave Jennifer and Michelson an odd look, and did not reply for several long seconds. Just as Jennifer was about to try again, the woman answered.

"I do apologize. Mr. Li is in a meeting in his office at the moment. I do not believe he is expecting other visitors," the receptionist replied in clear English, with a faint British intonation, very similar to Mr. Li's. The receptionist met Jennifer's gaze for a moment, as if to make her point, but then looked down at her desk in mild, deferential embarrassment.

"Yes, I understand Mr. Li is in a meeting right now. He is probably in with one of our colleagues. We traveled here together, but took separate cars from the airport. We are to be in the meeting as well, but we are just a few minutes late," Jennifer tried explaining. The receptionist again made no immediate response, but looked down at a flat panel monitor on her desk, presumably reading Mr. Li's schedule again more closely to be sure she was interpreting this apparent scheduling conflict appropriately.

"I am very sorry that there appears to be come confusion, however, you are not on Mr Li's calendar. May I have your names again please?" She asked in a polite, but more forceful tone. Jennifer, resisting the urge to become a very ugly American and go ballistic on this infuriating woman, clearly and calmly repeated her and Michelson's full names. As if he could sense her frustration and wanted to be close by to help avoid a scene if needed, Michelson, who had been standing slightly behind and a few steps to the side of Jennifer looking out over the city and surveying the impressive architecture and décor of the bank office tower, stepped next to her and put his hand gently on her arm as if to say 'stay calm'. The receptionist picked up the phone. She dialed a quick extension number and whispered in Mandarin to someone at the other end. After a short exchange, she hung up the phone and looked at Jennifer.

"Please wait for a moment. You may have a seat if you like," the receptionist motioned to a set of chairs by a glass coffee table

193

near the wall of windows. Jennifer chose to stand near the desk, in an effort to signal to this receptionist that she did not expect to be kept waiting long enough to sit down. The receptionist's phone rang. Answering, she again had a few brief exchanges in worried-sounding, hushed tones. Michelson gently pulled on Jennifer's arm.

"Let's have a seat and relax for a moment," he said, nodding his head towards the waiting area, and giving Jennifer a very deliberate look. They walked over to the edge of the glass windowpanes where the chairs and coffee table sat, looking as if they were seldom used.

"They really aren't expecting us. But Carty is quite certainly here and meeting in Li's private office somewhere on this floor," he said.

"The receptionist has been told to stall politely for a few minutes while someone else, presumably Li's personal secretary, figures out what he wants to do."

Jennifer continued her gaze out the window and nodded in acknowledgment. Obviously, her suspicion that Michelson was fluent in Mandarin was correct. Just at that moment, Jennifer's mobile phone rang out, uncomfortably breaking the serene silence of the executive suite. The number didn't register from her contact list due to the complexities of the international switch the call had been routed through, but Jennifer could tell from a quick glance at the end of the long line of numbers that it was B.W. calling.

"Hi B.W. I really can't talk right now," she answered, hoping to head B.W.'s worrying pleas off.

"Jennifer! Look, while you've been gallivanting around the world spending the last few dollars we have, I've been taking care of business. I managed to get through to Li again just a few minutes ago, and I've gotten him to finally make some concessions," B.W. huffed at Jennifer.

"What do you mean by 'concessions'?" Jennifer asked, annoyed that B.W. consistently seemed more worried about fighting for a few table scraps from their office in Atlanta rather than also trying to figure out what happened to her father.

"I don't know exactly what kind of offer he is going to lay on the table, but Jennifer, you listen to me, and listen good: when he does, you take that offer, and be done with this," B.W. directed, giving Jennifer a taste of the tongue lashing she had seen B.W. lay down on many others over the years, but had never been the recipient of herself.

Jennifer grew red in the face and her hand began to shake in rage at B.W's order. But she also felt terribly alone. B.W. had been her safe harbor amongst the tumultuous and terrible events of the past few days. Knowing he was back in the office, perhaps not always in complete agreement with her, but at least fighting for the same outcome, had been one of the few things keeping her on course. Without that support, she sensed impending failure on all fronts. She would lose the project, lose the money needed to save her company, and worst of all, never know what really happened to her father.

"B.W., I can't promise that, but you know I will do what is best," Jennifer answered, not letting on how angry she was at being ordered around or her growing disappointment in his selfish, tunnel vision.

"I have to go."

On the Atlanta end of the phone, B.W. continued to order Jennifer to take whatever offer was made as she hung up on him in frustration. Slowly pulling the phone away from her ear, Jennifer looked out thoughtfully over the city of Wuhan as she put her phone away. B.W. was a scared old man. Even though, on one level, Jennifer could sympathize with him, she could not agree with his order to just roll over and take whatever low ball offer Li and his bankers threw on the table. She knew they held all the cards, but she also knew this was just the kind of situation where her father would have played some masterful poker.

"If I can just buy some more time – even just a few weeks," she thought, "then this whole trip will have been worth it."

From across the room, the receptionist emerged from a hallway with the man who had met them in the airport. He was apparently Mr. Li's personal assistant. He waved Jennifer and Michelson over. Michelson flashed Jennifer a quick 'here goes nothing' smile, and they walked across the reception foyer to the meet the assistant. The man gave them a concerned look.

"I am so surprised to see you both here, but pleasantly so," said the assistant in his California accent. "We were quite concerned when we heard about the traffic accident, and have been calling hospitals all over town looking for you both."

"Thank you. It was quite a scene, but we wanted to be sure not to miss our very important appointment with Mr. Li, so we rushed over here on foot," Michelson answered, sounding quite sincere, and obviously wanting to head off Jennifer who had opened her mouth to speak. If Michelson did not believe the fake sincerity of the assistant, he certainly did not show it. They followed the PA down the hallway to a highly polished, wooden, double door with large brass fixtures. He pushed open one of the doors, and with slight bow, beckoned them into the room.

"You are expected. Please enter," the PA announced. Jennifer and Michelson walked through the door into an open, two-story, corner office, with a commanding view of Wuhan. In the center of the office behind a large glass and metal desk sat a diminutive, balding, Chinese man. In a chair in front of the desk, sat Carty Wallingford-Rolle. Upon seeing Jennifer and Michelson enter, both Carty and the balding Chinese man stood up.

"Ms. Bullfinch, Mr. Michelson, I am Mr. Li. We heard about your terrible car accident. We were so concerned about you. But please come in and join us," the banker said in his clear, slightly British accent that Jennifer remembered so well from their first, unpleasant phone call. Mr. Li motioned to two empty chairs next to Carty.

Jennifer smiled a forced smile and walked over to the center chair. She was determined to follow her game plan: buy more time. Michelson followed her and took the third seat. If he was nervous or uneasy, he didn't show it. In the commotion and rush of getting here, she had not really had time or the mindset to coordinate with him. Hopefully, he would just go along with whatever she said. Carty looked over at them as they sat down, a look akin to quiet amazement on his face.

"Are you OK?" Carty asked, with convincing concern. "And where is our friend Mr. Steele? I hope is he fine as well?"

"Oh, Mr. Steele is just fine," Michelson answered quickly. "He's just at a nearby café, probably having a drink to settle his nerves after our accident. He'll meet us after we're done."

"Very well, then. Please let's get down to business, as our American friend might say," Mr. Li broke in with a very slight, robotic smile. He subtly jerked his head at the assistant, who backed out of the room and closed the door, leaving them to get started. Mr. Li took his seat. There was a stiff, formal nature to him. He sat very straight in his chair, so although he was not particularly tall, he seemed large in stature from behind his imposing desk. He was impeccably dressed in a dark suit, an anchor print Salvatore Ferragamo neck tie, and a contrast collar blue striped shirt with silver cuff links, also of miniature anchors. Jennifer thought to herself in a brief moment of internal levity that he and Carty must shop at the same tailor on Savile Row. His dark hair, although sparse, was slicked back. He gave off the well-manicured aura of sophistication and slickness that said 'investment banker' anywhere in the world.   He sat looking at Jennifer, but said nothing further. She knew the negotiation had begun.

"Mr. Li, you called this meeting, through Mr. Wallingford-Rolle, and here we all are in China at your request. I admit I was surprised, given how you ended our last conversation. So, what can I do for you?" Jennifer asked, putting on her most business-like tone.

"Professor Michelson, Ms. Bullfinch, we know all about your supposed oil field, the 'MICAL Formation' as it has come to be called," Li said with a sly smile. He got up from his chair and walked over to the window, taking a few moments to look out over the skyline. The sun was getting low on the horizon, and shadows on the trees along the streets and parks of Wuhan were growing long. He turned back to look at Jennifer, Michelson and Carty.

"I have spoken with Mr. Wallingford-Rolle about this. I now make my proposal to you. The China Global Development Bank will foreclose on the Mayaguana project as scheduled in a matter days. We have made our own assessment of your supposed oil field. While there may be some deposits, they are deep underground, and of little economic value. The island itself is - pardon my bluntness in regards to your home Mr. Wallingford-Rolle - worthless. It will take billions of dollars to develop anything of value there, and your little, private company has no chance of ever succeeding or seeing a return, much less paying back the full amount you owe my bank," Li slowly walked back to his desk as he spoke. He pulled out a check and a legal letter that looked like a contract from a drawer and slid it across the desk to Jennifer.

"This check is for ten million dollars. It is a gift. I fear you will try to tie up the foreclosure with cheap lawsuits. I cannot stand for delays, as I must clear this bad loan off my books before year end and move on to other business. Hand over all documents, sign this release of any claims of ownership you or your company may ever have on the island or any property or equipment there, and do not return to Mayaguana ever again. I will clear your company of your loans. You may take the ten million to make good on any other final expenses and start over," Li produced a gold fountain pen from his suit pocket and set it on the release letter in front of Jennifer.

"There will be no negotiation. No second chance. Please sign this now, so we may conclude our business."

Jennifer looked down at the check and the legal release. She could feel Carty and Michelson looking at her, as Li stood peering down at her from the other side of his desk. B.W. had been crystal clear in communicating his wishes on this matter. Ten million dollars in the bank and the crippling debt of the Mayaguana project erased from the books would indeed allow Jennifer to pay the few other debts the company owed back in Atlanta and start over.

But without ever returning to Mayaguana, she would have no hope of ever finding out what happened to her father. In her mind, there really was no choice at all: no deal and no giving up at any price until the mystery of her father's disappearance was solved. She looked up at Mr. Li, who was still peering down at her. She stood up slowly from her chair so she could look him in the eye.

"Mr. Li, thank you, but I must decline," Jennifer said calmly and forcing herself not to blink.

Li returned her an even icier stare, as Carty sat in stunned silence. Michelson also sat quietly, but with the slightest hint of an amused smile on his face as his eyes darted back and forth between Li and Jennifer. After a few moments, Li drew himself up, walking slowly back over to his apparent favorite spot at the window and looked out over the city. He stood at the window a few moments, and then without looking back at his visitors, he spoke in a quiet voice.

"Very well. I will be on my yacht in Abrahams Bay to personally oversee the foreclosure process, which I intend to enjoy immensely. This meeting is adjourned."

Chapter 25

Colin Steele pulled the hood of his sweatshirt over his head as he walked through the quiet neighborhood in the Wuchang section of the Wuhan. He had gone in the opposite direction of Jennifer and Michelson, hoping if anybody was following them, they would come after him so Jennifer and Michelson could get to the bank. He knew that was unlikely, since obviously, Jennifer was the target of the staged car accident ambush. So, he was not trying to be completely invisible, just in case a few of their assailants happened to pick up his trail again. He was not impressed with whatever group was behind the attacks, since clearly they could not seem to accomplish their objective of retrieving the information on Jennifer's cell phone, even after two attempts.

Colin made a turn off the street entering a tree-filled public park, wanting to stay where there were plenty of other pedestrians. Up a small hill was a museum he had been in once before on a previous reconnaissance trip to Wuhan many months prior. The museum was a memorial to a 1911 uprising in Wuhan against the oppressive Qing Dynasty. A series of historical buildings, including an elaborate tower, called the Yellow Crane Tower, were crowded with people. The inhabitants of Wuhan loved this park, so even on this chilly winter afternoon many were enjoying the open spaces. A group of locals practiced Tai Chi, while another performed a traditional dance routine. Colin walked up the hill towards the tower, doing his best to look like a Russian expat worker. It was an act at which he had become exceptionally good over several previous visits to China. He passed a street vendor selling *jianbing*, a pancake snack made with green onion. He purchased one with some spare *yuan* he kept in his wallet from a previous visit. Finding a park bench, he sat down for a minute, taking a few bites of the *jianbing* and pretending to look around at the visitors to the Yellow Crane Tower.

Colin checked his phone. No messages from Jennifer, or anyone else for that matter. For now, he would take that as a sign that she and Michelson had made it to the bank headquarters building. That gave him about an hour. He turned the antenna off on the phone's settings menu.

From the hill where he sat enjoying his *jianbing*, he could just see the river, and his next objective. Along the river ran the Ziyang Road. Between the road and river lie a quiet, but immense industrial complex. Colin knew this complex well, and had observed it carefully over his several trips to Wuhan. It was the Wuchang Shipyard - the heart of China's nascent industrial capability to build a variety of military platforms, including recent work on the country's first aircraft carrier. Of particular interest to Colin, this shipyard housed the nation's most modern and innovative submarines for the People's Liberation Army Navy, or PLAN. From his vantage point, he could see a dry-dock area, with a large submarine in it under construction. The dry-dock was covered by a series of aluminum panels and large canvas sheets, making it difficult to see the work going on underneath, and probably impossible to see with any clarity from a satellite image.

His first few reconnaissance missions here had not generated much information about the new submarines. However, he had been able to get up close to the facility on a few subsequent visits, and had developed a decent understanding of the work going on by the PLAN. This trip had, of course, been a surprise to him. But now that he was here, even with the extra heat on him, he had to take this opportunity to get another look at the shipyard.

Anyone who was not Chinese stood out conspicuously in Wuhan. There were still few tourists or foreign business travelers, although that was changing quickly. Colin's best way to blend in was to look like a mid-level, contract technician doing work at one of the many factories in the area. He deliberately shopped for clothes, shoes, and his travel backpack from non-US stores with non-American brands. This time, he had not had the chance to bring the right disguise with him, and he was very conscious about it. He could feel people taking more notice of him than on past visits. The attention was making his spine tingle as he left the park and walked down a moderately busy secondary street towards the river and the shipyard. He kept the half eaten pancake in its wax paper wrapper in one hand, for use as a prop if needed, and walked at a measured pace along the road, trying to give the impression he might be on a light dinner break in between shifts. His other hand, in his pocket, held his phone.

He would follow the same plan he had done several times now, walking down this street until it emptied out on a riverfront road that led to the entrance of the shipyard. From a few hundred yards away, he would pretend to have a phone call, and then have trouble with reception, holding the phone up in the air a few times. In reality, he would take as many pictures as he felt comfortable with the phone's built-in camera. Then, he would pretend to get reception back, and continue walking down the street as if listening to a call. This simple rouse had worked remarkably well for him so far. Munching on the pancake with one hand, while talking quietly into the phone every now and then, gave him a leisurely presence that had allowed him to photograph a lot of valuable information at the Wuchang Shipyard.

Colin turned the corner and emerged onto the riverfront road. He looked sidelong down the street towards the shipyard and was pleasantly surprised. The winter season had left a lot of the trees bare of leaves, allowing him an even better view of things than his previous missions. He walked slowly along the street, pulling the smartphone out of his pocket. Pretending to pull up the phone menu, he activated the camera. He put the phone up to his ear for a few moments, and then held it up away from his face, using his thumb to tap the photo icon several times. He put the phone back to his ear and walked further down the street, talking in accented Russian into the phone in an imaginary conversation. Soon, he had walked past the entire front entrance gate of the shipyard, and had taken a series of pictures of the submarine under construction. Since it was early evening, the shipyard was quiet, perhaps in between the day and evening shift. An idea popped into Colin's head to get more conclusive evidence of exactly what was going on in that shipyard. It would be a gamble, but worthwhile if it worked.

He knew of a small, quiet side entrance just on the far side of the shipyard. It was hidden from most of the traffic, being closer to the bank of the river and lower than street level. He put the phone back in his pocket. Having a clear field of vision for the next phase of his recon would be more important than having the camera ready as a cover act. Finishing his pancake, he picked up his pace to get to the small staircase leading down to the side entrance.

Colin arrived at an eight foot high, metal turnstile cut into the cinderblock wall that surrounded the perimeter of the shipyard. He fumbled in his pocket for a minute, hoping he gave the impression he was looking for an access badge. The coast still looked clear. The few passersby on the street did not seem to notice him or care that he was by this gate. Through the metal turnstile, he could tell the shipyard was relatively quiet. Sparks flew from a lone welder working on scaffolding near the forward section of the massive submarine. Pulling out his camera again,

Colin quickly took a series of photos. Putting the camera back in his pocket, he started to turn back towards the main street.

Suddenly, something at the gate caught his well-trained eye. The turnstile's electronic latch had a key pad and a card sensor with two lights: one green and one red. Very softly, the red light was flashing. Colin quickly looked closer at the gate and nearly laughed out loud at his stroke of luck. The door latch had been caught ajar, and the red light was flashing to indicate it was not secure. Colin knew he could not let this chance pass him by. He walked to the turnstile gate and pushed. It rotated inwards and Colin found himself inside the shipyard.

Deciding it was still best for him to hide in plain sight, he looked around quickly and found a catwalk leading towards the river that afforded an excellent view of nearly the entire shipyard. He headed for the catwalk, taking in as much of the scene as he could, trying to mentally catalogue everything about the submarine.

This particular submarine was for carrying ballistic missiles. He could see the missile tubes being worked on near where the welder was creating all of the sparks. Colin's skills at reading Chinese characters were quite good, and he began to read a series of signs around the shipyard indicating what work was done in that particular area. There was a sonar section, a missile tube section, a propulsion section, and several other workstations organized around the major portions of manufacturing to be done on this submarine. Within minutes, he had taken in a lot of good intelligence. He could tell it had sixteen ballistic missile tubes, and that despite its large size, it was probably more maneuverable than any submarine currently in the Chinese inventory. He could tell they had made some improvements to the propeller system that they had copied from a recent US Navy upgrade, which would make it much quieter than just about any submarine active today, including the very quiet diesel models.

It also seemed to have a few industrial or mining attachments to it, like long boom arms that could be used to conduct underwater construction. He could also see that, based on his past visits, they would be finished with this submarine in a matter of weeks. He had people back in the US who would need to know what he had discovered, and see the pictures, as soon as possible.

At the end of the catwalk was a small, glass windowed office, like a foreman's crow's nest, from which the project managers could survey the work of their teams and hold coordination meetings. Colin couldn't resist the urge to see what he might find in the office. His heart was pounding, and he was starting to get very nervous that he had truly pressed his luck far beyond what was healthy. But taking a breath, he quickly looked around once more to confirm he was still un-noticed, and walked to the office at the end of the catwalk.

"Jackpot," he whispered to himself as he walked inside and saw a set of plans displayed on a laptop monitor sitting on a table with papers, clipboards and handwritten meeting notes scattered about the small office. Sensing no time to waste, he took out his phone and began to feverishly take pictures of everything. The plans indicated the submarine model was the 09/7, and it was clearly a game changer – the most advanced PLAN submarine in their fleet. Once completed, its new features would make it much more formidable than most subs currently facing off against the US Navy. He surmised this new intelligence was unprecedented, and he was certain if he could report this information back to his headquarters, it would go to the highest levels of the US government - maybe right to the President - for decisions on how to address this threat. He worked diligently, efficiently and quickly to capture the most critical data.

Colin Steele was suddenly snapped from his intense information gathering by the sound of the action of a semiautomatic handgun being pulled back to charge the weapon. Colin froze, knowing he was caught and not wanting to be shot by spooking his captors with any sudden movements. He slowly looked up to see two PLAN marines standing in the doorway of the office. One was a lieutenant, who held a pistol trained directly at Colin. The second was a marine sergeant, who held an AK-47, also trained on Colin. The enlisted marine, a little younger and clearly less experienced, looked nervous, but the lieutenant was tough looking and furious to have caught an intruder in his facility. Colin knew this officer's security detail was responsible for watching over the entire Wuchang Shipyard. Even though Colin was captured, it would reflect poorly on the officer that someone could get in this high security place.

"On your knees! Put your hands behind your head, now! And slowly!" the officer barked at Colin in Mandarin. Colin thought about playing dumb and pretending he didn't understand, but a glance into the steely eyes of the lieutenant told Colin it was better to follow orders. He obeyed, kneeling down on the floor next to the table he had been using to photograph the handwritten submarine production notes, slowly placing his phone on the table. Thoughts flashed through his head of interrogation and prison. He had to try something to avoid that scenario. He hung his head and did his best to instantly adopt the demeanor of a snooping, but generally harmless, Russian technician.

"I was only looking for a set of plans I lost. My boss will kill me if he finds out I left them somewhere," Colin said in perfect Russian with a Vladivostok accent he had worked on for several years. He looked up at the Lieutenant, fairly certain he spoke no Russian, but hopeful his tone and demeanor would get the point across and most importantly hide the fact that he was an American. To complete his act, he tried saying the same phrase again in broken Mandarin but with his Vladivostok accent. The Lieutenant gave him a suspicious and slightly confused look. Then with a jerk of his head and a quick command he ordered the sergeant to his side, still keeping his AK-47 trained on Colin. Colin maintained his browbeat demeanor. It was practically natural as his dread grew at what was about to come.

The Lieutenant holstered his pistol on his utility belt, and began to reach for a handheld radio on his other hip. Fear and excitement pulsed through Colin in an instant, realizing the officer was going to call in this incident. He also realized this might be his last and only chance at an escape. He only had one weapon pointed at him now instead of two, and that was good enough odds for Colin to go on the attack.

Colin sprang up from the floor in a swift, fluid motion. With his right forearm he swiped the muzzle of the AK-47 away from himself and towards the Lieutenant. He landed his right foot down hard on the sergeant's shin, causing him to double over crying from the sharp pain. Colin ripped the butt of the rifle out of his hands, and swept it up into the chin of the doubled-over marine, who began to crumple to the floor. Before the sergeant hit the ground, Colin jabbed the barrel of the AK-47 forward into the hand of the Lieutenant. As the officer pulled his hand back in pain, Colin lunged forward into him, pushing him off balance and on the floor. Before the Lieutenant could recover, Colin gave a swift, hard kick with his left foot smashing the man's head into the concrete floor. Colin pivoted back to the sergeant and gave him a powerful, full-force kick to the throat.

Seeing both men were still, he quickly crouched down keeping his head just level with the glass windows of the office, listening for any sounds of alarm or more guards. He heard and saw nothing but the sound of the welder in the shipyard. He took his phone from the table and he sighed in relief as he put it back in his pocket.

Colin stood up, looking around the room to make sure he hadn't missed any key information, and headed for the door. Suddenly, an alarm sounded and a red light began flashing from atop a watchtower along the high cinderblock perimeter wall. Colin knew he was blown. He ran back to the Lieutenant, grabbed his ID badge, ripped the AK-47 off the floor next to the sergeant, and sprinted down the catwalk to the turnstile gate. Over the blare of the alarm, Colin heard the sound of many footsteps echoing off the concrete floor of the shipyard as the guard force began scrambling to cover the exits. Colin ran faster and was only a few yards from the gate.

The rhythmic sound of automatic gunfire broke over the alarm. The whine of bullets ricocheting off the wall near Colin made him duck instinctively as he ran. He waved the officer's ID card in front of the scanner, and flung himself against the turnstile. He was outside the facility without a moment to spare. More marines appeared behind the turnstile gate. Colin turned quickly back towards the gate and jammed the AK-47 into the turnstile. The first marine trying to rush through the gate found it wedged and immobile. But Colin wasn't there to appreciate that his quick work had bought him some time. He bound up the stairs to the main river front road where, just a few minutes before, he had been pretending to enjoy his pancake while snapping photos.

He threw the ID badge into a clump of bushes at the top of the stairs and sprinted down the road to the first side street.

Brushing by throngs of workers on their way home at the end of the work day, he had to get off the street fast. The marines would be swarming out of the other exits and combing the streets for him in seconds. There would be plenty of helpful bystanders to show them which way he had gone. In his second stroke of incredible luck of the day, a green and white taxi cab sat just a few yards from him. He rushed over, and opened the door. A middle-aged cab driver looked at him from the rearview mirror. Colin sat back in the seat, instantly changing his demeanor to look as relaxed as though he had just left a local restaurant. In a calm, but firm voice, he directed the driver in perfect Mandarin, "Tianhe Airport, please." The taxi driver nodded and pulled away into the never-ending stream of cars running through the streets of Wuhan.

Chapter 26

Jennifer, Michelson and Carty emerged from the elevator into the cavernous first floor atrium of the China Global Development Bank headquarters as dusk began to turn to night. The brilliant lights and neon signs of Wuhan's business district began to shine against a deepening purple sky. Jennifer paused for a moment near the security desk and pulled out her phone.

"Just a moment. Before we head outside, let me text Colin to see where he is," she said, tapping away a quick note. Mr. Li's assistant had offered his car to bring them back to the airport, but Michelson had quickly chimed in to politely decline. As they waited a few moments to hear from Colin, Carty wandered around the lobby, as if he were lost in thought.

Michelson stood nearby looking at a large, flat panel, digital screen which had a running slideshow of advertisements and public relations for the bank. On the screen was a digital photo of a meeting of China Global Development Bank executives. They were dressed sharply in suits and ties sitting around a conference table. But sitting at the conference table in a professional looking pant suit was a familiar female face.

"It can't be…" Michelson said softly to himself as Dominique's beautiful face smiled at him from the advertisement. Could she really have been working for Li and his bank all along? The thought that she might know too much, or may have entertained ideas about selling the MICAL information had occurred to him before, but he kept a careful eye on Dominique, and had never caught her red-handed at anything other than playing her silly, sexy, head games with him. And he had enjoyed that too much to want it to stop despite his occasional suspicions.

The advertisement photo slideshow continued on, and the picture of Dominique faded away to be replaced by a photo of a woman happily using her mobile phone to conduct her banking. Michelson looked over at Jennifer and walked away from the screen towards the exit to draw the other's attention away.

"Have you heard from Colin?" he asked Jennifer.

She shook her head no.

"Let's catch that cab to the airport now. He's a big boy. He will meet us there like he promised," Michelson said walking to the entryway revolving doors. Jennifer and Carty followed, and soon they were in a taxi on the way to Tianhe Wuhan Airport.

Jennifer checked her phone several times on the way to the airport, but she got no text back from Colin. She began to get nervous that whoever had attacked them during the car ambush had found him. It was a quiet, awkward cab ride to the airport, with each of them lost in their own thoughts. The reverse trip was faster since the traffic had lightened a bit. Soon, they pulled up to the curb at the very end of the terminal where they had gotten into the black sedans just a few hours earlier. Jennifer, Carty and Michelson climbed out, and Michelson conveniently handed the driver enough *yuan* he somehow had in his billfold to cover the trip.

No sooner did the cab pull away, when a nearly identical green and white taxi pulled up. Colin Steele emerged from the cab, smiling grimly at Jennifer. She suddenly realized how worried she had been about him and how happy she was to see he was back with them and OK. The thought made her blush a little as she smiled back at him.

They all entered the airport terminal building and soon found themselves looking at the same immigration officer who had stamped their passports into the country. Their two Bahamian pilots emerged from the pilot's lounge. The power of the China Global Development Bank to get them into the country with such ease seemed to hold. Their passports were soon stamped, departures fees paid, and they were in the Gulfstream jet and on the way within a few minutes. Jennifer held her breath until the pilot announced in his comfortable, Bahamian accent that the jet was clear of Chinese airspace. The plane's return flight plan was taking them to Providenciales, Turks and Caicos. From there, they would be just a quick hop back to Mayaguana.

Many hours later, the plane touched down at Providenciales International Airport and taxied to the small private jet terminal next to the slightly larger International Terminal, which after being in Wuhan, looked like a quiet, municipal airport. After refueling, Carty intended to fly directly back to Nassau to make the final preparations for his Secession Movement vote in Parliament. Michelson was heading to his boat, docked at the container port near the Five Cays district, where he said he needed to gather up his geological research records. Jennifer wasn't sure what she was going to do, and Colin had been quiet about his plans. The uncomfortable silence among them had driven her crazy the entire return flight, so she decided to address the events of the disastrous China meeting head-on before parting ways.

"Well, gentlemen, it seems as though we are at a cross roads. I have no intention of simply handing over this project to Mr. Li, and I would never have just accepted his money to give up looking into my father's disappearance. I expect help from all of you, even if that means postponing MICAL's secession," she announced as they stood outside on the tarmac underneath the shade of an awning hanging off the executive terminal. Carty, absorbed until that point in memorizing his triumphant, secession-vote victory speech, spun around angrily to face her.

"Ms. Bullfinch, you have crossed the line!" he roared in a tone that Jennifer didn't think was in his toothy-grinning, politician's nature. He looked at her with anger smoldering in his eyes, and then continued.

"I am truly sorry about your father. I have no idea what has happened to him, but I do know what we are about to accomplish is bigger than any one person. It's about a new county, and freedom for a small, but very dear people who have been downtrodden, overlooked, and taken for granted two hundred years. So make no mistake. I will not let you selfishly ruin everything that we – including your father - have all worked so hard for over the last thirty years."

"I'm not trying to stop anything, or ruin the rise of this great new nation of yours. But I will find out what happened to my father. And I will not let a greedy bunch of old men walk away with everything my father worked for. If Dad was truly betting every penny he ever made on this crazy oil field, if it even is for real, then I am not going to let all that go without a fight. If you knew him as well as you say, you can be certain he would have expected me to do no less. But if you go ahead with your plans for secession, you won't be in charge of the MICAL region...Mr. Li will be," Jennifer told Carty, stepping in closer to him to emphasize she would not be shouted down.

"Carty, I do think it seems like you're throwing in with the wrong lot," Michelson stepped in between them. "You, and Langford, and I – we all worked together since the day we figured out there might actually be something valuable underneath that forgotten ocean. Yes, you have worked hard and now you've staked your reputation on MICAL independence. But Langford and I have risked a lot too. I've spent my entire career luring oil company geologists away from here, even when I knew it made me an academic fraud. Langford made a lot of money making some huge bets in real estate. He could have just walked away from this whole thing and retired a wealthy man. But he didn't. He bet his whole fortune on this because he believed in it, and in us."

Colin, who had been listening intently, looked at Carty, "I have to say, it seems very suspicious to me too, as an interested third party, that now that Langford's money is gone, you've decided to jettison everyone else and leverage your government ties to keep you in good with Mr. Li and his flock of investment banking vultures. They're fighting awfully hard to get clear control of what they claim is a worthless project - that is unless they know it could also be worth billions of dollars in oil money."

"I never told Li and his bankers anything about the MICAL formation. Does he know? Was he just bluffing up in his office when he said Mayaguana was nothing more than a useless, desolate rock? You want the answer? Yes, he knows about the oil field - but not from me," Carty blurted out in anger. For a split second, a look of surprised regret flashed across his face, as though the words had just slipped out, but he stood firm.

Michelson said nothing, but looked at the ground. Jennifer glared, too angry to speak.

"That's right," Carty pointed a finger at Michelson and continued, "And if I had to put my money on the culprit, then it would be on you. Li had a contact who told him everything. They knew all about the oil, how much work we had done for all those years…everything. I know it wasn't me that told them, and it certainly seems like it wasn't Langford. So that leaves you."

The group stood in silent shock. Jennifer looked back and forth between him and Michelson. Finally, Carty broke the silence.

215

"To hell with you all. You can think whatever you want, because I am done with this foolishness. I have a lot of work to do in the next few days. They are going to be the most important days in the lives of my people," Carty waved angrily to the two pilots, sitting quietly on a few plastic lawn chairs in the shade, to head to the jet. "Ms. Bullfinch, Mr. Steele, Ian…I don't expect or want to see any of you again, so I leave you with this parting thought: Mr. Li told you to get on with your lives, which you could have done quite comfortably with the money he offered you. When you refused, he warned you never to return to Mayaguana. I recommend you follow that advice."

With that, Carty Wallingford-Rolle climbed the stairs into the jet. The pilot started the engines. Carty disappeared inside, and the cabin door was closed. The Gulfstream taxied away, leaving Colin, Michelson, and Jennifer in the blowing dust of its engines. After the jet took off, climbing and then turning to the north over Grace Bay towards Nassau, Michelson looked over at Jennifer.

"Look. I know what Carty said about me has probably crossed your mind more than once. I had access to all the information about the MICAL formation. In some ways, I had the most to gain if I just sold the information to the highest bidder, to someone like Li and his bank. I can't blame you if you don't believe me, but I was always loyal to your father, and to Carty," he looked at her with a soft smile on his face.

"Do you know what happened to my father? I've asked you before, but I am asking you again now," Jennifer said to Michelson, watching the Gulfstream disappear over the horizon.

"No. I wish I did know something, but I have no idea. What I can tell you is this: he was on to something…something important. I don't think it had anything to do with our project or the MICAL Formation," Michelson said.

"What do you mean?" Jennifer asked, puzzled at this strange admission. Colin, who had been quietly standing nearby, perked back up and tilted his head slightly towards Michelson with a stifled look of curiosity on his face.

"I don't know, really. But when he came down to oversee the project, he seemed to have other things on his mind, some other agenda that had nothing to do with the Formation or MICAL independence. We never had a chance to talk about it before he disappeared."

"Time to come clean then, Ian. When Jennifer came down to the island, how come you took off for London?" Colin asked, taking the words right out of Jennifer's mouth.

"It really had nothing to do with Jennifer, but everything to do with the MICAL data I had been collecting. I began to suspect someone had been hacking into my computer. I had to get back to London to secure the files personally," Michelson answering, sounding quite frank. "Before you came to my office, obviously, I had been attacked. Someone forced their way in to my office to physically steal whatever data files they hadn't taken already."

"Well, from the looks of you when we found you at your office, they were successful," Colin said.

"Yes – the truth is most of the data about the MICAL Formation is gone. The only good news is that over the years, I backed up some of the data in another location. At least that's a starting point to rebuild the oilfield map," Michelson said, rubbing his jaw as if being reminded of the attack on him in London brought the pain back.

Colin looked at Jennifer, with an 'uh-oh' look. Jennifer thought for a second, and then realized what he was getting at.

"Ian, do you keep the backed-up data on a server at an apartment in Austin, Texas," Jennifer asked, knowing the answer and dreading his response. Michelson turned white.

"Oh no…how do you know that?" he asked in an amazed tone.

"When we put two and two together about your OSRI front organization, we went to Austin looking for you before we came to London. The CPU was gone from the apartment when we got there," Colin told him. Michelson walked, nearly stumbling, over to the plastic lawn chairs where the pilots had been, and collapsed into one of them. He looked like he had aged several years in just a few days and this was a blow he had not foreseen.

"Well that is a setback indeed. Though I can't say there was much very valuable in those files. It was a lot of the distracting data I had removed from the oilfield map, like some of the old military and NASA undersea communications equipment, from around the island. But at any rate, I guess it's gone," Michelson heaved a sigh.

"So now, 'they' really do have the upper hand. Somebody has the entire set of data about the MICAL formation, which is sure to be on its way to Wuhan by now. In a few days, Li will own most of the property on the island, and he'll have the newly minted Prime Minister in their back pocket," Jennifer reasoned aloud.

"Right," agreed Colin quietly from his chair, "and whether Carty was the one who told them about the oil formation or not, we need to figure out how to stop them, or we're all in trouble."

Michelson stood up and took a deep breath. "I can't say I know how we are going to do that, but maybe I can fix my own part in this whole mess. I'm going to my boat, comb through my files one more time, and see if I can piece together exactly what Li knows and doesn't know."

Colin sat down next to Michelson. He also looked exhausted. Jennifer knew she needed to rally the troops.

"OK. Colin, I think you and I should get a flight to Mayaguana," Jennifer said. She was still suspicious of Michelson, and wary of him going off on his own, but happy to see things moving again. "I want to get back on island and have a last look around before Li arrives on his yacht."

"Good. I'll text you when I am on the way over," Michelson said. "Good luck, and do be careful. If it wasn't safe for us in London or China, I get the feeling our own backyard may be even more dangerous."

With his parting line of typical, understated sarcasm, Michelson trudged off to catch a taxi to the docks, leaving Jennifer and Colin to find a charter pilot to take them on the fifteen minute flight to Mayaguana. They asked every pilot they could find, but on a lazy morning in the Turks and Caicos, they didn't find many pilots hanging around the private jet terminal, and none willing to take them on short notice to Mayaguana, quick hop though it may be. They sat back down in the plastic chairs under the awning.

"I don't want to be stuck here in Provo all day. What do we do?" Jennifer asked, reverting back to Colin's local expertise in The Bahamas and Turks and Caicos.

"I think we do what I always do in a tough spot around here: call Obie," he answered, a broad grin breaking out on his face. "It's nearly a guarantee he knows someone around here who can fly us over." Colin pulled out his phone to dial Obie. As he tapped on the screen and hit the send icon, the phone powered down on him, dead after the marathon of use he had put it through taking photos at the Wuchang Shipyard.

"Hey, my phone just died. I'm going to have to charge it because I have some important emails to send," he told Jennifer, who had no idea just how important those emails might be to the entire national security of the United States. "Can I borrow your phone?"

Jennifer, lost in thought about what final, Hail Mary steps she could take before Li arrived on the island, absentmindedly handed him her phone. Colin dialed up Obie, but got no answer. Not uncommon, especially if he was on Mayaguana.

"I'm going to text him, sometimes those get through easier than a call," Colin told her, and tapped on the text message icon. Jennifer gasped, and reflexively grabbed for the phone, but it was too late. Colin looked at her phone and his eyes grew wide.

"What the hell is this?" he asked angrily. "There's a data file attached to the text message from your father on the very day he disappeared. You haven't said anything about it? Why?"

"Because it is none of your business. Now give me my phone!" she demanded. She never had an older brother to play 'keep away' from her as a child, but she imagined this was how it felt.

"Not just yet, because I think it is my business. I've been helping you get around the entire world, literally, to try and find out what happened to your father, and here's a clue you have you didn't feel I needed to know. Does that sound fair to you?" he demanded back. Jennifer said nothing, but in her heart she knew Colin was right. Colin shook his head, and handed the phone back to her.

"I'm not going to read that file against your will, but I think you ought to consider the situation. We've been attacked in broad daylight twice now, and both times, that phone was what the attackers were after. But it's not really the phone they're after…it's whatever information is in that file. I'm asking you to trust me," Colin said, sounding hurt.

Jennifer could see he was making sense. She still had no idea what the message from her father meant. Colin probably wouldn't either, but clearly there was more to Colin than she initially guessed. He had come along with her this far, so perhaps he deserved her full trust. Slowly, she handed him back the phone.

Colin tapped on the text message from Langford to his daughter sent barely a week ago. He read the message, and had to admit, there was probably no way Jennifer would ever have made heads or tails of it. But to him, it started to connect the dots that had been popping up over the past few months. 'MICAL' the first part of the message, was clear enough to get Jennifer, who knew little to nothing about what her father was up to, pointed to the right part of the world. The second bit of text, 09/7, now made perfect sense and confirmed his earlier suspicion when Jennifer had mentioned the text message in Wuhan. The submarine plans he had just photographed in Wuhan had been labeled as a Type 09/7 model of sub.

He tapped on the text message attachment to the data and a series of numeric codes popped up on the screen. No doubt, this would also have meant nothing to Jennifer, Colin thought. It didn't mean much to Colin either, but it was obviously some kind of code important enough for someone to go through a lot of trouble to recover. The meaning and function of cryptic codes like this were very hard to guess, but coming from Langford, and given the 09/7 possible submarine reference, Colin thought he might just know what they were. He handed the phone back to Jennifer.

"Thank you," he said. "I don't take your trust for granted, but I wish you had shown this to me the day we met."

"Why? Does it tell you what happened to my father?" she asked, having trouble containing her excitement.

"Not entirely. But some people I know will be able to make more out of the message, and I think they may have some clues that will help solve the mystery," Colin answered truthfully, but wishing he had been able to look at the message and tell Jennifer what happened to her father.

Jennifer opened her mouth to ask just who these people might be, but before she could speak, her phone rang. It was Obie calling back. She handed the phone back to Colin. He tapped the answer icon and put the phone on speaker.

"Obie, it's Colin and Jennifer. I have you on speaker. We're sitting outside the airport in Provo," Colin spoke loudly in the direction of the phone.

"Man, I thought you were abducted by aliens. I heard you two had a bit of a shake up a few days back out front of Mr. Wallingford-Rolle's offices. Everything OK?" Obie asked. It did not take long for news to make it to every corner of The Bahamas.

"Sure, we're fine. We did need to use your car, though. It's at the airport parking lot. Should be OK. What's been going down on Mayaguana since we left? Everything quiet as usual?" Colin asked.

"Not at all - not at all quiet. You might want to get back over here soon. Don't want to say much more over the phone, though, you know," Obie said, and his tone became a bit hushed over the slightly static connection.

"We're trying to do that right now. That's why I called. We're trying to get a flight back from Provo. Is Tony or anybody else around who can get us?" Colin hushed his own tone in response.

"Man, it's just too hot for you to fly in right now. Be at Turtle Cove Marina in one hour. I'll see you there," Obie whispered as he hung up.

"Too hot?" Jennifer asked, looking at Colin.

"I don't know exactly what he means, but I get the feeling he's not talking about the air temperature. Sounds like we'll find out in an hour. Let's catch a ride over to the Marina," Colin shrugged as they walked towards the front desk to get a taxi.

Chapter 27

Mr. Li Hong stood looking out the windows of his office atop the headquarters of the China Global Development Bank. The skies were growing dark, and the lights of the city, which Li had seen grow exponentially over the past few years, lit up the sky. Having just ushered out the LIC partners, he was unhappy with the progress made in the past few days. Presently, but not unexpectedly, his personal cell phone rang.

"Li here," he answered.

"Li, what happened at the meeting? I expect the woman took your offer and we can move forward without further nuisance," inquired a distant voice at the other end of the line.

"She rejected the offer," Li answered, the frustration evident in his voice.

"Very disappointing. And you were not able to retrieve the phone?" the voice pressed Li.

"No. Nor could we successfully hack into it given the short amount of time it was active in our building. The entire operation, luring them all here to Wuhan, was a failure. And after the debacle trying to ambush them on the way to the offices, I dared not attempt further violence while they were here. We must find a way to get at them another time," Li said, angry at himself for not personally taking charge of the whole visit. Letting his subordinates handle matters had kept him safely disconnected from things, but his team was screwing up so badly, it was now down to the wire.

"We are running out of time! Wallingford-Rolle is pushing ahead with the MICAL independence vote as soon as he returns

224

home, and we must be ready to take full control of the island at that time. When do you arrive to Mayaguana?" asked the voice, clearly as annoyed by his failure as he was.

"I will be there tomorrow. I am heading to the airport now," Li answered, seeing his helicopter approaching the private helipad on the office tower roof. Just then, his 'red phone' land line rang from his desk. Picking up the receiver, he listened to a frantic report from an officer on duty at the Wuchang Shipyard. An intruder had been discovered gathering top secret information about the latest submarine, the Type 09/7, assaulted the guards, and escaped into the city. By the time Li hung up the phone, he was shaking with rage. Somewhat reluctantly, he relayed the report to the voice on his personal cell phone.

"Li Hong, you are failing us both, after many long years of preparing for this day. We may never have another chance to get the phone from the woman. Send Dominique to search the professor's computer system again. Perhaps she can find something hidden in his data files that will help us," the voice urged.

Li wasn't sure this was the right thing to do. It seemed Dominique had already squeezed every bit of information possible from the lonely professor. Li didn't want to have to explain that his latest raid on the professor's office had led to a confrontation with him in the heart of London. The chance of these espionage missions becoming headline news was growing with each blunder. However, he agreed quickly and quietly to avoid further embarrassment.

"Fine. That settles it. I will meet you in Mayaguana myself. We will both be there to ensure our final plans are executed. There will be no further failures," said the voice firmly. The line went dead as he hung up, not waiting for Li to respond. Li yelled harshly for his personal assistant.

"*Myan-bow-shi-fu* shall meet me at the yacht in MICAL. Have the necessary preparations made while I am en route. Is my jet ready as I ordered?" Li barked at his assistant. The assistant nodded yes, looking scared.

"Good. Call Wu and tell him I am on the way to Mayaguana," Li ordered as he departed for the helipad.

Chapter 28

Michelson stepped out of a ragged taxi at the container port on the end of South Dock Road, Providenciales. Unlike the other marinas on Provo, the small, quiet, container port had almost no slips, and no open air, thatched roof bars with tourists sipping umbrella drinks. This was a working port, the only one on the island. Michelson had established a good relationship with the owner many years ago, as a regular customer. It was more secure and secluded, and that was exactly what Michelson wanted. He'd spent many nights tied up to one of the few small docks waiting out bad weather. He had opted to leave his boat here on his way out to London a few days ago, thinking he might be gone quite a while.

As he walked through the chain link fence he saw his boat right where he had left it. He gave a wave to the marina supervisor sitting at his desk inside the dock master's office as he headed down a sand path to the small, rickety, wooden dock. It was always an odd feeling to him, but after spending so many years working on this little boat, it felt like arriving back at a vacation home when he first saw it. And as any vacation home owner, he was glad to see the boat seemed in good order.

Michelson walked on to the dock, hopping over the side of the boat and onto the back deck at the console, where he'd spent many hours at the helm. Suddenly, he noticed someone down in the cabin. Whoever it was had been caught by surprise, stood up from the desk. Michelson peered down the stairwell and saw Dominique's familiar long, black hair whirl about as she quickly stood and turned towards him.

"Hello, darling!" she cried out, sounding as if she had been longingly expecting him. She came up the stairs with her arms outstretched, coming to give Michelson a welcoming embrace. Just a few days ago, he would have deeply desired that, and been looking forward even more to what would follow. But a lot had changed in the past few days, and the digital picture of Dominique that had smiled back at him along with the crowd of other executives around the conference table in the China Global Development Bank was seared in his mind. He had suspected he was being used before. Now there was no doubt. She had been spying on him, probably since the very first day she showed up at his office in London.

But what was it she really wanted? He had wrestled with this question all the way back from China. Dominique had access to nearly all of his files and records. She didn't really need to sneak around behind his back to steal data about the MICAL formation. It had all been at her fingertips all along. Michelson backed away from her, his guard up. Sensing his apprehension, Dominique hesitated at the top of the stairs to the cabin.

"What are you doing here? I left you on Mayaguana," Michelson began his inquiry, forcing himself to manage at least a weak smile, lest Dominique clam up entirely.

"Oh, you know me. I couldn't stand having nothing to do on that quiet little rock, especially when there was work. So, I hopped a ride with one of the local fisherman coming over here to buy supplies. I hope you don't mind I slept here on the boat," she gave a simple, but rehearsed sounding answer.

"What work? " Michelson asked quickly. He knew there was really nothing left for her to do. And although competent, she had never been enthusiastic about long hours. So now that there seemed to be critical analysis she thought needed to be done...well, Michelson found that hard to believe.

"Oh, you know, I thought some of the files needed organizing. You'd asked me to do that, and I hadn't gotten to it yet," she offered up with a hopeful smile.

Michelson looked her in the eye, hoping he could read some kind of clue from her expression. Suddenly, he noticed her eyeballs twitch as something caught her glance behind him. He spun around to see three men with handguns drawn running towards the boat from around the corner of the dock master's building. Michelson looked back over his should at Dominique, who stood frozen in the door. Shots rang out across the marina. Bullets ripped through the console cabinet shattering the fiberglass windshield. Michelson hit the deck, as he heard a blood curdling scream from Dominique.

Dominique doubled over in pain. She stumbled to the side of the boat and swooned. He looked back in to her eyes, but they had turned glassy. She began to fall, putting a hand out to catch herself against the boat railing. She leaned momentarily at the edge of the boat, and then fell backwards overboard, disappearing under the water.

From the deck floor, Michelson peered up to see the men sprinting at full speed towards the boat. The keys were in the ignition at the console and his machete was clamped to the wall by a large magnet next to him. He knew he only had seconds to act. With a lunge, he flung himself towards the console, grabbing the machete off the wall. He slashed the machete with all his strength at the rope securing his boat to the dock, cutting it with one blow. Scrambling to the console, he turned the ignition key, and the engine turned over. He pushed on the throttle, gunning the engines. The boat lurched forward, pulling away from the dock. Ian turned to see the three men bounding on the dock, so close he could see their faces. He recognized them from the crew that worked on the Mayaguana for Mr. Wu. The boat sped from the dock, too far for any of them to jump aboard and too fast for them to hope to catch him swimming. He smiled to himself – another escape in a long line of close calls.

Shots rang out again and he ducked his head. He felt a thud smack his shoulder up against the console, like a cinder block had hit him in the back. The dull thud was followed instantly by a stinging pain. The console cabinet turned red. Looking down at his shoulder, he saw a growing red stain in his shirt, and he realized he had been shot.

Michelson looked back at the dock. The three men stood at the end of it, watching him head out to sea. He pulled out his cell phone after he had gotten far enough out to sea to feel safe. He tried to dial Colin's number, but the signal was too weak.

Michelson felt himself getting woozy from blood loss. He would have to motor to Mayaguana and warn them in person. He powered up his GPS, hit the "home" waypoint, which was Abraham's Bay, and steered the boat on to course for Mayaguana, locking the steering wheel. He needed to get a bandage on his shoulder fast. Looking down into the cabin, he saw the first aid kit on the wall. Struggling to see straight, he took a step towards the cabin stairwell, slipping in the puddles of blood and salt water splashed on the deck. He fell down the stairs and onto the floor of the cabin, unconscious.

Chapter 29

Jennifer and Colin sat at the Tikki Hut bar at the Turtle Cove Marina, on the north coast of Provo at the very east end of Grace Bay. It was the closest, full service marina to Mayaguana. Jennifer, ever the responsible member of their nascent team, sipped a diet Coke with a rather dry slice of lime and a few tiny cubes of ice. Colin was on his third scotch and soda. His phone sat on the bar, plugged in and charging in a nearby outlet, and he couldn't seem to take his eyes off it. He was tapping his foot continuously on the wooden plank floor. Jennifer pretended not to notice, but it was driving her insane. Colin had also ordered a basket of conch fritters, which he was dipping in hot sauce and chowing down on feverishly. The conch fritters were huge, deep fried, and pleasantly full of freshly chopped conch. Jennifer picked at a conch fritter, mostly out of boredom. Obie was running late, so they had been at the bar for almost two hours. In America, they would have worn out their welcome, but in the Turks and Caicos, on a sleepy late morning, the bar tender watched a cricket match between Trinidad and Saint Vincent on the television, nearly oblivious to them. Presently, Colin stood up from his bar stool, and looked at Jennifer for a moment as though he had a profound announcement. It was, not surprisingly to Jennifer, not profound.

"I'm gonna go take a leak," he told her unceremoniously, with just the faintest hint of slur in his speech. He got up from his stool, drained his tumbler of the last swallow of scotch, unplugged his cell phone, and took it from the counter before heading in the direction of the restrooms. Jennifer was mildly relieved at getting a break from the nonstop tapping of his foot, and refocused herself on learning as much as she could about cricket by watching the game along with the bartender.

Colin walked around the corner towards the restrooms with a slight stagger. Colin could have found his way from the bar to the men's room at the Tikki Hut in pitch black, since it was one of his few haunts near Mayaguana. He and Obie had run the boat over to the marina many a Friday or Saturday afternoon to spend the evening drinking and hitting on the tourist women who happened to venture to the Tikki Hut from one of the local resorts. As he turned the corner out of view of the bar, the stagger disappeared from his easy gait. He pulled out his cell phone and dialed a long number. After a long connection time and a series of faint clicks as the line transferred from various switches, a voice came on the line.

"Fort Lauderdale Imports, this is Shelly speaking," said a cheerful voice on the line.

"Seven five zero six Mike Mike Yankee, go secure please," Colin told 'Shelly.'

The line went quiet, Colin was promted to enter a security code, and a new voice answered the phone. "Station Six here, what can we do for you?"

"This is 7560MMY, I need to be connected to Agent Constantine at station AUTEC, Andros Island, immediately," Colin told the duty officer on the other end. The line went silent again for a moment, and then another voice, this time one Colin recognized, answered the line.

"Colin, what's going on? I haven't heard from you for a while. All quiet on Mayaguana?" a friendly voice came on the line.

"Hey Chris, I can't talk for long, because I'm out in the open. But there's something I think you need to know about," Colin said with a little more urgency in his voice than he usually liked to reveal from his cool manner, but feeling relieved to hear Chris's voice. Chris Constantine was the closest thing Colin had to a best friend. They had been working together in the Caribbean, Florida and Central America for several years, and had more than one close call together. Publicly, AUTEC, or the Atlantic Undersea Test and Evaluation Center was the US Navy's testing base for submarines, near a deep channel called "the Tongue of the Ocean" just off the Bahamian Island of Andros. Less publicly, it was also a center for counternarcotics and gathering and monitoring all types of undersea activity for most of the southern coastline of the United States. Colin and Chris used AUTEC as a home base of sorts for their covert operations together, and reported in to the senior intelligence officer there.

"I'm listening. Go." Chris said knowing that Colin Steele did not hit the panic button unless there was something very important in play, and the full force of the United States government was needed to draw things to a successful conclusion.

"I'm going to forward you a series of photos from my cell phone. I took them on a recon trip yesterday. Once you see these, everything we've been struggling to figure out on Mayaguana will make a lot more sense," Colin said, just over a whisper.

"What do you have?" Chris asked, confused.

"I saw the 09/7 submarine, and it's complete. They're going to launch it soon. I have a set of the plans. You'll get them off the photos I'm going to send. You may have to get one of the computer geeks there to blow up the images so you can read the specs, but it's all there," Colin said, almost breathless in his excitement at delivering this news to his friend and colleague.

"Jesus, Colin. We've picked up an intense uptick in activity out of China in the past 24 hours. It's like somebody smacked the beehive with a broomstick. From what we can tell, an infiltration team killed two Chinese at the Wuchang Shipyard yesterday and the PLA wants blood. Tell me you weren't involved in that?" Chris asked, but knowing the answer already.

"Involved? I was the team, and I did have to take out two guards who found me, but I didn't think I killed them. Anyway, I got enough information about that submarine to make sure we'll know every nut, bolt and weld on the ship," Colin answered, already getting nervous his call was taking too long and a trace could get put on him somehow.

"Hang tight a minute. I need to get Captain Karnes on the line," Chris told Colin, sounding like a just couldn't believe his ears. Before Colin could protest, he heard Chris set the phone down and call for Karnes. Captain Karnes was the commander of the AUTEC facility as well as for an outpost on Great Exuma Island, another Bahamian island a few hundred miles to the north of Mayaguana. Captain Karnes and Colin Steele had never seen eye to eye on most things. Colin had been operating undercover in Karnes' geographic area of responsibility for several years. Karnes was as straight laced and by-the-book as they came and Colin's methods were just too much on the edge for his liking. They had been in more than one knock-down, drag-out argument when Colin went outside of the boundaries Karnes felt were acceptable. However, Colin's record had stood on its own. No one else had brought down more drug rings, human traffickers, and money laundering operations in the region than Colin, and that tempered Karnes, who couldn't argue with success. For Colin's part, although he didn't have much respect for Karnes as an operator, he had to admit, that guy was a technical genius. He knew more about the technical side of US networks, countermeasures, and capabilities than any other intelligence officer Colin knew, and Karnes' knowledge of enemy systems was even more impressive. Colin heard some muffled conversations in the background of the small command center at AUTEC where he had been forced to show his face from time to time for a briefing or to handle administrative requirements. Presently, Karnes and Constantine came back on the line.

"Agent Steele, what in God's name were you doing in China on a recon mission without my approval?" Karnes demanded.

"Deep under cover, sir," Colin answered, trying to keep the disdain out of his voice at being questioned like that and getting in the only military courtesy he planned on extending to Karnes for the rest of their interaction. "I would have let you know, but it was impossible without blowing my cover. I've put too much into this one to give myself away just to keep you happy."

"Oh yeah, well, I'd say your investigation is just about up. After killing those two Chinese, you've caused a major international incident. I want you back here ASAP. We need to debrief you, and I suspect you won't be here long, because our brothers in Washington are going to be demanding to see you too. Somehow I knew you'd get us all in deep trouble with your half-baked conspiracy theory," Karnes was furious. Colin knew he would have to play this perfectly, to buy himself a little more time.

"I will be on Mayaguana in just a few hours, and I'll clean up my tracks there, and then report in as you ordered. But I think you may change your mind, and it definitely justifies all the trouble in China," Colin softened his tone, just a little.

"So what did you find out in Wuhan? Constantine tells me you've got something on the 09/7 sub?" Karnes asked, clearly disgusted with Colin, but feeling the same sense of urgency about keeping the call short.

Colin quickly retold his findings to Karnes, growing more nervous by the second. But he knew Karnes' buy-in would be important. Captain Karnes had staked a lot of his reputation on the idea that the PLAN were developing new technology that would allow them to counter the United States Navy's underwater detection system that ran along the entire coastline of America. The string of sensors could detect underwater activity and trigger a warning if a foreign submarine entered US territorial waters. The islands of The Bahamas, since World War I, had been linked closely to the United States anti-submarine strategy. In the early days of underwater warfare, the islands had served as forward operating bases for US and British submarines, which navigated into hidden coves and could lie in wait to ambush German and Japanese subs. During the Cold War, as technology advanced and detection systems became more reliable, small Bahamian submarine outposts became the sentries of the US coastal defense network. If an alarm sounded because an enemy submarine had been detected near the underwater, invisible fence line of sonar, US submarines could be quickly dispatched from places like the AUTEC base on Andros or Exuma to investigate. Mayaguana Island itself lie situated just inside this invisible "fence" making it strategically speaking, a point of interest for the US Navy. When Colin got wind of a large contingent of Chinese doing large-scale construction on the island from Obie, his best contact in the Bahamian Defense Force, he knew he needed to investigate.

But this was where Agent Steele and Captain Karnes ran against each other. Karnes was certain whatever was going on down on Mayaguana was not related to the underwater detection fence line at all. His analysis concluded the Chinese work on Mayaguana was at most a rouse to keep the US Navy focused on this unimportant island five hundred miles from the US coast. Meanwhile, the PLAN focused its real efforts on using new, next generation sonar technology to find holes in the US coastline defenses. All of Colin's investigating so far suggested that whatever the PLAN was doing on Mayaguana was no rouse, but some kind of critical, top secret operation.

The problem was Colin had not been able to determine what exactly was going on at Mayaguana. His carefully crafted cover story, that he was a paving contractor with expertise in paving runways, had gotten him on the island full-time with a seemingly legitimate reason to be poking around. The intense Chinese security, all supposedly in the name of construction safety practices, had prevented him from seeing anything past the chain link fence of the Abraham's Bay construction operation. He had turned up no new information. He had made multiple trips to the Wuchang Shipyard in Wuhan and turned up nothing concrete…until now. Now Colin was certain he was right. His hunch that there was a direct connection between the work on Mayaguana and the new 09/7 submarine was substantiated with the text message and file on Jennifer's cell phone.

The huge warehouse on the edge of Abraham's Bay the Chinese work crew had supposedly built to support the infrastructure needed to turn Mayaguana from a sleepy, forgotten island outpost into a major, mega resort destination was a cover story. That building had nothing to do with any future resort, and was more than just a simple warehouse. Exactly what was going on inside, Colin wasn't sure, but his instincts were telling him the China Global Development Bank, the Wuchang Shipyard, and this new PLAN submarine were all connected somehow through that warehouse.

"Send us those photos as soon as possible. Be up here within 48 hours for your debrief. I think you are wrong about the sub, and I can tell you your career is on the line here. Good intelligence or not, you're going to answer for the mess you created in Wuhan," Karnes huffed at him, handing the phone back to Chris.

"Colin, there's something else you should know about Li Hong and the China Global Development Bank. Our contacts in the PLAN tell us Li is an Admiral like we suspected, the CGDB is a money laundering front for his operations, and every worker on Mayaguana is under his command," Chris told Colin hurriedly.

"I guess that's not a surprise now," Colin said, his suspicions confirmed.

"Hang on. There's more," Chris concluded. "Our contacts in the PLAN know all about Li and the new 09/7 submarine. But they insist there are no operations anywhere near the Caribbean. It looks like Admiral Li has gone rogue."

Chapter 30

Obie's boat motored into the marina as Colin put his phone in his pocket, heading back toward the bar. He only had two days to figure out the real story, or he'd be working a desk for the rest of what promised to be a brief conclusion to his career. As Obie hopped out on the dock, and Jennifer paid the bar tab, Colin sighed to himself. He was going to have to tie up a lot of loose ends fast, not least of which was this woman who'd become entangled in a mess much bigger than she realized. Colin's job had never let him hold together a relationship for more than a few months, but sharing these past few days of adventure with her made him think how nice it might be to lead a more normal life when this was over and share it with someone like her. He put the thought out of his mind, and made a conscious effort to keep himself focused on the task at hand. He was going to have to explain to Jennifer his real reasons for being on Mayaguana, but not yet.

"Hey dog! Good to see you back so soon. And you too, Ms. Bullfinch," Obie said, grinning at them in his usual, cheerful manner. Despite his smile and typical easy manner, it was clear Obie did not want to hang around the marina for long. Rather than tie up the boat, he stood on the dock holding the rope fastened to the rear eyehook on the boat railing. Jennifer and Colin both were eager to get back to Mayaguana, too, having waited several hours for Obie to cross the Caicos Passage in his small fishing boat. Obie had a very nicely maintained twenty-eight foot long, center console Cobia boat, with a blue Bimini top for keeping the sun off. He kept it meticulously maintained and it ran well. However, if the winds were strong, as they happened to be at that moment, crossing the passage could be a little treacherous. While a boat of twenty-eight feet might seem large around the coast, in open seas, it was a small craft, and to avoid capsizing over some of the larger swells, the Cobia had to keep a slow and steady speed. It was only about twenty-five miles across the passage, but it could take a few hours of pitching and rolling over the waves to get from the marina to Abraham's Bay. Jennifer and Colin hopped aboard the Cobia, and Obie shoved them off.

Within a few minutes, they were motoring past the west end of Providenciales. The stiff winds aside, it was a gorgeous day in the Caribbean. The sky was perfectly blue, and the water a deep turquoise. As Obie steered the Cobia along the coastline, they went past a row of private beach homes, each more elegant than the next. Jennifer and Colin sat on a bench just behind the captain's chair where Obie perched looking out over the horizon.

For Colin, the beauty of the Caribbean was normally lost in the daily grind of his job. He'd spent many a night lying in the sand staking out a host of unsavory criminals, and many a day sifting through the records of sleazy money launderers in their ill-gotten, beach-front compounds. Looking at the white sandy beaches and over-the-top mansions usually made him wonder what kind of shady, criminal dealings had financed these *nouveau riche* monstrosities – because in his experience, nearly all of the money in the Caribbean could be traced to a criminal activity of some kind. When all you could see was blood money in this tropical paradise, it was time to go. His conversation with Chris and Captain Karnes had struck a nerve. The growing realization that he needed a change was something he could no longer ignore.

Colin made up his mind, amidst the sinister beauty of the island growing smaller on the horizon. He was leaving undercover work, leaving the intelligence community altogether. He would start a new chapter in his life, preferably somewhere there were seasons. His sun-baked brain needed a change. The game of chess between major military powers, criminal cartels, and terrorist organizations would never end, but still, he wouldn't leave without at least getting this current mission to a decent hand-off point. Out of the corner of his eye, he saw that Jennifer was watching him stare out over the ocean.

"We're going to get you back to Mayaguana like you wanted. I have to admit, I'm not sure what you plan to do once you get there," Colin said over the rumble of the Cobia's motor. The waves were picking up, and Obie was continually easing back on the throttle to make sure they crested the waves at just the right time and speed. Jennifer sat back against the deck wall of the boat to brace against the waves. She shook her head indicating she wasn't sure either.

"Let me suggest a starting point then," Colin said. If Jennifer had been sent important, top secret information about the 09/7 submarine by her father, then it might be useful to start enlisting her help more openly. "Why don't we investigate the large warehouse right on the edge of Abraham's Bay?"

"That sounds like as good a starting point as any," Jennifer agreed.

"I think that may be harder than either of you think," Obie chimed in, briefly breaking his intense focus on steering the boat across the Caicos Passage. "In the few days you have been gone a lot more workers have arrived. That warehouse area is buzzing like a beehive."

"How did they get to the island? By boat?" Jennifer asked, knowing that in the current condition, no plane much larger than Tony's six-seater could land on the Mayaguana runway.

"That's even more interesting. No one seems to know how they got to the island. No planes landed, no one saw any large boats arrive to Abraham's Bay. But somehow there are an additional fifty people working twenty-four hours a day around the warehouse," Obie answered. A particularly large swell heading towards the Cobia grabbed his attention and he turned his intent gaze back out over the ocean.

"That settles it. We've got to get a look inside that warehouse. There's something odd going on there. Maybe it will show that the China Global Development Bank has been doing things that might have caused the problems my father was having with the project. If I can find enough evidence, at least I can try and delay Mr. Li's take over," Jennifer said, a determined look on her face.

"Right. But I'll bet we're going to find more than that. I can't say for sure what we'll find, but I think it may shed some light on his disappearance too," Colin ventured.

The waves and swells on the passage began to slowly subside, indicating they were getting close to Mayaguana. Soon, the tip of the small radio and cell tower in Abraham's Bay came into view over the horizon. Obie picked up a set of binoculars from the dashboard of the Cobia's center console. He scanned the horizon.

"Colin, you'd better take a look at this. We've had a visitor arrive since I left to pick you up in Provo," Obie announced, handing the binoculars to Colin. Peering through the lenses, Colin observed a gleaming white mega yacht near the break in the reef at Abraham's Bay. Colin estimated it must be at least 300' in length, with four floors. It was more like a cruise ship than a yacht, he thought. He handed the binoculars to Jennifer and showed her where to look on the horizon.

"Mr. Li's yacht is here, and sooner than we thought," Colin said, unable to hide the disappointment and concern in his voice.

"Get down, Colin! You too, Miss Bullfinch!" Obie cried suddenly. "There's a helicopter coming up behind us. Better you two stay scarce." Jennifer and Colin ducked under the captain's chair. Obie threw a blanket he pulled from the stowage compartment over them, and lifted up a deep-sea fishing rod he had laying against the boat deck wall. He killed the engines, threw out the fishing line, and reclined back in his chair with his feet up on the console, looking every bit the typical out-island fisherman looking for a school of tuna. Within a few seconds, the blades of the helicopter could be heard getting louder. Soon it roared overhead on its way north towards Mayaguana nearly skimming the water it was flying so low and fast. As it flew past the Cobia, Obie gave a lazy wave to the helicopter so that hopefully he didn't look too anxious. The roar of the helicopter faded as it went past without incident, and the only sounds were the breeze and the waves lapping against the side of the Cobia. Obie risked picking up the binoculars and followed the helicopter. He gently kicked the blanket on the deck with Jennifer and Colin under it.

"All clear you two. Colin – take a look at this. That helicopter is landing on the yacht out there by A-Bay," Obie said, handing the binoculars to Colin as he and Jennifer emerged from hiding. Colin honed in on the helicopter just at it touched down on a helipad at the aft station of the mega yacht. He showed Jennifer, and sat back in the captain's chair to think for a moment.

"That helicopter could only have come from the airport at Provo. I think it's clear Mr. Li was not far behind us, and has just arrived on his yacht as promised," Colin said.

"I'd say you're right. Good call Obie, getting us out of sight. I think it's better Mr. Li and the Chinese crew on the island don't know we're back, especially if we are going to try and get a look inside the warehouse," Jennifer agreed.

"So, in that case, I recommend we take a wide turn west, and come in towards Devil's Point. We'll be out of sight from anyone in Abraham's Bay, including your good friend Mr. Li," Obie suggested.

"Good thinking. Let's wait it out a bit here, until closer to sundown, and we'll come in at dusk," Colin added. "Do you still have our diving gear on board?"

"Of course, man! Who do you think you're talking to? This ain't no rookie team!" Obie laughed, kicking open the door to the hold revealing a full load of equipment and supplies.

"Good. When we get to Devil's Point, I'm going in the water. I'll find out what's in that warehouse tonight, from the ocean side. Then the fences and locks and all of the workers shouldn't be as much of an obstacle. I might be able to find a way in," Colin said.

"You mean 'we', might be able to find a way," Jennifer said to Colin, "because I'm quite a diver myself, and you are not going alone."

Colin started to protest, but Jennifer just held up her hand, pulling out gear from the hold. He shook his head in disbelief and Obie laughed his hearty laugh. As they set out two full sets of gear, the winds of early afternoon began to die, the waves became a gentle roll, and the three companions waited for the sun to set.

Chapter 31

Michelson stirred from unconsciousness on the floor of his boat to the quiet sound of waves slapping the sideboards. He tried to lift himself up and pain shot through his entire body. He gingerly touched his shoulder but recoiled in pain immediately. The gunshot wound would not normally be life threatening, but without a doctor's treatment, Michelson wasn't sure he'd make it much longer. Lying on the deck of his boat, somewhere out in the ocean was a death sentence for sure, and he knew it. He had to get up and figure out what had happened. With his one good arm, he grabbed hold of the leg of the small desk. Overcoming searing pain shooting through his entire body, he pulled himself to an upright position.

Michelson closed his eyes, took a deep breath, planning his next few actions, which might take all the physical and emotional energy he had left. He needed to get to the console and figure out where he was and how to get to shore fast. He reached for a hand hold near the table and tightened his grip on it. With another effort, he pulled himself up to the galley bench. Exhausted, Michelson leaned his head back against the wall, closed his eyes, and took a few deep breaths. Sleep was beginning to overcome him, but knew he should not let himself slip back into unconsciousness. Forcing his eyes open, he looked at the screen of his laptop, still glowing brightly with the last screen Dominique had been viewing.

Michelson focused on the screen. It was the underwater sounding data they had been gathering together over the past few months. But for some reason, she had been going through and highlighting some of the locations in red text. He thought for a moment about the places highlighted in red. He pulled up the mapping program he used to plot the data points they recorded of the ocean floor, and loaded in only the red highlighted points. The map page loaded, and Michelson gave a curious look at the computer screen. The row of points formed a long line, running north to south, from near the Turks and Caicos running past Mayaguana, and onwards towards Grand Bahama Island, to the Florida coastline of the United States.

This was unexpected. Michelson had assumed he would find that Dominique had been highlighting the best spots for oil wells to tap. But this had nothing to do with oil. It looked far more sinister than just corporate espionage. Even in his semi-delirious state, Michelson's mind was incredibly sharp, and he began connecting the disparate data points in his mind rapidly.

While taking his geographic readings over the years, he had also come across other information about the undersea activity of the Caribbean. In particular, he had located underwater sensors used by the United States to track submarine activity in and out of their territorial waters. For Michelson, this had been useless information, and he ignored those sensor points. They cluttered up his important, geographic readings that were going to make him a rich man when the MICAL formation was tapped.

But a conversation, that seemed innocent at the time, between he and Dominique now flashed across his mind. One evening, when she had been working for him for just a few weeks, Dominique came up quietly behind him as he was working. In her seductive way, she draped her arms around his shoulders, and put her head next to his, whispering in his ear.

"What are you doing, my darling? It looks like you are erasing some of our readings?" she asked.

"Oh, right," he replied absentmindedly, thinking more about how wonderful her breasts felt pressing into him than her question. "I'm deleting the superfluous information."

"Superfluous?"

"Yes, you see, we sometimes pick up readings of things under the sea that don't have anything to do with my geological work. So, I go through and remove that data. Clean it up, so to speak."

"Ah, I see. It must take a lot of time to clean up your data. You've been working at it for hours."

"Oh, yes, it can take some time."

"Then teach me to do it, and then I can be a good little assistant," she bit playfully on his ear.

Michelson had done just that. He taught Dominique how to interpret the soundings, and pull out the underwater detection sensors, as well as other types of noise that interfered with his oilfield related geographic data. After a few times checking her work, he never found a mistake in Dominique's work, and managing that data had indeed become her job.

It was now clear that she had been saving the information about the US Navy sensor locations. When combined with the data stolen from his apartment in Austin and his office in London, Dominique would have had three decades worth of data on the US Navy's top secret electronic fence line.

On a shelf above the table where he sat was a bottle of rum. Michelson reached for the bottle, bit the cork out of it, and took a swig. He poured a little on his shoulder to wash away some of the dirt and dried blood. Taking a deep breath, he prepared mentally for his next effort.

The events at the container port in the Turks and Caicos were coming back to him more clearly. Dominique had not been working alone. The Chinese men that had emerged from the dock master's office with guns blazing had not meant to hit her.

They had been trying to stop him from getting to the boat and motoring away. They must have known the final piece of information Dominique was about to retrieve from the files on his laptop were critical and needed immediately. Otherwise they could have waited for him to return with the research boat to Mayaguana. But they took the risk of attempting to steal the data in Provo in broad daylight.

Michelson quickly checked the sent files from his email. The file with the last of the data had successfully been sent over the Wi-Fi at the container port. It must have been the last thing Dominique did as she saw him approaching the boat. Michelson knew now that Dominique had worked for Mr. Li and his bank, and that Li's interest went beyond the MICAL Formation. Li wanted to know about the US underwater detection network of sensors. He was controlling the henchmen on Mayaguana and around the world who had been trying to get at this information and at Jennifer Bullfinch. Clearly, she also held another piece of the puzzle that Li needed for his plans. Michelson felt a charge of energy run through him at this realization. He needed to warn Jennifer and Colin of this right away.

Michelson remembered his satellite phone on the console on deck. Having rested a second, and feeling a little better from the effects of the rum, he pushed himself up, and slowly began working his way up the stairs towards the outside deck of his boat, holding closely on to railings, handholds, and the wall to keep steady. He emerged outside and felt the warm air hit his face. He was in the middle of the ocean, with nothing in sight as far as he could see in any direction. He looked at the pilot's console. The fuel gauge read "E." He kicked a small, red plastic can under the console, which was the emergency gas tank. It shuddered slightly, and the sloshing of gasoline inside gave Michelson a brief glimmer of hope. The gas in the emergency tank might power the engines for one or two miles, just enough to get him to shore if he eventually spotted land.

He picked up the satellite phone to dial Colin or Jennifer and warn them. The phone was dead, and no spare battery. He found the charger nearby in the glove box, and plugged the phone into the socket of the pilot console cigarette lighter. He'd just have to pray that his boat's battery didn't die on him before the phone was charged enough to make one call. Looking at his wrist watch, he was surprised to see it was 5PM. He'd been out cold the whole day. How long the boat ran unpiloted before the gas ran out, he had no idea. Not wanting to risk the battery charge for the satellite phone, he didn't turn on his GPS. He eased himself into the pilot's chair, and leaned his head back against the seat rest, relaxing again. He picked up the charging sat phone and looked at the LCD display – nothing yet. He set the phone on his lap and closed his eyes, waiting. He drifted back into unconsciousness.

Chapter 32

The sun began to set off of the port side of Obie's Cobia. They had drifted about for several hours a few miles south of Mayaguana, with Jennifer and Colin trying to stay out of sight, and Obie pretending to fish as he surveyed the mega yacht through his binoculars. In actuality, Obie did do a little fishing in between recon work, and had even caught a few wahoo, which he threw in the cooler to bring back to the island. Now it was time to start for Devil's Point, a small peninsula of Mayaguana island that jutted out into the Caicos Passage and marked the far west end of Abraham's Bay. From Devil's Point, the Cobia would be out of view of anybody in the bay, as well as from Li's mega yacht. Getting in the water there, Colin and Jennifer would not have far to swim along the coastline before coming to the construction zone of the project and the warehouse they intended to investigate.

Obie cranked the engines and the Cobia glided over the waves heading northwest towards Devil's Point. As the last rays of the setting sun glint off of the ocean, which had calmed to a brilliant, red, glassy lake, Obie cut the engines on the Cobia just off Devil's Point. Jennifer and Colin planned out the recon mission to the warehouse as they put on their wet suits.

"When you looked around the warehouse, did you notice the cameras at each corner?" Colin asked.

"I did. But if I remember right, they hadn't put cameras on the waterfront corners yet, so we should be out of view if we keep low along the water's edge, right?" Jennifer said, thinking back to her first morning in Mayaguana. She wished now she'd taken more time to really look at everything. Jennifer zipped up her wetsuit and fastened a weight belt around her waist.

Obie looked over at Jennifer as she pulled out a wristwatch dive computer and programmed in the proper data. "You look like a master dive instructor. Where'd you learn all this stuff?" he asked, clearly impressed.

"Oh, I've been a diver my whole life. My mother hated scuba diving, but my father loved it, so we went all the time. B.W. used to dive with us also. Off the same boat that's in Abraham's Bay now," Jennifer answered, smiling at Obie as she thought about her father and his insistence that she learn how to dive much to the chagrin of her mother, who could never feel comfortable underwater.

"Who's B.W.?" Obie asked, helping her with the oxygen tank.

"He's my father's business partner. He's back in Atlanta pulling out what's left of his hair trying to stop Mr. Li and his bank from taking over everything. And, being frustrated with me, too. I think he looks at my efforts as a lot of globe-trotting with no results," she said with a mild sigh as she clipped the dive computer around her wrist and turned around to look at Obie.

"In between his negotiations with the bank, he's been calling Jennifer to keep tabs on her for the past week!" Colin said to Obie, laughing. "But you haven't heard from him recently, so maybe he's gotten used to you hanging around with the wrong crowd."

"If I know B.W., he's been frantically calling Mr. Li's office to try and override my decision not to take the money he offered," Jennifer mused.

"Ha! He must speak Mandarin, if he's getting anywhere with that crowd. I haven't found many that speak English on this construction crew, even from the supervisors," Obie joked along.

"You know, he does speak some Mandarin, actually," she said laughing along.

Colin's expression went serious for a moment. "Are you joking? How would he have learned Mandarin?"

"During the Korean War. He was a prisoner of war. His captors were Chinese, not North Korean," Jennifer answered, "He never spoke about it himself much, but we found out from another old veteran back in Atlanta named Ray Barnes. They had served in the same unit."

"Huh. Interesting," said Colin, giving a quick look over at Obie, who nodded back subtly. "Well, we've got work to do. Are you ready to get in the water?"

"Ready," Jennifer replied, making a last check on an underwater camera to document anything they found in the warehouse that might help her case and show some mis-management or wrongful conduct on the case of the construction workers. Jennifer and Colin sat on the edge of the Cobia, and with a final 'goodbye and good luck' from Obie, they fell backwards into the sea.

Jennifer had been on several night dives, but this one was unusually tense. Secret recon mission aside, Obie had given a warning before they left that the locals considered the waters off Devil's Point to be dangerously infested with sharks – hammerhead sharks to be precise. Jennifer had seen many sharks in the water diving before and knew to stay calm. However, it was not easy. Obie was right. Dozens of hammerhead sharks cruised silently through the waters, some of them large enough to be truly menacing. Jennifer guessed the largest might be fourteen feet long or more. Colin didn't seem phased at all. It wouldn't have surprised Jennifer to learn he picked the dive route in from Devil's Point through the area known to be the most precariously inhabited by man-eating sharks to ensure they didn't encounter anybody else on their swim to the warehouse.

The light rays from the rising moon began to illuminate the white, sandy floor of the bay. Coral heads shimmered, and smaller fish flitted by like neon streaks in the crystal clear water. Colin and Jennifer stayed low to the seabed. From the surface, to anyone who might have been looking, they would be difficult to detect. An occasional rise of bubbles from their oxygen tanks erupted quietly on the surface, but in the dark of the evening, they were very stealthy. It took about twenty minutes of constant swimming to reach the construction area in Abraham's Bay, and their first setback. Even though night continued to fall and the skies above grew darker, the water grew continually lighter the closer they got to their destination.

Soon Jennifer could see that underwater lights had been emplaced around the bay along the construction port. Li's mega yacht was also outfitted with underwater lighting, which drew schools of fish towards it. From behind her mask, Jennifer looked over at Colin. He nodded as if to say 'I see it too' and then indicated with his hand that they could keep going, moving closer to the coral formations near shore. They were in shallow water now, just a few feet deep in some locations. It was a more dangerous route, since they could be spotted more easily. But with the bright light in the deeper water emanating from the mega yacht, Jennifer had to agree that Colin was taking the best course.

They closed in on the warehouse site, which was unfortunately also lit as bright as day. Despite the danger of being spotted, Colin continued their mission. As he pointed out various areas of interest, Jennifer took photos. Soon they were within a hundred feet of their objective. To Jennifer's shock, when viewed from under water, it was obviously not a warehouse at all, but some kind of covered docking facility. The dredged channel, about forty feet deep and nearly one hundred feet wide, ran from the break in the reef directly to the warehouse entrance. A huge set of doors on a guiderail system could be pushed aside to allow access into the docking facility for even the largest ship. A set of markers had been emplaced, enabling ease of navigation into the docking facility.

Colin led the way along the sandy floor of the dredged channel to the doors. He pulled on the doors, but they were secure and didn't budge. He pulled out his spear gun, aimed it at the door where it ran along its track, and fired. The spear lodged into the rail. Colin pushed, pulled and pried, but still nothing moved.

As Colin struggled with the spear, Jennifer took a full set of photos of the entire underwater complex. She looked at her dive computer. They had been underwater much longer than planned. Colin began leading them back towards Devil's Point now that they had gathered as much information as possible from this reconnaissance mission.

Suddenly, Jennifer heard the sound of rushing water. Looking back towards the construction site, she saw three jet skis skimming towards them. Colin noticed too, and motioned frantically for her to follow him towards the shore, leaving the spear from his gun still wedged in the door track.

Swimming as fast as possible, they made it to a narrow stretch of beach. But they were only half-way back to Devil's Point, and the three jet skis must have spotted them. The lead jet ski made a sharp right turn towards the beach, kicking up a mist of water against the night sky, and gunning the engine of his craft as he headed directly for them. The other two jet skis followed close behind. Knowing they only had a few moments, Jennifer ripped off her fins and mask and ran up the beach. Colin did the same and ran at her side.

With clearer vision, now that she wasn't looking through a diver's mask, she could see the three men on the jet skis were carrying machine guns. Her blood went cold. Colin seemed to have a route in mind, so she followed him through a thicket of tall beach grass the locals called 'baycaner' grass, and into a small thatch palm grove.

"We'll never lose them," Colin said coldly as he turned and looked back at the beach. Jennifer did not reply, but it seemed like he was right. The other two men had now beached their jet skis, and all three were running towards them at full speed. Shots rang out and branches of the thatch palms began to fall as bullets severed them from the trees in the grove. Running further inland, Jennifer and Colin barged their way through thick underbrush until the route was blocked by a wide, marshy, salt pond. A large driftwood tree trunk lay at the edge of the salt pond. Colin and Jennifer jumped behind it, sitting quietly for a moment, well-hidden in the dark.

"We have to split up. I'll draw them away back towards Abraham's Bay. You take the camera and head west to Devil's Point and find Obie," Colin said, breathing hard from the sprint.

"Why are they shooting at us for looking at a warehouse?" Jennifer asked.

"To protect the same secret that could be compromised by the text files on your smart phone," Colin whispered.

Jennifer looked at him, still puzzled. "Why should Mr. Li care about that file anymore? They've stolen all the information they need about the MICAL Formation from Michelson."

"Not exactly. The text from your father mentioned the phrase '09/7.' That's the model of a brand new, next generation submarine being built by the Chinese navy. While you were at your meeting in Wuhan, I went to a shipyard there and saw one almost completed in a dry dock."

"So what does that have to do with my father and this island?" Jennifer asked, momentarily putting aside her surprise at Colin's confession about his whereabouts in China.

"That 'warehouse' we just photographed wasn't a warehouse at all. I think it is a docking facility being built to hide one of their new submarines. I think your father had figured that out," Colin whispered, peering over the driftwood to see if the three men were nearby. All was still and silent on the salt pond. "Get back to Obie with the camera. Tell him what I just told you. He'll know what to do."

"What do you mean 'he'll know what to do'? Obie is a construction worker. I thought you've been helping me to save your construction company, right?" Jennifer fumed at Colin with biting sarcasm as she pieced together Colin's true occupation.

"Look, I've been working undercover here for months. I've staked a lot on getting to the bottom of this. Obie has been working with me for a long time," Colin explained.

"What you really mean is you've been spying on my father for months!" Jennifer retorted angrily, and a bit too loud, forgetting their precarious position in her anger.

"This is no time to argue and I don't have time to explain the whole situation," Colin hissed.

No sooner had he finished, than the underbrush off to their left cracked and rustled as the three men blundered through the scrub searching for them. It looked like Colin was right. If they didn't split up, they were sure to both get caught. But separately, at least one of them might escape.

"Follow the salt pond to the west until it ends, then turn towards the beach and follow the shoreline until you reach Obie. Go - now!" Colin whispered.

Before she could protest, he got up and sprinted to the east, towards the bay. As he did, he let out a deliberate yell, as though he had been jabbed by a branch. She saw the shadows of the three men freeze, then rush towards Colin. Realizing he had let out that yell to create the diversion for her, she ran as quickly and as quietly as she could towards the west. The salt pond ended after a few hundred yards at the foot of a small rise. Stopping momentarily, she looked back along the edge of the pond.

To her horror, she saw Colin kneeling in the mud at the eastern edge of the pond, with his hands on his head. The three men had their machine guns trained on him. She thought they might shoot him right there, but instead, two of the men pulled him to his feet and roughly handcuffed him. They began dragging him back towards the beach. Jennifer wanted to help, but she knew one unarmed person against three heavily armed guards was useless. Turning slowly to the west, her heart filled with worry for Colin, she headed to find Obie at Devil's Point.

Chapter 33

Obie stood on the deck of the Cobia as it rocked gently in the calm, evening waves off Devil's Point. This whole day had been unsettling. Despite the aura of island-time lackadaisicalness that Obie spun into an effective cover, he was a meticulous, precise operator. He'd been working with Colin Steele now for a few years, and had grown accustomed to Colin's sporadic, unpredictable methods, but that didn't make it any easier for Obie to work with him. Today was a perfect example. Colin disappeared off the face of the earth for days without a word to Obie, then calls up out of the blue, needing help. And, since they were unable to coordinate anything in private, Obie was forced to bumble along, loosely adhering to his cover in front of Jennifer, unsure of how much she knew, and what information Colin had shared with her. It really irked him, but he didn't let it show. He was just too professional.

His phone chimed with a text message. Obie read the message and sighed to himself. A huge ceremony was just announced for the very next day, to be held in Abraham's Bay. The MICAL secession vote had gone before Parliament that very afternoon while they were out pretending to fish in the middle of the Caicos Passage. The Prime Minister of The Bahamas, the Governor General, and of course, Member of Parliament Carty Wallingford-Rolle were all coming to the island. The official signing of the Grant of Independence was to happen right there on the beach. Carty was widely expected also to be voted in as the very first Prime Minister of the newly independent country in a public election held immediately following the signing ceremony.

As the entire Mayaguana National Police Force was just five officers, the Bahamian Defense Force had been called upon to provide security for the event. Obie couldn't help but feel it wouldn't be the last time the BDF would have to help police this new country.

Even though he was on this undercover assignment, the concluding order of the long text message he had just received from Commissioner Crawford told him to be prepared to head up the security operation. He had a long list of things to get done in a very short amount of time. If things took a long time to get done in Nassau, on remote, little islands like Mayaguana...well, it would take a miracle for him to be ready in time for the ceremony.

Obie put his phone down after reading the message from Commissioner Crawford, and turned on the AM radio on the Cobia's dashboard. He tuned in the national radio station, ZNS, which was the only radio station he could get, and listened to an evening political talk show. The subject of the show, of course, was the MICAL independence ceremony.

Obie sat sketching his plans for tomorrow, when suddenly he heard a splash in the water near the beach over the sound of the waves against the iron shore off Devil's Point. He put his notepad down on his lap, glancing toward shore. If the splash had been a fish, he thought it might jump again, and he'd throw his line out for some night fishing. There was something large moving in the water. Obie strained his eyes against the darkness to make out what it was. After a few seconds, there could be no doubt that it was not a fish: it was a person.

Without taking his eyes off the swimmer making its way towards his boat, he quietly and slowly reached for the spear gun on the bench next to him. He positioned himself to be blocked from view of the swimmer and trained the spear gun on his target. The swimmer approached, and Obie could tell that although swimming quietly, the swimmer was moving quickly towards the Cobia. Suddenly, a ray of moonlight caught the water, and what Obie saw made him both surprised and worried. It was Jennifer Bullfinch. She didn't have any diving gear and she was alone. Obie knew in that instant that something had gone terribly wrong on the night dive recon to the warehouse. He set the spear gun down and went to the side of the boat to give Jennifer a hand out of the water.

"Miss Bullfinch! Where's Colin?" Obie asked, helping her sit down on the bench and handing her a towel. She looked worried and had cuts and scratches over her face and body.

"I don't know where he is now, but he's been captured by the workers from the warehouse," she answered, with a concerned look on her face and a confused, exasperated tone in her voice.

"What do you mean by 'captured'?" Obie asked, fearing Colin was in even more danger than Jennifer might think.

"I mean, he was taken away at gunpoint by three men who came at us on jet skis!" Jennifer cried out.

Obie didn't reply, but looked down at the notebook on which he had been sketching tomorrow's security plan. This was a serious and unexpected setback. The contingent on the island was becoming bolder and more brazen now that their numbers had been reinforced. And with the formal signing of the Articles of Independence tomorrow, they were clearly determined not to let anything or anybody get in the way.

Obie had been keeping this island under surveillance with Colin for a long time now, and they had both voiced concerns about 'something' amiss. But, they had never been able to prove just what was going on, or the involvement of this group of Chinese. Since the big shots in the Bahamian Government had quietly been happy to let this burdensome group of nearly deserted islands go off on their own, any scant evidence of odd happenings went ignored.

He looked over at Jennifer, sizing her up, and what Colin had told her, what she knew already or had guessed on her own, and most importantly what he should risk sharing with her now. She looked up from the bench at him, and beat him to the punch.

"Obie, Colin told me that you and he were working together, and not as construction workers paving the runway. He said you were agents of some kind, and you had been spying on my father when he disappeared," she said quietly.

"We were," Obie answered quietly in return. He didn't let on his surprise at Jennifer's statement. But it did make things a little easier for him. If Colin had shared that information, even under duress, he must trust Jennifer, which, in Obie's experience in working with Colin, said a lot about her. It also cleared his conscious that he could start treating her like a part of the home team, rather than a suspect in the investigation.

"Well, I guess I can understand why after all this. Colin also told me to tell you what we found in Abraham's Bay. The warehouse at the edge of the shore is a covered docking facility. Colin suspected it will hide a new, secret submarine the Chinese Navy has developed. What do you think is really going on here?" she asked.

"We began our investigation here because there was a lot of suspicious activity - underwater activity. We figured it had to do with the reputed oil field your father, Professor Michelson and Carty Wallingford-Rolle had discovered," Obie answered honestly. "I don't know anything about the docking facility or any new submarine. But what I can tell you, is that tomorrow, the Prime Minister, your banker Mr. Li, and our esteemed colleague

Mr. Wallingford-Rolle himself will all be here on Mayaguana. Carty pushed through the independence vote in Parliament today, and the final documents are to be signed in Abraham's Bay tomorrow in a grand ceremony."

Jennifer stood up in surprise. "Carty must have wasted no time." She looked up at the sky over Abraham's Bay. The lights of the banker's mega yacht lit up the dark bay making the water around the yacht glow a bright turquoise blue. Aside from that bit of artificialness, only the stars and a crescent moon cast shadows along the coastline. Jennifer thought about Colin, and wondered what might be happening to him.

The quiet of the night sea was disturbed by a faint sound in the distance. Obie and Jennifer both heard it and fell silent trying to make out what it was. Soon the faint sound became the more distinct whirring and whining of a turbine engine. The chopping sound of blades beating the air became noticeable.

"It's that helicopter," Obie said, looking out to the horizon. Soon, the faint red and green position lights of an approaching helicopter were visible heading towards Mayaguana from Providenciales. "Look like some other VIP is arriving to Mr. Li's mega yacht."

"Or they called it back from Provo to take someone off the island!" Jennifer exclaimed.

"You mean Colin?" Obie concluded, sounding worried. "I figured those goons were just holding him for twenty-four hours so he couldn't cause any trouble during the big Independence Ceremony tomorrow. You think they'd airlift him off the island?"

"I don't think we can take the chance they might," Jennifer said. Her resolve had come back at the thought of letting Mr. Li and his henchmen whisk Colin away secretly in the night. Given that they had been attacked several times now, and that Colin was actually some kind of government agent, he could be in grave danger. She made up her mind what had to be done.

"Obie, I'm going back to rescue Colin. Right now, before something terrible happens to him or he's taken away in that helicopter and we never see him again," she said. She set the towel down on the bench and headed to the stowage hold to look for another set of diving gear.

"Miss Bullfinch, you are crazy. I'm going to have a full security detachment from the Bahamian Defense Force here in just a few hours to help with security for the ceremony tomorrow. They're on their cutter cruising this way now. They'll help us find Colin. Trying to do this on our own is pure foolishness!" Obie shook his head at her in disbelief.

"Obie, in a few hours Colin may be dead. I think these guys really mean business. You haven't been with us getting attacked by armed biker gangs and shot at in broad daylight in the middle of a city. But if you had, you would know we don't have a moment to lose. I was pretty shaken up when I got back on board, but I've recovered. And we need to act," Jennifer said, pulling another oxygen tank off the sidewall rack.

"Well just what are you planning to do?" Obie asked with raised eyebrows.

"Colin must have been taken back to the mega yacht. I'm certain that helicopter came back to land on the deck to whisk him out of here. I need to get to that yacht and find him," she said commandingly. It did occur to her as she said it, that she really had no idea how to pull this rescue mission off. But too late now. Time had run out for waiting and investigating.

"What are you going to do if you even find him on board?" Obie asked.

Jennifer didn't really know, so she said nothing. Obie waited for a few moments.

"Well, maybe I can at least make myself useful while you're out swimming. Did you get a good look at that warehouse before getting nabbed?' Obie asked.

"We didn't get inside, if that's what you're asking. But we got up close enough to learn a few things," Jennifer said pulling out the underwater digital camera. She turned on the camera, pulling up the photos for Obie. He whistled through his teeth in awe as he looked at the photos.

"You see – here's the channel dredged right up to the edge of this supposed warehouse from the cut in the reef," Jennifer showed Obie the first set of photos.

"I see. Clearly the priority is to bring vessels right up to the warehouse, or whatever it is," Obie reasoned.

"Exactly. Now look at this. Those are doors. Underwater doors that can slide to either side and open up the building so a ship could follow this channel from the reef and go right inside – actually inside! – the warehouse," Jennifer continued excitedly.

"And then no one would ever know what was going on with that ship. It would be hidden from sight inside this gigantic, covered seaport," Obie said.

"And here's even more of a puzzle. The channel is marked along the seabed - under water," Jennifer told Obie zooming in the digital photo to show a set of underwater markers indicating the dredged channel and the entrance to the covered seaport.

Obie rubbed his head for a moment, deep in thought. Then he picked up Colin's phone from the dashboard and tapped the photo file icon again.

"I think", he said slowly, "that I am starting to put two and two together here. I probably shouldn't show you this, but it seems the cat is out of the bag on my and Colin's true identities, and you seem to have been deputized. So here goes." He pulled up the photographs of the submarine being finished in dry dock in Wuhan, showing the phone to Jennifer

"Colin took these photos while you were in China yesterday. He never had a chance to explain them to me, but I can tell you, he has suspected for a while that the supposed warehouse was going to be a secret submarine base for the Chinese Navy, also known as the People's Liberation Army Navy, or PLAN," Obie explained.

"Just before he was captured, he told me he saw a new type of submarine being built by the PLAN. Those must be photos of what he found in the Wuhan shipyard," Jennifer said.

"It looks that way from the date time group on them. Now, this particular submarine is quite advanced for the Chinese. There have been rumors that it may have the ability to go undetected by your government's network of underwater sensors. That line of sensors runs right by our little island here. And Colin has suspected all along this new submarine might hop the fence so to speak, right here, and use Mayaguana as a quick hiding place," Obie explained.

"I guess that makes sense," Jennifer said, her head swimming a little with this new information. She was trying to reason out what role her father might have had in all this.

"Colin saw what he thought were submarine components shipped to the island hidden in among all of this heavy construction equipment and building materials. He thought the PLAN might be creating a small prepositioned stockpile of supplies, and using the warehouse to hide them. The Chinese contractors were also over-billing your father for these expensive works and materials, which Colin thought was on purpose to drive him to bankruptcy," Obie continued, flipping through the digital photos Colin had taken in Wuhan.

"Then he's in even more danger than I thought. He's not just interfering with the independence ceremony, but he knows things that could put a lot of people in precarious situations. I have to save him right now," Jennifer said, pulling on her oxygen tank and adjusting the regulator. Obie looked at her shaking his head.

"I think you're going to get yourselves both killed. By my rights as an agent of the Bahamian government, I can stop you. This is still my country, at least until tomorrow," Obie said, giving Jennifer a more serious look than she had seen from him.

"You wouldn't do that, would you?" Jennifer asked. She waited, and Obie paused for a moment, looking down at the photos on Colin's phone as if weighing his options.

"Colin's a pro. He certainly wouldn't expect us to put this intelligence at risk just to save him. But on the other hand, we both owe him a lot," Obie said looking at Jennifer. "You seem to think he's being held on Mr. Li's yacht. I need to make sure whatever is on this island can't put my Prime Minister at risk tomorrow. So I need to pick up where you and Colin got nabbed and take a close look at that warehouse…or whatever it is," Obie reasoned. He handed Jennifer her cell phone and a small waterproof sack.

"Put your phone in this and tuck it in your wetsuit. When you get to the boat and find Colin, text me, or call if you can. I'll try and figure out how to pick you two up with the Cobia," Obie said.

"Thanks, Obie. I'll be fine," Jennier said, trying to sound confident and tucking the phone in her wetsuit. Slipping on her fins, Jennifer backed to the edge of the Cobia. Sitting down on the side, she made a few last adjustments to her diving gear, and pulled the mask over her face.

Obie walked over to the side and handed her a small diving knife in a sheaf. She clipped it on her belt.

"Don't thank me. If you get caught, I'll deny I know anything about this," Obie said with a deadly serious tone.

Jennifer managed to give him 'thumbs up' and a weak smile from behind her mask. She leaned back over the edge of the boat rail and fell into the dark water.

Chapter 34

The dive from Devil's Point out to Li's mega yacht would be just about the same distance as her earlier trip to the warehouse, but heading out towards the reef, rather than inland towards the coast. Jennifer was more mindful of her surroundings this time. Without Colin's extra eyes, she was more alert to the potential of being spotted by guards. She was intently focused on her objective, barely noticing the sharks off Devil's Point. She figured being eaten by a shark was less of a threat than an unusually loud splash or a trail of bubbles bringing more of Li's henchmen her way.

As she approached the yacht, its underwater lighting began to cast noticeable shadows from Jennifer's movement through the water. She was certain she would be spotted approaching if she just swam directly for the aft diving deck where she planned to sneak aboard. Off to her right lie the MICAL barrier reef. It was the only cover Jennifer could use to hide her approach to the yacht.

She began making her way among the coral heads towards the cut in the reef and the mega yacht anchorage. While the reef may have kept boats protected, for a lone diver, it was a precarious situation. Strong currents, the occasional swell, debris, and schools of night feeding fish made for a difficult swim. More than one time, Jennifer was nearly swept into the coral by a strong current. In one particularly scary incident, her fin became caught in a rocky outcrop of a 'swim-through.' These holes in the coral reef were large enough for a diver to 'swim through', had been attractive waypoints for Jennifer. They gave her an opportunity to mask her route, should anyone be tracking her. It took her several minutes, and a lot of wasted air, to work herself free with the knife Obie had given her. Her heart was pounding by the time she finally reached a coral head a short swim from the mega yacht.

Jennifer peered out, imagining herself like an octopus hiding amongst the coral, to observe any activity around the yacht. It was nearly dawn. All was quiet near the boat and around the entire bay. She watched for several minutes, with not a soul in sight. Her oxygen was running out, and it would be getting light soon. She had to make her move or it would be too late. She kicked furiously to swim the final leg across the open, brightly lit waters between her hiding place at the reef and the mega yacht's aft diving platform.

Jennifer found a small ladder. Grabbing hold, she quietly pulled herself on the platform. The aft deck of the yacht was a teak planked platform right at water level, about ten feet long spanning the back of the boat. Nearby, was another ladder about six feet long, leading up to the main deck of the mega yacht. Sitting on the edge of the platform, Jennifer hurriedly pulled off her tank, mask, fins and belt. There was a small 'Zodiac' boat resting on the platform off to the side. The Zodiac was a simple raft made out of two long, rubber, tubes with a small but powerful looking engine mounted to it.

'Finally some good luck,' Jennifer thought, noting what a perfect get-away boat that Zodiac would make. After stowing her diving gear inside the Zodiac, she climbed cautiously up the first few rungs of the ladder leading to the main deck. The coast was clear, and she continued up on to the deck. Walking very softly thanks to the soft rubber soled diving socks that covered her feet, she crept across the deck.

She had three choices: the deck to the port side of the boat facing land, the deck towards the starboard side facing the barrier reef, or the center door. The center door was an etched glass masterpiece leading into what appeared to be a luxurious lounge. She doubted Colin would be sitting comfortably on a sofa in the lounge. She didn't feel comfortable with the port side either, which might leave her exposed to guards patrolling the shore. That left the starboard side. Her mind made up, she walked quickly past the lounge chairs lined up along the deck of the yacht and down the side deck towards the bow.

After walking thirty paces past several large windows with elegant wood trim and another etched glass double door, she found what she was looking for: a utilitarian, metal door. It was oval with a plain, latch handle, and sat up off the deck a few inches so it could be sealed watertight. This looked like the kind of door that would lead to an engine room or control room in the underbelly of the yacht.

"Another stroke of good luck," Jennifer thought. "I'm on a roll – let's keep going!"

She pulled down on the latch door handle, pushing the door inward. It swung slowly open, revealing a stairwell along a bulkhead leading down into the hull of the ship. The stairwell was painted a dull, battleship grey, with black friction pads on the stairs to prevent slipping. The lighting on the bulkhead illuminated from thick glass globes covered with metal bars. At the bottom of the stairwell was another bulkhead compartment door similar to the one she had just walked through. Jennifer made her way quietly down the stairs and listened at the door. She heard the sounds of an engine and what sounded like a VHF radio transmission. Jennifer crossed her fingers, and opened the door. There at the other end of a small operations center, sitting on the floor and tied to the legs of a map table built into the yacht bulkhead, was none other than Colin Steele.

Forgetting the dangerous situation, Jennifer dashed into the room and over to Colin. A ripped cloth tied around his head gagged his mouth. She untied the cloth and threw it on the floor. Without thinking about it, Jennifer kissed Colin hard on the lips. After a moment, realizing what she was doing in the excitement of the moment, she pulled away from him. They gazed into each other's eyes and Jennifer sat back on her knees. Colin looked longingly at her for a moment, but the look faded from his face and was replaced by his typical, smirking smile. The longing smile on Jennifer's face faded, too. Now that the relief of seeing Colin was still alive had passed, she was furiously angry with him. She slapped him across the face on his right cheek and frowned at him.

"Why didn't you tell me you are some kind of spy? And, that you were spying on my father…with Obie…for months!" she demanded.

"Are you seriously asking me that now of all times?" he said incredulously.

"Well you can't go anywhere until I untie you, so maybe you should think about giving me a good answer before I change my mind and leave you here," she said, only half joking.

"I really couldn't tell you, or anybody for that matter. If you haven't figured this out by now, we are into something much bigger than your father's real estate project. This is a matter of national security," Colin said hurriedly.

"Not good enough…" Jennifer replied deadpan. "Maybe if you had trusted me, we could have figured this out quicker. Now I'm never going to find out what happened to my father. You're not going to be able to stop the independence of MICAL, or the occupation shortly thereafter by some kind of Chinese naval contingent."

"I don't think we could have stopped anything, but that's not really important right now. Untie me and let's get out of here!" Colin hissed at her in exasperation.

"Fine!" she hissed back, beginning to cut away at the ropes around his arms. "There's no way they know that I am here. It's completely quiet above deck, almost like this yacht is deserted."

"It's not deserted, and it has some of the most high tech surveillance systems in the world. If it will help hurry you up, they do know you are onboard," Colin said, with the odd, smart aleck tone he seemed to naturally adopt just to drive her insane.

"And how do you know that?" Jennifer asked, getting one rope cut away and starting on the next.

"Two ways. First, this room is the control center for the security operation, and I could see and hear you myself on the closed circuit camera monitors behind you," Colin answered as Jennifer gave him a 'give me a break' look trying to cut away the final rope.

"And second, Ms. Bullfinch, is that I am standing right behind you," an Asian accented, vaguely familiar voice chimed in amusedly.

Jennifer froze and glanced in Colin's eyes just as she cut through the last rope binding his arms. Colin closed his eyes for a moment and shook his head ever so slightly as if to say 'not again'. Jennifer slowly turned around to see Mr. Li standing in the bulkhead doorway. His two henchmen that had met them at the airport in Wuhan stood behind him quietly laughing at her.

"It's so nice to see you again, and in the gorgeous Caribbean setting, this time," he continued in his amused, faux politeness. "I have to admit, I did not expect we would meet again, and certainly not so soon. But you can believe me when I say that I do intend to fully take advantage of the fact that you are here." He nodded to his henchmen, who rushed in the control room, grabbing Jennifer roughly. With another nod from Li, one of the henchmen tied Jennifer and Colin with a thick chain to the same map table leg from which Colin had just been freed. The henchmen produced a small, bronze, padlock and snapped it closed around the ends of the chain link. Stepping back, he admired his work with a vicious sneer.

Jennifer was red with fury. How could she have been so naïve to be caught like this? Of course, there had been cameras and microphones, probably even on the outside of the yacht under the water. They had let her think the coast was clear to trap her and she had fallen for it completely. She was angry and disappointed with herself. Clearly, Li had plans for her, but what those might be, she shuddered to think.

Li walked further into the small command center, and leaned casually against a computer console with some keyboards built into it and the wall of flat panel screens displaying the myriad of surveillance cameras from around the yacht. As in his offices in Wuhan, Li was dressed impeccably, in a bespoke, dark, pin-stripe three piece suit, finishing off the look with what appeared to Jennifer to be his signature, anchor print Salvatore Ferragamo tie. He looked down at Jennifer with a sadistic smile.

"Ms. Bullfinch, your father sent you something. Something of great importance to me, but of little consequence to you, especially now, in light of your current situation. It was a data file he sent to your mobile phone number," Li announced.

"I have no idea what you're talking about. If you know so much about me, then you'll know that my father and I have had somewhat of an estranged relationship over the past few years,"

273

Jennifer bluffed, hoping she could stall long enough for her or Colin to come up with some kind of escape. The file her father sent was her only bargaining chip, and she was not going to just give it up yet, even chained to a desk in the hold of a ship.

"Ms. Bullfinch, do not lie to me. The message was sent to your phone. We know you at least opened the file. I sincerely doubt you would have deleted the message, given the potential significance to your company's future," Mr. Li answered, still smiling at her, but lowering his voice to a quiet coldness.

Jennifer steeled her resolve, closing her eyes as if to tell Li, without having to actually say it, that she would never surrender the file. Suddenly, her head snapped violently to one side. Her vision went blurry, as she slowly opened her eyes and tried to focus. Before she recovered or could see clearly, her head snapped violently again to the other side. Li's henchman – the one who seemed to be his personal assistant with a California accent - had smacked her twice, stepping away at a snap of Li's fingers. Her head fell to her chest and she went unconscious. For how long she was out, Jennifer couldn't tell. Revived with a splash of cold salt water against her face, she came to.

"Tell me where the phone is now, so I can get my file," Mr. Li ordered again in his quiet, evil intonation. "Then all this unpleasantness can end and you can be on your way."

Determined though she was, Jennifer felt close to giving in. She suspected what Li really meant by 'on her way' would be over the edge of the yacht in chains to drown in the ocean. That assumption kept her from talking…yet. She hoped if she could hold out just a little longer Li might reveal what had happened to her father. Then she would give him the phone. Thankfully, Colin spoke up, buying her some relief.

"She doesn't have it any more! I knew there was something important on that phone, so I took it from her. She just never realized it," he said, clearly worried what might happen if this interrogation continued. Jennifer tried to nod in agreement to play along, but her head was still swimming in pain. Mr. Li shifted his icy gaze from Jennifer to Colin, and seemed to give this prospect thought for a moment.

"Most chivalrous of you, Agent Steele, but somehow I doubt your story. And in any case, it doesn't matter. If one of you doesn't tell me where I can find my data file, it is going to be most unpleasant for you both," Li announced. He paced about the room for a moment with his hands clasped behind his back, as if taking a thoughtful, quiet stroll in the park.

"But fortunately, Agent Steele, I believe there is someone else who may have a more compelling effect on our dear Ms. Bullfinch's willingness to cooperate," Li said, looking towards the bulkhead door. As if on cue, the scuffle of footsteps could be heard coming down the stairs. Three figures emerged through the open door of the bulkhead: the two henchmen flanking either side of a third person they were dragging with them. Jennifer's vision was still a little blurry, but she strained to look at this new arrival.

It was a man whose head hung against his chest, his face turned from her view. He was well dressed in a three piece suit. He had grey, thinning hair, and expensive leather shoes. The shoes caught her attention, because they were very familiar. The henchmen abruptly threw the man against the computer console where just a moment ago Mr. Li had been leaning so casually. The elderly man barely seemed able to catch himself against the console, sliding slowly to the ground, as if semi-conscious. The shorter of the two henchmen walked over to the prostrate man, grabbed his head and held it up for Jennifer to see clearly: it was B.W.

"B.W.! Are you OK?" Jennifer cried out. She was snapped from her groggy, semi-conscious state by the horror of this new development and was now fully alert. B.W. held his head with both hands as if traumatized by a severe beating. He seemed to be heaving a bit, as though he might be crying from the pain and confusion. He didn't answer her, but just slowly shook his head 'no' as he moaned softly.

"So, as you can see, Ms. Bullfinch, I am done playing games with you and Agent Steele," Li announced, a hint of anticipated triumph in his voice. From inside his impeccable suit coat, he produced a small, black, semi-automatic handgun. Flipping off the safety with one finger, he pushed the barrel of the handgun into the back of B.W.'s head.

"Now, as they say, I am going to count three. Tell me where your phone with my data file is or your surrogate grandfather will suffer the ultimate consequences of your stubbornness. One...two..." Li began his count down.

"Jennifer, for god's sake, give him what he wants!" B.W. pleaded from behind his heaving sobs.

Jennifer opened her mouth to tell the banker the phone was in her wet suit pocket. It was one thing to never find out what happened to her father, and give up the last bastions of his business empire, but she could not continue to put B.W. in harm's way. Before she could speak, she heard Colin calmly speak up from behind her.

"Just so you know, B.W. has been working with Li and his bank all along. I don't think Li would really pull that trigger," he said.

Jennifer could actually hear him smirking even though they were chained back-to-back. If there was one thing Jennifer could count on Colin for, it was making her furious at exactly the wrong moment.

"What are you talking about?" she cried at him.

"He's in on this whole thing...I'm just telling you..." Colin said with an 'I know you don't believe me, but you should' tone. Before he could finish his thought, the back of his head banged abruptly and painfully into hers as one of the henchmen hit Colin with a sharp uppercut on the chin.

"Jennifer...Jennifer...just give these terrible people what they want so we can go home. I just want to go home and rest," B.W. moaned. He let out a particularly pathetic wail as Li pressed the barrel of his handgun harder into B.W.'s head.

"Three," announced Li, cutting through the conversation. With his thumb, he pulled the hammer of the handgun back. The metallic click echoed loudly against the bare walls of the small operations center. "Ms. Bullfinch, your time is up...pity."

"STOP! Please! Don't shoot!" Jennifer cried out. Li held the gun steady at B.W.'s head, turning to look at Jennifer.

"You win, Mr. Li," Jennifer said quietly, with tears welling up in her eyes. "All I wanted to do was find out what happened to my father. But B.W. might be all I have left of family. I won't let you hurt him anymore."

A severe smile broke out on Li's face. He slowly pushed the hammer on his handgun forward and let up the pressure of the barrel on B.W.'s head, but keeping the gun trained on him. "I thought you would be reasonable, Ms. Bullfinch. Now, my file," he said to her approvingly.

"I have it here. My phone with the text file my father sent is in this pouch," she nodded her head down towards the diving belt to indicate where she had tucked the phone in its waterproof bag.

Mr. Li snapped his fingers at the taller henchman, who quickly ripped the belt off Jennifer. The henchman unzipped the pouch, pulling out the waterproof bag to reveal Jennifer's mobile phone. He handed the phone to Mr. Li.

Li held up the phone with a satisfied smile. He tapped the screen a few times, and then looked at it intently for several long seconds, presumably reviewing the data file to ensure this was indeed the information he needed. Convinced he was now in possession of the genuine article, he locked the phone and tucked it neatly in his suit coat pocket.

"It has been a pleasure doing business with you, Ms. Bullfinch. Now, as much as I have enjoyed your company, I must get back to work," the banker announced happily as he re-engaged the safety on his handgun and placed it back in the vest holster inside his jacket. He stepped back from the console and helped B.W. stand up and neaten his rumpled suit. "We have much to accomplish today, do we not, *Myan-bow-shi-fu*?"

"Indeed we do, Li Hong. This will be a triumphant day," B.W. said, a broad smile on his face as he patted Li on the back in a congratulatory manner. He twisted his head around and rubbed his neck briefly as if to unwind from the uncomfortable position he had been assuming for the past few minutes, then neatened his tie. He looked down at Jennifer. "And you, my dear, should have listened to your new boyfriend."

Looking up at B.W., tears streaming down her face, Jennifer could only shake her head at him in disbelief. A thousand thoughts and questions were racing through her mind, but she could only manage to ask, "Why?"

"WHY?" B.W. spat with anger. "You of all people need to ask 'why'? I guess even with your fancy education you're still just a stupid child. Let me put it to you simply, then. For years, most of my life, I've worked for your father. It may have been his company, but without me, he'd be nothing. Just another dumb, country, red-neck trying to make a dime in a hard world. I protected him. I kept him out of trouble, got him the connections he needed."

B.W. began pacing about the small operations center angrily, getting louder and more angry with every word. "And while I sweated away, he squirreled away all the profit - for himself. And then…then he decided to launch his 'secret' plans using every single penny I'd ever earned for him to develop this worthless patch of sand into an oil well."

Jennifer sat listening to B.W. She wanted to protest, to tell him he was wrong, but she was so mad and confused she couldn't even speak. B.W. paced about the room growing more agitated.

"He jettisoned me. In favor of those two other morons – Wallingford-Rolle and Michelson - who by dumb luck stumbled onto something as teenagers. Well, if he thought I was going to stand for that, your father had another thing coming. And I'll tell you something, sweetheart, he jettisoned you, too. His own daughter," B.W. said, lowering his voice and slowing his rant for a moment to look Jennifer in the eye. She said nothing, and looked away, so he continued.

"Well, it just so happens I have a few secrets of my own, and some very powerful connections your dear father never knew about. It seemed like the right time to put those to use. So now, with the assistance of my old friend Li Hong here, I'm about to set this right," B.W. looked over at Li and smiled. "And I believe with this file in our hands, we can finally execute our plans to take

279

control of this island, the MICAL Formation oil field, and much more. Is that not correct, Li Hong?"

"Correct indeed. Dominique came through as usual. She was able to transmit the remaining sensor locations from the professor's data readings from his boat in Providenciales."

B.W. regained his composure. He turned to Li Hong. "Perfect. Let's get going then. I believe you need to load the transponder codes from Ms. Bullfinch's phone in the system before we can be fully operational. No time to waste." He motioned to the henchmen to head upstairs. He and Li turned to follow them above deck. Just as B.W. stepped through the bulkhead doorway, he turned and looked back at Jennifer.

"Oh, my dear, I suppose you're wondering what's going to happen to you. Well, let me tell you. We're not going to risk anything drastic until the nice Independence Ceremony is over and the crowd of witnesses, or...dignitaries, have left the island. After that, I'm afraid you and Agent Steele will be finding yourselves a new set of friends. The hammerhead sharks out in the reef are looking forward to getting to know you much better," B.W. chuckled to himself, slamming the door shut as he went up the stairs.

Chapter 35

Jennifer and Colin sat in stunned silence, chained together in the small, bare operations center in the hull of Li's mega yacht. Jennifer wasn't sure what to do next. The idea that B.W., whom she considered family, had been undermining her father for years in a quiet, jealous rage was simply unfathomable. Straining for a moment against the chains, she tried to look up at the wall of monitors nearby displaying the yachts closed circuit camera surveillance system. The exterior cameras views told her the sun had risen. Soon, the dignitaries from around The Bahamas would arrive to sign the Mayaguana Articles of Independence. Looking up at the highest screen, she recoiled as a sharp pain pricked her head. One of those darn bobby pins she was always losing in her hair was caught between her head and Colin's.

"Ouch," he exclaimed. "No need to make the pain worse," he tried a weak joke to break the somber mood.

"Sorry, I was looking up at those cameras. We have to do something. We're running out of time to stop the Independence Ceremony."

"I admire your ambition, Jennifer. I have since the day we met. But I think we're out of the game. The ceremony is in just a few hours. I don't see how we can stop it now," Colin said, sounding unusually negative.

"We have to find a way. I'm not giving up," Jennifer said, gritting her teeth. The shock of betrayal by B.W. was turning to anger and a desire to stop his plans at all costs. She owed it to her father, and to herself.

"Do you know what was on that file that we just gave to Li?" Colin asked, implying he did. Jennifer didn't answer, so he continued.

"Secret codes. Codes to underwater transponders that United States Navy submarines use to identify themselves as friendly," Colin explained.

"Obie mentioned something about this when I found him after you were captured last night," Jennifer reasoned back to him. "He said that it was like an underwater invisible fence line, and that the line went close by this island."

"That's exactly right. It's actually a very old system called the Sound Surveillance System, or SOSUS, that's been around since World War II. When submarines without the proper transponder code cross the line of sonar sensors, the US Navy is alerted there are potential enemy submarines prowling around US waters. They know where the submarine crossed into US waters, hunt it down, and find out what it's doing," Colin continued. "If the Chinese Navy wants to operate secretly off the coast of the United States, using these codes, they could cross the fence line, and not trigger any alarm bells. Crossing the line of sensors would then allow them to hide, lay low, so to speak, in Abraham's Bay."

"And if they docked the submarine in the covered warehouse, then even satellites couldn't locate it!" Jennifer followed his thinking.

"Exactly. It's a new twist on an old trick. The Germans tried the same thing right after the US established the SOSUS. They found a wealthy Nazi sympathizer who happened to own another Bahamian island with a nice bay, a lot like Abraham's Bay. He let them hide a submarine just inside the SOSUS detection line. That sub did a lot of damage until an informant told the US Navy what was going on and they launched a seek-and-destroy mission to take it out."

"Wow. Was that on another remote island like Mayaguana?" Jennifer said.

"No, actually, the German sub was hidden in what is now one of the most popular marina's in the world – Hurricane Hole on Paradise Island!" Colin said, his mood lifting a bit in telling the story. "Mr. Li has the same idea for Abraham's Bay, and he knows the location of every sensor in this area thanks to Michelson's detailed readings of every rock and coral head under the ocean for a few hundred miles around the MICAL Formation. With the data file off your phone, they will look like a US submarine when interrogated by the sensors they can't avoid," Colin explained.

"What does an investment banker want to do with all this? Li and his China Global Development Bank are all about money and investments. What do they care about undersea warfare?" Jennifer asked.

"In China, the military funds a lot of its own operations by running businesses, so a general or an admiral may be conducting a battle one day, and heading into an investor conference as a CEO the next. Not that long ago, military-fronted companies dominated a lot of the shadier businesses in China like prostitution and gambling. But recently, they've moved into more sophisticated industries like banking and manufacturing," Colin said.

"I had no idea. So you think the China Global Development Bank is actually run by the military?" Jennifer asked.

"Yes, and I'm certain that Li Hong is actually an admiral in the PLAN, and he presides over a multi-billion dollar military-industrial and financial empire. He is also the head of the Wuchang Shipyard, in Wuhan not far from the headquarters building of the China Global Development Bank where you met with him. That shipyard is building a highly advanced, next generation submarine. I think they intend to refit here at Mayaguana," Colin said, excitement and energy beginning to creep back into his voice. "But after talking to my contacts, I think the situation may be even worse."

"Worse? Really?" Jennifer asked incredulously.

"Over all of the months I have been learning about Li's plans for his submarine base on Mayaguana, something just didn't fit. The Chinese government has been investing billions of dollars in the Caribbean, and at first, I thought this was just another of their state-run investment strategies to keep a steady supply of natural resources for their economy. But Mayaguana didn't fit the mold. Everywhere else, the government was much more transparent. Jamaica, Trinidad, and even other places in The Bahamas, there were diplomats and dignitaries and lots of photo ops. But the work on Mayaguana was completely off the radar. And once we figured out the construction might be for military purposes, then things really made no sense. The PLAN would never support such brazen actions like the activity on this island. What Li is doing will clearly provoke the United States and maybe even start a war. It appears that Beijing knows nothing about Li's operations here. He's gone rogue."

"That settles it. We have to find a way out of here and stop that Ceremony!" Jennifer exclaimed. "There's too much on the line to just sit here and do nothing."

"Not to mention if we're still here when B.W. comes back, we're shark bait," Colin laughed, signaling to Jennifer he was recovering his spirits.

Jennifer pulled against the chains binding their arms to the desk, there was no play, and she didn't see any way possible to slip free. The padlock was secured tightly.

"There's no way I can slip free. The chains are too tight. What can we do?" she asked, hoping he had an idea.

"Well, this padlock...I wonder," Colin said as if reasoning aloud. He angled one wrist, holding the lock in place with his right hand, and pulling at it with his left. "If only I had something metal. I can reach the tumbler of this padlock just barely, and I'm usually pretty good at picking a lock."

"Yes, I remember," smiled Jennifer thinking of how smoothly Colin had picked the lock on the door to Michelson's apartment in Austin. "Wait a minute! I've got something!"

"Really? What is it?"

"A bobby pin!" Jennifer exclaimed, remembering the stray pin that had just stuck her in the head.

"That just might work. Where is it? Can you get it into my hand?" Colin asked.

Jennifer gently pressed her head back against Colin. She could feel the pin on the left side of her head. She rubbed her head up and down to see if the pin moved. She could feel the bobby pin work its way lower down the strands of her hair.

"If I can work it loose, it should drop to the floor near our hands. Be ready to grab it," she said with a hopeful tone. Moving her head up and down, and back and forth, the pin finally dropped to the floor.

Colin edged himself over a few inches, straining against the chains and the desk leg. Out of the corner of her eye, Jennifer could see his fingers clawing for the pin. Finally, with the middle finger of his hand, he got some traction on the pin, sliding it closer to him. She could feel him pick up the pin between his middle finger and thumb.

"Got it!" he announced victoriously. He began to wriggle his hands as he worked on the bronze padlock. Jennifer held her breath, letting him concentrate. After what seemed like a very long time, she heard the lock snap open. Colin pulled his arm up, the chains sliding to the floor. They were free.

Chapter 36

Jennifer and Colin carefully eased open the stairwell door and were met with a breath of fresh ocean breeze and the rays of the morning sun. They paused, holding their collective breath, and anticipating a guard might slam the door shut on them and raise an alarm. But only the sounds of the waves crashing against the nearby reef and gulls calling to one another as they hunted among the coral could be heard. Colin pushed the door further open and Jennifer peaked around the corner. She nodded with her head towards the aft deck where she had left her diving gear stashed in the Zodiac boat. Looking both ways up and down the promenade, seeing no one in sight, they quietly made their way towards the Zodiac.

The droning hum of a propeller sounded in the distance. It grew louder and after a few moments overpowered the quiet, morning calm of the bay. Jennifer looked up to see a Britten-Norman Islander flying over the mega yacht at a low level. The Islander banked to the right and began its final decent to land on the unfinished airstrip just beyond the ridgeline that had protected the old US air base.

"That's the Prime Minister's island hopper," Colin said as the plane descended out of sight below the ridgeline.

"We don't have much time, then," Jennifer said, walking over to the diving platform, and hopping down onto it. She untied the rope that tethered the Zodiac to the yacht as Colin made a quick survey of the growing crowd on shore around the government dock.

"There's a lot of activity going on out there. Looks like everyone is scrambling to get ready for the ceremony. The Prime

Minister seems a little early," Colin said, shielding his eyes from the sun to get a better look at the shoreline.

"Perfect. People should be distracted when we take this Zodiac across the bay to the warehouse. I'm not giving up until the ink is dry on the Mayaguana Articles of Independence. If we can find even one more shred of evidence, it will be worth it," Jennifer said pulling the small boat into the water.

By this time, Colin knew better than to argue, so he hopped into the Zodiac and pulled the starter. The motor sputtered to life. There were a lot of small boats in bay, since many local fishermen had motored over to watch the ceremony, and no one seemed to notice them. They cruised across the bay directly towards the east side of the warehouse and a set of rough hewn stairs cut into the iron shore. Jennifer steered the Zodiac as Colin scanned the shoreline to see what was happening.

"Carty and B.W. are heading towards the airfield in the Land Rover, probably to meet the Prime Minister and give him a ride over to the government dock for the ceremony," Colin announced, "But I don't see Li anywhere."

"I'm sure he's going to stay out of sight during the ceremony, especially with the Prime Minister here. I doubt he wants to raise any questions about why he's on the island right now!" Jennifer reasoned aloud.

She opened the throttle on the Zodiac motor to get to the shoreline quickly while everyone was distracted with the VIP arrival. The little boat bounced off the waves, jostling the oxygen tanks Jennifer had left in the boat. She took the risk of the noise and louder engine for more speed, and soon they were cruising up to the stairs. The iron shore at the warehouse area in the bay was about three feet above sea level, so as long as they stayed crouched down in the Zodiac, they were hidden from view.

Jennifer cut the engine, and they coasted right up to the stairs. Colin reached out, grabbing a piece of iron rebar hammered into the iron shore to serve as a hand hold and place to tie off a boat. He tied a quick two half hitches with the Zodiac's rope around the rebar.

They scrambled out of the Zodiac, peering over the edge of iron shore rocks towards the warehouse doorway. From the edge of the water, they could just squeeze through a narrow gap in between the end of the chain link, barbed-wire topped fence that surrounded the warehouse on the land, and the exterior wall of the warehouse itself.

"Hurry! We've got to get through that gap in the fence and inside the warehouse! The Land Rover just returned to the government dock with the PM. Things will settle down once they get the ceremony started. We need to be inside before that happens!" Colin whispered urgently to Jennifer.

She led the way along a narrow strip of iron shore to the gap in the fence. Just down the bay, the dull hum of the crowd was called to silence, and Carty stepped up to the podium to begin his speech. Then the Prime Minister would also make some prepared remarks, and then finish with the Articles of Independence signing. All eyes were on the podium, so she squeezed through the gap in the fence and made a mad dash to hide behind a large, twenty foot long shipping container. Colin followed, flattening himself against the long wall of the container next to Jennifer. They were hidden from view of the crowd at the government dock, but anyone moving about the warehouse yard would surely see them. A door leading inside the warehouse was directly in front of them. A keypad mounted on the wall next to the door indicated a security system locked the entrance.

"How fast do you think you could figure out a way past that lock?" Jennifer asked hopefully.

"Not fast enough to get us in before someone would probably notice," Colin said, looking about the yard to see if there was another way in.

"Well, you'd better pull some of your secret agent skills out of the bag fast, because we are sitting ducks out here, and we're running out of time, even if Carty loves to hear himself give a speech," Jennifer snapped at her companion.

Colin made another scan of the fenced yard. He rested his head back against the metal container wall with a quiet thud, looking vaguely towards the roofline of the warehouse as if to admit, without saying so, that he was out of ideas.

After a few seconds of awkward silence and growing frustration, the handle of the door began to turn as somebody from inside the warehouse was about to walk out. Colin grabbed Jennifer's arm and they sprinted to the wall of the warehouse, just to the blind side of the opening door. The door was held open a few inches, probably by a curious guard trying to listen to the ceremony. Colin grabbed the door and flung it wide open, gambling that there was not an entire crowd of workers on the other side. The door swung towards the wall. Jennifer caught it just before it would have slammed very loudly and alert the whole island something was happening in the warehouse yard.

Colin's gamble paid off. A lone, startled guard stood in the doorway. Colin grabbed the guard's arm, and in a fluid movement twisted it behind his back, forcing him on to his knees where a powerful chop from Colin's right hand stunned the man into unconsciousness. She winced a little in sympathy to the man's pain, but quickly followed Colin through the door as he dragged the unconscious guard inside, laying him on the ground against the wall of the warehouse. Jennifer quickly and quietly closed the door, crouching next to Colin. Jennifer looked around the cavernous building. It was brightly lit inside with rows of fluorescent lights hung from the ceiling, humming quietly.

But it was not the lighting that had Jennifer's attention: running nearly the entire length of the long building was a huge submarine.

The sub looked just like the one Colin had taken pictures of in Wuhan, except this one appeared completely operational. It sat in the water, moored to the concrete slip poured along a deep trench that had been dredged inland about 200 feet past the sliding, underwater doors Jennifer and Colin had explored the evening before. An auxiliary generator of some kind was running, sounding much like a large air conditioner. Jennifer could not help but be impressed. The submarine base was simple, but very effective and well organized. Along the concrete slip were pallets of spare parts, supplies, and numerous long, square boxes. The submarine bay seemed deserted, so Colin walked over to the suspicious looking boxes to investigate.

"Torpedoes," he announced quietly, turning to look back at her. "This is much worse than I thought."

"Is that submarine armed?" Jennifer asked.

"I can't say for sure, but it could be within a matter of minutes. This entire dock is lined with ammunition ready to be loaded on board," Colin said.

"Now they have a fully capable submarine with all the information it needs to travel undetected anywhere!" Jennifer said, realizing why her phone was so important.

"Yes. It could be launched, armed with torpedoes, explore the Caribbean and the US coastline undetected, or…" Colin continued.

"…Or serve as an armed escort for the soon-to-be flourishing oil industry right here on Mayaguana," Jennifer finished his thought. She realized they needed to do something fast to stop the independence ceremony.

"If we make a mad dash for it and make enough noise, maybe we can get the Prime Minister to come see this before he signs away the island. We only have a few minutes!" she said.

"I understand we need to stop the ceremony but I need to get on that sub. A quick look to learn about its capabilities could save thousands of lives. I may not have another chance," Colin said, walking towards a gangplank that led aboard the submarine. Jennifer stood at the edge of the dock, looking angry.

"If we don't stop that ceremony, I may never find out what really happened to my father. I'll go make a scene, while you search," she said, turning on her heels to head for the door.

"Jennifer – stop!" Colin said angrily. He looked at her for a moment, and then softened his tone. "I may need your help. And don't forget, we are not on American soil. Before the diplomats work everything out with this mess, Li and his crew could scrub this sub clean. It'll look like some kind of research vessel to study coral reef bleaching or something. There's a lot at stake here, beyond just your own personal interests."

Jennifer paused, her hand on the door handle.

"Five minutes. I'll help you search the submarine for five minutes, then we go put a stop to all this. Maybe then I can find out what happened to my father and be rid of Li and his bank for good," she said, walking to the gangplank. "But if we get to the ceremony and it's too late, Obie will be investigating your disappearance."

Colin started to laugh, until he saw the angry look on Jennifer's face. "We won't be too late. I promise. Let's get going. The hatch is open right here," he said looking down below. He started down the narrow, iron stairs with Jennifer following close behind.

As they entered the submarine, Jennifer was surprised how modern it felt. She had been expecting lots of iron work, pipes, and steam vents, with dull red lighting. The corridor they found themselves in was sleek, with access panels lining the walls, and LED lighting running along the ceiling as well as the floor. Flat panel computer monitors, inset into the corridor wall at regular intervals, presumably provided information about the systems in the access panels nearby. It was thoroughly modern, and the overall effect reminded Jennifer of the Apple Store in Boston.

The corridor emptied into a larger room, which must have been the control room. The walls of the room were covered with flat panel screens, similar to those in the hallway, only much larger. Swivel stools bolted to the floor were stationed at each of the panels. The computer systems looked powered on and running, as if the submarine was booting itself up and running final built-in-tests before the main engines came on and it took to the sea.

On a translucent, back-lit map table, set Jennifer's phone. It was connected via a USB cable into a computer processor bank. A monitor above the table was alive with a stream of never ending numbers running across it as it loaded up the classified sonar transponder codes.

"My phone!" she exclaimed, running over to the table. Colin, following closely behind, pulled the cable out of the phone. The stream of data running across the monitor stopped abruptly.

From behind a thick, stainless steel column running from the floor to the ceiling of the control room came a semi-conscious moan. A weak voice called out, "Jennifer? That can't be you!"

With a stunned look of amazement, Jennifer walked over to the stainless steel column, and looked behind it. Sitting on the floor, hands cuffed behind him to one of the bolted swivel chairs, was Langford Bullfinch.

Chapter 37

Jennifer rushed to her father, hugging him tightly and crying with joy. She looked him over to see if he was alright. He was much thinner, and he had some bad cuts and bruises over him, but nothing looked life threatening. Colin set to work immediately on the handcuffs, and freed his right hand immediately. They helped Langford carefully to his feet, where he rested against the chair. He gave Jennifer a broad, happy smile, and she was sure he would be fine.

"I don't know how you figured this out, but you got here just in time. Li was just here with his sub captain getting that file I sent you loaded into the computer," Langford said sounding relieved.

"Dad, I don't know how much you know. But I think there may be some pretty disturbing things for you to hear about," Jennifer said, wondering how she would break the news about B.W.

"Jennifer, I know you've been upset with me, but give me some credit," Langford said, giving her a sarcastic look from under his scruffy face.

Jennifer caught a slight smile grow on Colin's face, and she realized how similar she must seem to her father in her mannerisms. "OK. So you knew all about B.W. and Li, and this whole secret sub base then?"

"Well, I can't say I knew everything, but I had started to put the story together. That's when I contacted some old friends of mine in the intelligence business. I can't say I knew for sure that Colin here was anything more than another pain-in-the-ass contractor, but I had some suspicions. As for B.W., I have to admit, that caught me by surprise, maybe because I just couldn't bring myself to believe what was happening. One day, when old Wu let his guard down, I snuck a peek in his office. I found schematics for this submarine, and the transponder code files on his laptop. I copied the file to a flash drive I had, and then deleted as much as I could from his laptop. When I looked through his phone log, he had a call from B.W.'s personal cell phone. That's when I knew I was in real trouble. I should have just sailed away right then, but I decided to wait for the evening and head out under the cover of darkness. But by then it was too late."

"Is that why you sent that message to my phone?" Jennifer asked.

"Yes. I hated putting you in a dangerous position, but if B.W. was involved, I knew I couldn't send anything to him. I'm truly sorry you had to go through so much, but you were the only person I could trust. With only a few seconds to get that text message to you, I couldn't tell you everything you really needed to know. But I knew you'd figure it out," Langford told his daughter, with a proud look.

"Thanks, Dad, but this is not over yet. If we don't get out to the government dock, Carty Wallingford-Rolle is going to take this island over. Mr. Li and his crew will be in control of their own oil empire, with some pretty impressive security backing them up," she said.

Using Jennifer's recovered phone, Colin snapped a few photos of the control room, grabbed a hard drive that happened to be on another console, and then started to hand Jennifer back the phone, but stopped himself.

"I'm sorry, Jennifer. You and this phone have been through a lot together, but I'm going to need to hold on to it for a little longer," he said apprehensively.

"Let's get going, and you'd better hope we're not too late," she said, ignoring his confiscating her phone, and helping her father down the corridor towards the hatch to the deck.

Chapter 38

Michelson woke from his unconscious slumber, sitting up in the captain's chair. He remembered his satellite phone, which he had been waiting to charge when he passed out. It sat next to him glowing, with a full battery. He powered it on and it searched for a signal. Sunlight bathed the deck of his boat, and he imagined he had only been out cold for an hour or so. As the phone turned on, the digital clock displayed the time on the screen: 8AM.

"It's morning?" Michelson thought to himself. "That can't be right. Have I been out for over twelve hours?"

He slowly got up from the chair, looking out over the dark blue ocean waves and expecting he was out far at sea. To his amazement he saw land, and a familiar radio tower in the distance. With his good arm, he pulled out a pair of binoculars, peering through them to the horizon. There could be no doubt that this was Mayaguana Island and he was looking at the radio tower in the settlement at Abraham's Bay and the government dock. It was a familiar and heart-warming sight. A gleaming white mega yacht anchored along the reef.

He set the binoculars down for a moment, considering the scene. The mega yacht could only belong to Mr. Li. Michelson picked up the binoculars for another, closer look. He scanned the government dock area, and could make out a crowd of people around it. It dawned on him what was going on: the onlookers were gathered for the Independence Ceremony.

He flipped a switch on his dashboard, turning on the emergency gas tank pump. He'd only had to use the tank a few times. It wouldn't get the boat far, but he felt confident it would get him to shore. He turned the ignition key, saying a silent prayer that his battery would still be strong enough to start the engine after keeping his laptop running for nearly 24 hours and charging his satellite phone. The starter turned over a few times, and the engines cranked to life. He let the engines rumble happily at idle for a minute, a sound that brought joy to his ears.

Steadying himself against his captain's chair, Michelson set his jaw for what was likely to be a jarring ride for his injured shoulder, and pushed the throttle forward. The engines groaned as the boat crashed through a growing surf. He gradually pushed the throttle to full power and his boat sped across the waves. As flying fish jumped at the sides of the boat, Michelson glanced back to see a long trail of white foam left in his wake. The line of hills protecting the airport and surrounding Abraham's Bay became taller on the horizon as he closed in quickly. Wind rushed through his hair and the spray off the ocean hit against his face. Michelson smiled grimly to himself, glad to be alive.

Chapter 39

Jennifer flung open the door leading out of the building, emerging into the bright morning sun of The Bahamas. The Prime Minister was concluding his speech from the podium in front of the crowd of onlookers at the Government Dock.

"Follow me! We're just in time!" Jennifer exclaimed, heading for the gate in the chain link fence that led towards the dock.

"Ms. Bullfinch, what a surprise to see you on land. And here I thought I left you secure on board my yacht," the familiar voice of Mr. Li called out. From around the corner of the building, Li emerged with his henchmen. The two men who had beaten Jennifer onboard the yacht held small machine guns at their sides inconspicuously, but carefully trained on the escaping prisoners.

Jennifer froze. Langford closed his eyes in disappointment at being caught just steps away from freedom.

Li stepped closer to them and sneered. "This really has gone far enough. You and your father have caused far more trouble than I anticipated. But leaving you both alive is a mistake I am not going to make again."

He barked an order in Mandarin to the men and motioned to the doorway. He turned to leave.

"You don't think we're just going to go quietly, do you, Mr. Li?" Jennifer called defiantly after him. Li paused but did not turn back around. "Because I don't believe you would really have your men shoot us here in broad daylight. I'm not going back into that warehouse to be killed."

"Ms. Bullfinch, if you think I wouldn't kill you in broad daylight for one hundred years of free oil and unlimited access to any port in America for my submarines from Boston to Brownsville, you may want to reconsider your calculations," Li said, giving the armed henchman closest to Jennifer a wave to open fire.

"She doesn't have to think about it, Li. We're stopping this now, no matter what the math says," Langford Bullfinch stepped away from Jennifer and Colin and turned quickly towards the crowd.

Before Li and his henchmen could shoot, the roar of engines, which had been getting louder during their conversation, became overpowering. Leaping over the waves of the shallow bay, Professor Ian Michelson's boat bounded towards the government dock. With a last whine of the engines, the boat hurtled off the top of a cresting wave and ran up the beach in between the ceremony and the sub base, a grinning Michelson at the helm.

The crowd, which had broken into cheers and applause as the Prime Minister had finished his remarks and had gone over to an elaborate table with gold pens laid out for he and Carty to sign the Articles of Independence, went quiet. Hundreds of onlookers turned from looking at the ceremony to looking at the warehouse to see what was going on. The crowd gasped collectively as Michelson, covered in blood and soaking wet, flung himself on to shore. Li gave a subtle nod to his crew, who concealed their weapons and began to slowly melt away into the submarine base. Langford capitalized on the commotion.

"Mister Prime Minister!" Langford bellowed at the top of his lungs, "Stop this ceremony now, and do not sign the Articles of Independence. You've all been lied to!"

Langford walked towards the chain link fence as all eyes turned towards him. His clothes were tattered and stained with blood. A black steel handcuff was still locked around his left wrist, and the other handcuff dangled, jingling when he moved, against its chain at this side. His scruffy beard and his wild, uncombed hair, gave him the look of a marooned Robinson Caruso rather than a wealthy business man. But his demeanor hadn't been beaten out of him. He stood tall and straight, and spoke with an air of assumed authority that was unmistakable.

"Prime Minister, it's me, Langford Bullfinch, and I am very much alive. You are about to sign away much more than you know."

The Prime Minister put his gold pen down on the table and looked over at Carty, who gave him a nervous smile and shrugged his shoulders.

"And although I am ashamed to admit it, I and my business partners planned to keep a great discovery we made all for ourselves. But our own greed made us blind, and we are paying the price. Luckily for us all, it is not too late, and I intend to tell you the whole truth right here, right now," Langford continued solemnly. Before he could go further, Carty began yelling over him.

"Prime Minister, this is rubbish. We must ignore these charlatans. We've worked on this agreement for months. The people of the MICAL region want this; the people of The Bahamas want this. Let me put a stop to this foolishness right now, and let us get on with the important work we have at hand," Carty Wallingford-Rolle preached from the dais, his gold pen still in hand. B.W. sat silent, looking distraught from his front row seat at the ceremony, but said nothing.

"Just what is going on here?" the Prime Minister asked, sounding a bit bewildered, but keeping his cool, leadership presence in front of the crowd.

Jennifer stepped up next to her father, "I think I can help explain, Mister Prime Minister. There is some undeniable proof that things are about to happened in your own backyard I don't think you would like. Mr. Li, the banker whose yacht you see out in the bay, is actually Admiral Li. His crew of construction workmen on this island are actually sailors and marines under his command."

The Prime Minster looked doubtful, "And the undeniable proof?"

"There is a submarine docked in a secret sub base built on this island….right behind me," she called out.

"Well I guess we'll see about that. But before we all go tour this secret submarine, exactly why would anyone want to do this on Mayaguana?" asked the Prime Minster.

"There is more to Mayaguana than meets the eye," she continued loudly, "This island sits over a massive oil field that extends for many miles around it and out to sea. I admit my company may have been hoping to keep this quiet, but without our knowing it, Mr. Li arrived on the scene and had even more sinister plans."

"Ms. Bullfinch, I appreciate your candor," the Prime Minister said, "but when you've been around these islands as long as I have, you hear things. The oil rumor has been around for years, and I have no doubt there may be some small deposits here and there, but nothing worth the money of drilling."

"I'm sorry Prime Minister, but you're wrong," Michelson announced, slowly making his way up the beach towards the stunned crowd. "And I know because I've played a very big role in making sure you and the rest of the world thought just that."

303

"I'm afraid you have me at a disadvantage, sir. And you are?" the Prime Minister asked, eyeing Michelson in mild disbelief.

"Professor Ian Michelson. I've been taking geological readings of this area for years to prepare for drilling. The geological makeup of this area, called the MICAL Formation, may be one of the largest oil fields ever discovered. But every time somebody else came this way and began to suspect that very thing, I made sure to throw a lot of contrary data and findings out there. It was easy for me to throw them off the scent," Michelson answered, unable to keep the pride out of his voice during this exposition.

"And the involvement of Mr. Li and his bank came about how?" the Prime Minister asked, slowly beginning to realize he might be hearing the truth.

"That is my fault, I'm afraid," Langford said shaking his head. "I let easy money get the better of me. Little did I know it was a set up by old B.W. over there to give his long time friend, Admiral Li, a strangle hold on the island.

"And they planted a mole in our operation. They too, know every square inch of the ocean around here, and can tap into the rich oil deposits quite easily. I have some email traffic I believe might just prove that," Michelson added. Then he turned to Carty. "They've been using you, just like Dominique used me. Admiral Li and B.W. were never going to just let you run your own empire. You'd have been disposed of, probably sooner rather than later."

Carty looked at Michelson, and opened his mouth to speak, but for the first time, Carty Wallingford-Rolle was at a loss for words.

"And the submarine you mentioned?" asked the Prime Minister, walking slowly towards the fence.

"That was the real victory for Admiral Li," Colin spoke up. "B.W. had been held captive by the Chinese during the Korean War, and his interrogator was none other than Mr. Li Hong. B.W.'s turned traitor and became a sleeper agent. When B.W. felt betrayed by Langford, he reignited his connection with Li, who just happened to run a bank along with his fleet of submarines. Mayaguana looked like the perfect place for Li to take control and base his own secret operation, with an inexhaustible supply of fuel resources around the island to support his fleet."

"Well, you're going to have to have real proof of all of this. Let's start with this submarine that's supposedly behind door number one!" the Prime Minister stepped down from the small dais where the Articles of Independence sat, unsigned. He walked towards the building as the curious crowd began to edge forward along with him.

Before the Prime Minster and his entourage took ten steps, the sound of bending and breaking metal echoed across the bay. The advancing, curious crowd stopped in their tracks. The giant building housing the docked submarine shuddered and shook. The steel doors that blocked the submarine from escape into the dredged channel began to bulge. Rivets popped and ricocheted dangerously off of machinery and ripped into shipping containers. The hinges finally snapped on one side of the door and the sleek, grey hull of the 09/7 submarine emerged from the building, slowly but steadily heading through the channel and out to open waters.

Chapter 40

Admiral Li Hong had played a daring game, but the Bullfinch girl, her father, and Agent Steele had just turned the tables in their favor. As he stood listening to Langford Bullfinch explain the situation to the Prime Minister of The Bahamas, Li sent his men to the submarine with a subtle command. They were well trained, and smart, and he was sure they would anticipate his intent. Moments later, he heard the engines of his new submarine quietly come to life. Li smiled to himself, and waited for his chance to slip away.

Li quietly walked to the door of his sub base, slipped inside, and locked it behind him. Allowing urgency to overtake propriety, he ran up the gangplank, barked for the two marines guarding the main entry hatch to push the plank onto the dock, and headed down the hatch into the submarine. He sprinted to the control room, forcing himself to slow to a brisk walk just before arriving in the room. His men were at their swivel chair stations as he anticipated, frantically preparing for departure.

"Captain Wu – Immediate departure. I expect to be pulling away from this dock within the next sixty seconds," Li ordered his captain.

"Yes, Admiral Li, we are ready for immediate departure, however…" Wu stammered at Li.

Li gave his sub commander an icy glare, "Yes, what is the problem?"

"It's the sliding steel doors. I've engaged the electronic switch to open them, but they will not open. We are trapped in here," Wu explained.

Li bound over to one of the computer consoles, where a young, sharp-looking sailor manned a panel of security cameras placed around the submarine base. "Pull up the underwater camera view – at the sliding door exterior."

The sailor quickly pulled up a monitor view showing the sliding doors with as clear a picture as you might see looking at the doors in real life. Using a small joystick, the sailor panned the camera view along the doors.

"Stop! There! Zoom in on that silver object," Li directed. The camera picture zoomed in on a long, thin line of silver, glinting in the water as the morning rays of the sun bounced off of it. It was the stainless steel spear of a diver's spear gun, left compliments of Colin Steele and his reconnaissance mission. The door was jammed shut.

Li thought for a moment. This morning was certainly not going according to plan. But being captured in this submarine in a secret base obviously constructed for a military purpose, right in the United States' back yard, would be as unacceptable to Beijing as much as it was to himself. Not only would he be humiliated on the world stage, but if he ever made it back to China, he would face a court martial and likely the firing squad. He made up his mind.

"Captain Wu, bring the engines to one hundred percent," he said calmly.

"But sir, I can't tell you for certain we will break through those doors, and even if we do, the stress could cause the ship's hull to fracture, and the entire building will just collapse on top of us!" Wu protested.

"I understand. It is a risk I am willing to take. It is a risk we all must be willing to take," Li answered, sitting in the nearest swivel chair and staring vacantly ahead.

Wu knew questioning this order was in vain, and perhaps the Admiral was right - better to go down trying to make it to open waters than simply sit there at the dock under siege and wait to be boarded. He gave the command to his helmsman, preparing mentally for the worst.

Chapter 41

As the hull of the submarine pushed its way through the steel doors of the warehouse, the crowd at the government dock descended into a chaotic mob. The sub ripped free of the doors and pulled forward. As it did, the structural integrity of the entire building gave in, and the roof collapsed with a tremendous bang. Seconds later, a pallet of ammunition began exploding from the impact. The island shook with explosions. The crowd of onlookers roared in mass hysteria.

Carty Wallingford-Rolle sat in stunned silence at the document signing table, staring morosely at the Articles of Independence he was supposed to have signed. Beneath the polished exterior, he had always been a scrappy fighter. If the years of battling and living by his wits had taught him one lesson, it was to never give up. Following that guiding principle had led him to prevail in more desperate situations than he could remember. If ever there was a desperate situation, this was it.

Michelson's boat, lying half in the water right behind him, caught his eye. Cuba was just a few miles to the west, and Carty had a lot of friends there. The miles of uninhabited shoreline would be a perfect place to lie low for a while and regroup. He'd made that journey many times before and knew the way across the passage and into a small inlet called Boca de Tanamo. From there, he could make his way through beautifully secluded inland mangrove-lined salt ponds to the small town of Nicaro. For many years, Carty had kept a rather large and magnificent hacienda on the beach on the outskirts of town, as a kind of vacation home. Now it would be the perfect safe house. And Nicaro's small airport was the perfect place to pay a charter captain to fly him to other parts of the Caribbean quietly and discretely.

The delegation of reporters, the local islanders, and a few other curious onlookers who had heard about the ceremony and boated to the island for something to do had scattered. Carty stepped off the dais and sauntered to Michelson's boat. The coast was still clear. He jumped over the sidewall and onto the deck. He was startled by the condition of the boat. There were bullet holes and broken glass everywhere, with smeared blood stains covering the floors, walls and console. He shuddered a little but continued to the captain's chair. He turned the ignition key, ready to take back control of his destiny. Nothing happened. The sounds of the warehouse collapsing, the dull roar of the submarine's engines, and the yells and screams of surprise and fear from the people around the dock were all he heard. A shockwave of panic spread through Carty's entire body. He tried the ignition again, and again, and again. The clicking sound of the battery making contact echoed in his ears, but the engines didn't make a sound.

"It's out of gas, old friend. Just like your plans," a quiet, familiar voice said from behind him. Carty spun around to see Michelson - tattered, blood stained, and pale - but looking more resolute than Carty could remember seeing him in the thirty years they had known one another.

Carty looked at him with a fiery glare. "This wasn't about me. It never was. I am a liberator, a freedom fighter. I am delivering respect, dignity, and pride to these lonely islands that have been cast aside, forgotten and ridiculed for too long. They call these islands God's back, well I'm going to make them God's backbone."

"Don't preach to me, Carty. I've spent most of my life on these islands over the past thirty years. You came back here when it suited your own political needs, but precious few times otherwise. The greed for all this oil drove you, just like it drove me and Langford. And driven by that greed, you betrayed us – your closest friends. So you can't fool me with your talk of noble causes," Michelson said, shaking his head at Carty's distorted pride.

Over the din of the excitement, the sound of a lone set of clapping hands arose from the government dock. Michelson and Carty turned to see the Prime Minister emerge from the tangled mess of equipment, folding chairs, and bits of blown limestone, conch shells, and coral.

"Wonderful performance, gentlemen. Well played indeed. I have to admit, Carty, I almost believed you right there. And professor, I really have no idea what to make of you," said the Prime Minister stepping up to them, his two security guards close behind him. Surprised, Michelson and Carty silently looked back at him.

"But I suppose as I am watching a Chinese submarine cruise away from a base carved into the bay of one of my very own country's islands, all here without my knowledge whatsoever, I can't say I am quite sure what to make of anything at the moment," continued the Prime Minister.

"Now, Carty, tell me about this phantom oil field. The one you seemingly ignored during our many conversations and debates. The same oilfield you, good Professor, swear is quite real," the Prime Minister said, looking back and forth at them.

"Well, PM, you see, no one really can tell about these things. I mean, the professor has done a lot of research, but, well, who knows what really…" Carty began to explain.

But he was cut short by a particularly loud explosion from the warehouse as a pallet of torpedoes ignited and blew. The ground shook, and a great cracking sound filled the air, like boulders being dropped on one another. From the back corner of the warehouse yard, a great hole in the earth ripped open, and seconds later a gushing geyser of black, crude oil burst into the sky.

The Prime Minister's eyes opened wide, and after staring at the towering gusher for a minute, he turned back to Carty, "You were saying…"

Chapter 42

When B.W. saw the hull of the submarine pushing its way out of the warehouse and through the channel to open ocean he knew he had just been marooned by Admiral Li. He also knew if he was arrested by the Bahamian officials, he'd be extradited back to the US within hours and facing serious charges. He had crossed a line from simply betraying ungrateful business partners to actions that could be considered treason. Spending the rest of his life in prison, or facing the death penalty, were not options B.W. was willing to accept lying down.

"Well, if Li Hong thinks he's going to leave me behind here to take the fall, he's sorely mistaken," he thought, looking around the government dock to see how he might make his escape. The 09/7 submarine had cleared the warehouse wreckage completely, and was beginning to pick up speed as it made its way for the cut in the reef that would lead it to open ocean. It was too shallow anywhere inside the reef for Li and Captain Wu to risk diving, so the sub cruised along with the upper exterior deck just a few feet above the water. If only B.W. could make it to the sub before it reached the edge of the reef, he could climb aboard and get inside the sub through the top deck hatch.

In the confusion and hysteria, B.W. saw his opportunity. A Zodiac raft with a small but powerful motor sat tied at the edge of the water near the exploded and collapsed warehouse. He recognized it as the one from Li's mega yacht. Using the raft, he would be onboard the submarine in no time.

At a full sprint, B.W. jumped down the rough-hewn stairs to the where the little boat was tied to the shore. The Zodiac was indeed in fine condition, with a set of oxygen tanks stowed in the bow. B.W. hastily undid the rope, and threw it to the shallow bottom of the boat. With one foot on the edge of the Zodiac and one steadying himself on the iron shore stairs, B.W. cranked the engine and prepared to shove off.

"B.W., before you head out on that raft, I think we owe each other some explanations," Langford called to him, walking down the stairs to the water's edge.

"Langford, I think the time for explanations is past. You, of all people, should understand the behind-the-scenes power play. Your crazy ideas for this island just happened to intersect with the interests of some friends of mine, and I saw a way to profit from it. You'd have done no different," B.W. laughed mockingly at Langford.

"You're wrong. You had the opportunity to work with me on this. The irony is that you didn't trust my judgment. I swore an oath with Ian and Carty that I would never tell another soul about the MICAL Formation, and though it pained me not to tell you the full story, I was good to my word. If you had only had more faith and stuck by me, you would have shared in the final reward. And I never would have betrayed you like you did me, and your country," Langford answered.

Out of the wreckage of the destroyed warehouse, Jennifer and Colin ran to find Langford. They stopped at the edge of the iron shore, shocked to see B.W. in the Zodiac.

"Well, just in time. I suppose I have you two to thank for all this," B.W. waved at the flames and explosions around the yard. "You know, I should have taken care of you myself when it was clear you weren't going to leave things alone."

"Mr. Baker, I am placing you under arrest. Step out of the boat and come ashore," Colin broke into the escalating conversation.

314

B.W. gave him an odious look. He glanced over his shoulder to see the submarine picking up speed and making its way further from him on the path to open waters. From inside his suit jacket, he pulled out a small pistol and aimed it up at Jennifer.

"Well, it looks like I must conclude this charming reunion, as my ride is leaving. But before I go, I think I have just enough time to settle the score," B.W. said derisively, and pulled the hammer back on his pistol.

As he was about to pull the trigger, a thunderous explosion from the warehouse fire rocked the island. B.W. cringed and covered his ears. In the aftershock, Jennifer lunged for the pistol. B.W. fought back with a strength and ferociousness she had not expected. As they wrestled, B.W. twisted the barrel of the pistol at Jennifer's head, and she expected to hear a shot ring out at any second. Before he could pull the trigger, the pistol was ripped from his hand by Langford, as Colin broke B.W.'s lock on Jennifer. With her last remaining strength, she freed herself from his grip, but began to slip into the spinning propeller of the Zodiac's engine. In a fluid motion, Colin caught her and pulled her back safely to the iron shore. Momentarily free, B.W. kicked the Zodiac off the iron shore and out into the bay with all his might, toppling into the bottom of the small boat as it cruised out to sea.

"He's going to get away!" Jennifer exclaimed in disappointment. She stood up and looked out towards the reef as the whine of the Zodiac engine began to fade in the distance. Langford and Colin stood up next to her. Langford put his arm around his daughter and smiled lovingly at her.

Langford laughed. "I don't think he's going to get very far."

"Hey Langford, what happened to the handcuff that was still locked to your wrist? I was going to get it off for you, but you seemed to have slipped it yourself," Colin asked.

"I did. And I put it to some good use," Langford said quietly. Then he looked out to sea. "I believe those are your friends heading this way!"

Jennifer looked out past the reef to see three large naval ships heading at full speed toward the fleeing submarine. She strained her eyes to see the flags. Through the smoke of the explosions, they appeared to be two US Navy destroyers and a Bahamian cutter. At the bow of the Bahamian ship, calling out orders to a crew preparing to launch a skiff, was Obie Gibson.

Chapter 43

Admiral Li peered through the periscope from the control room of his new submarine. The approaching US Navy destroyers and the Bahamian Defense Force cutter grew large in his sight picture. He could see boarding teams of highly trained Navy SEALS preparing to launch, and large cannons at the bow of each of the ships were trained right at him. He slammed up the handles of the periscope in disgust.

"Admiral, there are several large vessels blocking the cut in the reef. Our only path to the open ocean is blocked!" announced a nervous sailor.

Li turned from the periscope to look at his crew with a defeated scowl across his face. "Captain Wu, prepare to dive. We will go under the blocking ships to get out of the reef."

"But, Admiral...we are in a very narrow and shallow trench until we get past the reef line. If we dive now, before we get out past the reef, we'll hit the bottom," said Wu incredulously.

"If we continue at sea level, we will ram those ships. Were it just one ship blocking us, we might be OK, but with three, the other two will engage us with cannons. I see no choice. Dive. Now!" yelled Li.

"Admiral, we are defeated. I think we have no alternative than to shut down the engines, sanitize as much secret information as possible, and prepare to surrender," Wu disagreed angrily.

"You are relieved of command, Wu. I will handle this myself, and deal with you later," Li shouted at his captain. He ran to the submarines helm and pushed aside the helmsman. Admiral Li pushed forward on the steering column, and his submarine angled sharply downwards, catching most of the crew by surprise.

"Wu – call out our depths and tell me when we are clear of the reef so we may go to a full dive angle," Li barked.

Wu walked to the depth reader, shaking with rage. Before he could call out any numbers, the vessel groaned and began to shudder. With a searing rip, the submarine ground its way into a limestone and coral rut in the shallow bottom of the channel. The engines quickly over heated, as red flashing alerts lit up the panels and a warning siren blared through the control room. Wu smacked an emergency stop button with his elbow. It was too late.

The nose of the submarine had caught on the floor of the ocean, and the rear of the sub had jackknifed up and out of the water from the impact.

"You fool. You've run us aground," Li screamed uncontrollably at Wu.

"No, Li Hong. You and your hubris have run us aground," Wu answered calmly, silencing the warning siren.

The submarine was completely quiet for a moment. Then a small explosion broke the silence. The clanking sound of the main hatch being torn from its' hinges echoed into the control room.

A bullhorn rang out: "This is the Bahamian Defense Force acting in cooperation with the United States Navy. You are unauthorized by international law and treaty to operate in these waters, which are Bahamian sovereign territory. We have you surrounded. Exit the vessel one at a time with your hands up!"

Chapter 44

B.W. opened the throttle to full speed ahead on the Zodiac engine, bouncing over the waves on his way to freedom. He was angry he didn't have the ultimate satisfaction of having killed Bullfinch and his daughter, not to mention their secret agent companion. But at least he'd escape to fight another day, and exact his revenge when they would least expect it. He looked ahead to see the submarine following the channel out to sea, but his eyes grew wide with fear when he saw three large military ships approaching fast, and blocking the submarine's route. No matter, he was nearly to the back of the submarine, and when he reached it, he could run his Zodiac right onto the deck and make his way to the hatch.

He looked back at the sub, realizing that for some reason, it had angled downward, and stopped suddenly with its tail up in the air. The propellers that drove it were splashing violently at the surface of the water, like two gigantic saw blades. B.W.'s blood ran cold - he was just feet away from the spinning blades. To avoid running into them, he pushed hard on the rudder to veer right. The rudder didn't budge. He shoved frantically with all his strength on the engine rudder, but to no avail. The Zodiac continued furiously straight ahead. It zipped across the white frothy churn of the submarine's propellers, heading right for them.

Out of the corner of his eye, B.W. caught the glint of blackened steel chain. The handcuffs used to imprison Langford Bullfinch were somehow wrapped around the rudder, locking it in place. B.W. swore out loud and stood up to jump from the Zodiac, but it was too late.

The front of the Zodiac hit the spinning propeller, exploding the oxygen tanks. The rest of the boat, and B.W. with it, plowed into the propeller system. The propellers whirling rhythm was slowed for a brief second at the Zodiac and B.W. were ripped through, and then resumed spinning evenly and loudly against the surf.

Epilogue

Jennifer was resting on the deck of the Maelstrom as it bobbed gently up and down in the calm and safety of Hurricane Hole Marina. The towers of the Atlantis Resort loomed in the background, and a line of very tall, royal palm trees waved gently back and forth in a light, easterly breeze. The cool of the "Florida Winter" that could sometimes leave Nassau crisp in January was staying away, and the warmth of the late morning sun was delightful. After the craziness of the week before, she was completely enjoying having a morning to lounge on her favorite deck chair and read a magazine she had picked up at a gift shop. She flipped absentmindedly through the magazine, and smiled to herself remembering the story Colin Steele told her that this very marina was where the German navy had hidden their secret submarine almost eighty years ago.

Once the BDF and the Navy had arrived and hauled away the 09/7 submarine and its rogue crew, Colin had disappeared out of her life as suddenly as he had arrived. The next morning, after hours of questioning, Jennifer and her father had been left on their own recognizance. They set sail soon after, heading north to Nassau. After a few days of refit, Jennifer planned to sail back to Savannah. It was an uneventful trip, for which she was very grateful. And it had given her and Langford a few days to reconnect after the years of strained relations over the Mayaguana Project, including a pleasant Christmas Day at sea.

She looked up from her magazine to see a familiar black SUV with two small Bahamian flags mounted to its hood fluttering in the breeze. It was followed by a green and white police cruiser. Two policemen on motorcycles led the way towards the Maelstrom, pulling to a stop. Jennifer sat up in curiosity. The door of the SUV opened, and the Prime Minister stepped out, followed by his two body guards. He looked around the marina, spotted Jennifer, and waved to her as he walked toward the sailboat.

"Ms. Bullfinch, so good to see you again, and under much more pleasant circumstances," he beamed at her as he hopped onto the deck. Jennifer greeted him and noticed that none other than Obie Gibson and Colin Steele had just gotten out of the police cruiser and were following behind the Prime Minster.

"Ah, well I'm sure you remember these two scoundrels as well!" the Prime Minister laughed seeing the look of surprise on her face. "I am here to thank you, on behalf of the people of the Commonwealth of The Bahamas."

"To thank me, Prime Minister?" Jennifer repeated inquisitively.

"Why, yes. You see, you have given new hope to the entire country. Having natural resources at our command will form a critical, and much needed, third pillar to our economy beyond tourism and banking. You can take my word, that whatever your company's involvement in Mayaguana in the future, the people of the MICAL region will no longer find themselves the poor, backwater of The Bahamas. So, you were just in time, it seems, to prevent me from 'giving away the farm'."

"Well, I'm glad I could be of help, but really, I was only worried about finding out what had happened to my father and trying to save our company. I can't say I had the interests of your country as a primary concern," Jennifer said candidly.

"All the same, I thank you," smiled the Prime Minister. He held up a copy of a newspaper he had tucked under his arm for her to read. "I wondered if you had seen today's headline in the *Nassau Guardian*?"

Jennifer looked at the headline: "MICAL stays with The Bahamas! Region to be Headquarters of new Bahamian Petroleum Industry" was above the fold. Below the fold was a smaller article entitled "US Navy and BDF say High Intensity Joint Training Exercise in Caicos Passage a Great Success." The article went on to describe how the use of very loud artillery simulators made for a realistic training scenario. There was also a quote from the Bahamian Defense Force chief apologizing that the training did unfortunately disrupt a local government meeting.

"When officials in Beijing heard about your friend, Admiral Li, well, let's just say they were surprised to say the least. He's back home already, and I don't think we'll be seeing him again in The Bahamas. As for my old colleague, Carty...well, he's cooling his heels under close watch until I figure out what to do with him. Everyone seemed to agree this story on the front page would 'save face' for all involved," the Prime Minister said, lowering his voice a bit.

"And, as a token of our thanks, I have a small gift for you. Who knows, perhaps it may have some real value."

He handed her an envelope, which she opened. It was a certificate for 1,000 shares of a company called "Bahamas State Petroleum Limited."

"That is our newly formed, state run oil company. But we are issuing some shares, and I am happy to present you with this certificate."

Jennifer thanked the Prime Minister, and tucked the envelope carefully into the fold of the newspaper.

"And now, I have to head to the airport. I have an important meeting with the OPEC ministers. It appears The Bahamas has some new found respect on the world financial stage," the Prime

Minster turned to head back to his SUV. "Oh, I almost forgot to introduce my new Commissioner of Police. I thought you'd agree with his qualifications!" The Prime Minister slapped a beaming Obie on the back.

"It's good to see you safe and sound, Ms. Bullfinch," Obie laughed. "After you headed back to find Colin, I was able to make a few quick calls and talk with your Mr. Raymond Barnes back in Atlanta. After a few memory jogging questions, it seemed he recalled quite a bit about Bennett Wilson Baker's stint as a POW in China, and how when he finally came back to the unit, he was a changed, and some might call it brainwashed, man."

"Yes, our new Commissioner did some quick detective work there, and after relaying all this to the US intelligence folks working with Agent Steele at AUTEC, turns out the unknown 'insider' they had been trying to uncover was your own General Counsel," the Prime Minister concluded, obviously proud of his new head lawman.

"Captain Karnes and Agent Constantine could get the quick reaction force to join our own Bahamian Defense Forces and head to the rescue! But thankfully, you took care of rescuing yourself, your father, and Colin without our help" Obie concluded.

The Prime Minister gave a final wave and headed for his SUV, as his body guards courteously cleared a path through a growing crowd of curious onlookers. Obie followed the PM and drove away in the police cruiser to escort him to the airport.

Colin stood at the edge of the marina wall, looking up at Jennifer on the deck of the sail boat, "Permission to come aboard, ma'am?" he asked hopefully.

Jennifer sighed, and against her better judgment waved him aboard. Colin hopped onto the deck, and the two stood looking at each other in awkward silence. Colin held out his hand to present Jennifer with a box. It was a brand new phone.

"I'm sorry you can't have your old phone back. It's important evidence now, and I think it may already be in a lab somewhere in Virginia for analysis. It's been a crazy few days, and we've been kind of quarantined down at AUTEC," he started the conversation.

"Yeah, well. I'm used to not getting the whole story from you, so I guess just save it," Jennifer said, sitting down on the lounge chair. More awkward silence followed. Colin apprehensively set the box down next to Jennifer's chair.

"So, uh...where are your dad and the crazy professor?" Colin asked, obviously hoping to re-break the ice.

"They're up in the Atlantis, probably at the bar in the casino. Ian was airlifted up here for the gunshot to his shoulder, but it must not have been too serious. He found us here last night. He has some theory that when he was testing all of his sounding equipment and algorithms back in the United States, he located vast underground wells of oil and natural gas under the mid west, in North Dakota or somewhere," she laughed, despite being mad at Colin.

"The next venture?" Colin asked, laughing with her.

"We'll see. My father has a lot of things to think about. Now that the China Global Development Bank appears to have been a front operation for the Chinese Navy, the loans and bankruptcy issues we faced are a whole new legal ball of wax," she explained.

"No kidding. So your company may not go under after all?" Colin asked hopefully.

"Maybe. We've got a team of very expensive lawyers back in Atlanta trying to get some answers," she said, picking back up the newspaper and pretending to read the front page story.

"Oh. And are you heading back to school up in Boston?" Colin asked, hoping to keep the conversation rolling.

"Eventually, I guess. I may take the semester off and start again in the fall. I'm going to sail up to Savannah and put this boat in for an overhaul. It's long overdue for one," Jennifer said casually.

Colin thought for a moment. The awkward silence continued.

"Jennifer. I guess I really need to apologize. I should have been a lot more honest with you from the start," Colin said earnestly.

"Well that sounds just great, Colin. Or whatever your name really is," Jennifer said coldly, not willing to let him off the hook just yet.

"Right. Good point. I get it. And my name really is Colin Steele. It's just too hard trying to stick to an alias and travel around the world like we had to," he said, sounding serious, but cracking just a small smile.

"So what is it that you want, Colin Steele?" she asked sharply, setting the newspaper down.

"What I want is, I think, it would nice if we could start things over between us. And this time, no secrets and no cover stories," he stammered.

326

Jennifer stood up and looked Colin in the eye for a moment. "I think that sounds like a good start," she said. She was still angry with him, but she couldn't help but smile at his nervousness. He smiled back, letting out a deep breath.

"You know, I hear a great way to get to know someone is to sail around Nassau on a beautiful afternoon," Colin said moving close to her and holding her hand. "Can you use a good boat captain?" he asked.

Jennifer paused, and gave him a sly smile. "No, I can captain my own boat just fine, thanks."

Colin's smile faded and he looked deflated for a second. Jennifer let a few breathless moments of silence hang in the air between them, and then continued, "But I could use a good first mate."

Colin regained himself and smiled, then on cue untied the sailboat's lines from the slip. The sails unfurled in the gentle breeze, and with Jennifer at the helm, they set sail into turquoise blue waters.

THE END

www.ingramcontent.com/pod-product-compliance
Lightning Source LLC
Chambersburg PA
CBHW030017180626
46810CB00001B/90